## Praise for *Intercept*

"What happens when the courts spring a bunch of bad guys? A retired Navy SEAL has to clean up the mess. This fast-paced thriller ranges from the Hindu Kush to northwest Connecticut in a plot as relevant as tomorrow's news."—Rich Lowry, editor of the *National Review*

"In all, *Intercept* is a fun read. . . . A good book for a summer evening on the front porch swing. . . ."—*Conservative Monitor*

" . . . an exciting action packed. . . . The story line is fast-paced through-out . . . readers will be hooked. . . ."—Harriet Klausner

"Robinson's *Intercept* is definitely a page turner . . . Readers who are fans of Vince Flynn's novels would likely find this a book worth reading."—*New Mystery Reader*

## Praise for *Diamondhead*

"*Diamondhead* is a fabulous action-packed thriller. . . . Mack [Bedford] is terrific as an obstinate hero . . . "—*Midwest Book Review*

"The plot is as fresh as today's news."—*Cape Cod Times*

## Praise for Patrick Robinson

"One of the crown princes of the beach-read thriller."
—Stephen Coonts, *New York Times* bestselling author of *The Assassin*

"Gripping."—*Tampa Tribune*

"Inspired."—*San Jose Mercury News*

"Patrick Robinson has tapped into our fear."—*Herald Express*

"Robinson [crafts] a fast-paced, chilling, yet believable tale."
—*San Francisco Examiner*

"If you like your techno-thrillers in ripping yarn form, you'll love . . . [Patrick Robinson]."—*Guardian* (London)

# THE
# DELTA
# SOLUTION

*An International Thriller*

# PATRICK
# ROBINSON

Vanguard Press
A Member of the Perseus Books Group

Published by Vanguard Press
A Member of the Perseus Books Group

Set in 11 point Minion Pro by the Perseus Books Group

Library of Congress Cataloging-in-Publication Data
Robinson, Patrick, 1939–
The Delta solution : an international thriller / Patrick Robinson.
p. cm.
ISBN 978-1-59315-647-3 (hardcover : alk. paper); ISBN 978-1-59315-663-3 (e-book) 1. Pirates—Somalia—Fiction. 2. Hijacking of ships—Fiction. 3. United States. Navy. SEALs—Fiction. 4. Special operations (Military science)—Fiction. I. Title.
PR6068.O1959D45 2011
823'.914—dc22
2010044323

ISBN 978-1-59315-711-1 (mass market)

Vanguard Press books are available at special discounts for bulk purchases in the U.S. by corporations, institutions, and other organizations. For more information, please contact the Special Markets Department at the Perseus Books Group, 2300 Chestnut Street, Suite 200, Philadelphia, PA 19103, or call (800) 810-4145, ext. 5000, or e-mail special.markets@perseusbooks.com.

10 9 8 7 6 5 4 3 2 1

# PROLOGUE

▼

T HE MOST REVERED SQUARE OF BLACKTOP IN ALL THE
United States military somehow looked even blacker beneath
a pale, quartering moon, which was presently fighting a losing battle with heavy Pacific cloud banks.

Its name, "the grinder," could give a man the creeps. It was a
place where men had, for generations, been crushed, their spirits
broken, their will to succeed cast asunder. It was a place where
dreams were ended, where limitations were faced. It was a place
where tough, resolute military men threw in the towel, publicly,
and then slipped quietly away.

It was also a place that represented the Holy Grail of the US
Navy SEALs, the place where their battle had begun and ended
with the awe-inspiring moment when the fabled golden Trident
was pinned on the upper left side of their dress uniform.

No member of the US Navy SEALs has ever forgotten that moment. And for all their lives, the holders of the Trident strive to live
up to its symbolic demands. Everyone who receives it expects to
earn that honor every day throughout the entire tenure of their
service.

Such a man now stood alone on the north side of the square.
Commander Mackenzie Bedford was back where he belonged,
right here on the grinder, the place where he had once stood as his
entire class voted him Honor Man, the young officer most likely to
attain high command in the world's toughest, most elite fighting
force.

There were only twelve of them—the survivors of a six-month ordeal, which had seen 156 applicants crash and burn, most of them DOR, or Dropped On Request. They were good guys who just couldn't make it—couldn't take the murderous training, the endless pounding along the beach, the cold Pacific, the swimming, the rowing, the sleep deprivation, the log-lifting, the elephant runs. Not to mention the stark SEAL command, *Push 'em out*—shorthand for a set of up to eighty eye-popping, muscle-burning, brutal nonstop push-ups. For most of them it was just too much.

But the SEAL instructors do not want most of them. They want only the elite, the young iron men with the indomitable will to excel, the guys with the strength, speed, and agility, who would rather die than quit.

Not to mention the brains. There are no stupid SEALs. Seventy-five percent of them have college degrees, and they fight and struggle their way through outrageously demanding courses: weaponry, marksmanship, Sniper School, navigation, map reading, unarmed combat, mountaineering, parachute jumping, even medical courses, in preparation for battlefield duty.

SPECWARCOM commanders have one everlasting comment about the dreaded BUDs course that bars entry to their establishment: *It's harder to get in here than to Harvard Law School. Different, but harder*.

Commander Bedford, dressed in dark blue for the first time in more than a year, walked quietly across the grinder, relishing every step. He'd dreamed of this moment since his court-martial on a charge of mowing down innocent, unarmed Iraqi civilians on the banks of the Euphrates River.

The officers who presided over the legal proceedings did not believe the Iraqis were innocent, unarmed, or even civilians. And the SEAL commander was found not guilty. However they had issued an "officers' reprimand," which finished him in the United States Navy.

There was not one member of the SPECWARCOM community who believed this could possibly be fair. But it took a year to reinstate him under the most extraordinary circumstances. Last night, he dined with Rear Admiral Andy Carlow, the newly promoted commander-in-chief special operations command, and had agreed he should begin the second half of his career as a senior instructor.

And now he was on his way to a meeting in the office alongside the grinder with six of the instructors, including the chief, a Southerner named Captain Bobby Murphy, a veteran of the Gulf, and a man who would always hold a special place in Mack's heart.

The instructor had stepped forward to shake his hand when Mack received his Trident. He'd said simply, *I'm proud of you, kid. Real proud.*

Since then, they had become friends, trained together, and served together on the front line in Baghdad. And now he was going to see him, to take up his new appointment, a six-month stint as a senior BUDs instructor.

It was slightly unusual for a newly promoted SEAL battlefield commander to work as an instructor. But Mack had requested the position to test his fitness and to bring his vast combat knowledge to a new generation of SEALs who might one day serve under his command in another theater of war.

Bobby Murphy was awaiting him in the brightly lit office across the veranda, where the DOR guys leave their helmets and ring the bell before leaving Coronado. The grinder, the veranda, the hanging brass bell, the line of helmets. This was a place of SEAL folklore. Just the sight of it caused Mack's heart to miss a beat.

He entered the office and was taken aback when all six of the instructors stood up and applauded. Each one of them shook his hand and welcomed him home.

Captain Murphy had already formulated a game plan. "Mack, old buddy," he said, "I think you should start as proctor to the next BUDs class when they begin INDOC. It'll be useful for them to start their training with a decorated combat veteran. Let 'em hear some real words of wisdom."

"Fine with me," said Mack. "But right after that I'd like to take a different set of guys through Phase Three, if there's no objection."

"Mack, there's no one I'd rather appoint, if you're certain about your own fitness." Bobby Murphy was very serious, considering, of course, that Phase Three BUDs—Demolition and Tactics, Land Warfare—was the most demanding ten weeks in the program. And the instructors were revered as the toughest, fittest men on the base.

"I'm good for it," he said modestly.

"You're good for anything," grinned Murphy. "Matter of fact, I very much like the idea of you coming in to finish them in Phase Three. Especially if you stay with them 'til Sniper School at the end. If I recall you were pretty good at it yourself."

"Yup, not too bad," replied Mack, both of them knowing full well he had been voted Sniper Class Honor Man unanimously and to this day was reckoned to be one of the greatest SEAL stealth marksmen there had ever been.

"Anything else?" asked Captain Murphy. "Like how do you want the students to address you?"

"I think *Instructor Mack* would be fine," he said. "I'm a SEAL, and I'm well known around here. I prefer first names among the brotherhood."

"I agree," said Bobby Murphy. "I'll make it known that from now on, you're *Instructor Mack*."

▼

AND SO, THREE DAYS LATER, at 0500, Commander Mack Bedford jogged down to the grinder where Captain Murphy introduced the new class going into INDOCTRINATION—prior to the start of BUDs proper. He told them that Commander Bedford was a decorated SEAL combat commander in Iraq and Afghanistan and, as their proctor, would guide them through the first weeks of their training.

He then formally handed over the students to the care of his old friend, the teak-tough officer from Maine. "One hundred and seventy-two assigned," said Captain Murphy.

"*HOO-YAH, INSTRUCTOR MACK!*" roared the class, with one echoing voice.

The words split the dawn air, and the sound reverberated through Mack Bedford's soul, because they were words he thought for so long that he would never hear.

He stood before them like Alexander the Great inspecting his legions. And then he stepped forward and said quietly, "*Push 'em out.*"

# CHAPTER 1

▼

I T WAS NOT QUITE ON THE SCALE OF THE CHILLING RHYTH-
mic war chants of the massed Zulus lined along the hills above
Rorke's Drift. But there was menace in the air along one of the
world's longest beaches, where crowds of Somali tribesmen
clapped, cheered, and chanted in that uniquely African style of uniform mob excitement.

The sound of high anticipation. The disciplined clapping. The
repetitive chorus, echoing out over the turquoise water. The sound
of pounding feet and stamping dulled by the sand.

The grim occasion was lessened by the frequent shouts of laughter rising from the crowd. On reflection, it probably sounded more
like Kinshasa in distant Zaire on that October night in 1974, when
the anthem of the faithful rose to the skies, *ALI, BOMA YE!*

That too was somehow joyful but edged with menace. The
words meant "Ali, kill him!" which was a bit harsh toward big, af-
fable George Foreman, who landed on his backside in round eight,
with the howls of the swaying, chanting mob in his ears . . . *ALI,
BOMA YE!*

The 1,000-mile long Somali beach was filled with about three
hundred people—men, women, and children—gathered beneath
a burning East African sun, all singing and jumping, forming a vast
crescent around twelve tall, lean, tribesmen, each with an AK-47
strapped across his back, manhandling a couple of thirty-five-foot-
long, scruffy white skiffs into the surf.

The barefoot boat crews all wore cheap shorts and shirts, but there was nothing cheap about their two huge Yamaha engines, 250cc and $15,000 apiece, bolted onto the stern of each of the old skiffs, befitting the equipment of oceangoing bank robbers.

The majority of the crowd had arrived in a convoy of vehicles now parked behind the remote and desolate beach. They were mostly new, 4 × 4 SUVs, but there were a few rough village carts drawn by oxen, which stared blankly at the arid sand dunes.

The wooden skiffs were heavy, the bows up on the beach, the 600-pound engines seaward, and the sweating, heaving crews were hauling ass trying to get them afloat. Every time they heaved in unison, the boat moved a couple of feet, and the crowd let out a deep, rhythmic note that sounded like *WHOMBA!*

And their hopes were bound together, the crews working in time to the breathless chant, the spectators willing them to reach sufficiently deep water: *WHOMBA! CLAP-CLAP-CLAP!* . . . *WHOMBA! CLAP-CLAP-CLAP! H-E-E-E-E-Y! WHOMBA!*

As far as the eye could see, there was only flat, vacant, hot sand, stretching for miles and miles, north and then south. This was Somalia's Empty Quarter-on-Sea, without Bedouins or camels.

The Indian Ocean, which washed against its long eastern frontier, was much the same, a vast unbroken seascape of gently breaking surf, lazily rising and crashing down on this African edge of the fourth largest body of water on earth.

On this day it was utterly without activity; unbroken solitude all the way to its great curved horizons. No oceangoing freighters, no Gulf tankers running the oil down the African coast, not even a local ferry. No pleasure boats. No fishermen.

There was but one tiny blot on the surface. About a mile offshore was a dark-red 1,500-ton tuna long-liner. If you could read the faded black letters, she was called *Mombassa*, but there was none of the Indian Ocean's rich harvest of bluefin tuna on board, nor any deep-sea fishermen.

The *Mombassa*, stolen a couple of years ago from a Thai fishing fleet, was crewed strictly by Somali brigands. The gear, stowed both below and on deck, comprised rocket propelled grenades, Type 7 with handheld launchers, RGD-5 military hand grenades, spare AK-47 rifles, dynamite, grappling irons, ropes, and nets. Boarding nets, that is. Not fishing nets.

The four-man crew was awaiting the arrival of the local hit men, the pirates who had terrorized the high seas the past dozen years, growing bolder by the week, as international shipping corporations paid up in exasperation. Millions of dollars were often dropped from fixed-wing aircraft or helicopters in fluorescent orange containers right on the decks of the captured vessels. Tax free.

The tuna boat, stolen, like almost everything else on the Somali coast, ran on a single-shafted diesel turbine, with a good range of more than 2,500 miles at 20 knots.

Her master was Captain Hassan Abdi, a black-eyed former fisherman from Puntland, close to the tip of the Horn of Africa on the Gulf of Aden. Up there, the ocean waters were annually decimated by pollution from industrial dumping by Western corporations. And trying to catch billfish had proved increasingly difficult, not to mention a severe blow to Captain Hassan's ancient family business, which had been harvesting the warm ocean for approximately 7,000 years.

And once more, the bloodthirsty monster of twenty-first-century capitalism had smashed asunder a historic way of life. The reason was simple: It cost $1,000 per ton to dump hazardous waste off the coast of Europe and only $2.50 per ton off the coast of Somalia.

Which made a perfect, well-reasoned, bottom-line business model for the mighty brains of Harvard, Wharton, Columbia, and the London School of Economics. It was obviously a complete catastrophe for the Hassans and hundreds of families like them.

In the end, the short, burly Somali seaman had given up and joined the pirates, abandoning the billfish for the dollar bills cascading into the pirate ships.

Captain Hassan agreed to come south and work out of the new pirate HQ of Haradheere, a small coastal town north of Mogadishu on this sunbaked coastline, a couple of clicks north of the equator.

Haradheere, a town of three or four thousand souls, is a pirate stronghold. One section on the seaward side stands as the equivalent of Beverly Hills when playactors first started earning fortunes in the 1920s. But perhaps a better example might be the beautiful white-painted clapboard captains' houses skirting the cobbled streets of Nantucket off the coast of Cape Cod. These were the custom-built homes of the wealthy whaling captains, men who went down to the sea and sailed great waters.

Little thought is given, of course, to the fact that Somalia is, even without the pirates, probably the most dangerous place in the world, destroyed by a seemingly endless civil war. It is a lawless country where the capital city, Mogadishu, has been effectively levelled. There is no government and no protection for the citizens, who live in fear and terror of tribal warlords, rampant diseases without medicines, and the ever-present threat of starvation in an agricultural desert. Thousands have fled to neighboring Kenya and Ethiopia.

There are only two truly safe enclaves in the entire place. The first is the wide, expansively built quasi-government and political region on the seaward side of Mogadishu, off-limits to the populace but protected by 4,000 soldiers, who form a peacekeeping force. This private army, backed by the UN-sponsored African Union, controls the seaport, the airport, and all main routes into town.

Somalia's other safe haven is the southeastern corner of Haradheere, world headquarters of the Somali Marines, a highly disciplined pirate organization whose chain of command reaches upward to the dizzying ranks of Fleet Admiral, four-star admiral, vice admiral, and head of financial operations.

All of these ranks square off nicely with that of the late Ugandan dictator and former British Army sergeant Idi Amin, whose normal working rig was the full, heavily medalled dress uniform of a field marshal.

Amin would have enjoyed the luxurious part of Haradheere—big, new opulent houses, heavily guarded and occupied by the new economic elite—men mostly between the ages of twenty and thirty-five, professional pirates who have money, power, new cars, and big guns. They married the most beautiful girls on the entire coastline and dined on grilled fish, roast meat, and freshly made spaghetti. Usually they scorned the traditional native camel and goat meat, preferring instead imported beef and lamb, which was affordable only to them.

Alcohol was plentiful, too plentiful, but it fuelled a prosperous local industry despite the strict Islamic ban that applied to almost everyone in the country. Except them. Nothing applied to the pirates because they made up their own rules, and they had the money to protect a way of life that grew increasingly lavish with every passing year.

They were able to share the wealth, making deals with the local warlords, which bought them protection from any other authority. They created businesses in the town, designed to cater to their needs. They patronized a local shipyard, which serviced and built their boats.

They handed over substantial sums of money to a local authority which they controlled. This in turn built a hospital in Haradheere and funded doctors and nurses. It also provided the best school in the country with textbooks and teachers shipped in from Nairobi and Addis Ababa.

Haradheere, with its dusty dirt roads, is without doubt East Africa's boomtown, and at the heart of this prosperous black Wild West, there is a brand new stock exchange, selling shares and bonds in the pirate operations.

The locals refer to it as "a co-operative." But in every sense, it is a stock exchange. The modern office is situated in the heart of the pirate lair, and all criminal activity perpetrated by the sea gangs is funded from this financial center.

Each and every pirate operation comes through here. Newly formed gangs arrive with their "business plans," which normally involve a leaky fishing boat and a few lethal weapons that could in the fullness of time kill them all. But if the exchange directors like what they see, they advance cash to the fledgling pirates in the form of a bridging loan.

When the boat is brought up to scratch, and more effective modern weaponry is purchased, the exchange deems the young men in good enough shape to go out and risk their lives trying to capture a ship and its crew in order to demand a multimillion-dollar ransom from the owners. Then the Haradheere Stock Exchange begins to issue shares in the operation. Typical is an issue of 100,000 stocks, priced at $10 each. Anyone can buy shares, and not for just cash. The exchange takes anything that could be useful to the pirates, in the form of equipment and especially weapons. In turn they issue stock to the client who then sits back and waits for a return.

If the ransom comes in hot and heavy, say $5 million, it all goes into the central exchange, and the original loan, plus a low rate of interest, is taken off the top. Very often the value of the stock multiplies five times.

One local lady, a twenty-five-year-old divorcée, came in with a brand-new missile launcher plus two Stinger ground-to-air rockets given to her by her husband in lieu of alimony. Originally stolen from the Russians in Ethiopia, the rockets were worth $5,000 minimum on the open market. The lady was given five hundred $10 shares, which ultimately traded out, after the operation, at $50 each.

The merry divorcée rolled over her profits into a new operation involving a Greek-owned VLCC (very large crude carrier) and cashed out just before Christmas for $78,000. She subsequently bought a new house and a smart four-wheel-drive automobile, and once more the local Haradheere economy boomed.

Her story is not unusual. The stock exchange stacks away money faster than any bank in Africa, almost all of it in hard cash, delivered by air to the decks of the captured ships.

Every pirate operation on the coastline is backed by the exchange. There are an estimated eighty "maritime corporations" attached to the operation, and twelve of them have pulled off at least one successful hijack. The Somali Marines Inc. is the biggest and the best of them, with probably four or five notches on their AK-47s.

Not all of the shares issued by the exchange make a profit, and from time to time, pirates get shot or killed. But the success rate is so high, and so many people are making good money, that hope springs as eternal as it can get in the sand dunes.

The exchange is open twenty-four hours a day and transactions are conducted through the night, stock certificates issued to the music of the loud SUV horns blaring in the potholed streets outside. The profusion of alcohol has brought an even more lawless edge to nightlife around Haradheere. This is where East Africa's Wall Street meets the wild rhythms of the tribal hordes in the most dangerous country on earth.

Inevitably, from an operation that risky and that brilliant, there emerges a heavyweight brain who keeps everything moving. In Haradheere he was the thirty-eight-year-old Mohammed Salat, who started in the export business up in the north, shipping agricultural products to Europe.

In fact, Salat started his career in the United States, having gained his master's degree in finance at the revered Ross Business School at the University of Michigan. The guy was a Wolverine in the sand dunes, a lawyer's son from the Puntland Peninsula, and he was in command of the most notorious illegal operation on the planet. He was the Godfather of the Dark Continent.

Salat was wearing a grin as wide as the African equator as he watched his twelve tribesmen leap aboard the skiffs in readiness for the one-mile dash out to the waiting *Mombassa*. These were the Somali Marines, his favorites, and they always brought home the bacon.

It seemed they had everything in their favor. They knew the ship they were seeking, and there were no visible warships in the area; no signs of that heavily armed but ineffective European Union fleet, which was supposed to offer protection in the shipping lanes.

Indeed, just that morning Salat had received a communication from a Somali mole deep inside the EU that even more laws were being drawn up to protect the human rights of the pirates.

The trembling, liberal heart of the EU was concerned as ever with those brigands who may have suffered an unhappy childhood, deprivation, or poor schooling. And their latest laws were specifically designed to discourage, if not forbid, trigger-happy navy gunners from opening fire on the raiders, even as they held crews and passengers at gunpoint all over the Indian Ocean.

Mohammed Salat loved those guys in Brussels, loved them with all of his heart. And his stock exchange had an ample budget to hire London's best human rights lawyers, and they were confident they could get the Somali Marines out of trouble, any time, any place.

Life for him was as happy as it could be. He lived in a sixteen-room, walled compound, which included his private mansion, adjacent to his combined office, operations room, and strong room. This in turn adjoined the armory, where all of the ammunition and assault equipment was stored under permanent guard, 24/7. These three heavily constructed buildings occupied the entire north side of the compound.

Salat had full control over all of the millions and millions of dollars in his care. He had married the beautiful Miss Somaliland 2006, who was fifteen years his junior, and the golden couple was guarded day and night by a staff of armed servants, many of them ex–Somali military.

Of course, a man of his intelligence was very aware the roof could fall in on his world any time. If an international shipping company ever became seriously angry, he could quickly find himself shot, bombed, or incarcerated.

But he had made his arrangements. There was an ever-growing Swiss Bank account, an unobtrusive residence on the shores of Lake Como, and access to a private aircraft out of Mogadishu airport.

His friends in the Somali arms business owed Salat so many favors they had lost count. Their only permanent obligation was to ensure that a private plane was ready at all times to whisk Mohammed and his lovely wife to Nairobi and then to Europe at a moment's notice.

The pirate crews had started the Yamaha 250s with echoing roars across the water. The departing assault troops were waving, and the helmsmen were revving. On the *Mombassa*, Captain Hassan gave a couple of whoops on the ship's klaxon to signify the operation was a go.

"*WHOMBA!*" yelled Mohammed Salat. And he clapped his hands in rhythm with the crowd, as they pressed forward down the beach. "*H-E-E-E-E-Y WHOMBA!*"

▼

EIGHTEEN HUNDRED MILES to the east of this joyous gathering on the Somali shore sits the US Naval Base of Diego Garcia, situated right in the middle of the Indian Ocean. The island, a large coral atoll in the Chagos Archipelago, is owned by the British. However, the US Navy leased Diego Garcia from the Crown for many years, and the island stands under two flags: the Union Jack and the Stars and Stripes. It has a wonderful deepwater harbor and provides regular support for even the biggest American warships, including the 100,000-ton Nimitz-class aircraft carriers.

The place is a strategic masterpiece, around 8,000 miles from major US Navy bases on both the Atlantic and Pacific coasts—Norfolk, Virginia, and San Diego, California. It is a safe haven for US submarines, with facilities to refuel and service. Its unique location makes Diego Garcia a modern gateway between West and East. Geographically, the base is situated on the Maldive Ridge, almost 1,000 miles off the southern tip of India, and 1,700 nautical miles east of the Somali coastline.

Its remoteness in this vast ocean makes it very nearly impregnable. The seas around it are swept by the most powerful radar systems in the US Navy, and their ever-watchful fighter-bombers hammer their way through azure skies above the sprawling archipelago at all hours.

The entire place is flat—no mountains and no hills. Its perfect naval airfield stands only nine feet above mean sea level. The largest bombers and freighters can land and take off with ease. The forty-mile-long island is an electronic paradise, home to the US Space Tracking and Satellite Surveillance Station. It even boasts an emergency landing facility for the space shuttle.

Diego Garcia, once a bucolic, rural outpost for a couple of thousand Hindu farmers, stands today as a somewhat secretive modern naval and military city. It is unusual for any merchant marine vessels to call here, except for those delivering US aid to stricken communities.

The US is always the first to offer the hand of friendship, always the first to recognize the scale of the problem, always the first to make big, practical decisions to bring in relief, food, shelter, fresh water, medicines, and skilled workers.

Even Somalia, the cause of so much catastrophe, so much self-inflicted heartbreak, counts on the United States for help.

Yet another crop failure, yet more starvation, sickness, and disease, had again caused a weary America, fighting back from its own financial ills, to step up to the plate for Somalia. Which was why the 18,000-ton Mars Class combat storeship *Niagara Falls*, deactivated and under civilian command, had just spent four days on the jetties at Diego Garcia being loaded to the gunwales with aid—food, tents, water, medication, and relief workers hoping to save Somali lives in the north.

It was a big ship, over forty years old and a veteran of many conflicts but capable of transporting 2,600 tons of dry stores plus 1,300 tons refrigerated. Under a full load, her 22,000-horsepower turbines would propel her through the water at a comfortable 12 knots for 10,000 miles before needing to refuel.

She was probably the most capable of the US aid ships, fully equipped with freight elevators and on-deck cranes. She took her orders from the heart of Washington, DC, from deep inside the spectacular Ronald Reagan Building on Pennsylvania Avenue, headquarters of USAID.

This building is one of the most majestic landmarks in DC, set beneath a domed rotunda with an eight-story foyer. The building is an everlasting symbol of America's massive generosity to its neighbors near and far, allocating billions of dollars annually for global food programs under the direct guidance of the US secretary of state.

Millions of underprivileged people all over the world have reason to thank the kind and thoughtful administrators of the US aid programs. And yet, the tide of evil that so often emanates from the profound envy of the Islamic Middle East recognizes no good in anything that comes from the West.

And in Room 609, near the top of the towering edifice of that entrance foyer in the Reagan Building, lurked a mole—a thirty-two-year-old US-educated Somali named Yusuf Kalahri, a computer programmer by trade. Kalahri was on the payroll of Mohammed Salat.

His task was one-dimensional: to report the global positions, directions, and destinations of the big US aid ships as they carried out their missions of mercy around the world. This applied even when those ships were steaming toward the shores of Yusuf's homeland, trying to help those who could no longer help themselves.

The *Niagara Falls* was carrying a multimillion-dollar cargo to thousands of destitute, still virtually homeless people in Somalia's north. The enormous resources of the US Navy had been seconded to load her, on specific instructions from the Pentagon, via the secretaries of defense and state.

She was unarmed and bound for Mogadishu with its improved harbor facilities. But whether or not her priceless food and aid cargo ever completed the 500-mile land journey north was essentially in the hands of the gods. African gods, that is, which too often come in the form of tribal warlords, men whose grasp of normal decency hovers permanently around the zero mark.

The US aid, currently in the huge cargo holds of the *Niagara Falls*, might or might not be stolen directly off the potholed, sandy highways of this lawless land. US government officials, who are inclined to treat tribal cutthroats as if they are mild-mannered midwestern bank managers, felt, in this case, that an armed naval escort would not be required since the supply ship was on a mission of mercy, trying to help Somalia itself.

Right now she steamed west-northwest in waters 10,000 feet deep under the command of her veteran master, Captain Fred Corcoran. Fully laden, *Niagara Falls* was making around 12 knots, holding a course of three-zero-eight under clear skies and calm ocean waters. The temperature hovered near 102 degrees Fahrenheit. Every air conditioner on board was running hard as they headed up to the equator.

Since Diego Garcia stands just north of the seven-degree southern line of latitude, and Mogadishu almost directly on the two-degree northern line, the big freighter moved three degrees closer every day to the hottest temperatures on earth.

Captain Corcoran barely left the bridge and stood between his first and second mates, Charlie Wyatt and Rick Barnwell, who constantly scanned the enormous horizons for signs of maritime activity.

For forty years, Captain Corcoran had plied the world's oceans, mostly the South Pacific and Indian Ocean cargo routes, normally taking the Red Sea-Suez-Mediterranean journey back to Europe. After a ten-year spell driving tankers, he was one of the acknowledged experts on the Indian Ocean and was growing more wary by the month of the dangers of piracy.

Reluctantly he had acquiesced to the US recommendation that no formal naval escort was required since the Somalis were unlikely to hijack a massive cargo bound for their own starving people, entirely free of charge.

Fred Corcoran was not entirely certain about that. And after his second request had been discouraged, he fired off an e-mail to the Ronald Reagan Building confirming he understood the executive point of view, and that he hoped a cruising naval warship might be close enough to come to his rescue if rescue was needed.

Without telling a soul, he had acquired an M-4 rifle—a light machine gun—and, with the kind of dexterity that comes with a lifetime spent on oceangoing ships, he smuggled it on board expressly against the advice and authority of about 10,000 European Union and US protocols and bylaws.

He stowed it in a locker on the bridge, fully loaded with a new magazine. There was no way any bunch of half-naked savages was going to take his ship without feeling a few volleys of hot lead. Fred Corcoran was a big, redheaded fellow, with an Irish temper to match his size, and he was ready to defend his vessel at all times.

Right now the *Niagara Falls* was close to 750 miles west of Diego Garcia on a hot, dry morning, with more than 1,500 fathoms beneath the keel. So far they had seen a couple of fishing boats, probably from the Inner Islands, which guard the northern approaches to the Seychelles.

But Captain Corcoran's course would take him through lonely waters, running a couple of hundred miles northeast of the main Seychelles shallows, and then taking a straight shot across the deep

Indian Ocean basin, and picking up the north-running Somali current that swirls up the Kenyan coast to Mogadishu.

They were in peaceful waters right now, more than nine hundred miles southeast of Mogadishu, and although pirate attacks out here were almost unknown a couple of years earlier, the much better financing and solid success rate of the Somali operations had made the area dangerous.

The American first and second mates, Charlie Wyatt and Rick Barnwell, while lacking the rearmament skills of their leader, were nonetheless aware of the inherent danger in these waters and had a couple of baseball bats tucked away on the bridge.

They were both ex–US Navy petty officers who had seen combat in the second Gulf War and could be relied upon to come out swinging if the chips were really down. But pirate gangs generally came in heavy-handed, usually with a twelve-strong boarding party, all armed.

However, Charlie Wyatt in particular believed that if the skipper opened fire first, and he and Rick stood by on the ship's rail to repel boarders with the Louisville Sluggers, someone was going to find it real tough to board the *Niagara Falls*.

Their second line of defense was to have everyone go immediately below on the freight elevators and seal off the rest of the ship. This would keep them safe for a while, but it would hand the vessel over to the Somali attackers and Rick Barnwell, a former offensive guard at Penn State, preferred to stand up and fight in the event of a piratical visit.

It was beyond his comprehension that any attackers could get close enough without the *Niagara*'s watch-keepers locating an unknown ship. The big ex–US Navy supply ship had outstanding long-range radar fitted in the Norfolk Navy Yard's ISC Cardion SPS-55 surface-search I-band.

But Captain Hassan also had state-of-the-art radar, purchased with the bridging loan Mohammed Salat's exchange had advanced

the Somali Marines. The Somali captain also had a newly recondi-
tioned engine running sweetly in the stern of the ship, driving her
forward on one powerful single shaft.

The *Mombassa* may have looked like a wreck, but that was the
idea. In truth she was a supercharged rogue pirate ship, armed to
the teeth in the style of an eighteenth-century privateer and hell-
bent on big prize money and a triumphant homecoming. She was,
effectively, a guided missile in need of a few coats of paint.

The crew had rigged up a tarpaulin to provide shade from the
burning sun. Young Kifle Zenawi, a twenty-four-year-old native of
Haradheere, was second in command of the ship but not the operation. He and the pirate chief, Ismael Wolde, a native of Ethiopia, had
jury-rigged the shaded area and now sat with their colleagues sipping
cold fruit juice. Captain Hassan did not allow alcohol on board.

Wolde was a critical team leader. He had attended the National
University in Addis Ababa, Ethiopia's capital city, where his father
had owned an agricultural machinery import business. Wolde, father and son, spoke fluent English, but Ismael sought fortune and
adventure. Not secondhand tractors.

Also in the group was the thirty-five-year-old missile director,
Elmi Ahmed, who had seen active service with the armies of the Somali government in their endless fight against the militant Islamists.
Ahmed had found himself in command of a Brigade in the suburbs
of Mogadishu, when the fighting was ferocious in early 2009.

Commander Elmi Ahmed preferred the less dangerous life of
an oceangoing pirate to the murderous artillery and machine gun
battles that had just about flattened the capital city of his country.

Ahmed's skill with guided missiles was outstanding. While his
principal duty was to fire rocket propelled grenades across the bows
of the pirate target without setting the ship on fire, he was also occasionally required to slam a missile straight into the upper works to
discourage unarmed merchant captains from making a run for it.

Like Kifle Zenawi, Ahmed was a native of Haradheere, and the two families had been friends for generations. A long time ago they were all fishermen, before the huge foreign factory ships, especially those from Japan, ransacked the local waters of their stocks, thus adding to the general destruction caused by their toxic waste dumping.

For the Somali people, everywhere they looked there was destruction, by land and by sea, none of it their fault. And there's no reasoning with people who believe they have been robbed of everything. You could talk to the people of Haradheere for a thousand years and they'd never understand why it was illegal to hit back at the foreigners, any foreigners, and somehow make them pay for the damage they had done.

Captain Hassan, protected from the sun by a bulletproof reinforced roof to his control room, ran with his wide windows open and the hot breezes rushing through. At the helm was Abadula Sofian, a native-born Somalian from Mogadishu who had a dual-purpose role on the mission. An experienced gunner from the government forces in the south, he was a skilled fisherman and knew how to drive the boat. He was also a veteran assault trooper and would go with Ismael Wolde, the Ethiopian boarding expert who would lead the opening attack on *Niagara Falls*. If and when they found her.

Stationed on the stern end of the deck was Hamdan Ougoure, another Somalian from Mogadishu and Wolde's head of ordnance. He was currently checking through the arsenal of weapons, which included a twenty-one-pound machine gun with a stack of ammunition belts, all smuggled out of Afghanistan after an al-Qaeda attack on a truckload of US Marines.

The big gun had arrived in Haradheere on the usual route, by road to Iran and by air to Yemen, in an expensive arms shipment financed by Mohammed Salat, who, it must be said, wanted only the best for his pirate teams. Arms flights landed by night in Mogadishu from Yemen's international airport on the north side of

Aden—a 660-mile journey due south, straight across the Horn of Africa.

Ougoure was also in command of the RPGs and packs of TNT and dynamite. Wolde's commandoes always attempted to capture a ship by "peaceful" but threatening behavior. But when they went in, they were never joking and, if necessary, fully prepared to carry out their threats.

The powerful commercial overtones that surround acts of piracy mostly ruled out violence because everyone was wary. The kidnapped boat crews were mindful of the laws they would be breaking if they decided to shoot their attackers; the pirates themselves accepted that the world was hostile but, so far, not too hostile since no one had yet been murdered; and the shipowners themselves were always anxious to pay up and get on with the regular business of making money.

Only the US government had ever threatened to become a total pain in the ass to the grab-and-ransom Somali operations by refusing to negotiate or even speak to the pirates. The US preferred to let the commercial interests work it out for themselves.

The possibility of an attack on the aid ship *Niagara Falls*, however, was a sensitive area because it would throw the hawkish US Navy into direct conflict with shipping executives who just wanted to pay up and be damned.

The two ships were still some 850 miles apart and closing. On board the *Mombassa* there was much to be done. The two skiffs had been hauled inboard and made fast to a couple of jury-rigged davits fashioned from the outboard fishing net "arms," which still betrayed a former life as a trawler.

Those skiffs were critical to the operation. The *Mombassa* would be no match for the *Niagara Falls* if Captain Corcoran opened his throttles and elected to repel boarders. The skiffs were there for a fast, quiet approach, coming in from Corcoran's stern arcs in the dead of the tropical night.

The trick with an illegal boarding is speed. Tangled ropes might be fatal. The well-organized pirates had a couple of very slick rope ladders with brass rungs, also attached to grappling lines. These would enable even the least experienced climbers to make it on board the aid ship in quick time.

These hot, sultry equatorial days invariably heralded calm seas, and the Indian Ocean, while never as aggressive as the Atlantic or the Pacific, was especially good for fast, effortless running.

All through the day, Captain Hassan posted a lookout on the bow: a young Somalian named Bouh Adan who sat on deck astride a rail post and peered out at the horizon using a pair of Russian binoculars. Every couple of hours he was relieved, and then the captain relied on the sweep of his radar to locate traffic. But he was an old-fashioned skipper and liked to have human contact at all points on the ship.

Bouh Adan also had dual duties on these missions. At twenty-two, he was extremely athletic and could scale the side of a target ship like a mountain goat. When the pirates boarded, Bouh climbed right alongside Ismael Wolde with an AK-47 slung over his back in identical manner to his leader.

Hassan kept the speed at a steady 15 knots all through that first day and all through the night. The morning passed slowly, but by noontime they had covered almost four hundred miles. And all the while, the *Niagara Falls* was steaming hard toward them. With her huge load, she was not as fast, but she was three hundred miles closer and some 150 miles from the spot on the ocean where Yusuf had forecast she would meet the *Mombassa*.

▼

ON THE BRIDGE OF THE AID SHIP, Captain Corcoran spent much time staring at the first mate's computer, in which Charlie Wyatt had installed software that highlighted every site of every act of piracy since the Somali Civil War had begun in the early 1990s. "Nothing much to worry about, sir," he said. "There've only been two hundred ships captured. We'll be alright."

Fred Corcoran had tried to avoid the irony and countered with, "I know. I know. But how many have happened out here . . . What are we, 650 miles off the coast of Somalia?"

"'Bout that," replied Charlie. "And the answer is about fourteen, all of them in the last five months. And thirteen of 'em paid the ransom money. No one died."

"Jesus Christ," said Fred.

Able Seaman Jimmy Tevez brought them tea and a big jug of iced lemonade in the late afternoon. By this time, Second Mate Barnwell had the helm, and the engineer Paul Schuyler, an ex–US Navy PO, was asking what time he could reduce some of the power being pumped out by the generators.

"I guess the temperature will drop some after dark," said the captain. "We could try then. We don't have a problem, do we?"

"Nothing yet," said Schuyler, "but those generators have been going flat out for a lot of hours and it'd be a real bitch if one of 'em got tired."

Jimmy Tevez was basically hanging around to check up on the latest baseball scores. He was from Santo Domingo in the Dominican Republic, the same Caribbean island as Boston Red Sox slugger David Ortiz, and he believed that this geographic revelation made him a world authority on America's national pastime.

His devotion to the cause of the Red Sox brought him into good-natured conflict with Yankees fan Paul Schuyler, while Charlie Wyatt, from the baseball-gripped city of Baltimore, home of the Babe, considered both of them to be Johnny-come-latelies—guys who had latched on to a team when it was winning.

Whereas he, Charlie, was a *real* fan, born a few streets from the Babe's actual birthplace, and a supporter, with Orioles blood in his veins, since childhood. He considered Camden Yards to be the cathedral of the game and believed that one day the deified Orioles would rise to their rightful place in the baseball firmament.

Right now, Charlie was trying to avoid any mention of the Orioles 9–0 loss to the Detroit Tigers, but he still had time to comment on the fact the Red Sox had blown a 5–0 lead to the Blue Jays and were slipping games behind the Yanks every day.

▼

DARKNESS FALLS VERY SUDDENLY on the Indian Ocean. As night closed in, there was still no "paint" on the radar. It was the loneliest of seaways. Rick Barnwell had the screen on long-range mode, accurate to twenty-five miles in all directions, but the steady green-colored arm of the system just swept endlessly around, showing precisely nothing in the way.

It was much the same in the *Mombassa*. But Captain Hassan at least had a target area, and he knew he was approaching it steadily. The captain and his staff in the *Niagara Falls* were basically groping around in the dark.

They took turns taking two-hour naps, and as midnight approached they were just about thirty miles from the spot Yusuf had forecast the two ships would meet. The *Mombassa* was already in the area, making a lazy racetrack pattern in the water. She showed no lights and transmitted nothing, but she'd picked up the American aid ship on her screen and made a ten-second check every half hour.

The *Niagara Falls* had also spotted her, but the US radar had also located another fishing boat twelve miles off her port beam, which they thought might be Japanese. The much smaller vessel was obviously fishing and Captain Corcoran was not concerned either way. In his mind, pirate ships would be very obvious. Every major hijack out here, way offshore, had been conducted from the "base camp" of a "mother ship"—quite often a stolen freighter or small tanker, and Fred Corcoran's radar had located no vessel of that size.

The slow-moving trawler was showing no radio or radar transmissions. It was plainly harmless and very small compared to his 18,000-ton merchantman.

The result of all this radar cat-and-mouse was that the *Mombassa* was somehow watching the Americans, but the Americans were paying little or no attention to the former longline tuna boat from Thailand.

As the powerful freighter from Diego Garcia rolled ever forward, Captain Hassan steered out to a position eight miles off the *Niagara Falls*'s starboard quarter. From there he could watch the screen as the Americans went past. And now he came around, facing south in a slightly rising sea, beneath a bright moon and phosphorescent water.

Hassan could see her starboard lights as she steamed along the horizon, making that same steady 12 knots she'd been recording throughout her journey.

By now Ismael Wolde was standing next to him staring through the Russian binoculars. "We come straight in on her stern?" he asked.

"We don't have much choice," replied Hassan. "We don't fire across the bows. We move up on them very carefully. This is a bright night, and I don't want them to see us. I'd recommend the skiffs track him for a couple of very quiet miles, no lights. And then close in at high speed for the final five hundred yards, staying in the portside shadow of the ship for the attack."

Captain Hassan fell in astern of the *Niagara Falls*, about eight miles off her starboard quarter. His plan was to track the Americans for maybe twenty-four miles, drifting to his portside, closing all the way, until the *Mombassa* was only a mile back and dead astern. Then they would lower the skiffs and move unobtrusively in for the attack. No lights, no revs, quiet running until they came alongside their quarry.

The Americans might catch a "paint" of the tuna boat, but they would not see the skiffs moving in below the radar, showing nothing on the screen for the last mile. Captain Hassan turned off all of his electronics and they proceeded forward in dark silence.

Captain Hassan opened his throttles at 0100 and came in much faster to his chosen spot, making 18 knots through the water for the six-mile journey. It took him less than twenty minutes, and there was heavy activity on deck as Ismael Wolde's men prepared to lower the two fully laden skiffs over the side.

As long as they were on board, Captain Hassan gave the orders, and at 0140, he called down, "Okay, Ismael. Lower away."

The skiffs reached the water with two men already aboard each one, and the Yamahas kicked into life. On either side of the ship, Ismael's men moved expertly down the rope ladders. The pirate leader came last, climbing down to the starboard skiff, which would be helmed by Abadula Sofian.

Also in this boat was the slim, athletic Somali lookout, Bouh Adan, and the missile director, Elmi Ahmed. Two other young bloods from the old fishing fleet completed the six-man crew. Each boarding pirate carried an AK-47 plus two grenades.

On the portside, Hamdan Ougoure, Wolde's head of ordnance, would take the helm. Omar Ali Farah would ride with the big machine gun and the veteran Somali army sergeant Ibrahim Yacin would be first up the grappling ropes. Gacal Gueleh, a former fisherman from Mogadishu, was in charge of fixing the rope ladders up the side of the *Niagara Falls* just as soon as the first grappling hook sailed over the gunwales.

Somalia's pirates had learned the hard way that rope ladders were about a hundred times quicker to climb than having the men climbing ropes, hand over hand, their feet struggling to find a grip.

And now, with everyone seated and the boats low in the water,

Captain Hassan cast off and sent them away. Three of the departing pirates had cell phones with open lines to Hassan's bridge.

The skiffs moved through the water at 20 knots. They were barely a mile behind the US aid ship, which was, as ever, making 12 knots. Gaining eight miles an hour, that meant a seven-minute run for the skiffs to catch her, and Wolde was confident they were under the radar.

The stern lights on the *Niagara Falls* grew closer, and the men from Haradheere could see the silhouette of the 18,000 tonner in the moonlight as she rode the long swells toward the coast of Africa.

It was 0155 when they hit the first rough chop from the freighter's mighty bronze single screw. Wolde, in the lead boat, ordered Abadula Sofian to steer into the smoother water to the portside and then run in along the hull, cutting the speed and holding position in the shadows.

This was easier said than achieved. There was by now a bow wave rolling back, and the *Niagara Falls*'s quarter deck was higher than Yusuf's sketch e-mailed from Washington, DC. It was, in fact, an old military helicopter landing pad, and immediately forward the deck dropped down to its lowest point. There was a fifty-foot "window" to throw the grapplers. It was up to the helmsmen to hold the skiffs at zero speed relative to the forward motion of the freighter.

The upper works too were higher than Wolde had expected, but the deck was much lower and the Somali pirate king assessed the grapplers needed to fly fourteen feet above the water in order to clear the rails and grip. The good news was there was not a sound from the crew of the *Niagara Falls*, most of whom were sound asleep.

Wolde's boat was right where he wanted it. Abadula had the skiff balanced. The engines ran softly. The only sound was the occasional clink as the grappling men stood clear of their shipmates, waiting to throw, awaiting the command.

Hard astern, Hamdan Ougoure was having minor problems getting Skiff Two balanced against the hull, and the sea was now rising perhaps four feet on the swell. But his team was made up of experts. The grapplers were ready. The crew stood back for the throw.

Ismael Wolde positioned himself on the stern to ensure his command would be heard by both boats.

"Ready?" he snapped.

"Affirmative," called Ibrahim Yacin, a former Somali gunrunner who believed he was the reincarnation of General Rommel.

"LET'S GO!!" called Wolde. In the same split second, four grappling hooks whirled around three times and then flew upward. Each rope was marked with a thick red wool tie, showing the precise place the throwers should tighten their grip to avoid the grapplers rolling around on deck.

The irons hurled by three of the pirates landed perfectly over the rails with a clinking noise, but the fourth one got away, flying up way too high and landing with a thump, clatter, and rumble as it shot back to the rails and smacked into the metal post.

Charlie Wyatt, wide awake and with the air-conditioners cut back, was sitting below an open window on the port side. The clatter caused by grappler four caused him to jump out of his chair.

"What the fucking hell was that?" he shouted. Fred Corcoran, dozing on the whiplash hair trigger of a veteran ocean master, came out of his chair like a bullet. Rick Barnwell had been reading on the far side of the bridge and did not hear the racket. But he heard Charlie Wyatt.

"We've fucking hit something!" he shouted. "Either that or the goddamned radar just fell off the roof."

Charlie craned out of the window and could not believe his eyes. There in the moonlight, illuminated by the light from the upper-works entrance, two figures could be clearly seen clambering aboard the *Niagara Falls*.

Ismael Wolde and Bouh Adan were up and over. And before Charlie Wyatt had time to collect himself, the rope ladders and their separate grappling hooks were flung over the rail by the dead-eyed Gacal Gueleh, which signalled the moment when everyone, all eight of the remaining men, jumped on to the ladders and climbed up with every ounce of their strength.

"HOLY SHIT!" bawled Charlie. "We're being boarded. Get the fucking baseball bats, RITCHIE! This is it!"

Captain Corcoran already had the loaded M-4 machine gun in firing position and had joined Charlie at the window. The full crew from the *Mombasssa* was not yet over the rails, but both Fred and Charlie could see four heads coming up the ropes, with the two lead climbers, Wolde and Bouh, pulling their Kalashnikovs off their shoulders.

Fred opened fire in a reckless and inaccurate volley of flying bullets. More by luck than anything else, he hit and killed young Bouh. Wolde rushed for cover, and Charlie and Rick charged down the stairs wielding the Louisville Sluggers. The fact they were facing gunfire with baseball bats did not faze them since they both believed they may be fighting for their lives.

Fred Corcoran pinned Wolde down behind the portside bulwark. He unleashed another furious volley of fire from the high window but hit nothing. Bullets ricocheted in all directions. The assault troops at the top of the ladders froze since to move forward would be suicide.

By now Charlie and Rick had both reached the bottom of the companionway, and Charlie rushed out onto the deck, where he could see the stalled incoming climbers still on the hull of the ship. Charlie swung hard and caved in the skull of Gacal Gueleh. The former fisherman from Mogadishu, who was trying to fix the rope ladders, toppled backward into the warm waters of the Indian Ocean.

Charlie was just on his backswing to end the life of Elmi Ahmed when Ismael Wolde stepped out of the shadows and gunned him down, four quick-fire bullets straight into his back, instantly killing the first mate from Baltimore.

Up on the bridge, Captain Corcoran's magazine was empty and he could not locate another. Jimmy Tevez locked them both in, and down below, with Charlie Wyatt dead, the raiders swarmed over the rail. They'd lost Bouh and Gacal, while Hamdan and Abadula were still on the helms. That left eight fully armed pirates against Rick Barnwell and his baseball bat.

Right now, he was tucked behind the deck-level doorway to the upper works, uncertain what to do. Ismael Wolde knew he was there and not carrying a firearm and, very carefully, the Ethiopianborn pirate chief solved the problem.

"Sir," he said, "I know where you are. And I command you to throw out that baseball bat and then come out yourself with your hands high. I'm giving you five seconds, and then I shall throw a hand grenade through that doorway."

Somehow Rick understood that his old friend Charlie was dead. And he guessed the captain had run out of ammunition. He tossed out the bat and walked out onto the deck.

"Stand against the wall," said Wolde icily. "We do not like bloodshed and I regret your colleague opened fire on us from the high window. Two of my men are dead and one of yours. There will be no more killing. Although if there is further resistance from either you or your crew, my warriors are ordered to shoot to kill. Do you understand me?"

"I understand you," replied Barnwell.

"And now you will lead me and three of my colleagues to your communications center on the bridge, and we will sort out our business together."

He then ordered four of his team to secure the ship and assemble everyone on deck. Wolde was counting on there being no armed personnel on board except for his own men. He and Elmi

Ahmed, in company with Omar Ali Farah, the pirate with the big machine gun, made their way up the companionway to the bridge, the door to which was locked and clipped.

"Tell them to open it," he commanded.

Rick Barnwell shouted, "May as well open it, sir. They killed Charlie, and there are eight of them, all heavily armed. If you don't open the door, they'll blow it open. They have hand grenades. Their CO has ordered no more killing."

Captain Corcoran understood he was beaten. He unlocked the door. His second mate walked through with his hands still raised. Wolde came next, his Kalashnikov levelled. Omar made a formidable sight holding the big machine gun. Elmi Ahmed moved to the front of the bridge and stood with his gun levelled, like his boss.

"I want all three of you to walk over there and stand with your backs to the wall," said Wolde. "And listen to my instructions very carefully. First of all, you will cut the ship's speed back until she is idle in the water, resting on the tide. Then you will call your owners, I think the time is five in the afternoon in Washington.

"You will tell them the *Niagara Falls* has been captured by the Somali Marines. And that you are powerless to fight back. You will tell them I will be in touch personally in the next thirty minutes to inform them of the ransom money—and that twenty-four hours from now, the crew will be taken into captivity on the mainland.

"For the moment that is all. Except of course to mention that if my demands are not met, you will all be shot and the ship and its considerable cargo confiscated permanently."

Fred Corcoran ordered Rick Barnwell to cut the engines back and open up communications to the maritime section of USAID in Washington. "It's Section 418," he said. "I deal with Frank Allard, but this may require the head of section, Eugene Marinello. Tell whoever answers that no one less will do."

Ismael Wolde walked across the room and picked up Fred's

empty M-4 machine gun. "I shall confiscate this," he said, admiring the former US military weapon. "And of course any other firearms we discover on board."

"You won't find anything," said Captain Corcoran. "This is a ship on a mission of mercy, carrying aid to your half-assed country. Except for my personal gun, we are completely unarmed."

"Then I have been very unlucky to lose two of my best men," replied Wolde. "Very unlucky. I don't like dead bodies on my ships, so we will take Bouh Adan home with us and place his body in our skiff. My crew will throw your dead man over the side. My other casualty is already in the water."

"It is traditional in my country that we too would wish to take our dead home, and for that reason I would ask that Charles Wyatt be placed in a body bag and . . . "

"Permission denied," snapped Wolde, pointing at both Tevez and Barnwell. "You're lucky I did not shoot you all, after your stupid reaction when we came aboard. You started the killing; don't make us finish it."

At this point, the line was opened to Washington and Eugene Marinello was located. Captain Corcoran took the receiver and said, very deliberately, "Eugene, the *Niagara Falls* has been boarded and captured by heavily armed Somali pirates. My first mate is dead, and we are, as you know, unarmed and without escort."

He looked across to Wolde and requested, "May I tell them our GPS position?"

"Certainly," he replied. "This is where they are going to deliver the ransom money."

Captain Corcoran relayed his precise position on the water and then informed the stunned section chief that the commanding officer of the Somali Marines would be in contact in the next half hour.

He did not, of course, know that the Somali mole Yusuf, currently on duty in the Ronald Reagan Building in Washington, had furnished Mohammed Salat with the phone number of the senior

US naval officer under whose command the *Niagara Falls* and all USAID ships were designated.

Wolde now ordered Omar Ali and Elmi Ahmed to guard the three Americans while he returned downstairs to the deck. And once there, he walked forward and telephoned Captain Hassan on board the *Mombassa* one mile astern.

"This is Ismael," he said. "We have captured the *Niagara Falls*. Bouh and Gacal have been killed, but we have complete control of the ship. I am calling Washington in a few moments with our ransom demands. I expect a favorable outcome. Please inform Mr. Salat."

Captain Hassan was saddened at the loss of his young Somali lookout but extremely pleased the mission was a success so far. "Well done," he said quietly.

While Wolde returned to the bridge, the *Mombassa*'s master called the private line of Mohammed Salat and relayed the news to him. The stock exchange boss was ever vigilant and summoned his driver to take him immediately to the office, one hundred yards away.

The place was open and doing business. The 20,000 remaining shares in the Somali Marines operation were trading at $20 each, having doubled the moment the *Mombassa* made contact with the target far out to sea. Salat himself had retained 15,000 shares.

Salat wrote down the stock bulletin and ordered a clerk to punch the sentence into the flashing electronic notice board. The crowd of perhaps thirty or forty local "investors," sensing an important update, surged forward.

They could see Mohammed Salat was there in person, and the Somali Marines' operation was very topical. In general terms they were aware the *Mombassa* must be within striking range of their target, but they knew no more.

The notice board went dark as earlier bulletins were removed. You could have heard a spear drop as everyone waited. Then the board flashed . . . *SOMALI MARINES CAPTURED THE 18,000-TON UNITED STATES FREIGHTER* NIAGARA FALLS *45 MINUTES AGO. ESTIMATED $100 MILLION DOLLAR CARGO. TEN MILLION DOLLARS DEMANDED FOR HER RETURN. ENDS BULLETIN.*

The roar from the crowd split the hot night air. Trading in the shares caused pandemonium. Salat's brokers opened at $35–$38: buy at $35, sell at $38. Traders were almost crushed by the stampede to buy. Everyone in the entire country knew the Somali Marines had collected four ransoms in succession—the big one from the Greeks just one month previous.

There was a risk and everyone knew it. Maybe the United States would refuse to pay. But the cargo had a value, so did the huge ship. And the stock market was reflecting pure optimism. The crowd could not possibly hide its elation.

The 20,000 remaining shares were snapped up in thirty minutes. No one was remotely interested in cashing out. Even the tribal elders at the back of the room wore wide smiles, as they contemplated building the new Haradheere School library with their share of the prize money.

All the modern muses of profits, gambling, risk, nerve, and greed, the driving forces that took down Wall Street in the autumn of 2008, were present in this economic outpost on the shores of the Indian Ocean.

But when the rhythmic throb of the chanting began, the sound rose up through the hot, still night air. It sounded like a thousand hours of practice, but it wasn't. It was spontaneous, and the people slipped into its lilting repetitive beat, stamping their feet, clapping, and smiling.

# CHAPTER 2

▼

LIEUTENANT COMMANDER JAY SOUCHAK'S LISSOME SEC-
retary, Mary-Ann McCormac, had a rising edge of incredulity
to her voice. "Sir, he says he's taken command of a US warship and
kidnapped the captain at gunpoint and will very probably shoot him
sometime in the next twenty minutes. He wants to speak to the
boss—and he's on the private line so I guess he knows something."

Not many outside callers manage to connect with the office of the
chief of United States Naval Operations up on Corridor Seven, right
off E-Ring on the fourth floor of the Pentagon. But someone had done
so, and with a message so utterly bizarre, it might just be true.

Souchak picked up the telephone. "I am Lieutenant Commander Souchak, executive officer to the CNO of the US Navy.
State your name and business real quick."

The reply came quickly. "I am the senior commanding officer
of the Somali Marines Assault Force. One hour ago my troops
boarded and captured the USS *Niagara Falls*, five hundred miles
off the Somali coast in the Indian Ocean. I am on this telephone
for you to inform Admiral Mark Bradfield of the terms I have decided for the return of the ship."

Jay Souchak's mind spun. He rammed his hand on the receiver and snapped, "Mary-Ann, hit that computer and pull up
the *Niagara Falls* in the Indian Ocean—she's a fleet auxiliary
under civilian command—and get me the name of the captain.
And get a trace on this call right now."

Mary-Ann, sensing real urgency when she heard it, dropped

everything and asked the main Pentagon comms center to get a handle on the phone call currently connected to the office of the CNO.

Jay Souchak asked the caller, "Where exactly are you personally?"

Ismael Wolde spoke very slowly. "Sir, I am on the bridge of the *Niagara Falls*. Captain Frederick Corcoran is unharmed, but he is my prisoner with everyone else. We are stationary in the water."

"Give me your GPS numbers."

"We are zero point seven-five south, five-two point three-six east."

"Hurry, Mary-Ann, for Christ's sake!"

"I'm getting it, sir . . . right now . . . *Niagara Falls* is under the command of Captain Fred Corcoran, Irish-born US citizen. The ship sails under an American flag. "She's in the Indian Ocean . . . Gimme her GPS numbers."

"This computer is fifteen minutes out of date: Last reading was zero point seven-five south. Five-two point three-six."

Given that the ship was apparently dead in the water, Jay Souchak knew instantly this was real, so long as the call was not incoming from anywhere in the US.

"*MARY-ANN!*" he yelled, "Find the boss right away and patch him through to my private line."

"Sir, the call is coming from outside the US—*wait!* They're saying India, no—*WAIT*—they changed that to East Africa—it's a cell—they have a frequency line—satellite—they just asked the Brits to help via Cyprus."

"Where's the boss?"

"He's in with the chairman. He'll be on the line right away."

Jay Souchak knew he needed to keep the caller on the line. "Do you have specific terms for the release of the ship?"

"Very definitely," replied Wolde. "But I am instructed to use this phone number and to speak to Admiral Mark Bradfield in person."

Lieutenant Commander Souchak, a former XO in an Arleigh Burke Class guided missile destroyer in Gulf War II, tried to imagine the scene on the bridge of the *Niagara Falls*. Questions ranged through his mind: *Had there been a firefight? Was anyone injured? Or worse, dead? Would the ship still run?*

Mary-Ann called from the next room: "Sir, they're saying definitely East Africa on that call, but the satellite connection is not good. Also, did you know the *Niagara* was an ex–combat support ship, and it's on an aid mission to Somalia?"

"Why would you seize an aid ship heading for your own country?" Jay Souchak asked Wolde.

"Sir, that is my business. Please put Admiral Bradfield on this line."

"Admiral," snapped Souchak, "it is after 6:00 p.m. here in Washington, and the admiral attends a conference every evening at this time. I have located him and we will not keep you long."

"Then tell him to move fast," replied Wolde. "Because you may force me to shoot someone else."

"What do you mean someone else?" demanded Souchak. "Who have you already shot?"

"I believe you call it the fortunes of war," said Wolde. "Please put Admiral Bradfield on the line."

At which point the CNO came on the private line in the outer office and said crisply, "Okay, Jay, what's happening?"

"Sir, I have a fucking Somali pirate on the other line, and he says he's boarded and captured a United States aid ship, the *Niagara Falls*, under civilian command and would like to discuss terms for her release with you personally."

"How the hell did he get this number?"

"Darned good question, sir. I've checked him out. He's not only waiting, he's genuine. There's no point in my talking to him further. He has terms to offer but only to you. You want the call patched through to the conference room on the second floor?"

"Good idea, Jay. Then get down here and bring Mary-Ann. This might get very complicated. Gimme half a minute."

Ismael Wolde connected with the head of the United States Navy exactly five minutes after he dialled the number Yusuf had provided.

"Sir," he said, "my assault troops have taken command of the *Niagara Falls*. Captain Corcoran and his crew are my prisoners. And so is the ship, which I understand contains many millions of dollars in cargo, such as food, medication, and shelters.

"My price for the return of all this is 10 million US dollars. Payable in cash, at sea, delivered by air. At that point my troops and I will evacuate the *Niagara Falls*, and she will be free to continue her voyage with little harm done."

"You sound like an experienced man," replied Admiral Bradfield. "And thus you must be aware that the United States Navy does not, will not, under any circumstances, negotiate with pirates."

"Of course, that is a matter for you to decide," said Wolde. "However, there are just a few points I should make. I have already negotiated a very good price for half the cargo to my own government. I am proposing to sell the other half to the Ethiopian government. And because there is some urgency with refrigeration, I will need to move swiftly."

"What about the ship?" snapped Admiral Bradfield.

"We shall of course keep that, and if you do not wish to negotiate, we will have little choice but to execute the crew. We will not do that immediately, since there is the possibility of ransoms being paid through families and other connections. We are businessmen. And, as you probably realize, we do have something quite valuable to sell."

"I cannot make any decisions without conferring with my superiors," said Mark Bradfield. "I am thus going to suggest you call again in one hour and I will give you the official position of the US Navy."

"Okay, admiral," said Wolde. "I'll be back. But I should warn you, if you refuse any negotiations, we shall execute your officer called Rick Barnwell, followed by a seaman named Jimmy Tevez. The remainder on the crew will be taken into captivity on the mainland. For now."

Lieutenant Commander Souchak and Mary-Ann arrived at the conference room doorway and the CNO signalled them to come in. The secretary plugged in a laptop and pulled up the latest data.

"*Niagara Falls* is an ex–US Navy combat storeship," she said, "and she's now under civilian command for the USAID agency."

"So she's not under our control anymore?" asked Admiral Bradfield.

"No," replied Jay Souchak. "But she's under a kind of USAID permanent charter, which is as much US government as we are. And that shuts off our option to negotiate, unless someone wants to change policy real quick."

"Hmmmm," muttered Mark Bradfield, "there are some unusual circumstances here. First off, we got a left-wing president, and his concern will be the huddled masses in Somalia, starving kids with no food, water, or shelter. That's going to pull a lot of weight with him."

"Okay," said Jay. "And he just might say we got $100 million worth of aid in that ship, and for Christ's sake give these bastards what they want to free it up and save a lot of totally innocent people."

"Also we need to think about that ship. She's a big and very useful freighter."

"Not to mention the captain and the crew," added Jay.

"It says here that *Niagara Falls* was unarmed," said Mary-Ann. "And I guess these Somali Marines were all carrying machine guns."

"You get a dozen of those guys boarding your ship, and they're not afraid to open fire. You don't have a prayer." Admiral Bradfield was visibly concerned by these events.

"I have to tell the chairman," he said. "And he must inform the president. And the defense secretary has to be brought in. And then

I guess State. Jesus Christ, right there we're looking at a prairie fire of goddamned words."

"Sir, they're going to ask us for recommendations," said Jay. "And they're going to want them fast. They'll ask us if we can rescue them."

"Yeah," said the CNO, "and how long that'll take. And they'll want to know if the SEALs can do anything."

"Trouble is," said Jay, "They're all politicians and desperately light on brains. The best course of action is to get the goddamned price down to $5 million then pay it. That Somali aid already cost the US government upward of a $100 million.

"And five mill solves the problem, right? That's the commercial decision. A fucking monkey on a stick could work that out."

"It's also why the goddamned pirates are so rich. And if we pay 'em, they'll do it again next week. The politicians believe they have to be stopped soon, and it might as well be now—*if* the US government could come in with a show of strength."

"I guess so," replied Jay Souchak. "But my instinct would be to pay them, free up the ship, and then flatten their fucking hometown. Haradheere, right? The pirates' lair?"

"I know, Jay. But it's not going to happen. This is going to be a protracted negotiation unless we can somehow swing it onto a civilian course. Get it paid. But not by Uncle Sam."

"I sense the germ of a major idea," said Lieutenant Commander Souchak. "We better have a couple before the entire government starts demanding answers. Because they're all going to duck and dive for cover and then tell us it's the navy's problem."

"I know. And it isn't even our ship anymore, right?"

Just then the chairman's buzzer sounded, and Admiral Bradfield picked up a private line to the highest office in the US military.

"Sir?" he said.

"You finished with me?" replied General Zack Lancaster, the

craggy ex–Rangers C-in-C who had occupied the chair since returning from Afghanistan three years previously.

"Sir, I haven't even started," replied Mark Bradfield. "I better come in and bring my XO and his secretary with me. Because you are gonna need answers."

General Lancaster really liked his chief of Naval Operations and he chuckled that deep confident laugh of his, the one that all his troops had loved at even the most diabolical briefings in Helmand Province, the one that implied, *Take it easy, kid, we'll be alright.*

Big Zack was every inch the US warrior. An ex–West Pointer, he was enormously popular and he had political ambitions. Owing to his propensity to show total exasperation with lesser intellects, however, the popular view was that Zack would last about ten minutes in a diplomatic situation.

Still, there were those in the Pentagon who thought much the same about Admiral Mark Bradfield, but the truth was, if you really wanted to get something done, these two formed one hell of a starting point. It was common knowledge that Admiral Bradfield would himself become chairman of the Joint Chiefs when the fifty-four-year-old General Lancaster retired.

He led Jay Souchak and Mary-Ann into the inner sanctum of the Pentagon. The chairman immediately stood up and greeted Mary-Ann first, remembering her name with that unfailing certainty that had made him a prince among army commanders. Every soldier who fought under his command anywhere in the world thought he was General Lancaster's best friend.

He was six feet four inches tall with neatly clipped, greying hair and very blue eyes. A New Englander and the son of a Connecticut timber merchant, he had a deep voice and a slight air of irreverence about him. He was a man to whom others had naturally deferred throughout his career. If he'd not chosen a military career, his father would doubtless have employed him as a lumberjack.

"Okay, lay it on me," said the general, reseating himself behind his vast antique desk. "No sugarcoating. I know it's gonna be bad."

"Sir," said Admiral Bradfield, deferring to the chairman's rank in front of the other two, "Somali pirates have just captured at gunpoint the USS *Niagara Falls*, an 18,000-ton aid ship in the India Ocean."

"Is she still navy or under civilian command?"

"She's still navy. But under permanent charter to USAID."

"Does that let us off the hook?"

"Negative."

Lieutenant Commander Souchak stepped in while the senior officers gathered their thoughts. "Sir, he said, "They're asking 10 million dollars for her return. Her cargo's worth well over $100 million, and the pirate chief intimated that there may have been casualties. He is of course threatening to shoot everyone if he doesn't get his bread."

"Better remind the little sonofabitch it's not his bread right now. It's ours. And he's playing with fire. Mark, did you speak to the SEALs yet?"

"Not yet, sir. I thought we'd better have a strategy meeting first. Before we make definite decisions."

"Well, we know the policy of the US military for the last thirty years since President Reagan: We never negotiate with terrorists, which is what these guys are. So I guess we better start thinking about an attack policy."

"It's not easy, sir," said Mark Bradfield. "We do not have a Special Forces platoon anywhere near. There's nothing at Diego Garcia or at our base in Djibouti. Nearest SEALs are in Bahrain and that's 1,500 miles to the north. Also we don't have a platform within a thousand miles of the goddamned ship, in any direction."

"If we did, how would a rescue be attempted?"

"Well, I don't think we could come in by sea and board the *Niagara Falls*. Too dangerous, and too hard to get covering fire. The guys would be sitting ducks climbing the hull. Carlow would never sanction it.

"So I guess we'd need to come in by air. That would require a big helo, probably a Chinook, plus a serious gunship to cover them while they landed. All of it miles from help."

"Hmmmm," said the general. "But what about that operation in the Arabian Gulf two or three years ago? When the SEALs shot three pirates who'd captured the US captain?"

"That was very different, sir. The pirates had taken the captain off. He was an important US citizen from Vermont as I remember. And they had him at gunpoint for several days, held prisoner in a lifeboat. Our guys had a target, and they had the ship as a platform from which to attack. It was only a short distance to the lifeboat."

Mary-Ann said, "Wait a moment. I'll pull it up."

"There's probably a dozen heavily armed pirates on board the *Niagara Falls* right now," said Admiral Bradfield.

"I think we'd take unavoidable casualties if we stormed the ship either by sea or air. And I really don't want that to happen. For a start, the public would hate it. They think SEALs are gods."

"So do I," said the general.

"Here we are," interjected Mary-Ann. "She was the *Maersk Alabama*, a 17,000-ton container ship. Captain was rescued on Easter Sunday night. She was owned by a private shipping line and operated by a steamship company. She was only thirty yards from the lifeboat. SEAL snipers."

"The trouble with the public," said the general, "is they know very little. But they have good memories. In their minds, the way to end a hijack at sea is to send in the United States Navy SEALs. They did it last time. Ask 'em to do it again."

"But this is different," said the admiral. "If you want my opinion, it would only be possible if we accepted there would be a lot of dead SEALs in the Indian Ocean. And Andy Carlow will not send his guys on a suicide mission. The answer is obvious. We get the price down and then pay the sonofabitch pirate. Get the ship moving, get that cargo to the people who really need it. No dead bodies."

"When's this friggin' Blackbeard coming back to us?"

"'Bout half an hour."

"You going to take control?"

"No choice. He won't speak to anyone else. And he says he'll shoot the second mate plus an able seaman immediately if we don't agree to his terms."

"Bastard," grunted the general. "Listen, you guys get back up to the navy offices and deal with him when he calls. I'm going to scout around and see if I can find a way to pay the ransom. It's no good chasing up blind alleys. We need to go with what might work."

"Okay, sir. Meanwhile, you want me to touch base with Admiral Carlow? SPECWARCOM needs to be kept informed. Just in case."

"Good plan," said General Lancaster.

Before the three navy personnel were even out of the doorway, General Lancaster had summoned the youngest of his three personal assistants, Air Force Major Harry Blythe, a thirty-four-year-old ex–fighter pilot, veteran of the current Afghan strife, and native of Memphis. He'd once been shot down in the Iraqi no-fly zone but escaped and made it back to base, dressed as a tribesman, riding a camel. Harry Blythe was very smart and cunning as a Tennessee fox.

General Lancaster briefed him carefully and concluded by saying, "Harry, we want to pay up and get that ship free with no more bloodshed. The strong-arm route is no good to us, not right now. I want you to locate a civilian organization that will pay the ransom for us.

"I don't like it, but I am not ordering SEALs to die for no reason. And we need to move fast. See what you can do."

Harry moved fast. He Googled the ship and located data on the captain, who was, thank god, an American citizen. Then he spoke to the duty officer at Military Sealift Command and then the head of the US Navy Fleet Auxiliary, both in Washington navy yards. That was *Niagara Falls*'s former life. Now in effect, she was civilian, and Harry needed advice.

The Fleet Auxiliary controls more than one hundred ships, which provide combat support, oilers, hospital ships, cable repair vessels, research, and surveillance. The senior command was of a high order, and Captain Jack Carling suggested he contact the Seafarers International Union of North America out at Camp Springs near Andrews Air Force Base.

This was the main trade union, an umbrella for several other seamen's unions, representing deep-sea personnel and the crews of merchantmen that worked the Great Lakes. It took Harry less than a half hour to get the chairman of the union on the line. Everyone in America jumps for the Office of the Chairman of the Joint Chiefs. The word "Pentagon" is apt to make people very nervous.

He outlined the problem and confided in the union boss that he, the US Navy, and the chairman himself believed this was a time to pay up and free the ship. Any other course of action, under the circumstances, was a stupendous pain in the ass and may fail.

The union's chairman wanted to know what role he was supposed to play.

"We would like you to pay the ransom," said Harry.

"Who me?" exclaimed the chairman. "How much is it?"

"Somewhere between 5 and 10 million dollars."

"You must be out of your mind."

"Sir," said Harry, "we'll give you the money. We just can't be seen to pay off pirates. The policy of the United States is that we don't negotiate. So in this case, the lives of the crew will be saved by the Seafarers International Union, which has nothing to do with the government.

"If the ransom's, say, $6 million, you get $6.25 and you can keep the change. We'll take care of the delivery, just so long as you arrange the cash and handle any press announcements."

"So the party line is the ship is a civilian merchantman on an aid mission to Somalia? We just stepped in to save our personnel."

"Precisely. I expect they're all members anyway."

"They will be. I just tapped in the name of Fred Corcoran and he's one for a start. Major, this is very good for us. And I'm grateful you called."

"No problem," said Harry. "I'll call you as soon as we know the precise sum negotiated. Then you can send your bankers in to see us, and we'll get it done."

Five minutes after Harry Blythe had relayed the good tidings to General Lancaster, the phone rang in the CNO's office two floors above. Admiral Ismael Wolde was on the line, direct from the bridge of the *Niagara Falls*.

"Okay, sir. I have been in conference with my people," he told Admiral Bradfield. "And we have decided to reduce our demand to 7 million dollars. Have you decided to cooperate, or will I just go ahead and shoot the prisoners and then sell off the cargo?"

"The attitude of the US Navy is not flexible," said the admiral. "They will not negotiate with you. So far as they are concerned, you can go right ahead and kill anyone you like, because we believe it will be a very small price to pay if we can reduce your future activities against innocent ships and their crews."

"Is that your last word, sir?"

"No," replied the CNO, "because we have a serious complication here. The *Niagara Falls* flies an American flag but is no longer a US Navy vessel. Which disqualifies us from paying out many millions of dollars for her release. She's not ours."

"Well, who are her owners?" asked Wolde.

"That won't help you," replied Bradfield. "She's on charter to a US aid agency. Which is also government and cannot negotiate. No one else cares. My high command, incidentally, is disgusted by your actions since the ship is bringing voluntary aid, millions of dollars worth, from my country to yours, as a gift."

"We are businessmen," said the assault chief of the Somali Marines. "We are interested only in the price. Not the morals."

"Evidently," replied Mark Bradfield, somewhat loftily. "However, we are still working on this and would like you to call back in thirty minutes. We may have a way forward."

"Well, that will be 0400 our time," replied Wolde. "Eight o'clock yours."

"Correct. Meanwhile I would like you to refrain from killing anyone else."

Wolde fell for it. "Our gunfire was in self-defense," he snapped back. "We had no wish to kill. Your captain opened fire and two of my men died. We in turn shot one of yours because there was no choice."

For the first time, Admiral Bradfield knew there had been a gunfight on board the *Niagara Falls*. He walked down to the chairman's office, where he was informed of Major Blythe's successful dealings with the trade union.

"That's excellent, sir. But just one thing," he asked, "Whose budget is this money coming from?"

"Oh, we'll just spread it around," replied the general.

"We could take a little from the carrier new-build program," said Mark Bradfield. "Those guys in Newport News are working with several billion dollars. We'll get a million out of the Fleet Auxiliary. They have a massive budget. We'll take a million from the navy aviation budget. They won't even miss it. Probably another million from that closure program."

"Hell, we've got enough money in here to hide 5 or 6 million without even thinking about it," said General Lancaster. "A SEAL operation to rescue the ship would cost more than that. And the *Niagara Falls*, just refurbished from deck to keel, is worth $20 million on the open market. It's the soundest decision, and this way no one's gonna get killed, which is the part I like most of all."

"By the way," said the admiral, "they just reduced their ransom demand from 10 to 7 million. I'm betting I can get 'em down more. Nonetheless, I think we better make arrangements to get escort ships out there from Diego Garcia. We have a couple of guided-missile frigates and a destroyer ready to go. The *Ronald Reagan*'s on standby fifty miles south of DG with eighty-four fighter aircraft consigned."

"Jesus, we could wipe out Somalia," said the general. "And if they don't start behaving themselves, we just might fucking well do it. This piracy bullshit has to stop. And if that skid-row government of theirs doesn't come into line real soon, we'll knock 'em into line. Crazy bastards."

It was a frequently expressed opinion that if Lancaster and Bradfield ever got into sole command at the Pentagon, a lot of America's most irritating foreign problems would vanish. Real fast.

The two men were unfailingly formal in front of the troops, but privately it was Zack and Mark. Right now it was the latter.

"Mark, old buddy," said the general, "how long before this Blackbeard calls again?"

"'Bout ten minutes."

"Okay. Let's get the deal done. And I'll have Major Blythe work out how to get the trade union's cash into a bag and air-dropped onto the *Niagara Falls*. Where's the nearest major bank?"

"Nairobi. Mary-Ann just checked it out. Barclays is the main bank in the city, and she says the British Embassy here in Washington will help. They still have a lot of clout in Kenya—they work from some colonial palace in Nairobi called the British High Commission."

"If we opened a place in Kenya called the United States High Commission, there'd be a fucking civil war."

"I know. But the Brits are real useful for us. They'll work with Barclays, and we can fly the money right out of Wilson Airport south of Nairobi. It's not so big as the main international terminal.

"I better go, Zack. But who's going to organize the Seafarers

Union? They need to make some kind of announcement to get the heat off the Pentagon—you know the stuff . . . *We are negotiating on behalf of our members, providing the kind of protection they deserve . . .*"

"You better do that. Since it's your money. I'll have Major Blythe send you a note. But I'll deal with Simon," he said referring to US defense secretary Simon Andre. "He can organize the president."

"Beautiful. I'll be back as soon as I speak to the pirate."

Admiral Bradfield arrived back on the fourth floor just in time. Jay Souchak had Ismael Wolde on the line as Mark walked in the door.

"He's on, sir," said Jay.

"I'll pick up at my desk."

But this was no longer the smooth, confident Admiral Wolde. This was a nervous, irritated pirate who had been waiting too long.

"Okay, 7 million dollars for your ship and crew," he said. "Give me a straight answer. Otherwise we're leaving and you will not see your people again . . . You are deliberately holding this up. Probably planning to attack the ship."

"Steady," replied Admiral Bradfield. "These things take time. You're looking at a lot of money, and there are a lot of people involved. But I can say we're making progress."

"*Progress! What's progress?* You have the money for me, or you don't."

"Okay, now listen . . . I told you the US government or military will not negotiate with pirates. That's never changed and it's never going to . . . "

"*Then you're wasting my time!*" yelled Wolde. "I'm going right back there to execute this Barnwell and Tevez. Then we'll see who's running this operation. *Do you understand me?*"

"You're not going to execute anyone while you think there's 7 million bucks awaiting you. Because if you pull that fucking trigger, you'll get nothing. Do you understand *ME*?"

Wolde, momentarily shocked at Admiral Bradfield's change of tone, thought of the cash and said, more calmly, "I understand."

"Good. Just so we're on the same page," said Bradfield. "And now you must pay attention . . . and the first thing is, since the US government will pay nothing, we had to find someone who would."

"That's good," interjected Wolde. "That's very good."

"And we have found an organization that will step in with cash. But not your 7 million . . . "

"How much?"

"They'll go to 5 million. No more. They don't have any more."

"Well, who are they?"

"They're the Seafarers Union. They are a civilian organization, very powerful, and very upset with you and your men."

"Five million is not enough."

"Okay. That's the end of it. I can't get more. The president won't allow negotiation. I can get you 5 million bucks for the release, under our terms. But if that's no good, you go right ahead and shoot the American crew and take the ship. Right after that we're gonna kick your skinny black ass. And that fucking rat-hole town you live in? We'll take it off the map. Now fuck off, you fourth-rate little murderer. Enjoy the last month of your asshole life."

Mark Bradfield, a surface-warfare commander at an unbelievably young age, twenty-nine, had an old-world charm about him when riled, even if he was only faking it. And now he rattled the cradle of the telephone. And he could hear Admiral Wolde yelling . . . *NO! NO! Sir, don't put the phone down. We can work with 5 million.*"

He gave it ten more seconds and then spoke again. "Five million is what we'll pay. Not a dollar more. And we have stringent terms which you must accept."

Mark was far more worried than he would ever let on about the lives of the crew and the possibility of losing the entire ship and its valuable cargo. Mostly because as the US negotiator, he would undoubtedly get the blame. The politicians would insure that.

"Okay," said Wolde. "You know my terms. What are yours?"

"First off, I want to speak to Captain Corcoran. For all I know you've already shot him. Secondly, understand there's no way we'll drop that 5 million bucks on the deck of the *Niagara Falls*, leaving you with the cash, the ship, and the prisoners, while we sit here in Washington with nothing. Get it?"

"Well, what are you proposing?"

"Subject to my talk with Captain Corcoran, you will order your assault team off the ship and out of the area, save for yourself and two armed guards. There will thus be three of you, armed with machine guns on board, with the American crew held in one place. You still hold all the cards.

"We will send over a military aircraft that will drop on deck a fluorescent bag containing the money, which you will retrieve. And all the while I shall be on an open line to Captain Corcoran. When the money is in your hands, you and your two guards will disembark onto a boat of your own, leaving our crew and our ship unharmed."

"Sounds reasonable," replied Wolde.

"However, I should warn you that if you make one unusual move, or harm any member of the crew between now and the drop, you will never get off that ship alive."

"If you hold to your part of the bargain, there will be no need for anything unpleasant," said Wolde. "But how do I know you won't attack my own ship once we clear the area with the money?"

"Mostly because we don't want to become more unpopular than we already are in East Africa," replied Admiral Bradfield. "We have no intention of indulging in any senseless killing. Certainly not by publicly bombing a fishing boat or whatever you use. Also, it's not our money."

"Okay, you have my word. I have yours," said Wolde. "I abide by what you say. I am ordering my boat in now to take off my men. We have one captain on board our own boat, and we had twelve in the assault force at the start of the mission. There are two dead, two skiff drivers are not here, and eight men are on board. Captain Corcoran will see five of them leave in the next hour."

"Put him on," snapped Admiral Bradfield. "Put him on the line."

Fred Corcoran was very subdued. "We never had a chance, sir," he said. "There were too many, all armed with machine guns. And two of them boarded us before we even knew they were there. We tried to fight, but it was hopeless. We had two baseball bats against seven rifles and one heavy machine gun."

"I'm sure you did all you could," said the CNO. "And we have arranged for someone to pay the ransom—your union, matter of fact, the Seafarers International, looking after your interests."

"Thanks very much, sir. We're all getting a little scared right now."

"Don't be. I will be talking to you whenever I wish. These bastards smell cash right now, and they'll do what we tell them. I gave that one a firm talking to."

"I know you did, sir. He's a quiverin' wreck compared to two hours ago."

"Okay, now they're taking five men off and keeping two guards with you. When we make the cash drop, they will vacate the *Niagara Falls*, leaving you and the crew to proceed. I've told them if anything goes wrong, they will not get out of this alive. Any of them."

"And what about the cargo? The aid for the Somalis?"

"Well, we're not driving that ship into a Somali port where she'll be surrounded by a different set of pirates. So screw 'em. That cargo goes right back to Diego Garcia under escort. We'll give it to someone else. And that will seriously piss off the Somali government. They might think we're soft. But we're not that fucking soft."

"Spoken like a Christian," replied Fred Corcoran in his rich Dublin accent. "Screw 'em."

By this time, General Lancaster had set in motion the procedures to handle any form of United States disaster on the high seas. He had walked up to the office of the secretary of defense, the fifty-eight-year-old Simon Andre, and informed him of the capture and hijacking of the *Niagara Falls*.

Andre, a calm, assured man who held a Harvard degree and had written books on naval and military strategy, had been a career diplomat, who, by a series of personal miscalculations, had somehow ended up in the US Embassies of Iraq, Saudi Arabia, Iran, Nairobi, Zagreb, and Beijing. Lancaster once said he'd seen more explosions than Rommel.

But today he was in no mood for heroics. There were a lot of things he found difficult, and one of them was announcing to the public the death of American military personnel. Dead Navy SEALs filled him with horror, and Andre agreed with Zack Lancaster's view that to attack the *Niagara Falls* in her present position, in the hands of heavily armed pirates, was tantamount to a suicide mission.

"We'd win in the end," said General Lancaster. "But in this case winning wouldn't matter. It's the death rate, men dying for a few bags of fucking wheat. That's the issue."

Simon Andre agreed. And he was delighted with the scheme for the Seafarers International Union to pay $5 million to free their members and reclaim the ship. He had not the slightest interest in where the money came from.

"The important thing is to keep the president out of this," said Andre. "And that will not be a problem because he will have no interest in discussing anything that makes the United States look like a soft target. He's got enough problems there without us making it worse."

"I'm going to suggest a very quiet announcement tomorrow morning early," said General Lancaster. "Just a short statement to be issued by the Seafarers Union that an unarmed American merchant ship has been attacked and seized by a small group of Somali pirates in the Indian Ocean, several hundred miles off the coast of East Africa. No mention of casualties. Just a confirmation that the pirate leader has been in touch with the ship's owners. And that a ransom sum has been agreed with the Seafarers Union whose interest is to protect their members."

"Sounds very good," said Simon Andre. "But I think it needs an optimistic forecast—something like . . . *Negotiations are scheduled to conclude today, and the ship, the* Niagara Falls, *is expected to be on her way within forty-eight hours.*"

"Excellent," said the general. "And I think we should put a rigid ban on further information leaking out. We do not need the goddamned press writing stories about dead merchant navy officers boldly giving up their lives for Africa's starving millions."

"In the next half hour, I plan to inform the usual military channels what's happening," added the general. "Admiral Bradfield is briefing the navy departments, including SPECWARCOM. I'll get a briefing into Diego Garcia and Djibouti. And we'd better tell State, plus the CIA, and the National Security Agency. You'll deal with the White House?"

"I will. And we'll confer at 0600 before the trade union's press release."

"Yes, sir," said Zack as he left the room. "I'll have someone draft it this evening. Then our friend the union boss can release it to Reuters, or one of the other news agencies, at 0900 tomorrow."

The general went straight up to the fourth floor to the navy department, where Mark Bradfield was heavily ensconced with Major Harry Blythe, and Mary-Ann McCormac's fingers were flying over her computer keyboard, rounding up every last detail on the crew of the *Niagara Falls*. She had two cell phones on her desk, both tuned to a push-button satellite route to the bridge of the ship. Conversations with Captain Corcoran were mere seconds away at any time of the night.

A third phone next to her keyboard was programmed to the cell phone of Admiral Ismael Wolde, whom Mark Bradfield had decreed could just "keep his black ass waiting" until the US Navy was good and ready.

Major Harry Blythe was through talking to the duty officer at the British Embassy up the hill on Massachusetts Avenue before 2030. He did not explain precisely why the Pentagon wished to enlist the embassy to help with a large transfer of money to Nairobi via Barclays Bank, but the young attaché on the line sensed it was sufficiently important to inform the ambassador right away.

Sir Archie Compton left an embassy dinner and promised Harry he would facilitate the operation immediately. "I'll have the High Commission in Kenya monitor it. You can pay us right here, which will save you a lot of trouble and a hell of a lot of time."

"As a matter of pure interest, in case I'm asked," said Harry, "how does the money actually travel?"

Britain's ambassador to Washington answered: "Pentagon wires to this embassy's bank account," he said. "I'll give you the address and IBAN. Then we'll have our local bank here wire to Barclays International on Wall Street. They wire to Barclays downtown Nairobi. It's a big branch right on Moi Avenue, at Kenyatta."

"Sir, how could you possibly know that?" asked Harry.

"Family lived there, old boy, my father was High Commissioner during the Mau Mau rising—damned nearly ended up with an assegai stuck in his arse."

Harry said, "I'm really grateful to you, sir. And, just so you know, when the 5 million comes in, it will be under the name of the Seafarers International Union."

"Wouldn't matter to us if it came from the account of the Mothers' Union," said Sir Archie. "Just get it in there, and we'll make sure it's bagged up, waiting for you in cash in Nairobi within two hours, tomorrow morning . . . Tell your chaps to pick up a couple of ours at the High Commission. They can go to the bank together. No mistakes that way.

"By the way, can you tell me what you want it for? Just for interest. Not starting another bloody war, are you?"

Harry Blythe entirely forgot everyone was sworn to secrecy and instantly decided to regard Sir Archie Compton as a member of the US team. "Sir, we just had an 18,000-ton aid ship boarded and captured by pirates in the Indian Ocean. They're heavily armed, we got one man dead, and in this case we decided to let the Seafarers Union pay up for their men."

"That's sometimes much better," said Sir Archie. "Rescues often cost more than ransoms. And people do get killed too often. How're you getting the money out?"

"By air, sir. Military aircraft."

"Tell 'em to work with our military attaché in the Kenya High Commission. And use the smaller airfield, Wilson that is, out along the Mgathi Way. We used to own the place."

"Thank you, sir. And will you have someone e-mail the British Embassy's bank account details to me here at the Pentagon, Office of the Chairman of the Joint Chiefs."

"Chairman, eh?" said the ambassador. "You chaps must be a lot more concerned than you're letting on. Anything else we can do to help, just call me on my private line. Give Zack Lancaster my best, will you?"

Harry Blythe had just received a short lesson on why Sir Archie Compton was generally regarded as the best ambassador in the entire British Foreign Service—because he was witty, unassuming, clued-up, well-connected, and vastly experienced. He'd plucked the truth out of Harry like a ripe plum on a tree. Effortless. Harry never even realized it had happened. Until he put the phone down.

"Holy shit," he breathed. "I shouldn't have told him all that."

But the money complication was over, and he had solved it. Right down to the point of collection at Barclays Bank on Moi Avenue in Nairobi.

Nonetheless, Harry was worried about how much he had revealed to the British ambassador. Though he need not have been. Because Sir Archie merely stored the information, understanding it was not necessary for his government to know. It had nothing to do with the Brits, or anyone else.

Meanwhile Admiral Bradfield and Lieutenant Commander Souchak were moving fast on the line to the US Navy's Fifth Fleet headquarters in Bahrain and operational command in Diego Garcia. It was plainly imperative to move at least two warships into the ops area around the *Niagara Falls* and have them stand by to blow the pirate ship out of the water if necessary. If the money drop went smoothly, they could then escort Captain Corcoran back to safe harbor in DG.

Right now it was also necessary to have on standby an aircraft capable of flying nonstop into Kenya, a distance of 2,200 nautical miles from Diego Garcia, which would mean a six-hour journey for a P-3C Orion with its 4,000-nautical-mile range. It would also mean refuelling, which the Brits would easily organize at Wilson Airport.

Mark Bradfield was also on the line to Admiral Andy Carlow at SPECWARCOM in Coronado, and the SEAL boss almost visibly groaned when he heard that a large former US Navy vessel had been captured by what he described as "a small force of Somali tribesmen with fucking blowpipes."

"How the hell did it happen?" he asked Admiral Bradfield.

"Mostly because our ship is a merchantman now and is not armed in any way," he replied.

"Valuable cargo?"

"'Bout $100 million worth."

"Is that all? What was it?"

"Aid. A USAID consignment. Food, medicine, shelters, and a few workers."

"Bound for? . . ."

"Somalia."

"Jesus Christ! You mean they hijacked their own stuff?"

"'Fraid it's not like that in their country. Everybody's fighting everybody else. The pirates are independent of their own government, independent of their own nation. They just act on their own. That goddamned Somalia's completely lawless. Even when we get aid through to them, it just gets stolen by tribal warlords. Hardly anything gets through to where it's supposed to go."

"Then what the hell are we doing sending it there?" snapped Admiral Carlow. "If they don't steal it on land, they steal it on the high seas. That's what you're telling me."

Admiral Bradfield had rarely heard the SEAL C-in-C quite so irritated. "Steady, Andy," he said. "I didn't send it personally."

"No, I know. It just really pisses me off. Not that the government is out spending millions of dollars of taxpayers' money on hopeless causes. But that we're not fucking ready. We're totally unprepared for this kind of attack. A bunch of goddamned savages in a friggin' canoe somehow seizes a huge modern American freighter while it's making 15 knots through the water out in the middle of the ocean."

"Just as you say, Andy, we simply weren't ready."

"And think how long it would take us to prepare a rescue operation. Just getting my SEALs in there, way offshore, attacking from the surface or from the air, without any specialist training. I mean right here we're in the fucking Spanish Main, and the truth is we're just not ready for sixteenth-century piracy."

"Look, on this occasion at least, it's a great deal easier and cheaper for us to pay the ransom and get the ship and crew back . . . "

"Don't tell me the White House has agreed to negotiate with pirates?" Admiral Carlow interrupted, "That's a real first."

"No, tell you the truth, we've had to be a bit light-footed," said Mark Bradfield. "And we're not planning to ask any of our commanders to risk the lives of their men. But how do you feel about sending in SEALs on operations like this?"

"Badly. Because people would get killed trying to get aboard from the ocean, unless we came in behind heavy rocket attack, and that would almost certainly kill members of the ship's crew and damage the ship itself."

"And that, Andy, puts us right back to square one. Except for that one time when your guys did get on board the captured ship, the *Maersk Alabama*, then shot the pirates to free up the captain in the lifeboat."

"I know, Mark. But that was a bit of a landmark. The guys we were after were not on the main ship. And the ship was unguarded. It was all a bit unusual. And everything was in our favor so long as my guys remembered how to shoot straight."

"Well, I called just to keep you in the loop. But we all have to think about this—because no one is more aware than I am that the payment of this ransom shows a serious weakness on our part. Tonight those oceangoing bandits understand that the US will pay up if our backs are to the wall. Yesterday they had no reason to believe that could ever happen . . . "

"I know, Mark. But you gotta win the fight you're in. Not the one next week."

"Guess so. Let's both give it some thought. Bear in mind, we can't send an armed warship to escort every US tanker or freighter in the Middle and Far East. It costs $60,000 a day to keep those suckers out there. But we have to come up with something."

▼

AT 0500 THE GUIDED-MISSILE FRIGATE USS *Ingraham* cleared Diego Garcia about ten miles astern of the 9,000-ton guided-missile destroyer USS *Roosevelt*. An SH-60 Sikorsky Seahawk helicopter gunship was embarked on board each of them, armed heavily with machine guns and hellfire missiles. The two warships were ordered to make flank speed for 1,200 miles directly to the point on the ocean where the *Niagara Falls* now wallowed, helpless under the armed control of primitive foreign invaders. It would take them less than forty-eight hours.

Five hours later, Britain's High Commission in Nairobi informed Britain's Washington Embassy the sum of $5 million in cash was awaiting collection by US personnel at the Barclays Bank offices on Moi Avenue.

Thirty minutes later, a P-3C Orion Navy Anti-Submarine Warfare aircraft came hurtling down the Diego Garcia runway and rocketed up into the clear blue skies above the base, banked hard, and headed due west for the shores of East Africa. At the controls was Lt. Com. Aaron Marshall assisted by his engineer officer and navigator, Lt. Raymond K. Rossi.

Behind them sat a special four-man navy guard, all qualified air crew, who would accompany them in two vehicles provided by the British High Commission for the round-trip from Wilson Airfield to the bank and back. The guards all carried M-4 light machine guns. Any one of them could fly the aircraft in an emergency.

Lieutenant Commander Marshall swiftly took the big Orion to its 30,000-feet cruising altitude and set her speed for 400 knots per hour. Lieutenant Rossi sat next to him in the co-pilot's chair. They would land in Nairobi at 1600 hours, and the two officers would be guests of the British High Commission overnight, with an ETD of 1800 hours the following evening.

The guards would remain with the aircraft and supervise the refuelling. There was no way the US Navy was going to air-drop that cash onto the deck of *Niagara Falls* before the American warships were in place, port and starboard. They were scheduled to arrive shortly before 2100.

General Lancaster and Admiral Bradfield caucused at 0600 as planned on the navy department's fourth floor. Lieutenant Commander Souchak, who had assumed a loose command, had been there all night, twice speaking to Captain Corcoran, both times conscious that Wolde was very happy to cooperate.

Thanks to the swift intervention of Sir Archie Compton, the finance was all in place. There was a report from DG that the Orion was scheduled to land in Nairobi in two hours, and the two warships had been steaming west for several hours.

The press release had been prepared and would be automatically e-mailed to Reuters from the Pentagon on behalf of the Seafarers Union, signed by the union boss himself. All future media inquiries were to be directed to the Seafarers' HQ out in Camp Springs. General Lancaster had a suspicion this would lead to pure chaos on an unprepared union switchboard.

But neither of the military chiefs cared about that. Chaos was good in situations like this when a smoke screen, not clarity, was the objective, and Mark Bradfield observed, "Well, they're making a very easy quarter-million for this. Might as well make 'em earn it."

Almost 7,000 miles away, the *Niagara Falls* was beginning to roll on the rising swell of the Indian Ocean. Without her forward propulsion, this was an unusual, exaggerated motion, and several of the crew were feeling decidedly ill. However the engines were still running and the generators were active as she pitched and yawed in the outer limits of the Somali current.

On the bridge, Captain Corcoran and Rick Barnwell were prisoners, but they were allowed freedom to walk around and keep an eye on the big machinery. They were guarded by Admiral Wolde and Omar Ali Farah, who sat on the floor with the heavy machine gun. Elmi Ahmed had the rest of the crew pinned down on the lower deck, while he sat at the top of the companionway.

The hours passed very slowly because there was nothing to do except wait for the US airdrop. Wolde spoke frequently to Captain Hassan who still had the *Mombassa* a mile astern. And he once called Mohammed Salat to inform him that terms had been agreed and that an American trade union was paying for the release of the men.

"How much?" asked Salat.

"Five million US dollars," replied Wolde.

"Excellent," said Salat. "The stock should increase significantly as soon as I post the news. Did your operation go smoothly?"

"No, sir. The captain opened fire and Bouh Adan was killed. We also lost Gacal Gueleh during the boarding. Two crew members came at us with baseball bats. I had to shoot one of them."

"Sounds very bad," said Salat. "I won't mention it until you return because we must always protect our businesslike reputation. All of our dealings must be strictly commercial. High finance. Not street fights on the ocean."

"Yes, sir, I very much agree," said Wolde. "But I wish you'd tell that to the Americans."

Back in Washington, managing the news totally preoccupied the principal players in this oceanic crisis. The press release went out on time, 0900, and like so many military press releases quite correctly sought to conceal the facts from the shark-cruising journalists.

The release was of course drafted for minimal drama. And for a half hour in this early part of the media's working day, no one was especially excited. First of all, the story was happening thousands and thousands of miles away. There were no pictures and zero possibility of getting any. It seemed unlikely there had been death or even the threat of death. Also the Pentagon plainly knew nothing and cared less.

The only person to whom the journalists could speak in the whole of North America was a guy who worked for a trade union, which was about as sexy as a pound of turnips.

It was not until the major shift change in the late afternoon that someone at Fox News tuned in to the possibility of real drama on the high seas. He was a senior editor, chief copy-taster, night news editor, a former foreign correspondent for Fox in Afghanistan, with a hair-trigger instinct for any kind of a break and a vivid imagination.

Ian Brodie was one of Rupert Murdoch's blue-eyed men, a fellow Aussie. In addition to being as sharp as anyone alive on a news story, Brodie was a gifted writer, capable of stepping beyond the bounds of a regular news report and delivering supple prose in the form of a colorful but understanding essay, always drawing on his depth of firsthand knowledge.

He'd seen the station's earlier bromide attempt to present the story. And while he was uncertain they weren't right in their judgment, something told him they were "all over the bloody place on this one."

Brodie reported for duty early, pulled up the original press release, and nearly hit the ceiling. Every journalistic instinct he had told him this was major. He stood up and yelled, "*What's going on with this hijack in the Indian Ocean?* A group of armed Somali pirates somehow boarded and captured an 18,000-ton freighter flying the flag of the United States of America.

"The Pentagon is lying through their teeth; that's bloody obvious. What's this '*received no report of casualties*'? Jesus, can't anyone sense they just don't want to tell us? Otherwise they would have written, *THERE WERE NO FUCKING CASUALTIES*! RIGHT?"

The Fox newsroom went silent. Ian Brodie was not only a revered television reporter and editor, he was a close friend of Murdoch's. People said their families had been friends for generations back in Melbourne.

And now he was in full cry. "Picture the scene," he snapped. "These comedians from Somalia, always armed to the teeth, somehow creep up on the freighter. They get alongside and the grappling irons flash through the night air over the rails. The crew hears the clang, but the pirates are up and over, swinging against the hull, the sea rising below them.

"There's a fight, someone gets shot, the crew surrenders. Right here we're dealing with terrified men, ruthless cutthroats from a lawless land, men who will kill without mercy. And the US Navy, furious, humiliated, sends for one of the most powerful warships in the world. I betcha she's steaming in there right now, guns blazing.

"Is there anyone is this room who does not think that is the biggest story of this week? Because if there is, he better get out of here right now and change jobs. Meanwhile, for Christ's sake get moving. Because if there's anyone in the other channels with a lick of sense, we're gonna get the shit knocked out of us on the evening news. Let's really start to move it."

Thus Fox jumped into the lead, bombarding the Navy Press Office in the Pentagon and meeting a wall of silence that inflamed their curiosity: *But you must be able to confirm the pirates took the ship by force . . . Were shots fired? You say no casualties, how do you know? Where's the warship? What's the name of the captain? Where's he from? Has his family been informed he's a prisoner of brutal killers?*

The questions rained in. And the press officers kept saying they had no information. They had no contact. And they could not reveal where they had acquired their minimal information.

But it did no good. When Fox News came out with their early evening bulletin, they ran a headline on the screen which read:

GUN BATTLE AT SEA
US FREIGHTER SURRENDERS
TO ARMED PIRATE GANG

It was, in every word, precisely what General Zack Lancaster did not want to hear. Because it announced what no one would dare admit—the United States was bargaining with terrorists.

# CHAPTER 3

▼

THE RAIN THAT HAD BEEN THREATENING FOR TWO DAYS finally swept in from the southwest, straight off the Pacific Ocean, and it lashed the long beach at Coronado. The wind rose and fell, and the squalls stung the faces of the BUDs class laboring along the tidal mark where the thumping breakers end their everlasting journey.

There were 162 men assigned, all of them wearing their canvas shorts, socks, and boots, the smart ones seeking out that narrow strip where the sand has hardened from an outgoing tide and is no longer being washed by the foamy water.

Running this beach is an art form. Too high up, the loose sand impedes every stride, doubling a man's energy output. Too near the water, boots hit unstable, shifting sand, and a man ends up splashing instead of running, a half ton of wet sand stuck to each boot.

Every morning is bad for a BUDs class. This one was awful. The rain was belting down, the wind was warm but strong, every few minutes rising to a peak that turned raindrops into shards of glass. But there was no complaining, no audible sounds of men having second thoughts about this test of physical stamina.

The run was four miles: two out, two back to the starting point. This was the first week, and the objective was eight-minute miles. There was, as ever, a pack of maybe a dozen good runners out in front, with a pack of perhaps forty right behind them, struggling, breathless, trying to come to terms with the insane level of fitness required of them.

Alongside the class bounded their proctor, a SEAL commander of massive presence, and he was running the third mile as if he'd just started, springing along the beach some ten yards wide of the second pack, watching for the guys who betrayed the critical signs, the ones that signalled they were not putting out. Not giving it *everything*.

Instructor Mack needed to sort these characters out real fast because they were wasting his precious time, and worse, they were getting in the way of the true iron man who wanted to become a United States Navy SEAL so badly nothing else on this earth mattered.

Mack ran the tough, deep, sandy course with an easy stride. He'd attained wild-animal strength and fitness on this very stretch when he was only twenty-three, and he'd never lost it. Of all the striving men on the beach, only he understood what was required—total mental dominance and lung-busting effort. Sets a man so far apart he might be accepted one day into the most elite fighting force in the world.

Above the rain squalls, his words rang out as he pounded the sand: *COME ON, YOU GUYS . . . LET ME SEE SOMETHING . . . I WANT YOU TO DIG . . . DIG DEEPER THAN YOU EVER DID BEFORE . . . FIND SOME MORE FOR ME . . . NOW RUN! RUN! RUN! YOU THERE, FRETHEIM! YOU WANT TO STAY IN THIS CLASS? YOU BETTER START PUTTING OUT . . . NOW HIT IT! LET'S GO! GO! GO!*

They were into the last mile and the going seemed to grow tougher as the rain soaked the sand and made it cling even more. Mack Bedford kept shouting, sometimes encouraging, sometimes berating. Six guys had already quit and could be seen walking away over the dunes toward the veranda, where they would place their helmets in that poignant lonely line before ringing the brass bell that hung from a beam, departing Coronado.

The rest floundered on, soaked through, most of them likely to fail the target time of thirty-two minutes for the four miles. Some would make it because of a God-given talent to run; others would make it because they would rather die than fail. And some, who had no real talent for hard distance running, would get there on sheer willpower, overcoming the pain, refusing to give in, no matter what.

These were guys Mack Bedford needed to locate. These were the United States Navy SEAL commanders of the future. They were men like him, men whose physical and mental boundaries reached so far away they were over the goddamned horizon. You don't need to be an Olympic runner to become a SEAL, but you need to believe you could be if the chips were down.

More importantly, every BUDs student needs to care profoundly about attaining objectives. Because if it's not a matter of life and death in each man's own mind, he may as well get himself a one-way ticket out of this terrible place.

Mack Bedford always ran the last three-quarters of a mile out in front of the pack so he would be waiting as the class battered its way up the home stretch. For these last three minutes, he always switched on his digital radio and ran to a track of "Night Train." Because he liked the beat, the hard, fast drumming that caused his boots to hit the sand faster and faster, carrying him clear of the pack. The way he liked it.

No matter how young his class, no matter how inexperienced and essentially unfit they were, Mack Bedford needed to be better, faster, stronger, the iron man of the training camp. It was not even difficult. But he still needed to prove it. Every day.

Mack ran on, hard, all the way to the line, opening up a fifty-yard gap between himself and his leading BUDs class group. At the end, he stared back down the beach and touched a button to switch off the music. The radio came on automatically.

*News bulletin: An 18,000-ton US freighter has been boarded and captured by Somali pirates in the Indian Ocean after a ferocious gunfight on board the vessel. The battle took place hundreds of miles off the coast of East Africa. The United States Navy is believed to be deep into negotiations with the pirates. It is the first time the Pentagon has ever bargained with terrorists, which suggests a very serious situation.*

Mack Bedford frowned but switched off the radio because he had more pressing business, like three more men quitting and informing his junior instructors they were DOR—dropping out on request.

Mack faced the leading group and thanked them for their efforts, giving them immediate permission to rest. The following bunch of fifteen, the hard-driving runners-up, arrived next. Mack said nothing. But he stood glowering at the third group, half-dead with exhaustion, fighting their way across the sand fifty yards back.

There were four young men among the twenty who Mack suspected were not "putting out," men who were quite good runners and could, perhaps, have gone faster but lacked resolution. Worse yet, one of the four was a very tough young officer and an extremely popular guy.

Mack Bedford bellowed at them, watching their eyes, watching the way some heads went down. "*You see that group up the beach resting?*" he yelled. "*Those guys are winners. And they're being rewarded for trying their guts out! You guys are LOSERS! Hear me? GODDAMNED LOSERS!*"

No one spoke. "*GET WET AND SANDY!*" bawled Mack. "*AND DO IT FAST—FOR A CHANGE!*"

The shattered group of twenty BUDs hopefuls responded, "*HOO-YAH! Instructor Mack.*"

They headed for the breakers, buffeting their way into the freezing Pacific, out through the first crash of the waves and into the second. At least, nineteen of them did. The young officer quit unconditionally, requesting permission to drop out and leave.

Mack Bedford nodded curtly. Unsmiling. The kid would never be back for another try. Surface fleet officers are only allowed one shot at becoming a SEAL and are formally regarded as guys who should have known better than to apply.

Mack watched the other nineteen. Two other instructors were already down at the edge of the water also watching carefully, both with stopwatches, ensuring the men were out of the water before hypothermia set in.

On the signal, the nineteen men came running out of the water, reached the dry sand and rolled in it, standing to attention as the chafing and itching kicked in. Each man was barely recognizable. Mack Bedford stood before them and yelled. *"FLUTTER KICKS!"* he ordered. *"GET IN THAT WATER AND SHOW SOME EFFORT!"*

The men rushed down to the shallows and hit the water, glad to wash away some of the sand. They then turned over and dropped onto their backs at the very extreme of the tide's reach, with only their heads and shoulders in the ocean.

They began their kicks, lifting both outstretched legs and pushing them up and down. It was, without doubt, the most brutal of all the disciplines and very nearly impossible for men who have run four miles and then treaded water, in the surf, for six minutes.

The pain was almost unbearable, burning thighs and lower backs. And every time a wave rolled in, the water washed over their faces, suddenly and unexpectedly. Men were coughing and spluttering, trying to breathe, trying to kick, trying to spit out saltwater, choking, struggling for air, some of them giving up.

After the rest of the class had straggled across the finish line, four of the instructors walked among the men doing the flutter kicks. Everyone except the first group of winners was in the Pacific Ocean in a kind of surreal disgrace.

The instructors knew precisely how impossible the kicks were, but they laid into the men verbally. *"GODDAMNIT! YOU'RE LIKE A BUNCH OF GODDAMNED FAGGOTS! ARE YOU SURE YOU WANT TO BE HERE? WHY DON'T YOU QUIT RIGHT NOW. GO AND RING THE GODDAMNED BELL!"*

By now, no one was capable of correctly performing the flutter kicks. The instructors, of course, did not care one way or another.

They cared who was trying; they watched for the men who would not give in, whose faces were set, whose jaws were jutting, whose fists were clenched, whose legs were still pumping, who spat out the seawater. They were looking for the ones who swore and roared with the pain. But who would not give in.

Almost every single one of the 162-odd guys who had set off along the beach an hour previously would be on his way home, or back to the fleet, sooner rather than later. Two more caved in and went DOR before the flutter kicks were concluded. Twelve gone before lunch—average for the first day of INDOC.

Instructor Mack lined up the rest into three groups of fifty, each with six lines of eight men, class leaders out in front. And even as the exhausted students struggled to make a decent formation, the soulful notes of the brass bell at the edge of the grinder chimed out across the sand dunes.

It was the sound of failure. It was the sound of reality. It was a sound from the very heart of the United States Navy that certain men had been found unsuitable for the precious responsibilities visited upon a Navy SEAL.

Mack understood the strange shock that the chiming bell had upon the entire group. And he spoke to them sternly. "No one chimes that bell for you," he said. "You chime it for yourself. That's the only way the sonofabitch rings. You decide whether you want to stay here or not. And I'm here to tell you it's gonna do a lot of chiming over the coming weeks.

"But that's not to say we think any less of you. Otherwise we'd end up hating several hundred applicants every year. No, we understand. And we ask only that you do not waste our time.

"If you have serious doubts about yourself, then quit right now. You leave with our best wishes for the future. And you may become top-class professionals in your navy careers. We all hope you do. Some of the best guys I ever met out here in Coronado rang that bell. One of 'em commands a US Navy destroyer in the North Atlantic.

"I want to issue one warning: We do not laugh at a man who quits. *EVER!* And anyone who gets caught doing so is expelled from the course instantly. That's because he's either too stupid or arrogant or does not understand team spirit. We do not need that person. Remember that."

At the top of the beach, the other instructors were in the process of moving huge logs the size of small telephone poles near the men. Mack was about to issue a regrouping when the cell phone in his pocket vibrated. He glanced at the small screen and saw the call was from the office of Rear Admiral Andy Carlow, C-in-C Special Operations Command. His ultimate boss. The Emperor SEAL.

The two men were friends, although Admiral Carlow was a little older and had always been senior. But they had fought their way together through the rubble in North Baghdad, run a thousand risks, and captured insurgents by the dozen. On one dark and terrible night, a vicious young Islamist had flown at Andy Carlow's throat with a curved tribal knife and, for once, the SEAL team leader was not looking.

In a split second, Mack Bedford had leapt forward, almost took the kid's head off with a thunderous blow from his rifle butt, and saved his buddy's life. Andy Carlow had never forgotten it.

"Mack?"

"Yup."

"I hear you're killing 'em down there."

"Nah. Just trying to keep 'em alert."

"Can you have lunch with me?"

"Sure. What's on your mind?"

"You hear about those friggin' pirates on board that US freighter?"

"Just did. On the radio."

"Buddy, you can trust me on this. Right there we're looking at big trouble. One of the crew, the 2 I/C, got fucking killed. And the problem is going to come home, all the way to Coronado. How about noon? My office."

"Roger that."

Mack clicked off the phone and turned to the sweating, heaving workforce on the beach, all of them trying to get the heavy logs in place. He could hear the instructors yelling *LIFT! LIFT! LIFT!* And he called down to them, "*SEE Y'ALL LATER—DON'T LET ME DOWN NOW.*"

And with that he turned back toward the grinder and began the long run up and over the dunes. There's no walking in Coronado, not for anyone associated with a BUDs training class. Everyone runs. Hard. And Mack Bedford covered the deep sand dunes with a short, punchy stride, driving forward, hearing the never-ending voice in his mind, still echoing: *Go, Mack, drive on, stay out in front. Be the best, always the best.* Thus went a true Navy SEAL from one place to another.

He showered and changed to meet the boss and arrived at two minutes before noon, never having forgotten the words of his own proctor on the first day of INDOC: *No matter what time I get here, ANYONE WHO ARRIVES AFTER ME IS LATE! UNDERSTAND?*

He walked into the office and found Andy pouring over e-mails downloaded from his computer, all of them on the same subject— the pirates of Haradheere.

"Okay, Mack, I ordered a couple plates of chicken salad and some fruit and yogurt. Is that okay for you?"

"Fine. In the absence of a big cheeseburger with onions and ketchup."

The admiral laughed. "I can't eat like that now I'm not on operational training," he said. "We gotta stay healthy."

"I'm healthy," grinned Mack. "I just ran about three hundred miles along the goddamned beach. This is a good bunch of guys in the class, by the way. A lot of them very serious and very determined."

"Christ, I hope so," said Andy. "Recruiting's getting harder every year."

"Now," said Mack, changing the subject. "What's all this Harad-heere bullshit?"

"Tell you the truth, it has not really affected us so far. The Pentagon's found a way to pay these bastards off, cheap, and get the ship under way. I'd guess they're real nervous about this officer getting killed."

"I bet they are," replied Mack. "Because when the news gets out the guy's dead, there'll be about twenty Republican senators demanding that the US cease to be humiliated by a tribe of armed savages and start laying down the goddamned law."

"Correct," said Andy. "As usual you're a couple of jumps out in front of me. But I guess I've had reason to be real grateful for that a few times.

"Mack, I'm going to walk us both through this. Because for a start, neither the public nor the media understands what the hell is going on off the coast of East Africa."

"I'm not sure I do either," said Mack.

"Well, this pirate bullshit is, in my opinion, here to stay. The sonsofbitches are making a fortune. Because it's always cheaper and easier to pay up and get out of trouble. In a way, the goddamned pirates have always played fair. When they get paid, they release prisoners and ships. Thus no one who mattered has ever died. But that just changed. Last night. Someone who mattered did die . . . "

"And the navy decided to open negotiations . . . " Mack interrupted.

"Right. And as God is my judge, the crap is about to hit the fan." Admiral Carlow was frowning. "Because the game just changed. And when that happens, a lot of people are going to want a lot of answers."

"I guess so," said Mack.

"The big question is going to be as follows: When the *Maersk Alabama* was boarded and the captain kidnapped, the US sent in the SEALs and the problem was solved. Three dead pirates, right? Game over. *Why can't we do that every time and put an end to this shit?* That's what they're all going to ask—reporters, columnists, politicians, and the rest."

"They don't understand, do they?" Mack mused. "How difficult that mission was. All the planning, the ocean drop, the sensational marksmanship."

"No, old buddy, they don't. But they're still going to ask that question. Why can't the SEALs go in, every time."

"Well, obviously, under certain conditions, we can't possibly go in. Because an attack by sea is sometimes impossible, and a helicopter attack is a pretty bad idea if the nearest US helicopters are a thousand miles away. The time factor can be a real pain in the ass."

"And there's something else I haven't told you yet," said the admiral. "Two of the pirates were also killed on board the *Niagara Falls*. The captain shot one of them with a machine gun he shouldn't have had, and one of his officers smashed someone's head in with a baseball bat while he was trying to board."

"You think that might make 'em a bit more vicious in the future?"

"Don't you?"

Just then a waiter came in with the chicken salads and fruit along with a fresh pot of coffee and two hot rolls with butter. Andy Carlow declined politely, so Mack gratefully began to devour both lunches, spearing hunks of grilled chicken as he went.

"This debate," said Andy, "which will begin in the media and proceed to Congress, is going to end up with no-nothing politicos saying stuff like, *What's the point of spending X billions on our Special Forces if we can't use 'em, can't even send 'em in to rescue our own ships and our own people?*"

"Well, they have to understand that not all circumstances are the same," said Mack. "Different locations. Different demands. Different threat levels."

"They don't," snapped Andy. "To them, a pirate attack is a pirate attack, so send in the SEALs to rescue everyone. And do it quick. That's the mindset, both in the media, and in a large part of Congress."

"And what are we going to do about it?" said Commander Bedford. "Reload our M-4s and go in all by ourselves? Show 'em how it's done?"

Andy Carlow grimaced. "Mack," he said, "this could get out of hand. They might *make* us go into a totally inappropriate theater of operations, and a lot of our best guys stand a hell of a good chance of dying. And I might not be able to stop the mission."

"I see that. What do we do?"

"We need an idea, something to surprise the life out of them. Something that makes us one jump out in front of them all. We need to make them look like amateurs in a very professional place."

"I'm right with you on that."

"Mack, how much do you know about DEVGRU?" asked the admiral, mentioning the most secretive, highly classified operational force in the United States Navy, the Naval Special Warfare Development Group.

"Not much. But I know what they do, and where they are."

"They're a sensational fighting group, the premier US counterterrorist teams, and they've had a lot of success. But the world is moving on. Fast. These damned pirates have changed the rules in the last two years.

"And the truth is, DEVGRU has become too big. It's too much like an army, too many people know what they're up to. And everyone knows when they move. They're really a joint services operation, and brilliant as they are, they're a state secret that's become loose.

"Right now, because of a zillion legal factors, we need to be much smaller. We need an outfit that can move very fast, in total secrecy. These days when DEVGRU moves, probably a thousand people know it's happened."

"They even had a book written about them, right?" said Mack.

"Yeah. And it was a pretty good book. But more and more became known. Right now they got Web sites all over the Internet. There's about four hundred people involved in DEVGRU, including support staff, combat teams, and a training team, and a huge hunk of real estate down at Dam Neck, Virginia Beach. Nations have gone to war with less frontline backup."

"What's changed so much, Andy?"

"Laws, Mack, goddamned laws. Things need to be done these days when *no one know*s what happened, or who did it. It's the new way, and it's going to become the only way. Because anyone gets caught fighting and perhaps killing in order to save their own people and ships, well . . . that someone is going to face some quasi-international justice. The US cannot allow that legal bullshit to happen."

"So what do we do?" said Mack.

"We need to form a kind of anti-pirate platoon, a highly trained, specialist force that is geared only to attack pirates. Guys who are at home on the high seas, guys who will become world experts at taking pirate ships, recapturing hijacked vessels, and then going in on land and knocking out their headquarters and beating the shit out of their high command. I'm thinking the most ruthless professional fighting force in the world."

"If you want it secret, where do you plan to put it? Qatar? Diego Garcia?"

"I haven't decided yet. But first this new platoon will need some intake from DEVGRU itself—guys who are already experts on boarding moving ships. Like the pirates, they will use grappling irons, and they will climb hulls and come in from the air in attack gunships—one to deploy our boarding party and one to give them heavy covering fire."

"Training them where?"

"Right here in the San Diego base. There are warships and submarines running in and out of here all the time. It's ideal. We can work with both stationary and moving ships, and we can establish this platoon and its senior command to form an outfit that deals with pirates only. The training will be absolutely sharp end, no distractions. And people in the base will hardly notice, since we work there fairly often anyway.

"This new Pirate Platoon will become the unchallenged experts on the subject. They say yes, then it's a go. They say no, and we reconsider. But at least we won't have politicians and journalists telling us what they think."

"You have any ideas about who might command this fighting force? As if I didn't know."

"That's my boy, Mack. This would be right up your alley. Take you back to the old days, oil rigs in the Gulf and all that."

"Well, it might. But they were swim-ins from the mini-subs. This is entirely different. Boarding a moving target."

"That's why you're here, Mack. Because we believe you can do what would be impossible for other men."

"Hmmmm. Let's give it our best shot. Which platoon am I having?

"Alpha, Beta, and Charlie are busy. I want to reform Delta. So from now on Delta is the anti-pirate force, and you're its commander. There's probably some special guys you want with you, and I regard this coming challenge as so urgent you can have anyone you like.

"But for the first time, Mack, we'll have a specialist group, ready to go in and attack the pirates, show 'em what happens when the SEALs move onto the international stage. But we better not fuck it up."

Mack was thoughtful. "Andy, we cannot just go in if a situation is honest-to-God hopeless. We'll get no marks for failing. And there will be situations that are beyond us—mostly because they're too far away offshore, and we cannot get there in time.

"Equally, we don't want to go in heavy-handed and start shooting pirates when it's not necessary. Our missions need to be chosen with care. But when we go in, we hit hard.

"As Navy SEALs, we are sworn to protect those who cannot protect themselves, so every mission is a mission of mercy, to rescue prisoners, to reclaim ships and property, to protect the innocent."

"Couldn't have said it better, Mack. I'm calling a meeting of senior instructors and commanders this evening. And then we go to work. Line up some top-class guys for the Delta Platoon. These goddamned pirates want to fuck about, we'll show them how to *really* fuck about."

▼

NINE THOUSAND MILES FROM CORONADO, the Navy's P-3C Orion took off from Nairobi's Wilson Airport right on time, bound for a remote stretch of dark sky high above the Indian Ocean, 0.75 degrees south on the GPS, 52.36 east. Behind the captain and the navigator sat the four navy guards. Between them were five large zip-up mailbags, fluorescent orange in color.

Inside those bags was a total of $5 million, packaged in stacks of fifty $100 bills. There were two hundred of these small, manageable stacks in each of the five bags, the handles lashed together with a wide unbreakable nylon strap.

On each bag, there was a flotation device and a satellite location beam, just in case the drop missed the deck of the *Niagara Falls* and landed in the water. The state-of-the-art locator, which would begin transmitting as soon as the bags landed, was similar to those carried by all combat SEALs operating behind enemy lines.

Their route took them over land, directly east, straight along the equator from Nairobi to the coast. And almost immediately the light began to fade, even before they reached the ocean, flying fast, making 400 knots away from the sun setting behind them over Kenya's Great Rift Valley.

By the time they reached the coastline, the inshore waters below were a dull pink color and then, almost immediately, they turned inky dark blue and then black. Out in front, high to starboard, they could already see their own personal badge in the sky, the bright constellation of stars that form Orion's Belt—their aircraft having been named after the mythological hunter.

The Orion's computer system was already showing distance to target. Right now it showed 483 miles to the drop zone, and the aircraft was knocking off one mile every nine seconds. Lt. Ray Rossi was opening maritime radio comms on the agreed frequency directly to the bridge of the *Niagara Falls*. Admiral Wolde had accepted this must be done between Captain Corcoran and the incoming aircraft that was transporting the ransom cash.

Ray Rossi had the connection as the computer ticked off the miles, now down to 420, only sixty-three minutes to the target, not allowing for the drop in speed over the final ten miles.

On the bridge, a tired Captain Corcoran spoke slowly: "Receiving you, Bankers One. We have speedboats ready to proceed to pickup at five minutes' notice. Both standing by, with Mombassa, one mile off our stern. Over."

"Roger that, *Niagara*. We show four hundred miles, ETA 2105 hours. Planning low-level flight drop, no parachutes, fluorescent orange night bags with flotation. We'll aim for the ship, margin for error no more than one hundred yards. Over."

"Roger that, Bankers One. We have your approach course two-seven-zero degrees. The wind's light southwesterly. I'll turn *Niagara Falls* into it. You'll come at us from astern, two-two-five degrees. Over."

"Roger that, *Niagara*. We will come in downwind and then

swing around the ship on your portside about four miles south. You'll see us okay. Probably at 2,000 feet and losing height. Over."

"Roger that, Bankers One. Check in thirty minutes. Over."

It was completely dark now and the Orion cut through the tropical night, still at her cruising height, crossing the earth's easterly lines of longitude. They'd been aloft a long time with a very small crew, and two of the guards were shifting the moneybags toward the internal bomb bays under the front fuselage.

The Orion is designed with external sonobuoy launch tubes, but no one was keen to have 5 million bucks in paper money hurtling through the windswept stratosphere outside the aircraft, beyond reach. Lockheed had not, of course, designed the great airborne warhorse of the United States Navy to deliver cash.

Half an hour later the computer showed fewer than two hundred miles left, and now, it seemed, the miles ticked away even faster. The cash was in place, and Lieutenant Rossi opened up communications to the bridge of the *Niagara Falls*. Simultaneously Aaron Marshall began his descent into the drop zone, coming five degrees south in readiness to bank left for the final approach.

Captain Corcoran came on the line to receive the terse message from the incoming US aircraft: "Bankers One—one-nine-zero miles. Steering course nine-five. ETA twenty-one-hundred and five hours."

"Roger that, Bankers One. Over."

The Orion was losing height. Minute by minute it slid down through the sky. With fifteen minutes to go it was at 15,000 feet and descending. Ten minutes from the target, which it would overfly, it was sixty-seven miles west-southwest of the US freighter and flying at under 10,000 feet.

Seven minutes later it was slowing down, only twenty-six miles from the ship, which was now plain on the radar screen. It was flying at only 2,000 feet, and four minutes later the pilots could see the lights of the *Niagara Falls*, six miles off through their portside cockpit window.

Lieutenant Rossi again opened the Orion's comms to the bridge. "Suggest you launch speedboats. Bring them in close to the vessel, port and starboard. That's us six miles off your starboard beam. We're running up for our one-eighty turn. You'll see the approach. Descending to one hundred feet for the drop . . . *stay* on the line, captain."

Standing right next to the ship's master, the pirate chief, Admiral Wolde, called the *Mombassa* and ordered Captain Hassan to send the boats away. Immediately the helmsmen, Hamdan Ougoure and Abadula Sofian, gunned the two skiffs directly at the distant freighter in readiness for the drop.

By now the area was becoming crowded and very noisy. Both the destroyer *Roosevelt* and the frigate *Ingraham* had arrived on station and were positioned close in to the captured freighter, lights blazing. On the stern of each warship was a Sikorsky Seahawk, rotors howling, ready to take off. Essentially there was enough US Navy hardware within a couple of hundred yards to conquer a small country—guided missiles, bombs, torpedoes, naval artillery, and machine guns.

The Orion was down to two hundred miles per hour. She was three miles past the ship, and Lieutenant Commander Marshall began the turn. The portside wing dipped as he banked hard left. He held her at 1,000 feet and then descended again, in 220-foot drops.

Rossi's last message to Captain Corcoran went through: "Coming in now at one hundred feet for the low-level drop. Will aim directly for the deck."

Inside the cockpit, Marshall held the huge aircraft steady, flying straight at the stern lights of the *Niagara Falls*. Her four turboprops screamed in the night, as Lieutenant Rossi called back: "Two miles . . . thirty-six seconds . . . twenty seconds . . . "

Marshall could see the outline of the freighter now, and he heard Ray Rossi's final call. His voice rose to a shout as he ordered: "*Okay, we're right on her . . . NOW! NOW! NOW!*"

The bomb bay flashed open and the orange bags fell out, tumbling straight down one hundred feet as the Orion thundered overhead. It was a great shot, but a rising gust on the southwester just caught it, and the five roped bags swooped over the starboard rail and landed in the Indian Ocean only ten feet from the ship's hull.

Abadula Sofian, his skiff positioned only a hundred yards away, watched the bags tumble from the giant aircraft, and he saw the bags hit the rail and almost slide down the hull of the stationary ship. He could see the bright fluorescent light floating on the surface of the water. He steered his narrow boat right onto the big waterproof bags and rammed a boat hook into the middle of the mass of handles and the nylon rope.

Abadula heaved, and the orange bags gripped. His crewmate leaned over to help, and there on the moonlit waters the two Somali pirates hauled aboard their five-million-dollar catch. In the far distance the lights of the Orion were back in view as Lieutenant Commander Marshall made his second 180-degree turn and headed back to Diego Garcia.

Back on the bridge, Admiral Wolde, on his cell phone, ordered his two skiffs to close in on the freighter, where the crew was already fixing nets for the disembarkation. On the other line, Admiral Mark Bradfield in the Pentagon was giving the orders, and he told Wolde to take his two guards and report to the deck. When the two skiffs pulled alongside, all three men were to disembark, using the nets, and proceed directly to the *Mombassa*.

When Wolde asked the admiral if he was permitted to have a word with his helmsman just to check the bags were actually full of money, he was given a curt but unexpected answer.

"No," snapped America's chief naval officer. "But I do have a couple of words for you personally. One's 'fuck' and the other's 'you.' Now get off our ship, and consider yourself damn lucky we don't blow that tin-can fishing boat of yours clean out of the water with all of you on board."

Ismael's grasp of colloquial English was not bad but by no means perfect. Even so, he definitely understood Admiral Bradfield's drift, and, secretly, he did consider himself lucky to be getting out of there alive.

"Sir, I have kept my word to you. No one has been harmed since we first spoke. The *Niagara Falls* is returned to you as it was when we found it."

"That's the only reason you're still breathing," gritted Admiral Bradfield, ungraciously.

"Then I bid you good-bye, sir," replied Ismael Wolde.

"For your sake, I hope I do not come across you again," rasped Mark Bradfield down the line from Washington, with an equally ungracious flourish.

The three pirates stepped over the rails, tossed down their weapons, and climbed down the nets into the skiffs. With a roar from the Yamahas, the raiders took off with their booty, speeding back to the *Mombassa*.

As they left, Ismael Wolde was on the line to Mohammed Salat with the shortest message: *Mission accomplished. Somali Marines coming home with 5 million dollars. Arrive Haradheere midnight tomorrow.*

When the same message flashed up on the bulletin board in the stock exchange, you could hear the roar in Nairobi. The village elders smiled as their stocks in the operation doubled in value, and the hospital would get its new X-ray machine.

It was almost 10:30 p.m., and the crowds on the dark streets thronged in and out of the bars. The SUVs roared around the town, horns blaring. Anyone who did not understand that the Somali Marines had triumphed must have been sleeping very soundly.

▼

MEANWHILE ADMIRAL BRADFIELD ordered Captain Corcoran to turn the ship around and head back to Diego Garcia. And even as he did so, Lt. Com. Jay Souchak came in with a signal flashed through from the USS *Roosevelt*, via the Indian Ocean Command Center: *Fishing boat* Mombassa *stands less than one mile off our port quarter. Have our orders changed? Do you want us to sink it now?*

Mark Bradfield, who knew *Roosevelt*'s commander extremely well, wondered for a split second if this was a joke. If it was, it was typical of Commander Bill Taylor. But he decided it wasn't and said to Jay Souchak, "Negative to both."

"Bit of a waste, sir, dropping 5 mill on the ocean floor," replied his XO.

"Bit of a drag, Jay, when tomorrow's newspapers right here in the US come out with a headline that reads:

US GUIDED MISSILE DESTROYER BLASTS
INNOCENT FISHERMAN IN INDIAN OCEAN—
MANY DEAD—PRESIDENT AGHAST. ORDERS
NATIONAL DAY OF MOURNING

Jay Souchak laughed. Unlike the dispatch team in the Orion, Mark Bradfield's cutting wit rarely missed its target. And while he was concerned at the way any US aggression would be treated by the media, he was a great deal more concerned about the real issue: Had the US government, for the first time, negotiated with terrorists?

Fox News would not take no for an answer. And the rest of the media was apt to follow, more slowly, but become more sure-footed in their suspicion that the Pentagon had paid up. Mark Bradfield knew his press office had to put out a statement announcing that the *Niagara Falls* had been recaptured and the pirates had vanished.

He also knew the tigers in the Fox newsroom would immediately ask whether the US freighter had been reclaimed by force or negotiation. If the latter, was a ransom paid? He called for Jay to contact the chairman of the Joint Chiefs. This, he decided, was too big an issue.

General Lancaster was even more concerned. "This is bigger than just a military decision, Mark," he said. "Because there are political overtones which will not go away. Many people believe we should never pay off pirates because it just encourages them to strike again, as they always do."

"Then we better stick to our guns, Zack," replied Admiral Bradfield. "A ransom was paid by the Seafarers Union, which was concerned for the lives of its members. I think we can admit we assisted them in their efforts, but the decision to pay a small ransom to free the men was theirs alone. We did not consider it appropriate to discourage them."

"Perfect," said General Lancaster. "Make sure the release refers all future inquiries to the union."

"Okay, boss," said Mark Bradfield. "Meanwhile we need to get a plan. Because, trust me, these bastards are going to come calling for another 5 million bucks sometime in the not-too-distant future."

"I know they are," replied the general. "The trouble is, our specialist fighting force, DEVGRU, has received almost no training to attack a moving ship from the ocean, not one that's been captured. Their instinct is always to save as many hostages as possible and then blow the bastard out of the water. We gotta get smaller. And get modern."

"Leave it to me," said Mark Bradfield. "I'll talk to Carlow in the morning. But we can't go on like this, always getting caught with out pants down every time a group of tribesmen decides one of our freighters is a soft touch."

"And don't forget the land, Mark. We may have to go ashore and knock the shit out of one of these pirate towns. That's what I like about Carlow's SEALs. They can operate anywhere."

▼

WHEN THE PENTAGON'S PRESS RELEASE went out the following morning, it was written in undramatic terms. By the evening editions of the newspapers, the story had slipped off the front pages and down the playlist for the news channels. And that's where it would stay, growing less significant by the day, until the name and address of the late first mate, Charlie Wyatt, was released.

The media and the public had lost interest. And the real seething curiosity now switched to Capitol Hill. Because there, in both houses of Congress, there was genuine concern about the USA's involvement in the payment of ransoms to pirate gangs off the coast of Somalia.

The successful action of the SEALs in freeing the captain of the *Maersk Alabama* had undoubtedly made matters worse—not because they had been obliged to blow the heads off three pirates but because they had demonstrated that fierce professional aggression against heavily armed amateurs paid off.

There were already rumblings in Washington that the US should cease to soft-pedal the growing problem and get in there and rescue any American vessel that was captured. Most senators were only marginally up to speed on the subject, and they were entirely ignorant about the iron hand of control exercised by the international insurance corporations.

The brokers understood there was an ever-present threat that even the pirates could sue for compensation if one of their number was shot dead. There were lawyers lined up to sue any national government that sent in armed troops that subsequently opened fire. Legal compensation could run into the millions of dollars, and law firms were making it abundantly clear they had no qualms about representing families of bereaved pirates.

And while insurers were happy to cover the costs of stolen cargoes, the cargoes were rarely lost, because all the cards were stacked in favor of paying out the ransom. No one likes a standoff with an insurance company. Least of all shipowners who, despite everything, understood their premiums would rocket upward if the US military started blowing away the tribesmen.

However, the US government remains the most powerful force in the world. All Congress needed was a law that banned foreign nationals from suing the US military in US courts for actions that take place either on the high seas or on foreign soil where the troops were protecting American interests.

And there were Republican senators and representatives all over the country who were about to demand this kind of law be enacted. These same politicians were also demanding that the US *never* negotiate with pirates, or foreign governments that harbored them, and *never* pay out ransom money to terrorists or pirates, whatever the circumstances.

But the sands were shifting. The demand from both the legislators and a riled American public was that not only should the new law be passed, but that the Special Forces go in, every time, and protect American citizens and property.

A groundswell of public opinion and congressional outrage had an energy all of its own. And the worst fears of Admiral Andy Carlow and Commander Mack Bedford were about to be realized. With a posse of journalists waiting outside the US Navy base in Diego Garcia, it had become impossible to withhold the name of Charlie Wyatt any longer. The navy press office was under siege, and the *New York Post* came out with an editorial that demanded: *Who the hell does the Pentagon think it is? Deliberately withholding from the public the name of a brave American merchant navy officer who died at the hands of Somali tribesmen while trying to defend his ship and his crewmates? What God-given right does the US Navy have to hide his identity?*

The two-column headline above the editorial read:

## CAN'T-FIGHT, WON'T-FIGHT US NAVY PLAYS POLITICS WITH THE FAMILY OF A VERY BRAVE AMERICAN

This was too much for Admiral Mark Bradfield, who asked Jay Souchak to get Admiral Carlow on the line from SPECWARCOM in Coronado, San Diego. And the conversation was terse.

"Are you announcing the first mate's name tonight?" asked Andy Carlow.

"No choice."

"You understand the media will probably go bananas? Guys outside his family's front door, cameras everywhere, interviews with Charlie's best friend, ex-girlfriends, school teachers, and Christ knows who else."

"And that won't be the worst of it," replied Admiral Bradfield. "Because right after that, they'll start ranting about the navy's reluctance to face up to a real gun battle at sea despite overwhelming odds in our favor."

"And they are not going to get put off real easy," added Andy Carlow. "Because they know this is a subject where we have to tread very carefully, and they can say anything they damn please."

"I don't expect to come out of this with flying colors," said Mark Bradfield.

"And I'm kinda braced for them to accuse us of letting everyone down. They're bound to do that after the *Maersk Alabama*. But I have a plan, and I'm putting it into operation starting tomorrow. It's a new anti-piracy platoon, geared to the recapture of ships and the attack on pirates who commandeer US ships and property."

"Hey," said Mark, "I like that."

"What I really like," said Andy, "is that the platoon will have a senior commander, and we can flag him up as a world expert on piracy, a man whose job is to destroy the raiders. It'll help us shut down noisy politicians and journalists. We just bring in our naval authority on the subject, and his word will count. Right now the media thinks we're only making excuses."

"Excellent. Can you get to Washington and brief us in person? I think Zack Lancaster would very much like to see you."

"Sure. When?"

"Tomorrow."

"No problem. I'll leave at 0700, arrive late afternoon."

"We'll meet you at Andrews. Return San Diego next day."

"See you tomorrow, sir."

"And, Andy, bring your new anti-pirate commander with you. What's his name?"

"Commander Bedford, sir. Mack Bedford."

▼

THE SCENE ON THE BEACH in front of Haradheere was a bacchanalian romp. Bonfires burned, goat carcasses were roasted on spits, African beer flowed, and almost the entire town was in attendance on the hot equatorial night. The most beautiful girls in the town, some married, some not, were dressed in their summer best, heavy on African jewelry, especially necklaces and bangles. In token deference to their Islamic religion—mostly Sunni Muslim—they also wore bright headscarves

Hundreds of local tribesmen danced to the throbbing beat of the drums, and they chanted words of praise and thanksgiving. Before their eyes stood the symbol of their triumph: the navigation lights of the *Mombassa*, moored four hundred yards offshore.

They'd bring it in at low tide and beach it on the soft sand, allowing it to rise with the incoming tide, with the option of leaving two hours either side of high water. Meanwhile the two skiffs had been lowered, and the massed revelers on the beach could see the flashlights as the crew disembarked and boarded the little boats.

Already the soft beat of the Yamahas could be heard across the dark water, and there was enormous anticipation in the air as the crowd pushed ever closer to the lazy breakers in the still of the African night.

The chant was resonant of the grand farewell that had echoed along the beach when the *Mombassa* had departed almost a week ago. But then there had been a note of anger, an unmistakable tribal sound of impending battle. This was different, full of laughter. But the clapping was the same and the words seemed simpler. Whatever they were singing held a disciplined rhythm, and it sounded like: *O-O-O-O-H SOMALI . . . S-O-M-A-L-I HAAAAH! H-E-E-E-Y WHOMBA!*

They jumped up and down on the sand in a chaotic rhythm, waving to the boat, calling out the name of Ismael Wolde, the pirate leader who was bringing back the wealth.

When the skiffs reached the shallows, the Yamahas were cut and tipped up. Tribesmen leapt out into the water and manhandled the boats onto the beach. Willing young men ran into the water to help. Others came down with bottles of cold beer for the heroes. Mohammed Salat, surrounded by six armed guards, walked through the crowd to greet the men he had financed on their mission.

Captain Hassan, Admiral Wolde, and Commander Elmi Ahmed stepped out onto the warm sand, dragging behind them the five orange bags that contained the $5 million. The crowd cheered rhapsodically.

Mohammed Salat stepped forward to shake the hand of each Somali Marine for their selfless and courageous actions in battle. Then he ordered the guards to load the bags into a 4 × 4 SUV parked down by the water, and the six men, in company with two of the village elders, climbed aboard. Salat, with his wife, boarded another vehicle farther up the beach, and the crowd roared as they set off in convoy to deposit the money in the vast vault of the stock exchange.

The men of the *Mombassa* joined the great throng for the midnight feast, the celebration of a battle hard won and so much extra wealth for almost everyone on the beach. All of their families were there, but in a very separate group, talking with Ismael Wolde, were the parents of the two local men, young Bouh Adan and Gacal Gueleh, who had been killed in the action.

There was a heart-gripping sadness, but Mohammed Salat was unfailingly generous to those who died for the cause. The Adans and the Guelehs would each receive a $25,000 credit at the stock exchange with the option to reinvest in the next mission of the Somali Marines.

Out on the waters, beyond the breakers, the dark hull of the *Mombassa* could be seen against the high equatorial moon. It was riding its heavy anchor, silent and without lights. Tomorrow it would be brought in and beached while a half-dozen local mechanics serviced, painted, and refuelled it.

The *Mombassa* would be ready for the next mission within a couple of weeks and would rest on the sand until new advice came in from Yusuf Kalahri, the mole in the Ronald Reagan Building. Or, alternatively, from someone else in the labyrinth of US government offices who received a monthly allowance from Mohammed Salat.

▼

ADMIRAL CARLOW and Commander Bedford touched down at Andrews Air Base in the late afternoon. A Cobra strike/attack US Marine helicopter transported them the twenty miles to the Pentagon. Lt. Com. Jay Souchak awaited them beside the landing area and escorted them immediately to the office of Admiral Mark Bradfield on the fourth floor.

They took a half hour for coffee and a general chat about the pure audacity of these pirates and then walked down to the office of General Lancaster, who was anxious to be briefed about the new anti-pirate operation.

They found him in a state somewhere between irate and thoroughly pissed off. He was introduced to Commander Bedford and greeted the SEAL officer with grace and enthusiasm. "I'm very pleased to meet you at last, commander," he said. "You've had an unorthodox but highly distinguished career. And everyone here has reason to be grateful to you—especially after those shenanigans in . . . er . . . Afghanistan . . . not to mention Connecticut."

"Thank you, sir. I just did what any one of my fellow officers would have done on a mission like that."

"There aren't many missions like that," grinned the general. "So we'll probably never know what anyone else would have done. However I know what you accomplished and, as I said, I'm personally grateful. You probably single-handedly kept Guantanamo Bay open! Sure as hell scared a few people around here."

But the general's levity was quickly over. And the pirate attack sprung right back to the forefront.

"You guys seen the latest editions of the newspapers?" He pushed several issues across his desk toward them and snapped, "Just look at this crap. They've got the name of Charlie Wyatt, the guy who died in the *Niagara Falls* attack, and now there's about four hundred reporters, cameramen, and who the hell else camped out in his parents' backyard right up the road in Baltimore."

"Headline's really great," muttered Mark Bradfield.

## US Navy Stands Idle
## While American Hero Dies

"They don't actually mention that our nearest warship was over a thousand miles away," he said. "They think the Indian Ocean's about the size of the friggin' Reflecting Pool."

General Lancaster nodded. "I read the interviews they're coming up with: *Charlie was the nicest guy in the world . . . the most popular . . . most brilliant . . . no one's surprised he's the one man who stood up to the armed pirates since the Navy SEALs went in to save the Maersk Alabama.*

"They can't get that fucking ship out of their minds. And they suspect we're lying about the ransom paid to free the *Niagara Falls*. So every damn thing they write is slanted against us."

"Well," said Mark Bradfield, "The one thing we can agree on is that something has to be done. All of this is very bad for the morale of the armed services. Damn newspapers coming out and nearly accusing us of cowardice."

Zack Lancaster grabbed another newspaper and pointed in outrage at the treatment of the story. "Look at this bullshit," he added, pointing to a new headline:

ORIOLES DEVOTEE CHARLIE
DIED SWINGING—HIS LOUISVILLE
SLUGGER GRIPPED IN HIS HAND

Zack shook his head. "I haven't yet returned a call to the defense secretary, mostly because I know he's been on the line to the president who's basically on the side of the goddamned pirates! But even he won't like being C-in-C of a fighting force that's under national attack for a lack of courage in the face of the enemy."

"Well, sir," said Admiral Bradfield, "I hope we have some enlightening news for you. Because the navy is unanimous: We can't go on without a specialized anti-pirate force. And Commander Bedford here is in the process of forming an elite SEAL platoon ready to go in and conduct rescue operations with whatever force necessary."

"Okay, gentlemen, let's sit down and give the subject a good airing," said General Lancaster. "Trouble is, it's a high-risk game, and the consequences of having our own guys die, especially SEALs, are very, very bad. Because the public hates it, and the media knows that. Commander Bedford, where the hell do we start?"

"Sir, the basic concept is rescue at sea, essentially trying to retake a fortified enemy stronghold. That's what a captured ship becomes. So we need to become experts on boarding, probably at night, a target possibly moving at 12 knots through the ocean. She may be slow. And she may be stationary, but we have to get on board with a minimum of uproar. Preferably in silence.

"I understand this may be impossible either because of sea conditions or an overwhelming pirate guard presence, but we still need to become world experts at such a boarding operation. Because there will be times when we must take that chance."

"How long to train guys to pull that stuff off?" asked the general. "I guess we're talking grappling irons and ropes?"

"Yessir. Probably take regular navy personnel about six months to master it. My guys? Three weeks."

"How about the approach?"

"Inflatables, sir. Quiet running. The way we'd go into a beachhead. But if we can get into a submarine, somewhere close, we might prefer to hitch a ride and then swim in, which is even quieter."

"Assuming you get the platoon on board, what do you consider the chances of complete recapture of the ship?"

"One hundred percent. With respect, sir, no SEAL team would be held up long by a bunch of overexcited, trigger-happy natives, would it?"

"Not hardly," replied General Lancaster. "And what about all these new rules about not attacking and killing pirates on the high seas? Mostly European, some international, framed by the insurance companies and their lawyers?"

"Sir, my men will be behind enemy lines for this. When they open fire, they shoot to kill. If we have to fight our way on board or fight to get off, we will spare no one. In this case we will fight only under the military laws of the United States of America. Any other rules of engagement would be entirely unacceptable.

"On a mission this lethal, the guys cannot be encumbered with regulations. If my men are not given a free hand to defend themselves and accomplish the mission, any way they see fit, I'm afraid they're not going."

"You are never going to meet anyone who agrees with you more," replied the general. "The operations will take place under the precise circumstances you have just outlined. Every mission you undertake will be classified to the highest possible level."

"We do have a built-in secrecy factor," said Mack Bedford. "Because all of it will happen far away from any observers—no press, no foreign diplomats or lawyers, no long-range photographers. No one will find out anything happened for several days."

"None of this will ever be put into writing," said the general. "But in the presence of two United States Navy admirals, I give you my solemn word that no member of your SEAL platoon will ever be prosecuted, court-martialled, or reprimanded for any action he may take on one of these missions.

"These fucking Somalians have taken the gloves off. They have issued their own set of rules. They have set up a cutthroat business of lawlessness on the high seas. And whereas other countries have moved to allow this, we will not. I have six very powerful senators on my side in this. And Simon Andre will back us all the way."

"I'm grateful for that, sir, really I am," said Mack. "The guys must have confidence when they go in. They need to believe in their moral rights, and they have to be sure their government backs them. One of the biggest worries SEAL teams have these days is that their own people, American media and lawyers, will turn against them. It's very dangerous for us if our team, subconsciously, holds back in the attack. We all find it very, very sad, this frequent disapproval by our own nation."

"Yeah," said Mark Bradfield. "In this case, we can't do anything right, and you get a regular guy like Charlie Wyatt whacks a pirate on the head and he's treated like Eisenhower."

General Lancaster chuckled. "You'll need air support?"

"Sir, there will be several times when a sea-launched attack is not possible. Then we'll have to come in by air. And we'll need two helicopters. A big guy to land the force and a gunship to provide heavy machine-gunfire cover while we land. There may be other times we need a decoy attack from the air while we board the vessel from the sea."

"Sounds militarily correct to me," replied General Lancaster. "And we want to be correct. No mistakes. No failures. No expense spared. We need to make this work."

"That's the spirit, general," said Mack jauntily. "Make the bastards play by our rules."

"For a goddamned change," snapped the chairman of the Joint Chiefs.

# CHAPTER 4

▼

M R. PETER KILIMO RAN THE OPERATIONS DIVISION OF Athena Shipping from a twentieth-floor office in New York's 570-foot-tall Olympic Tower on Fifth Avenue at Fifty-second Street. Peter's father, Omar, had worked as a butler for Aristotle Onassis, the man who was largely responsible for building the tower in the early 1970s.

The operations division in any big-city shipbroking house represents the heart of the corporation. It is the computerized engine room of the business—the room where the world's shipping lanes are tracked and the satellite signals come in, having located giant cargo vessels and tankers all over the globe.

There's nothing glamorous about this section of the work—guys in "ops" don't lunch in fancy Manhattan restaurants wooing potential clients. Guys in ops have their finger on the maritime pulse. They don't have time for lunch. But they can tell you in a split second if a 300,000-ton VLCC is likely to miss the tide when it finally turns up the Yangtze River toward Shanghai.

Peter had been in the shipping game all his life. Mr. Onassis had liked him from the start, this tall twelve-year-old son of one of his most trusted butlers, a Somalian named Omar Kilimo. And Peter, who had been born Ali, became Westernized and was schooled in New York while his father lived and worked in the sprawling Onassis residence in the Olympic Tower.

When the great man died in 1977, Peter Kilimo was headhunted by a rival shipping line that also had offices in the tower.

And while Peter subsequently made a respectable living, $250,000 a year plus annual bonuses that often ran to a similar sum, his loyalty to any corporation vanished with the demise of his friend Aristotle Onassis.

Peter was sixty years old now and probably knew more than any man about the world's shipping lanes and the enormous oceangoing vessels that rode them. He knew their cargo capacities and the seaports that could handle them. Tankers were his specialty. Massive tankers, that is. The VLCCs that take four miles to stop after someone applies the brakes.

Peter was a family man. He was married to a New York girl, and they had brought up three children in the outer suburb of Bronxville. And from them he harbored a very deep secret. In 2005, he had met a somewhat engaging financier at a United Nations reception for East African diplomats and been offered a private consultancy position, which would require little of his time but a certain amount of detail about voyages of crude oil and petrochemical tankers sailing out of the Persian Gulf.

It was a weekly task that Peter Kilimo could have done in his sleep. In recent months he had been disconcerted to notice that his e-mailed reports to his "chairman" contained the names of several big merchant vessels subsequently hijacked for heavy cash ransoms off the coast of Somalia. His chairman's name was Mr. Mohammed Salat.

It occurred to Peter that he may be becoming an important wheel in a major pirate operation. And soon he became an expert on the activities of Mr. Salat, who plainly ran an enormous illegal operation out of Haradheere and was very likely wanted by Interpol and God knows who else.

Every alarm bell in Peter's mind was sounding off. He could not possibly become implicated in such a nefarious world. He could be ruined, maybe even prosecuted. But he loved that $20,000 wire transfer that kept showing up in a private bank account he had opened in Westchester County. No one knew about that. Especially the IRS.

He justified his little sideline business by telling himself he had deep and abiding roots in Somalia. He had, after all, been born in Mogadishu and had lived there until his father, in 1958, accepted a position in the royal household of Emperor Haile Selassie in Addis Ababa before moving to Athens to work for Onassis.

It was only in very recent months that Peter, the highly respectable shipping executive who commuted into Manhattan every working morning, became really concerned about the intricate level of shipping details he was supplying to the pirate master on the coast of Somalia.

One ship in particular was on his mind, the *Queen Beatrix*, a 300,000-ton crude-oil tanker owned by the Rotterdam Tanker Corporation in Holland and currently on charter to Athena Shipping, the Greek-owned and New York- and Monaco-based brokerage that employed him.

Currently the *Beatrix* was 1,000 miles south of the Strait of Hormuz and past the vast estuary of the Red Sea with 345,000 cubic meters of Saudi crude in her gigantic cargo tanks. At more than 1,000 feet long, she was one of the largest visitors to the offshore Sea Island loading docks and was now well on her way down the northern coast of Somalia, making around 12 knots seven hundred miles from the shore.

Her route would take her straight down the sixtieth line of longitude before making her hard left turn and running south of the Maldives but north of Diego Garcia, en route to the Malacca Strait.

The final destination of the *Beatrix* was Zhan-Jiang, 250 miles southwest of Hong Kong and just about the first major oil port in China for a ship steaming north around the island of Hainan.

Zhan-Jiang was a very lucrative tanker route for Athena Shipping. Her giant refineries were in the heavily industrialized seaport, and under the current trading agreement, the China National Oil

Corporation had paid a full 20 percent deposit on this cargo and would settle the balance at $60 a barrel when the ship docked.

The *Beatrix* carried almost 2.9 million barrels, and she was one of a limited number of the world's biggest tankers to make the journey along the shortest route to the South China Sea, through the five-hundred-mile-long Malacca Strait, which divides Malaysia from the enormous island of Sumatra.

The strait is only eighty-two feet deep, but the almost new *Beatrix* was one of the first of a new breed of two-hundred-foot-wide, double-hulled VLCCs with a sufficiently shallow draft to enter this critical if narrow seaway, saving hundreds of miles each way.

But there was a problem deep in the massive heart of the *Beatrix*, an intermittent vibration on the main shaft, probably traceable to the stern tube bearings or the coupled flywheel at the forward end. Either way it was not life-threatening, but any minor problem that affects the shaft alignment needs to be examined by the engineering team sooner rather than later.

Bearing in mind the main shaft in a VLCC is about the size of a giant redwood tree, the vibration, to a wary skipper, sounded like a seven pointer on the Richter scale. And the problem, as on all super-tankers, was the same as always: Do we slow down right now, try to eliminate the vibration, and risk being late into Zhan-Jiang? Or do we press on hard, hope to hell it doesn't get worse, and get it fixed in China, where the company will almost certainly get royally ripped off by the local shipyard?

Answer: Let's see what our engineers can do.

Peter knew the giant ship was planning to slow down in the open waters of the Indian Ocean, probably at night. And because of the pressures of arriving on time, she may need to make two stops while her engineers attempted to make tiny adjustments in the engine room, millimeters rather than inches.

Because the huge ship was one of Athena's own, he had felt a severe pang of guilt when sending that last communiqué to Mohammed Salat informing him of the route of the *Queen Beatrix* and of the problem that would require attention in the next couple of days.

He had also informed Salat that the heavily laden ship was riding low in the water under the command of a Dutch captain, Jan van Marchant. In Peter's opinion the ship would not attempt to exceed 10 knots until the shaft problem was thoroughly solved and that right now she was running south 60.00E 10.00N.

She operated under a Liberian flag of convenience, and the majority of her crew were from the Philippines, except for the first officers and the engineers, who were all Dutch. He enclosed the phone number of Athena Shipping in Monaco, where he knew the Greek boss of the corporation was in residence.

For a pirate, this information was priceless because the *Beatrix* was carrying cargo worth $200 million on the international market. However, tankers that big are an extremely difficult target, especially when running at maximum speed. To board her was a death-defying maneuver, and her senior officers could be armed in defiance of the current rules.

The better news was the presence of maybe thirty Filipinos who owed not one shred of loyalty to the New York charter company and none to the owners in Rotterdam. Most of them did not know where Rotterdam was, and neither did they care. Theirs were well-paid but menial jobs—cleaning, cooking, laundry, stewarding, and occasionally helping with the docking. Nothing else.

Not one of them was interested in laying down his life for the *Queen Beatrix*, and if past acts of piracy were any guide, the raiders' biggest danger was being trampled to death in the Filipinos' stampede to surrender.

If the Somali Marines were to launch an attack, they would need their top team, and their number-one commander, Ismael Wolde, who had only been ashore for ten days since the successful attack on the *Niagara Falls*. But this was a huge opportunity. It was almost midnight local time when Mohammed Salat dialled Ismael's cell phone.

The pirate assault commander was at home working on plans for an extension to his six-room home on the smart side of Harad-heere. He planned to build a garage for his new 4 x 4 Honda, a billiards room, and a television room, with two bedrooms and two bathrooms above. Ismael was not married but he had a spectacu-lar-looking Ethiopian girlfriend. And they had two children.

He listened carefully to the hot news from Mohammed and confirmed that the *Mombassa* was fuelled and ready to go, except that Captain Hassan was very obviously drunk in the bar next to the stock exchange. Two other members of the marines, Omar and Abdul, were similarly inebriated. And they all had an excuse. It was Captain Hassan's birthday. Elmi Ahmed was with them but he never touched alcohol.

Ismael was an extremely ambitious pirate, and the vision of the stalled VLCC in open water in the dark, swarming with passive Filipinos and $200 million worth of crude oil in the holding tanks was almost too much for him to grasp.

"That's just beautiful," he said. "Do we have a fix on the ship's position?"

"Right now she's steaming south, down the sixtieth line of lon-gitude," replied Salat. "She's maybe seven hundred miles off the So-mali coast and probably slowing down. 'Bout ten degrees north."

Ismael smiled to himself. "You have all the weapons and am-munition?" he said. "In the armory, right?"

"Everything is ready. I have six men on duty, ready to assist any way you want."

"Sir, high tide is 3:00 a.m. That means the *Mombassa* needs to be afloat by 5:00 a.m. She's a big ship and we'll need a lot of people to haul her down the beach. If we're not under way by 5:00 a.m., we're stuck for another ten hours and that's obviously hopeless."

"How about the captain? He can't take command if he's shit-faced, can he?"

"No, but Elmi Ahmed can."

"Okay, can you get the marines together?"

"I think so. Omar Farah, Zenawi, Ougoure, and Sofian will be ready to go in an hour. The boat's freshwater tanks were filled today, but we'll need food, which I'll have to leave to your men. We'll load the three drunks with the provisions. They can sleep it off on board."

"Okay. I'll have the guards go door to door in the town, round up some guys to haul the boat to the water," said Salat. "How many will you need?"

"Maybe fifty men on the lines, if we can get the big winch to work and all four tractors will start. We'll first need to drag the winch down to the water."

"Okay, Ismael. Can I announce the new mission on the stock exchange?"

"I don't know why not. What's my bonus?"

"Two thousand shares on a $10 launch. Then your leader's share of the prize, 5,000 stocks at closing market value when the boats return."

"Can we rendezvous on the beach, say at 2:30 a.m.? It'll take a while to get everyone ready."

"Especially the drunks," said Salat. "I'm afraid we're reaching the stage where alcohol must be banned from all marine personnel.

"Our present information network is working so well," muttered Salat. "All key personnel must be on near permanent standby."

And so, in the small hours, the second major pirate launch from Haradheere in two weeks was under way. But this time there was no cheering and chanting. In the still of the hot, humid night, lines of men took up position on the ropes attached to the *Mombassa*. The SUVs, two of them hitched up on either side of the former longline fishing boat, were revving, ready to take the strain. Down by the water, the diesel engine on the big winch roared.

By 2:45 a.m., the gear was loaded on board: food, water, boarding equipment, machine guns, RPGs, ammunition belts, and grenades. The gas tanks were full, and the erect figure of Ismael Wolde could be seen standing next to the 1,500-ton beached vessel.

The *Mombassa* began to move after ten seconds. The fifty men pulled with all their strength, but the heavy muscle of the SUVs made a huge difference, and the old but powerful winch made up for a hundred men as it wound in the cable, dragging the boat down the sand to the water.

It took maybe seven minutes to get the stern wet. Because the engines could no longer drag it, the *Mombassa* had to be pushed the final yards with the tide washing in around everyone's ankles. Ahmed and his men hitched up the skiffs to the long ropes and drove them out into the breakers.

Everyone grabbed the lines and, on the command, heaved, waiting for the wave that would lift the boat and swing her around. Others rushed in and jammed their shoulders into the sweep of the starboard bow. Everyone pushed on that side; everyone else tried to pull without falling under the water, and the big Yamahas roared.

After three minutes, a bigger wave crashed and swept in, and the bow rose up. She swung out bow-to-seaward, and every one of the huge launching party now moved to the stern and pushed like hell. With a swish along the sand, the *Mombassa* was suddenly afloat, and the skiffs alone towed her into deeper water.

Elmi Ahmed jumped aboard from the little boat, and the helmsmen took both skiffs back into the shallows to collect the crew's personal bags. They also loaded the three semi-drunks, all of whom were sobering up fast, especially Captain Hassan.

Ahmed started the engines and positioned the *Mombassa* a couple hundred yards out. When the skiffs arrived, they were unloaded and then hauled inboard. The ship's instrument panel glowed in the dark as the crew made ready their sleeping quarters, some on deck, some below. They had three hammocks but the rest were trying to find places for sleeping bags.

At 3:28 a.m., Ahmed gave two short blasts on the ship's horn and opened the throttles, steering course zero-nine-zero, due east, in search of the *Queen Beatrix*. At flank speed, 20 knots on their expertly serviced diesel turbine, this meant one full day plus sixteen hours' running time to reach a point eight hundred miles offshore where they could pick up the giant Dutch tanker. Ismael thought they might find her on radar long before that, especially if she had come to a complete stop, as Mohammed Salat had suggested.

The moon was still high as they covered the first miles of their long journey. In the first two hours they passed only one ship, a medium-sized tanker, riding high in the water, obviously without cargo and headed north up to the gulf to load tens of thousands of tons of crude oil.

The sheer volume of money traversing these waters in the early twenty-first century was breathtaking. And the lion's share of that money was owned and controlled by the most powerful nations on earth: the US, Russia, China, Japan, the Gulf States, and the big hitters of the European Union.

The simple objective of Ismael Wolde was to ensure that his ravaged nation, withering on the burning east coast of Africa, should, in some small way, share in that wealth.

▼

MACK BEDFORD ELECTED not to relinquish his two-week position of class proctor for the INDOC students as they prepared to enter the full BUDs program. Captain Murphy had given him the option when he was told of the reformation of Delta Platoon.

But Mack had declined, saying he would like to finish his first task on this, his second tour of duty with the SEALs.

And, echoing a phrase he had once said to Mack so many years ago, Bobby Murphy grinned and said, "Ain't no quit in you, right, son?"

Every morning at 0500, Mack Bedford was at the grinder when the class assembled. When the men were still, and the unspoken ethos of the SEALs was once more settled upon them, Mack began the day.

"Drop," he said, without expression.

"*DROP!*" responded the class as they hit the concrete and snapped into the correct position, arms extended, bodies straight.

"Push 'em out," said Mack.

"Push-ups," shouted the class leader.

Thirty times the guys lowered their bodies to the grinder, and thirty times they forced themselves back up, arms straight, shoulders throbbing, muscles aching, hearts pounding.

The class leader shouted again: "Instructor Mack!"

"*HOO-YAH, INSTRUCTOR MACK!*" bellowed the class, still balanced on their hands and toes. Still rigid.

"Push 'em out," said Commander Bedford. The class once more went into the attack, pushing and striving to complete the discipline, trying to get past the throbbing pain barrier. One caved in, stood up, and requested immediate DOR. Without a word or a change of expression, Mack Bedford just nodded and pointed to the bell.

When the second set of thirty had finally been completed, the class, shocked by the severity of the first forty minutes of each day, stayed gasping on the palms of their hands, each man trying in his own way not to betray his pain, praying for the command to stand up and recover.

Mack Bedford left them there for six minutes. Two more men quit with only two minutes left to go, and again Mack just nodded and gestured toward the bell.

On the fourth day he told them they would be taking the five-point BUDs screening test in its entirety that morning. They had already completed sections, but now he wanted to see them put it all together.

The program was by any standards a vicious examination of men, both physically and mentally. It included a five-hundred-yard swim, breaststroke or sidestroke in twelve minutes and thirty seconds; a minimum of forty-two push-ups in two minutes and fifty sit-ups in two minutes; six dead-hang pull-ups; and a mile-and-a-half run in eleven minutes and thirty seconds wearing boots and pants.

Mack told them after four days this was compulsory. Anyone who could not stay with the program would be ordered to quit. "Most of you won't be here for much longer anyway," he said.

Without a word, he joined the class and four of his instructors, swimming powerfully out in front on the opening test in the pool. Then he ripped off sixty push-ups with the rest of them, except he used only one arm. Without even breathing hard, he completed a hundred sit-ups in the two minutes.

Mack completed his daily thirty-eight dead-hang pull-ups. On the mile-and-a-half run, Mack knocked it off in ten minutes, striding easily along the top of the tideline, as he had done for so many years.

Three more men went DOR during these tests, at the end of which Mack said quietly, "Thank you, gentlemen. Push 'em out."

While the depleted class fought and struggled with the last of their strength, he stood by, making notes in a small black book, logging, he later told the survivors, the guys who were really putting out. The guys who wanted it so badly they would die for it. The future Navy SEALs.

By now it was apparent that the issue of brute strength was critical. And much of that is God-given. You can make a strong guy stronger. Much stronger. But you cannot make a weak guy strong. At least not very often.

The same applies to the issue of speed. Given that everyone who survives Coronado is strong as hell, the honing of speed is probably more important than any other aspect of SEAL training. Because the guys have to be fast in every way, fast over the ground, agile on rough terrain, fast in their thoughts, fast to adapt to setbacks, excellent all-around runners, sprint and distance.

Mack Bedford understood that it's the issue of speed that truly sorts out a BUDs class. Before he left for his afternoon of surveying potential recruits for Delta Platoon, he issued a stern warning to everyone in the BUDs class.

"I'll be seeing you again tomorrow morning," he said. "And I expect by then several more of you will be gone. But just so you understand precisely what you are involved in, I want you all to hear the following:

"This is the most serious business there is. It's a school for warriors, for men who will, if they are successful, represent the frontline muscle of the armed forces of the United States of America, the true protectors of our people.

"There is no more vital business. Not oil, not mining, not industry. And you must understand the weight of responsibility this profession will force upon you. So if you even suspect you may not want to go all the way, for Christ's sake get the hell out now, because we do not have time for you.

"We prefer six guys who will lay down their lives for their country and their platoon than fifty whose hearts are somewhere else."

And with that, Mack Bedford was gone, jogging fast across the dunes, headed for perhaps the most brutal training ground in the world—Coronado's Obstacle Course, a fifteen-part open-air torture school, a place so hard on new recruits it is often used by fully fledged SEAL combat teams on their final warm-up before deploying to a war zone.

The O-Course is composed of rope climbs, a sixty-foot cargo net, climbing walls, barbed wire, gymnastic vaults and parallel bars, rope bridges, and places with sinister names like The Weaver. Mack's class would almost certainly show up there toward the end of the afternoon. But there were three SEAL teams shortly deploying to Afghanistan, and they were scheduled to work there right after lunch.

Mack grabbed a sandwich and then stationed himself right in the middle of the place where he could see and locate SEAL team members with special talents for climbing and agility; men with supreme balance, forearms made of blue twisted steel; men who could scale the side of a big ship that had been commandeered by armed Somali pirates.

After the first SEALs arrived, Mack watched the hardened combat veterans scale the eighty-foot climbing ropes and then slide down, fast but steady. No mistakes. This particular group performed the exercise three times, and of the thirty men who tackled it, Mack noticed just two. They were all outstanding, but these two were very fast, and one of them was, unsurprisingly, the team leader. Mack had no interest in removing him from his platoon just before they went into a theater of war.

The other man was Shane Cannel, a twenty-three-year-old, newly promoted petty officer second class from Orange County, California, surfer, athlete, and guitar player. Specialist: 200 meters, 21.2 seconds. And he could scale those ropes like a six-foot-tall Rhesus monkey.

Mack moved on to the cargo net, where men worked two or three at a time. Here he could make a comparison, and Shane Cannel was just as good in a discipline where everyone was very accomplished, since the net is identical to the one SEALs use to board and disembark ships and submarines.

Young Shane seemed to sense the big rope footholds. He might have been climbing a regular set of stairs. Never faltered. Went straight past both his Team Ten buddies, who were no slouches themselves. Neither of them even looked sideways, and Shane was up and over the big log at the top before the other two had reached the fifty-foot mark.

*Guess he always goes by 'em like that*, thought Mack, and he wrote down the kid's name.

Down at the swinging rope bridge, Mack found another young SEAL from the same Alpha Platoon, Team Ten. He was Josh Malone from Iowa, about six feet tall, a farm boy who graduated from Annapolis and served as a gunnery officer on a destroyer.

The swinging bridge makes everyone look bad, especially the big guys whose weight is inclined to swerve the main walking rope. Lt. Josh Malone stepped lightly across it under a full pack, as sure-footed as that character who tightroped over Niagara Falls. Mack had noticed Josh on the cargo net and selected him as the one guy who might have given Shane Cannel a run for his money.

Next stop was the wall, and Mack stood watching for almost an hour as teams of SEALs came thundering into its base, grabbed a rope and tried to walk straight up, a kind of backward rappel.

Watching an expert, it looked dead easy. And to a large extent they were all experts. But just as with most groupings, two out of ten are merely average, four are not bad, two are very good, one is excellent, and one is supreme. It was that last cat for whom Mack was searching, the one with automatic coordination, the one with strength and rhythm, no fear and no doubts about his ability.

All afternoon Mack Bedford checked out that wall, watched dozens of men climb it and drop down the other side. Only one of them caught his eye, a SEAL who was a little older than the others, Chief Petty Officer Brad Charlton from Colorado, a mountain man, climber, skier, son of a coal miner, aged thirty-one. Machine gunner by profession, SEAL Team Two.

Brad went up that wall as if he were merely going uphill, straddled and rolled the top beam and kind of walked at high speed down the other side. Mack followed CPO Charlton down to the rope bridge and witnessed another effortless example of battle-ground coordination, full pack and rifle, not a foot wrong.

Mack hit the buttons of his cell phone to run an instant check on the CPO and discovered he was a skilled marksman, Honor Man at Sniper School, a decorated veteran who served with distinction in Baghdad, and earmarked for officer training school after his next tour of duty in Helmand Province.

The following morning, Petty Officer Shane Cannel, Lieutenant Josh Malone, and CPO Brad Charlton were all informed they were to continue their final preparations for deployment with their teams, but they would not be accompanying their platoon to Afghanistan. When their teams began pack-down for their departure, they were to report instead to the newly formed Delta Platoon under the exclusive command of Commander Mackenzie Bedford.

No explanations were given, except an order to observe normal rules involving highly classified operations. And to await further orders from Commander Bedford.

▼

THE EQUATORIAL SUN ROSE SLOWLY above the eastern horizon of the Indian Ocean in a burning sphere of pure fire. It cast upon the water a deep-red, shimmering highway along which the *Mombassa* seemed to be travelling, directly into the inferno.

Captain Hassan had missed the first sunrise of this voyage while he was nursing a stupendous hangover with cold towels on his head and sufficient Alka-Seltzer to fizz up Lake Michigan.

He had recovered by lunchtime and took over the wheel somewhat sheepishly. Captain Hassan was one of nature's autocrats and was monumentally embarrassed at having been too drunk to drive his own ship. Still, he had not expected to be under way for several more days, and he felt obliged to make that clear to all members of the crew at regular intervals of approximately thirty minutes.

This applied especially to Ismael Wolde, who was making no

secret of his rank displeasure with the members of his highly paid assault team who had been clearly unfit for duty. The savior of the operation was Elmi Ahmed, the Haradheere-born former Somali brigade commander in the government army.

The thirty-five-year-old teetotaller had stepped right up into the captain's shoes and taken over the operation of the *Mombassa* from the start of the mission, checking out the oil and fuel levels, setting the instruments, taking the helm, and driving the ship carefully, slowly out through the shallows, then out beyond the crashing night breakers.

He had set her correct easterly course and stayed at the wheel for a total of ten hours before Captain Hassan took over. Before they left, Ismael Wolde had requested a formal promotion for Elmi, and Mohammed Salat had his guards deliver a personal citation to the beach.

It was printed on the Somali Marines letterhead, upon which there was a facsimile of Admiral Lord Nelson's coat of arms, posthumously bestowed upon the victor of the Battle of Trafalgar. The letter congratulated Elmi Ahmed on his devotion to the Somali cause and promoted him in the field, effective immediately, to Commodore Ahmed, signed by the Honorary Admiral of the Fleet, First Sea Lord Mohammed Salat.

Right now he sat at Captain Hassan's right hand. They were 580 miles off the Somali coast and pounding their way forward through the normal long swells of the Indian Ocean. At 0700 most of the crew were not yet awake, although someone was preparing fruit salad, North African flatbread, and canned ham for breakfast.

Captain Hassan forbade having a propane gas cooker on board. Not with high explosives around. So no one was in much of a hurry to rise and shine since there was no hot coffee, toast, or eggs. The only other crew member in action was Hamdan Ougoure, who had taken first morning watch on the bow of the ship, standing lookout for the skipper.

Commodore Ahmed was engrossed in navigation and the radar screen. He was trying to calculate precisely how far the *Queen Beatrix* might have travelled from her last known position 10.00N 60.00E. That had been around midnight, about thirty-one hours ago. And there was an air of approximation about those numbers, relayed as they had been from the computer screen of Peter Kilimo on Fifth Avenue in New York.

Armed with Peter's critical information about her course, that she intended to run south and then cut left somewhere between the Maldives and Diego Garcia, Ahmed was mildly surprised at the rapid progress they had made and how close the *Mombassa* must be to her quarry. Running twice as fast east, they had gained probably five hundred miles on her.

And they were still gaining. There was of course nothing on the radar screen yet, but Ahmed would not have been surprised if they picked up a paint late in the afternoon. At one point, Ismael Wolde made satellite communication with Mohammed Salat and requested an update on the *Beatrix*'s progress, given that the Indian Ocean is such a gigantic body of water.

But the First Sea Lord of Haradheere had declined to pursue that inquiry with Peter Kilimo since it would plainly frighten him to death, especially if they proceeded to hijack the 300,000-ton ship later that night. Salat did not wish to lose his principal New York eyes on the shipping world.

So Captain Hassan ran on through the dawn, and his boat came slowly awake. By 10:00 a.m. the crew was attending to its tasks in readiness for a possible assault. The priority was the ropes and grappling irons because the *Beatrix* would need to be boarded.

There was no question of stopping her by firing a couple of RPGs across her bow. The officers on her bridge were so far away from the bow they would hardly see it. As for stopping the ship by force of arms or threat of explosive, that was out of the question. No one could stop it, not even her captain; the oceangoing monolith would plow on for miles even with the engines at a dead stop.

If the *Queen Beatrix* had been balanced on her stern end, she would have been one hundred feet taller than the Eiffel Tower. She was two-and-a-half times taller than the highest point of Sydney Harbor Bridge. It was mind-blowing even to consider capturing her, except for three factors: (A) She might be stopped in the water or travelling at a very slow speed; (B) She would be riding very low on her lines, thanks to her colossal cargo of crude oil; and (C) Her unarmed crew, comprised 90 percent of foreigners, would most certainly not fight to save her from a marauding Somali Marine force, heavily armed with machine guns and hand grenades. The only difficulty was getting on board without being seen.

Wolde had studied a thousand plans of the world's big tankers, and he understood the boarding, if and when they found her, would have to be at the stern, where the entire crew would be stationed. To attempt anything at the bow end would be to invite disaster because every member of the assault group would somehow have to traverse the entire length of the ship, three hundred yards, with no cover.

If the captain or one of his officers did have a machine gun, Wolde and his men could be picked off like desert jackals as they raced aft along the barren steel roof of the vast holding tanks.

Wolde had a reasonably good drawing of the rear end of the ship and, fully laden, there were rails not too high off the water. This mission would live or die by the skill of his grappling-iron men, and he had already ordered Kifle Zenawi, Ibrahim Yacin, and Elmi Ahmed to work on those lines.

They needed to insure they were ready to go instantly, no knots, no tangles, no screwups. Setbacks such as these could occur all too easily in the drastically confined space of the attack skiffs. And the ropes needed to be carefully coiled and placed in handmade, square open boxes like thin, plaited snakes.

The cast-steel irons were the time-honored four-hook variety, unchanged in design since the US Army's Second Battalion Rangers Assault Group used them to scale the heights of *Pointe du Hoc* four miles west of Omaha Beach on June 6, 1944.

Those anchor hooks could grab into anything—rocks, boulders, sand, bushes, even trees with the right angle. The steel post and rails on the deck of a big ship were probably the easiest target ever invented. All Wolde's men needed was to clear the top rail on the first throw.

Omar Ali Farah was tasked with checking the weapons, especially the big machine gun, which could spell the difference between life and death. He also conducted a thorough overall of every Kalashnikov in the pirate arsenal, cleaning the barrels, fitting the new magazines, making certain the spares were laid out in order for each man. One malfunctioning rifle could be fatal for them all.

Lunch was probably the most boring meal ever created on any wealthy, working ship in maritime history—for the fifth time in a row, fruit salad and canned ham sandwiches utilizing African flatbread that was growing staler by the day and resembled, according to Wolde, the outer cardboard of a small ammunition box.

They couldn't even throw a line over the side and catch a fish because there was nowhere to cook it. Bottom-dwelling shellfish, which could be eaten raw, was out of the question since the ocean was about two miles deep.

They ran on under a sweltering sun all through the afternoon. Commodore Elmi Ahmed checked the GPS and made long pencil lines across his charts, plotting the possible course and position of the *Beatrix*. He figured she must be somewhere within one hundred miles of them. If she had stopped and examined her shaft, she might be fifty miles away. Either way, they had a fighting chance of finding her that night.

▼

CAPTAIN JAN VAN MARCHANT was a forty-eight-year-old life-long tanker man from the little south Holland town of Delft, a ten-minute train ride from the world's greatest deep-water oil terminal of Rotterdam. He was the son of a master glazer at one of the Delft china factories and spent his early years living in constant dread of ending up on the workbench next to his father, shining up the famous blue-and-white pots and figurines.

Jan van Marchant was on a train to Rotterdam at the age of six-teen to begin a two-year tour of duty as a deckhand on a 100,000-ton tanker before either of his parents realized he had gone. When he returned at eighteen, his father had died, and for the past twenty-seven years he had helped support his mother from his ample salary.

Van Marchant had his master's certificate before he was twenty-one, and his first overall command of a freighter at twenty-eight. He became a first officer for the Rotterdam Tanker Corporation at thirty-one and assumed command of his first VLCC two days after his thirty-third birthday.

Established shipping corporations could charter these gigantic ships from Rotterdam, but the *Queen Beatrix* could only be taken if Captain van Marchant stayed in command. He was widely considered one of the principal masters in the world oil business, a skilled navigator with a near-flawless record of having delivered a billion tons of crude all over the globe, on time, every time, barring engine malfunction or impossible weather. He was an expert entering and leaving a hundred different harbors and knew how to pull strings with every loadmaster on every crude-oil dock in the world.

When he retired at fifty-five, if he so wished, Jan van Marchant would do so with a full-salary pension for life and an agreed golden handshake of $5 million. Such was his reputation. It was never even contemplated that this tall, fair-haired athletic Dutchman would ever be challenged, never mind captured.

On every voyage stood his two closest colleagues, Johan van Nistelroy and Pietr van der Saar, both age thirty, first mate and bosun respectively. They formed a trio of very tough, competent world seamen, but they obeyed the law and never carried firearms, mostly because they thought this mighty oil fortress at sea was impregnable.

But Holland, befitting a country situated almost entirely below sea level, has an enviable record as a centuries-old naval power. Navy training is top class, and all submariners learn those instinctive reactions to heavy-duty machinery, functioning under the surface of the ocean.

Every one of their submarine crews learns to listen, and Pietr van der Saar was especially gifted. He could pick up an irregular beat on a camshaft in an instant. Same with a hydro-problem, a malfunctioning ballast tank, a "knock" on a generator. It was Pietr who picked up the vibration on the main shaft of the *Beatrix*.

And Captain van Marchant was only a few minutes behind him. He detected it while Pietr wandered down to the enormous engine rooms below the upper works just to see if he could get a handle on the problem.

But it was well hidden. And he returned to the bridge to find the captain, leaving Johan van Nistelroy at the helm. Deep down in the lower enclaves of the engine room, both men could hear the distant, deep shudder below the waterline. Jan van Marchant thought it not too serious. But they each thought someone should have a good look when sea conditions were okay.

As they pressed on toward the equator, it seemed to flatten out. But later that night, Pietr sensed it, rather than heard it, again. At this time he had the helm himself, but he thought the shudder sufficiently serious to hand over to Johan, awaken the boss, and once more go down to the engine room for a check.

As the gigantic ship ran on through the ocean, both men decided formally to bring it to a complete halt at first light when the watch changed, and then take the full engineering team below to make some adjustments.

They were 120 miles north of the equator, which was just about as far south as they intended to go. The captain backed eight degrees north of ninety, still heading east, straight at the northernmost point of land on distant Sumatra, gateway to the Malacca Strait.

The problem on the *Beatrix* was that the shudder seemed to come and go. There was scarcely time to make any mechanical move before it stopped. However this was the third time that both the captain and bosun had heard and felt a very definite problem on the shaft.

And while neither of them thought the rise and fall of the swell would have much effect on the ship, they agreed it would be better to conduct their investigation, and any repairs, in flat calm if possible.

It was mid-afternoon now, and the majority of the engineering staff would be reporting for what the US Navy calls the First Dogwatch at 1600. They'd give it a shot then, if the sea was subsiding in a dying afternoon breeze.

By 5:00 p.m. the engineers in the *Beatrix* had made minor adjustments. By 6:00 p.m. she was well under way, back up to speed and running approximately fifty miles ahead of the *Mombassa*, which was still going twice as fast, closing in on her starboard quarter.

Two hours later the *Mombassa* had covered forty more nautical miles. And the *Beatrix* had traversed only twenty, which made the distance between them precisely thirty miles.

A half hour later, Commodore Elmi Ahmed picked up a slow-moving radar paint on the screen he had been studying for so long. It was bright green, and it came and went in rhythm with the endless circular sweep of the electronic radar arm, near the edge of the screen, on the twenty-mile circle.

It was plainly a very large ship. A modern radar system easily differentiates between something big up ahead and something small. A trained operator will instantly catch a flock of seabirds five miles off the bow or even a small rain squall. A 300,000-ton VLCC does not look like either of those—more like the Taj Mahal just showed up in the Indian Ocean.

Elmi Ahmed knew this particular tanker was going marginally slower than normal. Its speed, direction, and GPS coordinates all precisely matched those both reported and forecast by Mohammed Salat's man in the New York shipbroker's Fifth Avenue office.

"We got her, boss," said Ahmed. "Right here on the screen, GPS fits, size is right, speed correct, direction accurate. It's the *Beatrix*, no doubt. Steaming twenty miles off our port bow. There's not another ship of that size anywhere near us."

Elmi was proud of his grasp of the ocean's highways, and the present route of the tanker coincided with his main pencil line on the chart. Captain Hassan replied, "Is she where you expected?"

"She is."

"Good. Better get Ismael in here."

Five minutes later the Somali Marines' assault team leader was on the bridge staring at the radar screen and the big green paint that showed up every time the indicator swept around.

Wolde checked the numbers and nodded thoughtfully. Elmi, smiling, muttered, "She's nearer than she was ten minutes ago. At this speed we'll catch her inside a couple of hours. Easy."

Wolde checked his watch. It was twenty minutes before nine o'clock, pitch-black outside and still hot. The pirate ship did not, of course, have air-conditioning, which, in this heat, made the *Mombassa* even more of a rough-and-ready working vessel.

"Start loading the skiffs," said the assault team leader. "Let's get the grappling ropes aboard, plus those rope ladders and the harnesses for the climbers. We're getting in close, and the water's calm right now, so we'll lower away with the boats loaded."

He then asked Captain Hassan whether it was likely that the control room of the tanker could see them on their own radar screen. The veteran Somali fisherman replied that he thought it unlikely.

"Any other ship on the seven seas I'd say yes," he replied, "but not those VLCCs. The standard of seamanship is very poor. They are so big, the presence of a small vessel is meaningless to them. They could run over a 1,000-ton boat and never know they'd done it. And when a routine task doesn't matter, in the end they ignore it."

Captain Hassan was right, but for different reasons. The giant ship was running in very deep water, hundreds of miles from land, on automatic pilot because all of the senior staff were below in the engine room, checking the turbine room, the camshaft room, the generators, the freshwater plant—every mechanical part that could have any bearing on the mysterious shudder that was so exercising the captain.

All the while, the *Queen Beatrix* was inexorably slowing down, her speed now at only 5 knots and dropping. There was hardly a ripple on the dark waters beyond her hull, and she rode up scarcely a couple of feet on either end on the gentle lift of the ocean's surface. Inside the cavernous area where the shaft runs aft toward the thirty-foot high propeller, the senior men stood and listened.

Pietr van der Saar was positioned on a gantry, feeling the vibrations on the soles of his feet, and Jan van Marchant was below him. The shudder on the shaft was more regular now, as if the fault had settled in and would systematically haunt them for the rest of their 6,000-mile journey.

The engineers felt helpless. There were small technical adjustments that could be made, and these were ideal conditions to try. On a flat calm, the speed of the *Beatrix* was still dropping. Also the radar screen was still unattended, despite showing the fast-approaching *Mombassa* as a clear paint.

At 9:45 p.m. Hamdan Ougoure, the pirate lookout man on the

bow, spotted the running lights of the tanker out on the horizon to the northeast, about five miles distant. He called up to the captain as he stared through his stolen Russian night binoculars and confirmed the presence of a VLCC steaming so slowly she looked as if she might have stopped altogether.

This came as some relief to Elmi Ahmed, who was just beginning to doubt the accuracy of his navigation. He had already decided that either he had made a serious miscalculation or the *Queen Beatrix* was doing something unorthodox. They were now headed for a point beyond the tanker's bow, not her stern, as planned.

Of course, the news that she was more or less stopped in the water solved everything. Ahmed advised Captain Hassan to come hard left, almost due north, in order to squeeze back toward the tanker's stern arc, rather than racing straight across her near-stationary bow.

Hassan pulled the *Mombassa* back through a northerly sixty degrees and kept going, knocking off a mile every three minutes. But then he cut the speed, and the noise, and ran in very quietly to a point two miles off the stern of the *Beatrix*.

Ismael joined him at the helm, and the captain pointed out the ship up ahead and the route they would take in order to get closer. He switched on his state-of-the-art shortwave radio system and tuned into the likely frequencies upon which he might expect some communication from a major vessel.

But there was nothing. The entire senior command of the *Beatrix* was still below the massive green deck, just forward of the island, checking out the running of the shaft in the pristine seclusion of the spotless engine rooms.

Captain Hassan's fishing boat was now positioned dead astern of the tanker with about a mile of ocean water between them. He ordered the crew to lower the two skiffs and watched as the assault party climbed down the boarding rope ladders on either side of his ship. There were as always six men in each skiff, and tonight Ibrahim Yacin and Abadula Sofian were on the helms.

By now the danger of being spotted onscreen was almost over because within a few hundred yards the small boats would be well under the tanker's radar, which transmitted from an electronic dish thirty feet above the high deck outside the bridge.

Ismael Wolde stayed to synchronize his watch with that of the captain and to insure that their satellite cell phones were just one push-button apart. He was the last man aboard the lead boat and gave the order to depart at 10:30 p.m.

The Yamahas roared into life for the first time since they had left the beach at Haradheere, and the bows of both narrow skiffs rose off the surface as they lurched forward, Wolde's boat indicating the speed they would travel. He was at first undecided whether to go for a fast approach or pure stealth in the pitch dark, and he kept his line open to Hassan just to establish there was still no radio contact with the *Beatrix*. The captain confirmed there was not a word.

Ismael Wolde could not believe their luck—that after a journey of hundreds of miles, effectively stalking the huge tanker, no one knew that two Somali Marine attack boats, filled with armed assault troops and high explosives, were within a few hundred yards of hurling the grapplers.

Abadula Sofian, driving Wolde's leading skiff, was ripping across the water at more than 28 knots directly at the stern since there was no wake behind the stationary ship. They came in almost under the overhang, which would have looked like a tower block if she'd been empty. But right now, hard down on her lines, the *Queen Beatrix* at close quarters was a much less formidable target. It was almost beyond belief that she could be so low on her waterline and yet more than a thousand feet long.

Sofian steered down her starboard side for only thirty or forty yards, and all six men stared up at the lowest point of the aft deck.

In was hard to assess the exact distance up to the rails, but in this stationary position it could not have been as much as twenty-five feet, well within the accuracy range of the hurlers, all three of whom were in Sofian's boat.

The helmsman made a 360-degree turn and came in twenty feet off the hull, holding the skiff motionless on the slight south-running current.

They listened carefully above the rhythm of the idling engine, making its familiar pop-pop-popping beat on the night air. Ibrahim Yacin held the second skiff off, right under the stern of the ship. And still there was no sound or movement from the *Queen Beatrix*. It was a ghost ship.

"Okay," snapped Wolde. "Let's go!"

All three men began to whirl the grappling hooks, each one in a clockwise circle, just as they had practiced so many times, counting the revolutions off . . . *one* . . . *two* . . . *three* . . . and then *NOW!*

On the fourth circle they let go and the irons flew upward, off a slight forward angle to the perpendicular. All three of them cleared the starboard rails and clattered onto the deck, chipping the pristine emerald-green paint.

Wolde, Zenawi, and Ougoure, their individual ropes clipped to their wristbands, seized the lines and pulled back. All three of the grappling irons hooked and held on the steel posts and chain rails. The three pirates leaned back and let the irons take the strain. Wolde's slipped a few inches and then snapped tight on the middle section.

Sofian twisted the helm and worked the skiff closer into the tanker's hull, while Zenawi and Ougoure shouldered their light, coiled hook lines and prepared to scale the side of the ship. At the top they would drop the lines back and then draw up the rope ladders, the ones with the brass rungs, which made it a simple task for the others to climb aboard.

Wolde was the only man armed as the first three pirates swung out beyond the skiffs and then slowly climbed the ropes, barefoot, using hands and feet for grip, up to the rails, where they swung over and landed on the green deck. It took another three minutes to secure the rope ladders in readiness for the mass boarding of the Somali Marines.

By now the crew of the *Beatrix* were back at their night stations. The shaft seemed to be turning smoothly and the engines were just beginning to increase power. But the luxury and efficiency of the ship was such that no one needed to go on deck at all. There were elevators, stairways, lights, and catering staff throughout all five stories of the executive island.

No one heard the pirates' grapplers clatter over the rails. Neither was there any longer a paint on the radar, denoting the arrival of either the *Mombassa* or her accompanying skiffs. In any event, no one was looking.

The only activity beyond the bulkheads was the sound of a couple of Filipinos walking up from the accommodation block with glasses of iced fruit juice, which they proposed to sip out on the deck. One of them thought he heard something.

"Who's that?" he called.

Ismael Wolde stepped out of the shadows, his Kalashnikov raised, and he answered calmly: "Raise your arms very high, both of you—otherwise I shall be forced to shoot you dead in the next five seconds."

The Filipinos had only a modest command of the English language but they understood. The tension nearly crackled as their glasses of fruit juice shattered on the deck's green paint, so urgent was the crewmen's desire to appease the ugly-looking black guy with an AK-47 machine gun.

# CHAPTER 5

▼

THE TWO FILIPINOS, MARCO AND PAUL, STOOD, HANDS high, almost in shock watching the bizarre events unfold before their eyes. The character with the Kalashnikov was quickly joined by two others carrying identical weapons and then, up and over the rails, swarmed seven more pirates.

Wolde spoke up. "How many on the bridge, including the captain?" he asked.

Neither prisoner answered, both pretending not to comprehend. Then Marco said something in Spanish, and Wolde shook his head. He ordered two men to stand guard on this section of the deck and four armed men, led by Kifle Zenawi, to enter the island with Marco at gunpoint and take the companionway down to the crew's quarters.

Their orders were to capture every crew member, asleep or awake, in the shower or eating supper, and then parade them on this deck in fifteen minutes. Any resistance would be met with brutality but not death. One more of the team would move over to the portside and assume command below the bridge, his Kalashnikov primed.

Wolde himself, in the company of two of his most trusted men, Elmi Ahmed and Hamdan Ougoure, armed with the heavy machine gun, would proceed with the prisoner Paul up to the bridge, where they would take command of the *Queen Beatrix*. Wolde was already assuming that the ship's high command would not be armed warriors.

In silence, Paul led the way to the executive elevator and pressed the button for the fifth floor. When they stepped out onto a carpeted foyer, a place where Paul had never before been, they were faced with a wooden door upon which brass letters proclaimed:

BRIDGE AND CONTROL ROOM
EXECUTIVES ONLY

"Knock and wait," commanded Ismael Wolde, and Paul tapped twice, waiting five seconds before Pietr van der Saar opened it. At which point, Pietr, Johan, and Jan van Marchant suffered the greatest shock of their collective seagoing years.

The door cannoned back on its hinges as Elmi Ahmed slammed his shoulder into the brass letters and knocked van der Saar flying. Ougoure was right behind him and crashed over the prostrate Van der Saar and fired a short burst into the sidewall, wheeling left with his rifle aimed at the bridge officers.

Ismael Wolde rushed across to the tall, white-shirted Van Marchant and rammed his rifle into the captain's rib cage, right below the heart. All three Somali Marines were shouting to intimidate, waving their rifles, demanding, unnecessarily, that the terrified officers of the *Queen Beatrix* shut up.

In the space of twenty-five seconds, Captain Jan van Marchant and his three executives, plus the deckhand Paul, had their backs to the wall, arms raised, without a word. Never in the entire history of ocean warfare had a ship this big been captured so swiftly by so few.

"Captain van Marchant," said Admiral Wolde, "you and your staff are my prisoners. The *Queen Beatrix* is now under the command of the Somali Marines and a substantial ransom will be asked for her return. No one has been hurt, so far, but if our demands are not met, we will begin shooting you all one by one and throwing you overboard. You understand your deaths are of no consequence to us whatsoever."

And he finished with a flourish. "Live or die, over the side or on board. None of it makes the slightest difference to us. I will never even think about you again. So you may as well obey my commands while you are still alive to do so."

His words had a more chilling effect on the highly paid officers than even Wolde imagined. "Well," said the captain, "what do you wish us to do now?"

"Sometime in the next ten minutes your entire crew will be brought on deck. I may as well inform you that I represent a force of ten heavily armed marines. We are in possession of both hand grenades and rocket propelled grenades and a very large amount of high explosives.

"If we wished, we could sink this ship. And out on the water we have two high-powered skiffs with trained helmsmen, plus a fast 1,500-ton vessel to take us home. Right now, I would like you to turn the *Queen Beatrix* around and begin heading slowly back toward the coast of Somalia, eight hundred miles to the west. I shall leave my three armed bodyguards with you, and should any of you do anything rash, their orders are to shoot to kill.

"For every indiscretion you commit, my men on the lower decks will execute one of your crew. But perhaps we will start with this man here who led us to the bridge. His usefulness to us is over."

Captain van Marchant could see no escape. There were only thirty-two men in his entire crew. No one was armed, and they were up against ten gunmen, cutthroats who had made it clear that they would kill without mercy. Like all masters of big ocean-going merchant marine ships, the captain knew all about piracy. He just thought it could never happen to him on a vessel this large.

He stared at Wolde and said quietly, "Very well. Since we have no choice, my crew will do as you instruct. I imagine you will require communications to transmit your ransom demands?"

"No need. I will speak to my own captain on the telephone, and the instructions will be relayed to Somalia and then to the chairman of Athena Shipping."

At that moment, Wolde's cell phone vibrated. Kifle Zenawi was on the line from somewhere in the bowels of the ship.

Wolde answered, and Zenawi's report was succinct: "Twenty-seven crew members held at gunpoint. I can't see any others. We're keeping them in the crew dining area for now. What next?"

"Keep them together. I'll be there in fifteen minutes."

Wolde turned to Captain van Marchant and asked, "How many in your crew total, including all five men in this room? I know how many we have prisoner, and if you lie to me, I will shoot this deckhand instantly."

Paul looked about as scared as any captured Filipino can ever be. "There are thirty-two men in my crew," replied the captain, "not including myself. Five of us, as you can see, are on the bridge."

"Thank you, sir," said Wolde, relieved that everyone was accounted for. He was now prepared to grant Jan van Marchant the respect of one senior officer to another.

"And now perhaps you'd face the ship to the west," he said. "And restrict her speed to four or five knots. I will return in a few minutes. What's through that door?"

"Just a small deck."

"Good," replied Wolde and walked outside, pushing a single button on his satellite cell phone as he went.

"Ismael?"

"Yes. It's me, Hassan. We have captured the *Queen Beatrix*. The captain and his entire crew of thirty-two are my prisoners, all being held at gunpoint. I am personally in command of the ship, standing outside the bridge. Elmi and Hamdan have the heavy machine gun. They are guarding Captain van Marchant and his senior officers. Everyone else is confined below to the crew dining room."

"Thank you, Ismael," said Captain Hassan, "and have you given orders for the ship to move?"

"Yes. I told them to steer due west and not to exceed five knots. Elmi is watching the controls."

"Very good, Ismael," said the master of the *Mombassa* and clicked off the line.

And while Admiral Wolde went below to organize the lives of the prisoners for the next few days, Captain Hassan opened up the satellite line to Mohammed Salat. It was a little after 11:00 p.m. in Harardheere.

"Sir," he said when Salat answered, "I am pleased to report the Dutch-chartered *Queen Beatrix* is under the command of the assault troops of the Somali Marines, led by Admiral Ismael Wolde.

"The captain and his crew surrendered fifteen minutes ago and are now held prisoner at gunpoint by our forces. I confirm the tanker is fully laden with crude oil, very low on her lines, and slowly heading west under the orders of Wolde and Commodore Elmi Ahmed. No casualties, and may God bless Somalia."

"That is excellent news," exclaimed Mohammed Salat, who always smiled at the way his pirates assumed the formalities of an international navy at moments like this, and he responded in kind.

"Please convey my congratulations to Admiral Wolde and his troops. I will open negotiations with the owners immediately. Stand by for further orders."

▼

CONSTANTINE LIVANOS, a distant relative of the greatest of Greek shipping family dynasties, was four time zones back from the central Indian Ocean when his telephone rang in Monte Carlo.

With a phone number supplied by the operations chief of Athena Shipping, Mohammed Salat was through the first time, on the landline to the sensational duplex Livanos kept at the most expensive block of apartments in the principality overlooking the harbor. It was twenty minutes after 7:00 p.m. and the tycoon was on his way out for dinner. His wife, Maria, looked like the empress of the entire free world.

"Mr. Livanos?"

"Speaking. Who is this?" The Greek shipowner was extremely curious about this call because it was on a line used only by his top executives and even then only in an emergency.

"My name is not relevant," replied Salat. "However, I am the commander-in-chief of the Somali Marines. I am calling to inform you that my troops have captured and now command your tanker *Queen Beatrix* eight hundred miles offshore in the Indian Ocean."

Constantine Livanos was temporarily stunned. And his mind raced. Somehow he needed to slow down this insolent African gangster. "I am afraid you have the wrong man," he said blandly.

Salat, who understood perfectly well that he had the right man, replied, "You are not Livanos of Athena Shipping?"

"I am. But we do not own the *Queen Beatrix*. She is merely under charter to us. Which means we have rented her for a few months."

"Mr. Livanos," said Salat, "You know as well as I do that we are not discussing the ship. We are talking about 2.9 million barrels of Saudi crude, worth $200 million on the open market. I imagine that is worth something to you."

Livanos kept playing poker. "It's insured. No problem. If you take it, I will claim for its value. Lloyd's of London, old man, ever hear of it?"

For the first time, Mohammed Salat sensed the mild chill of pending failure, and he was not especially enjoying this long-distance duel with a very smooth Greek multimillionaire.

"Then that's a matter for you," he said. "I will order my troops to wipe out your crew and scuttle the ship. I expect your compensation insurance will cover you for the irreparable environmental damage to those cheap little vacation resorts on the Maldives."

Livanos knew his insurance would not cover even a tenth of the potential damage. And he did not look forward to explaining why he had told the most notorious pirate gang in the Indian Ocean to go right ahead and shoot down his tanker crew in cold blood. In this short, brutal Mexican standoff, he blinked first.

"How much?" asked Constantine Livanos.

"Ten million."

"Too much. Far too much."

"Works out to three dollars and fifty cents a barrel, I believe."

"I told you: too much."

"Well, what's not too much?"

"I suppose $3 million."

"Don't be absurd. I could sell it to an empty tanker captain for twice that and keep the ship."

"Well, put a price on it to include the safe return of the crew, unharmed, and the ship in perfect condition, plus the cargo untouched."

"Okay," said Salat. "Seven million dollars, cash."

"Five."

"Split it?"

"Six it is."

"That's still cash," said Salat, whose fingers were racing over the buttons on his calculator. "Works out to only a couple of dollars a barrel—equivalent to a regular daily downturn on the world market."

"I am aware of that," replied Livanos icily, not betraying his slight smile while he considered whether to hit Rotterdam Tankers for a third or a half of the ransom money. Either way, things could be a lot worse.

"And how would you like to proceed?" asked Salat.

"Through my New York office. I can brief them now since they are five hours back and it's early afternoon on the East Coast of the United States."

"That's fine. Who do I deal with?"

"Ask for Tom Sowerby. He's my president in the US. You may instruct him where you want the money delivered. But what are your assurances that you will keep your end of the bargain?"

"Mr. Livanos, we have been conducting these operations very professionally for the past three years. If we were a Western banking business, we would be triple-A rated. Which, of course, is more than can be said for your own Greek National Bank or indeed the mighty Lehman Brothers in New York."

Constantine Livanos could not help being amused by the sheer brass of the maniac on the other end of the line. Had he not been about to drop several million dollars at the conclusion of the phone call, he might have laughed out loud.

"Since you do not wish me to know your name, I am at some disadvantage. But I should warn you that I will be requesting assistance in this transfer from the United States, where I have many close friends.

"My office will be in contact with the Greek ambassador this afternoon. And at the time of the exchange of money, there will be a military presence in attendance with the *Queen Beatrix*. Needless to say, if you do not free the crew and vacate the ship immediately, your troops will be unlikely to get out with their lives."

"That will not be a problem," replied Salat. "We are men of our word. There will be no need for you to pay this ransom until you are confident of your position.

"Of course, if you were to break your word or somehow attack my men, they are ordered to take three hostages, shoot the rest of the crew immediately, blow up the ship, and then escape the best way they can."

"I think we understand each other," replied Livanos. But as he put down the phone, he uttered a telling phrase of amazement, one that he had picked up during his formative years at Eton College in Berkshire, England.

"Fuck me!" said the Greek tycoon.

▼

TOM SOWERBY SAT WIDE-EYED in the Olympic Tower listening to the chairman of Athena Shipping on the line from Monte Carlo. He understood he must await a call from the pirate commander and then work out where and how the money should be paid. He should also try to touch base with Captain van Marchant. In the meantime, Sowerby was being told to call the Greek Embassy in Washington and inform both the ambassador and the naval attaché what had happened.

Livanos pointed out that the Greek military had no base of operations anywhere near the northeast coast of Africa and that US cooperation was vital if they were to free up the *Queen Beatrix* and get her on her way to the South China Sea with no harm done.

The least of Sowerby's problems was the $6 million. Big tanker corporations operate on such vast financial platforms that sums like that are completely dwarfed in the day-to-day running of their operations. A lot of Athena's money was kept in New York, including, incidentally, China's down payment of around $30 million on the cargo of crude currently stalled in the middle of the Indian Ocean.

The problem was, the Horn of Africa was indeed the skid row of the Middle East. Banking was apt to be slow, confused, prone to diabolical mistakes, and oblivious to the word "urgent."

Tom Sowerby called Athena's bankers in New York, JP Morgan, and spoke to the president. He immediately suggested Nairobi for big sums of corporate cash, declaring, "Barclays International is the best in East Africa. They'll get it done. I'll call them. You can do it all through us."

Relieved, Sowerby called the Greek Embassy in Washington and explained to Ambassador Petros Karamanlis what had happened. He requested formally that he assist them in persuading the Americans to help but was not encouraged by the response he received.

"Mr. Sowerby," said the ambassador, "I want you to pass on my very best wishes to Constantine Livanos, since we are old friends. But I must warn you that the Americans are awkward about dealing with pirates. They will not negotiate, they will not pay ransoms, and, given half a chance, they will happily blow the pirates and their ship out of the water. In these matters Uncle Sam carries a very big stick."

"We do not want them to negotiate or pay," said Tom Sowerby. "We have dealt with that satisfactorily. We would, however, appreciate the presence of a US warship somewhere in the vicinity when the pirates are due to vacate our ship.

"We only want it as an intimidating presence just in case they may be tempted to cut and run with our oil after they collect the ransom. It would be hell's difficult for us to get that ship back if these pirates are holding the crew hostage."

"I do understand that," replied the ambassador, "and I will certainly do all I can to persuade them. But I think we are going to end up dealing with the Pentagon, probably the navy department. So I will bring in our naval attaché, Rear Admiral George Argos. He's a personal friend of the top US admiral, Mark Bradfield. Mutual cooperation in the Aegean, you understand?"

"Pity it's not closer to Somalia," said Sowerby, good-naturedly.

"Sorry, Tom, we can't fix that," said Ambassador Karamanlis. "And I must warn you again: The Americans won't like this, you paying massive amounts of money to these gangsters and then asking for US protection. It's against their religion."

"I can only ask you to do your best, Excellency," said Sowerby. "Perhaps your man Argos could call me when he has some news. Get me on my cell, anytime tonight."

In the next two hours things moved very fast in Washington. Admiral Mark Bradfield said the US Navy had a destroyer in the vicinity, and he was happy to cooperate, mostly because it gave him another chance to get a good firsthand report on the pirates.

He did not, of course, know whether it was the same gang that had grabbed the *Niagara Falls* a couple of weeks ago. But he was incredulous that the Somalis had struck once more against such a massive vessel.

The first thing he wanted to know from Admiral Argos was whether the Greeks had agreed to pay up and get their ship freed. Or whether there was some kind of a standoff taking place. George Argos could not enlighten him, but he suspected the Greeks were in the process of stumping up a multimillion-dollar ransom to rescue their crude oil cargo.

Mark Bradfield did not much approve. But the memory of his own actions over the *Niagara Falls* was still fresh in his mind, and he chose not to remonstrate with this senior member of the Greek Navy. He did, however, call Admiral Andy Carlow out in Coronado to inform him that a gang of Somali pirates, believed to be the same marine corps that had grabbed the US aid ship, had struck again.

He told the head of SPECWARCOM everything he knew, but his information was limited.

"Are they asking us to attempt a rescue?" asked Admiral Carlow.

"No. They never even mentioned anything like that," said Mark Bradfield. "The Greek Embassy thinks they made up their minds about that several hours ago, but no one seemed to know the price."

"Well, if we're going to oblige them with a warship on standby, they probably owe us that information," said Andy Carlow. "But we're not nearly ready to send in Mack Bedford's specialists. It seems to me that no one in merchant shipping is anxious to get into a hot war with these villains, tempting as it may be."

"Sometimes I think the world would be a much better place, Andy, if it was run by businessmen. Because war, blood, and death is unthinkable to them. Gets in the way of making money. For 7 million bucks these Greeks can have their ship back and only make $33 million instead of $40 million on the run to China."

"It's pretty easy to see where those guys are coming from." Andy Carlow could be surprisingly philosophical. For a SEAL.

But in truth, both of these seasoned navy commanders were astounded at the nerve of the Somalis. Also, they were both fighting back the undeniable fact crowding in on them: There must be a master spy somewhere in the United States. Because not many people knew about that USAID ship, its course, destination, and position. And even fewer people knew about the *Queen Beatrix* with her private commercial cargo, her private ownership, and private charter.

And yet, the pirates had hit her a couple of days out of the loading platforms in the gulf. She was full to the gunwales with crude oil. No ship could carry more. And she was apprehended in one of the loneliest parts of one of the loneliest oceans on earth. According to Rear Admiral George Argos, she had been stopped in the water when the Somali Marines hit.

"You think it was a fluke?" asked the SEAL boss. "Because I don't. Those bastards knew who she was, where she was, where she was going, and what she was carrying.

"And suddenly this crowd of goddamned tribesmen comes rolling up in the middle of a million square miles of water at precisely the right time and precisely the right place. Jesus, you could search that ocean for a thousand years and never find the fucking *Titanic* if she was still floating."

Mark Bradfield could not help laughing. But Andy Carlow was not done. "Same with the *Niagara Falls*," he said. "She did not even have a schedule. She'd been hanging around in Diego Garcia for about three weeks. Finally she was loaded with sufficient gear, and the tide was right, so she left for Somalia. And what then? Right in the middle of fucking nowhere these guys turn up and capture her."

"I know," said Mark Bradfield. "It's almost impossible to believe they didn't have inside information. Someone must have told them where these ships were going to be. No doubt in my mind.

"And that's why this business is getting more dangerous and more costly by the day. These bastards have more goddamned money than God. And when you have that much, you can pay for the best information."

"That's why they win almost every war they fight," said Carlow. "I think they know the value of these cargoes before they start. And it doesn't take quantum physics to work out that a 150-million-dollar cargo is worth five mill of anyone's money to get it back."

Mark Bradfield was silent. And when he spoke, his words were weighty. "According to George Argos," he said, "the character who called the Greek shipowner was not even a pirate. He wasn't calling from the ship. He was calling from some kind of command head-quarters on the land.

"Can you imagine that? Some African tribesman going straight through to the private residence of a member of the Livanos family in Monte Carlo. Someone somewhere is feeding these guys the best possible information. Not even we could come up with a phone number like that, unless there was a full-scale war in the Aegean Sea."

"The truth is, Mark," said Andy Carlow, "we have to stop this. Because it's escalating so fast, it's out of control. Every time some-one pays them a big hunk of money, the problem accelerates. Be-cause the pirates can't wait to attack again, and they have thousands of dollars more to pay people who will inform them about the car-goes and routes of the biggest freight carriers and tankers in the world. You can guarantee a repeat assault on someone's ship every time these darned shipowners pay up."

"So what do we do?"

"Well, I guess we could start off by telling the Greeks we won't lift a finger to help them out with a warship because we cannot con-done their actions in paying the ransom."

"Don't you get the feeling that would open a whole political bag o' worms?"

"Of course I do," replied Andy. "I guess that's why you told Ad-miral Argos we'd help them. The last thing you need is an angry president on the line, complaining he's been given a right going over by the prime minister of Greece."

"That's the trouble when you get into this stuff too deeply," said Admiral Bradfield. "But tell me: If Mack Bedford's boys were ready, do you think they could go in and retake the *Beatrix*, if necessary wiping out the pirates, with no civilian casualties on our side?"

"Yes, sir. I know they could. But we're several weeks too early."

"Then I guess that makes the formation of the Delta Platoon all the more urgent. Because these African bastards are killing us. And what started off as a minor problem is now getting worse by the day."

"Judging by what you know, Mark, what would you advise if retaking the *Queen Beatrix* was a go: a sudden crashing attack on the ship or by stealth get the SEALs in and then tell them to take it from there?"

"Stealth every time," said the CNO. "It just happens to be easier to kill your opponents when they don't know you're there."

"The guys in Delta Platoon will be only top guys," replied Andy Carlow. "No one but the best."

"Look, I'm going to make a few more inquiries about this ransom before I commit a warship. Meantime, go to it, old friend. Tell Mack to pull out all the stops."

"You don't need to tell him that." said Andy. "He only fires when all the stops are out."

"Yes. I have noticed that in the past," said Admiral Bradfield. "We're damn lucky to have him back."

▼

BACK IN THE OLYMPIC TOWER, Tom Sowerby took it upon himself to inform the head office of Rotterdam Tankers that their prize VLCC was under the command of a gang of Somali pirates in the middle of the Indian Ocean. He was speaking only to the night duty officer, but the man reacted as if the assault was the responsibility of Sowerby himself.

He was plainly young, and he kept saying in the quasi-American accent the Dutch are inclined to adopt when speaking English, "This is down to you, my friend . . . this is nothing to do with us . . . she's your charter . . . it's your insurance . . . not ours."

Tom Sowerby, who had forgotten more about shipping rules than this Dutch hysteric would ever know, snapped back, "If these fuckers blow up the goddamned ship, the oil is our loss. Our insurance. And we are covered for the charter costs. But the ship's still yours. That's why you carry insurance on her. I have a copy of the document right here."

"Rotterdam Tankers makes no insurance claims for this kind of thing," said the Dutch-American voice. "No claims whatsoever. The ship is in your care. If she's lost, it's your problem. Trust me."

"Well, it seems no shipping company in the world is immune to the activities of the Somali pirates," replied Sowerby. "And right now, under the rules of the European Union, we're not allowed to have armed guards and certainly not permitted to open fire on the assault parties."

"I know," replied Rotterdam. "Only the Americans reserve the right to defend their ships by force of arms. As members of the EU, both the Dutch and the Greeks are bound by the rules governing human rights."

Sowerby relayed the GPS position of the *Queen Beatrix*. He supplied the times and dates as best he could and confirmed the number of crew members and that there were no casualties. He also reported that his chairman, Constantine Livanos, had come to an arrangement with the pirate's senior commander and that a ransom had been agreed upon.

He added that the Greek ambassador in Washington was talking to the Americans about a warship escort for the cash handover, and that Athena Shipping expected Rotterdam Tankers to make a $2 million contribution to the overall sum demanded by the pirates.

"That's out of the question," said the voice from the Netherlands, predictably. "The issue here is cargo. And so far as we are concerned, that's all down to you."

"So it may be," replied Sowerby. "Although that would depend upon how many times in the future you would like us to charter big ships from you. Think about it."

Outmaneuvered and outgunned by this rude bastard from New York, young Hans Cruyf, the twenty-five-year-old son of the tanker corporation's managing director, decided to make a name for himself. So he called the offices of Netherlands 3 Television and asked to speak to the news desk.

He identified himself as a director of Rotterdam Tankers and said he wished to provide an exclusive report concerning the capture of one of the biggest oil tankers in the world by Somali pirates. He provided as much detail as possible and confirmed that his family corporation owned the massive ship and that his father would be taking charge of the investigation.

He told the reporters that he believed a ransom had been worked out and that the Americans had agreed to assist his father with a warship on station next to the *Queen Beatrix*. By the time Hans had finished, his father, Jorgen Cruyf, sounded like the new ruler of all the oceans with Hans as his very obvious right-hand man.

But the grandiose family picture the young Dutchman painted did not affect the guts of the story. The 300,000-ton *Beatrix* had been commandeered by pirates, and this was the first news of the action on the Indian Ocean.

Netherlands 3 came out with the exclusive story on their 10:00 p.m. television news bulletin. The Reuters man in Rotterdam, Jack Hardy spotted it in a city bar and called his London office. In turn they called their man in New York, who checked in with their office in Riyadh. No one knew a single thing about such a maritime outrage.

Either the Dutch TV station knew something no one else did or there was a major hoax taking place. The trouble was the news bulletin did not name the tanker's owner, only that it believed it to be Dutch on charter to a Greek shipping corporation.

Which left the world's newshounds spinning around in circles. There was no point calling the United States Navy since they were not involved in the actual hijack. The Somali media was close to useless as it made no difference, and the ship had never even been to America.

The Reuters office in London searched online and checked out all media outlets broadcasting or publishing at night, and no one had a single sentence about the plight of the *Queen Beatrix*. The only lead the Rotterdam Reuters stringer had was the television station itself, and that was located on the outskirts of Amsterdam, thirty-five miles away.

So Jack hit the road north and burned rubber all the way up the E-19 highway, past Schipol Airport and into Holland's capital city. At Netherlands 3, he went in search of the news editor. It was almost midnight and the place was quiet, but they located the reporter on the phone.

Yes, he did have a note on the owners of the *Queen Beatrix*. She was owned by Rotterdam Tankers, which had a head office down near the docks. There was a phone number, and the name of the night spokesman was Hans Cruyf.

Apparently Hans's father owned the corporation, not to mention the ship, and this was a wild exaggeration for a man who owned a couple of thousand shares in the company and operated on an executive level similar to that enjoyed by Tom Sowerby at Athena Shipping in New York.

Jack Hardy tried to get Rotterdam Tankers on the phone but he had no private numbers, only the main switchboard. Hans was in there somewhere but it was midnight and he might be sleeping.

So Jack hit the road again, straight back down the E-19 to Rotterdam, taking the same route as his original night dash in search of the *Queen Beatrix*. It took him only a half hour to reach the offices of Rotterdam Tanker. There were lights inside but the door was locked. Jack rang the bell hard.

After five minutes someone answered and agreed to take the man from Reuters up to the office of the night duty officer. And after Jack had shown his press card, Hans Cruyf, plainly flattered to be the subject of international media attention, recounted all that he knew about the hijacked *Queen Beatrix*.

He even provided photographs of him and his father standing with the giant tanker. He furnished Jack Hardy with the names and staff photographs of Captain Jan van Marchant and his two senior officers, Johan Nistelroy and Pietr van der Saar. He provided home addresses for all three of them and confirmed the number of crew members.

Jack Hardy was astonished with gratitude. Because Hans Cruyf held back nothing. He'd provided the name and addresses of the chartering company, Athena Shipping, in New York, and provided a phone number and name for the boss there, Tom Sowerby.

He'd briefed Jack on the Greek ambassador and the connection with the fabled Livanos family. And when the interview was complete, he explained that the original communication had not come from a member of the pirate gang. It had come from their shore-based Somali commander, though he did not know the location of the base.

The man from Reuters left wearing a brand-new Rotterdam Tankerman baseball cap. And he went directly back to his office and made some calls. He failed to connect with Tom Sowerby or the Greek ambassador in Washington but he nonetheless filed his story. It was 2:00 a.m. in Holland, 1:00 a.m. in London, and 8:00 p.m. in New York.

And the Reuters story hit the print and airwaves like a pirate's RPG. The revered international news agency slugged it:

WORLD'S BIGGEST TANKER
SEIZED BY SOMALI PIRATES
*US Navy Answers Desperate*
*Appeal by Dutch Government*

There followed a knock-down-drag-out account of the giant tanker being boarded by the machine-gun-toting gang in the dead of night eight hundred miles offshore in the Indian Ocean and the crew being held at gunpoint.

Jack Hardy covered every base: the ransom demand, the threats, the hostages, the phone call to a member of the Livanos family who had the ship on charter. And the possibility that a ransom had been agreed to by the Greeks and the raiders.

When he'd completed the action part of his story, Jack Hardy filed another six hundred words on the recent history of piracy off the coast of Somalia, pulling up the Internet accounts of the *Niagara Falls* incident from only a couple of weeks ago.

He delved into the Reuters archives and pulled out another recent story about the lady who had traded her alimony rocket launcher for shares in two pirate operations and walked out with a $78,000 profit.

Emboldened by the new organization of the pirate raids, Jack took the opportunity to take a serious lead among journalists covering this murky world. He stepped out of the strict news and recap business and stepped into the speculation game.

And he ended his piece with a flourish:

Meanwhile out on the dark, hostile waters of the Indian Ocean, the *Queen Beatrix* and her crew could only await developments.

But mindful that the charter company Athena Shipping has world headquarters in New York City, US officials last night found themselves being dragged inevitably into the controversy and were considering whether this might be the same gang that captured the *Niagara Falls*.

Pentagon insiders believe there were many similarities between the two raids. The US Navy's top brass were also in conference last night with the CIA chief, Bob Birmingham, and the director of the National Security Agency, Captain James Ramshawe.

Jack Hardy acquired those names from a government directory on the Web. And altogether they added to a sparkling little cluster of facts with which he rounded off his world scoop.

Some of the "facts" might even have been true.

▼

THE FOLLOWING MORNING, General Zack Lancaster, Admirals Mark Bradfield and Andy Carlow, not to mention Commander Mack Bedford, were as furious as anyone can be without blowing a gasket.

Military people detest the glare of publicity, and the *Queen Beatrix* debacle was supposed to be kept strictly under wraps, mostly because the subject was hideously sensitive and the very mention of it riled the public, the politicians, and the media to a degree second only to civil war and mass murder.

Everyone involved had been hoping for a swift and silent payment of the ransom, which would send the *Beatrix* peacefully on her way into the Malacca Strait and then China.

But this suddenly huge story, incontrovertibly linked to the *Niagara Falls* incident, appeared in almost every news publication in the United States, many of which plastered it on their front page. There were pictures of the crew, pictures and diagrams of the ship, valuations placed on its cargo of crude oil, and quotations from executives.

Various publications had attempted to force a quote out of the Chinese National Oil Corporation in Shanghai. And one breathtakingly enterprising New York radio reporter had tried to get through to the private residence of Queen Beatrix of the Netherlands to find out how upset she was at losing her ship.

It all had the slightly crazed atmosphere that accompanies news stories when the journalists know only about one-fifth of the facts.

And now the admirals could expect the roof to fall in, once again finding themselves fielding press demands asking why this was being allowed to happen. That the United States, with the biggest navy in the history of modern warfare, could possibly allow a bunch of half-naked African bandits to run circles around them. Every week.

A police line was formed outside the Olympic Tower to prevent the media from launching a mass entry to the twentieth floor to find Tom Sowerby, who had been mentioned that morning in newspapers and news broadcasts more often than the president.

The Fourth Estate attacked from all angles. They stationed men outside the home of Captain van Marchant's mother in Delft; they ran to ground the families of the captured Johan Nistelroy and Pietr van der Saar outside Rotterdam; they besieged the apartment block in Monte Carlo trying to reach Constantine Livanos; they laid siege to the Greek Embassy in Washington, DC; and they fearlessly tried to smart-talk a whole fleet of lieutenant commanders in the United States Navy Press Office.

More than one spokesman was moved to ask inquiring reporters, "Why in God's name are you so excited about this? No one's in any danger, and we are doing everything possible to solve the problem. It should all be over in another day. What do you want from us?"

And the answer from all the reporters followed the same lines:

"Because it's in the public interest, our readers/listeners/viewers deserve to know the dangers present on the high seas. If these pirates can take a ship that big, they can take anything. This tanker is managed from New York City, and our readers/listeners/viewers need to know why the US Navy is apparently helpless."

By noontime, General Zack Lancaster was being pressured from the White House either to act or make some kind of statement through the DOD Press Office. But action was out of the question until Mack Bedford's trainees came on line. And any statement would be construed as vacuous.

The general's advice never varied: "Everyone keep their heads well down and keep repeating, 'It's not even our goddamned ship, and neither the owners, nor the insurance companies, nor the crew, wish us to intervene in any way.'"

Meanwhile he privately ordered Admiral Mark Bradfield to send in the destroyer from Diego Garcia to help the *Queen Beatrix*, if necessary, during the ransom payment operation. "Because if something goes wrong and people get killed," he added, "we, sure as hell, are going to get the blame right here in the US."

▼

THE GUARD ON THE BRIDGE of the tanker was down to just two men, Elmi Ahmed, with the heavy machine gun, and a junior pirate called Georgio, age eighteen, who carried only his Kalashnikov. Still in control of the ship, her navigation and propulsion, was Captain van Marchant with his two senior officers, Johan and Pietr.

Ismael Wolde had permitted the officers to eat in the private dining room on the fifth floor and had made it very clear that he and his commanders would use the same place for their own lunch and dinner. After one day dining in the company of Ahmed and Zenawi, Wolde estimated that he had rarely, if ever, been quite so well served.

The captain and his staff were never more than five yards from that big machine gun and had accepted there was nothing they could do about their plight. The remaining crew members were kept below in the accommodation block and had their meals in their regular dining area.

For the cooks and cleaning staff, it made little or no difference whether the *Queen Beatrix* was under the command of Captain van Marchant or Admiral Wolde. The work was much the same, except for the presence of the Somali Marine guard patrols, who prowled the ship constantly, unsmiling. They were a silent reminder that anyone attempting any kind of a revolt would be shot instantly.

Admiral Wolde was constantly on the telephone to Mohammed Salat and together they drew up the plans for the collection of the $6 million ransom. There was a spot on the deserted beach ten miles northeast of Haradheere that could be approached by a cart track over the dunes. No problem for a 4 × 4 SUV.

Rather than risk an ocean drop, possibly in the presence of warships, Salat favored telling the Athena executives to fly the money in, probably from Nairobi, and make a low-level drop onto the beach, where his men would retrieve it. The aircraft could then fly on to ensure an orderly disembarkation by the pirates from the *Queen Beatrix* and a swift clearance of the datum by all concerned.

Subject to the availability of a long-range military aircraft, this seemed reasonable to Tom Sowerby, and he cleared the operation with the Greek ambassador before speaking to Livanos in Monte Carlo. The Greek tycoon, however, had bigger things on his mind than a mere $6 million off the bottom line of one of his tanker cargoes en route to China. He ordered Tom Sowerby to make whatever decisions were necessary. But he was gratified to learn that his New York chief executive had just heard that the directors of Rotterdam Tankers were prepared to pay 33 percent of the ransom money since it was, after all, their ship. And Athena was, after all, one of their best customers.

The directors had already had a rather busy morning, having summarily fired Hans Cruyf for *indiscretion so appallingly judged* that it was unlikely he could ever occupy a position of responsibility in the somewhat reclusive world of international shipping.

Meanwhile the GPS numbers relayed to Tom Sowerby for the big drop were 4.40N 47.53E. According to the Greek ambassador, his navy was not strong on modern aviation, owning only old Orion aircraft. And he requested that Sowerby check with his friends at Rotterdam Tankers in search of a better aircraft. If not them, then perhaps the Americans, who, unhappily the ambassador guessed, would be seething after this morning's media blast.

"Perhaps," he suggested, smoothly, "we might intimate to the Dutch that they rather stepped on our toes with that unfortunate leak to the press. Inadvertently, of course, and no fault of the directors of the tanker company.

"But perhaps a word in the right place might urge the very well-equipped Dutch Navy to step in and assist us with the transportation. They might even like it to be known that when one of their great shipping corporations runs into trouble, they are indeed there to help and ensure rescue.

"I expect the Dutch captain of the ship might be persuaded to express his appreciation to them. Publicly, of course."

Tom Sowerby immediately understood that he had just been provided with an abject lesson showing precisely why men like this were awarded sensational jobs in Washington, elegantly representing their nation on the world's biggest stage.

Sowerby rang off, called the offices of Rotterdam Tankers, and had a discussion along the lines the ambassador had suggested. They informed him that they were knocking $2 million off the cost of two charters that were about to be contracted, and they were also sure they could prevail upon the Netherlands Navy for a modern aircraft for the long-distance drop on the East African beach.

Tom then spoke to the bank, which had the finances in order, much to the amusement of the manager in Nairobi who was becoming used to this one-way avalanche of cash being transferred to the local savages up the beach in Somalia. Nonetheless he stepped forward and had the cash ready and bagged for collection.

▼

IT TOOK FOUR DAYS for the pieces to fall into place. The main holdup being for the Dutch Navy to fly one of their state-of-the-art Lockheed Orion P-3C Mark IIs from a base in the south of France, where admirals were conducting a naval program of cooperation with the French.

They needed to fly first to Cairo, refuel, and then go on to Nairobi. The navy was willing but had to deal with the admirals first, and that necessitated a new aircraft being flown down from the Hague. But in the end it was all slotted together, and on a burning hot afternoon, six days after the *Queen Beatrix* was captured, four carloads of Mohammed Salat's staff were gathered on the beach northeast of Haradheere.

The commander-in-chief was in attendance along with eight of his palace guard. There were also two representatives of the village elders, plus two executives of the Haradheere Stock Exchange. This was the biggest business they had ever had, with $6 million on the line, and shares in the mission already trading at $40 each.

According to Salat's watch, the Dutch Orion was six minutes from making the drop. But quite suddenly, out over the flat sandy land to the southwest, he could see a tiny speck in the sky, an aircraft, flying low and not particularly fast. And somehow he knew this was the one.

No one spoke as the ASW Orion came howling high over the terrain in a giant circle. It made its pass perhaps a half-mile back, away from the water. And then it accelerated out to sea, further north and heading east directly offshore, until it almost disappeared.

Salat's already cold heart was chilled even more while he speculated that maybe everything was off and that the Europeans and the Americans had somehow joined forces and planned to attack the *Beatrix* and wipe out the Somali Marine force. The C-in-C knew how rapidly things could change in this lawless arena in which he saw himself as the undisputed ringmaster.

Salat was not sufficiently foolish to underestimate the power of his opponents. And he could easily imagine the major Western naval powers growing very seriously vexed at his constant and expensive harassment of the world's shipping operations.

Again he checked his watch—only three minutes to go—and through his binoculars he once more spotted the big gray military aircraft to the north that was turning directly toward him.

Without a word, Salat pointed, and every eye on the beach followed the direction of his arm straight up the tideline, perhaps only a hundred feet above the surf, and from here at least, it looked like it was travelling like a bat out of hell.

The Orion came screaming in, low and fast, 250 miles per hour, and a pile of six mailbags, all roped together, came tumbling out of its bomb bay. There was no parachute, nothing except the bags, and they turned over and over, swept backward by the slipstream as they fell.

They hit the sand at a shallow angle, about fifty yards north of where the party stood, kicking up a dust cloud. The ungainly pile came scuffing and rolling to a standstill. And the guards chased in to retrieve the bags.

Mohammed Salat stood and watched the aircraft bank hard left and head once more out to sea, gaining height as it went. The observers on the beach turned their eyes toward the palace guards dragging the mailbags across the sand.

They delivered the bounty to their leader, who unzipped one bag and thrust his hand inside. The bag was crammed with neat bundles of fifty one-hundred dollar bills, two hundred of them, the standard packing procedure designated by the manager of Barclays Bank on Moi Avenue, Nairobi, when preparing the pirates' bi-weekly ransom money for the private aircraft drop.

Salat stared down at the bags of money, six of them all checked and correct. He'd actually stopped counting halfway through the second bag because it was obvious each one was identical. Salat delved into each of the six and randomly selected a bundle and pulled it out for a check. No variation.

"Load the merchandise into the cars," he ordered. And then he called Ismael Wolde on his cell phone, speaking in what he believed to be clipped military tones.

"Ransom paid in full. Vacate the *Queen Beatrix* immediately and return to the *Mombassa*. We all await the arrival of heroic Somali Marines. Send ETA."

Wolde responded in the way he'd read was appropriate for battlefield commanders: "Roger that, sir," snapped the pirate chief. "Over and out."

▼

ON THE BRIDGE of the *Queen Beatrix*, Wolde dialled the number of the *Mombassa* and ordered Captain Hassan to bring the big fishing boat close-in for the marines to disembark. Then he turned to Captain van Marchant, offered his hand, and said that it had been a great pleasure to work with him. The master of the *Queen Beatrix* could not believe this farce being played out right in front of his eyes.

Nevertheless he shook hands with Admiral Wolde, politely said good-bye to Elmi Ahmed and the junior guard, and watched them leave the bridge, shutting the door behind them. They travelled down in the main elevator, and Ismael asked Kifle Zenawi to inform his troops that everyone was to assemble immediately on deck.

He formally saluted his 2I/C and was rather proud when

Ahmed returned the traditional mark of respect. And one mile away, over the stern rails, he could see the welcome sight of Captain Hassan's *Mombassa* charging in at flank speed behind a surging bow wave.

One way or another, Admiral Wolde would leave the *Queen Beatrix* a contented, fulfilled, and wealthier man. He'd enjoyed this mission and no harm had been done. So far as he knew, no one bore him and his men any ill will. The ransom was paid and the massive tanker was on its way.

He gazed over the water with some satisfaction as the *Queen Beatrix* made her turn back to the east and onward to the Malacca Strait and the South China Sea.

Wolde was a man of considerable imagination, easily visualizing military-style operations and able to work with his fellow commanders and combat troops. He was at home in planning meetings, fitting in nicely with the forecasts, hopes, and expectations of his C-in-C.

And their success rate was so utterly formidable that he now believed they could not fail. For Ismael Wolde, defeat had become unthinkable. He was also conscious of the sea change that consistently occurred in the minds and demeanor of his captives. Their opening hostile attitudes always dissolved into acceptance and then submission.

In the several days he had spent in the company of the captain and his Dutch officers, he had grown to like them. He was extremely gratified there had been a complete absence of violence—no one wounded, no one killed.

Wolde, in general terms, was in accord with the often-stated view of the Chinese despot Mao Tse-Tung: "Real power comes from the barrel of a gun." And indeed that had been his experience. The mere sight of that heavy machine gun, held by Somali warriors with ammunition belts slung across their chests, had always been sufficient to force a crew to surrender their ship.

The only time there'd been real trouble was on board the *Niagara Falls*, and that was only because the captain had panicked. It had been completely unnecessary.

So far as Wolde was concerned, his boarding and threat levels were as close to perfect as they could be. His men were trained to the minute and could be relied upon thoroughly. Their shore-based commander was a wise and accomplished planner and financier. The money was safe. The investment solid. The little marine fortress of Haradheere was close to impregnable.

Ismael Wolde, the newest admiral in East Africa, had it made. He was a master of his trade and commander of the oceans. What he did not know, however, was that 1,500 miles away, one of the most powerful shipowners in the world, Constantine Livanos, was about ready to kill him. And that 6,000 miles away in New York, Athena Shipping president Tom Sowerby would willingly have throttled him. And that two hundred miles south of New York, Admiral Mark Bradfield was planning to destroy the Somali Marines' forthcoming operations. And that 3,000 more miles away in San Diego, Commander Mack Bedford was making contingency plans to take the Somali pirates off the map.

Ismael Wolde had undoubtedly become a world military figure. But not in quite the way he had envisaged.

# CHAPTER 6

▼

C OMMANDER BEDFORD COMPLETED HIS TWO-WEEK STINT
as proctor to the BUDs INDOC class. He worked mornings
and spent the afternoons recruiting more outstanding SEALs to
join his clandestine Delta Platoon.

He raided the teams and watched the final tests being conducted
in the pool by more advanced BUDs classes, where there were several guys almost ready to join. He knew precisely who he was after
because he understood as well as anyone that there are people who
have a God-given ability underwater.

In Mack's opinion, this was one of several aspects of SEAL training that couldn't be taught from scratch. It could be honed but not
taught. Even he, the Moby Dick of a coastal Maine shipbuilding
and fishing town, had summarily failed at his first try at Pool
Comp.

He'd never forgotten that shameful day when they had ordered
him out of the water and sat him against the wall in the line of failures who could not cut it in deep water.

On reflection, his instructors may have been enjoying a well-
intentioned laugh just as a warning. They'd failed every member
of his class that day, but they'd permitted a select few to get back in
and try again. Pool Comp is traditionally the graveyard of BUDs
students.

And for Mack's forthcoming operation, boarding large ships
captured by pirates, he needed men who were perfectly at home in
the water. Because there would be setbacks. Men would end up in

the ocean, probably in the dark, possibly in rough water. But they would have all of the right equipment. They just needed to be those guys of whom his very first BUDs instructors had said, "For us, water is a sanctuary because no other armed force in the world can operate in it like we can."

Deep into the second week as proctor, he found such a character in SDV Team 1 in the final stages of preparation for a return to Afghanistan via the US base in Bahrain. They were in the huge training pool at the time, conducting some informal races, and there was one kid, way out in front, who could really swim. Even wearing his big SEAL flippers, he looked like an Olympic finalist, slicing through the water using that special SEAL sidestroke—long, dead-smooth power strokes. He looked more like a fish than a human being, the obvious result of about 10 million timed laps in this very pool.

His name was Barnaby Wilkes. He answered to Barney, and when Mack sent someone to pull up his records, he was unsurprised to see he'd been Honor Man in Pool Comp. He'd also been right up there over the O-Course and had done well as a sniper.

Barney was twenty-four, a petty officer second class, due for promotion probably before his Alpha Platoon left for the Gulf. He was from Morehead City, beyond the salt marshes of North Carolina's Atlantic coast, south of Cape Hatteras and about twenty-five miles northeast of the gigantic US Marine base of Camp Lejeune.

Barney was a SEAL warrior from his combat boots all the way up to the brown-and-green drive-on bandana he wore into combat. He was six feet three inches tall, 210 pounds, with a deepwater seaman's blue eyes, outlandishly strong, and as much at home underwater as he was on land.

His combat record was rock steady. He'd shown profound courage under fire and was widely rumored to be going to officer training school at the conclusion of his next tour of duty. In another parlance, he was judged to have "the right stuff" to become a commissioned SEAL commander, one of Coronado's chosen ones.

Thus young Barney was mildly surprised to be informed by his CO that he was not going back to Afghanistan after all, that he had been selected to transfer to the newly formed, highly classified Delta Platoon under the command of the legendary Mackenzie Bedford.

In the normal run of things, Barney would not have been overjoyed about leaving his team, but the reputation of his new CO was not much short of legendary. Mack Bedford was the SEAL officer who had single-handedly gunned down a large group of Iraqi insurgents on the Euphrates River and then been court-martialled in such a colossal miscarriage of justice that they brought him back when the verdict was publicly deplored by everyone at SPECWARCOM.

The story was not, of course, quite accurate, but it was good enough for the entire population of Coronado. Because out there, they don't have any public heroes, only private ones, known only to a few. Mack Bedford, on this base, had transformed that stereotype. Everyone knew who he was, and Barney Wilkes, swimmer, warrior, and southern raconteur, would be proud to serve under his command. *Darned proud. Yessir.*

Another recruit to Mack's Delta was Cody Sharp, a thirty-one-year-old native of North Dakota, chief petty officer with SDV Team 1 in Hawaii. Cody was old friend of Mack's. They'd been in Iraq together, and among his many talents he was an excellent boatman and qualified to pilot navy helicopters. He was a gunner by trade and had made Honor Man in his Unarmed Combat course.

Mack wanted him as a personal bodyguard—as well as everything else. The heavyset, laconic former cowboy from the northern prairies was real pleased to be joining his old teammate from along the Euphrates River. When Mack had been reprimanded by the judge at his court-martial, it had taken three very senior officers to persuade CPO Cody Sharp not to resign from the United States Navy and return to his father's cattle ranch in the Badlands.

Meanwhile, several other officers were helping Mack in his search for personnel. But they were on the other side of the country in Dam Neck, Virginia Beach, where the ultra-secretive but too-big DEVGRU operation was sited. These officers were anxious to dispel the obvious conclusion that top people were being cherry-picked to serve with the new Delta Platoon on the West Coast.

Thus several outstanding SEALs suddenly vanished overnight from Dam Neck on mysterious inter-naval transfers. No one knew where they had gone, and everyone knew better than to ask. The Navy SEALs' version of *omerta* made the average Sicilian Mafia don look like a chatterbox. That code of silence, drummed into them since BUDs, followed them throughout their careers in the branch of the US Navy where *everything* is classified.

So it was that Mack Bedford's platoon took shape, imperceptibly, with new arrivals training informally on the beach, practicing with the boats, the high-powered Zodiac inflatables, and in the pool. For one week Commander Bedford had them all transferred to the SEAL Jump School at Fort Benning, Georgia, where they secretly honed their parachuting techniques, especially the HALO system—high-altitude, low opening—involving freefalling from 26,000 feet.

In Mack's judgment there was a limited number of ways any combat platoon could board a ship, and one obvious scenario was a high-level parachute jump into the ocean, from where they would be retrieved by SEAL small-boat crews and transported to the ops area.

All of the personnel from DEVGRU were top class. Between them they could achieve anything they attempted, and within two weeks Mack had them integrated with the nucleus of his new group: Chief Petty Officer Brad Charlton, Petty Officer Second Class Shane Cannel, Lieutenant Josh Malone, PO2 Barney Wilkes, and CPO Cody Sharp.

Three more days working together, forming their swim partnerships and appointing team leaders, and the entire platoon would be decamping every morning for the San Diego Navy Yard, currently the biggest in North America and the hub for the warships of the Pacific fleet. The SEALs would travel by truck because it was more anonymous than by boat, driving straight across the two-mile long Coronado Bridge, two hundred feet above San Diego Bay.

There they would perfect the brutal SEAL team efficiency, which Admiral Carlow sincerely hoped would, in the not-too-distant future, frighten the living daylights out of the Somali Marines.

▼

IT WAS 0500 THE FOLLOWING MORNING when the forty-strong Delta Platoon drove out past the SPECWARCOM sentries and headed over the high concrete-and-steel gantry of the Coronado Bridge, directly to the US Navy's stronghold on the other side of San Diego Bay.

Nine thousand miles to the east, at precisely that same time, 4:00 p.m. (local), a hundred-pound ammonium-nitrate bomb, boosted with powered aluminum and TNT, detonated in the downtown end of Churchill Avenue in Addis Ababa, the predominantly Christian capital of Ethiopia.

It knocked down the grand front façade of a hotel, flattened a single-story supermarket, and blew four cars across the street, one of which hit a bus stop and killed everyone standing there. Altogether thirty-eight people lost their lives, not including the jihadist driver of the truck that carried the bomb.

Another 117 people were injured, some by a large container of baked beans that exploded in the supermarket and fired six-dozen red-hot cans straight across Churchill Avenue, mowing down the populace on the same side as the bus stop.

Addis Ababa was aghast, especially the Christian section, which had not been targeted by terrorists for a very long time. And now it had started again, and the city's police chief was convinced it was the work of al-Qaeda, operating from one of its bases in Somalia, almost certainly in partnership with the fire-eating, Taliban look-alikes of the ultra-extremist al-Shabaab movement.

The bomb on Churchill Avenue was classic al-Qaeda. A very powerful IED delivered by a suicide bomber in a thriving area of a big capital city with strong ties to the West. The traditional animosity between Somalia and Ethiopia was a useful smokescreen at the heart of the crime.

But the interlopers of al-Qaeda had been quietly encamped in both the north and south of Somalia for almost twenty years, cozying up to tribal warlords, befriending the fanatics of al-Shabaab, and fanning the flames of the endless war between the extremists and moderate Somali Muslims.

It was claimed that Osama bin Laden himself, forecasting world upheaval when he hit the Twin Towers, had personally ordered his troops into Somalia to start a new international base on the Dark Continent.

And now, by all accounts, on the Horn of Africa, the snake bite of al-Qaeda was once more on the loose, almost certainly delivered by the twin-headed cobra formed by their alliance with al-Shabaab.

The shock in Ethiopia's main city was profound. The president himself was on the line to his Washington embassy, anxious to re-cruit US military help if he found himself in yet another holy war with the jihadists. By 9:00 a.m. Washington time, the Ethiopian ambassador had briefed his military attaché to contact the US sec-retary of defense.

And now Simon Andre, the world-travelled, world-weary oc-cupant of the big office on the third floor of the Pentagon, was star-ing at his first briefing of the day, a sketchy account of the atrocity in Addis Ababa. He read the communiqué with the swift mechan-ical grasp of a career diplomat, tossing back and forth the ramifi-cations in his mind.

He noted with concern the immediate reaction of the president of Ethiopia, which, in his experience, was a sure sign that something most unfortunate had broken out. Not just the blast and the deaths of so many people and the pure misery it had unleashed, but also the political background of the event, including the likely culprits. And right there was the word he currently dreaded above all others: Somalia.

Andre knew all about the urgent formation of an anti-pirate attack force being masterminded in Coronado. And of course he understood the recent political history of the area, better than most as it happened. And he was especially aware of the plight of that benighted land beside the Indian Ocean.

God knows, he thought, they have enough trouble without fucking al-Qaeda starting a brand new war. Andre had been there, he'd seen the mind-blowing situation of a place ravaged by decades of war and terrorism, which in turn had led to brutality, oppression, poverty, and malnutrition on an almost unprecedented scale.

Over half a million people were living in makeshift camps. Hundreds of thousands more were living absolutely nowhere. Somalia represented the worst country on earth, with only a third of its population literate and 40 percent entirely reliant for survival on food provided by other charitable nations.

And in the middle of this terrible place, the evil of al-Qaeda was rising again, bringing yet more strife to a nation that simply could not cope. Andre Simon knew full well the strength of Ethiopia's armed forces—almost 300 main battle tanks, 400 armored infantry fighting vehicles, almost 100 fighter aircraft and helicopters, and 330,000 overall military personnel.

Hapless Somalia, bankrupted by other wars, would surely buckle and fold under an Ethiopian attack. And then the cycle would begin again. The United States inevitably being called upon by the world community to persuade their allies in Addis Ababa to stop the fighting and then to step in and help deal with the aftermath of the carnage.

Simon Andre could hear alarm bells everywhere: *If that beady-eyed Ethiopian president decides that bomb in his city originated in some godforsaken al-Qaeda training camp in the mountains of western Somalia . . . well, all hell might break loose.*

The dichotomy of his ponderings was not lost on the most sophisticated member of the US government. On one side Andre was trying to cope with the arch-villains of Haradheere, the Beverly Hills of East Africa, and on the other, he may need to smash into yet more al-Qaeda training camps.

"Jesus Christ," said the US secretary of defense.

▼

MEANWHILE, FAR AWAY in the burning hills of western Somalia, only four miles from the Ethiopian frontier, the al-Shabaab training camp was indulging in a day of self-congratulation. The bomb in Addis Ababa was judged a huge success and would almost certainly make world headlines. According to their sources in the city, the blast had caused unremitting chaos, with its spectacular detonation and fairly high death toll on Churchill Avenue.

The men of al-Qaeda had no regrets. And as permanent residents, their work reflected credit on the entire camp. The attack had been one part of their master plan, which would not cease until they had driven the infidel from the Middle East—not until there was a Muslim empire stretching west from the Horn of Africa all the way to the Atlantic coast.

The policy was primitive: We must keep killing and smashing the cities of the unbelievers until the intruders from the Western world pack up and leave. And in the execution of our master plan, we will eliminate the illegal state of Israel.

Ethiopia, with its Christian majority and long-standing ties to the US, Great Britain, and Italy, was merely an irritating neighbor that had to be brought into line. Neither al-Qaeda nor the warriors of al-Shabaab considered the possibility that the rulers of Ethiopia might unleash their very powerful military upon the terrorist camps in Somalia.

There is a uniformity to these training camps, wherever al-Qaeda pitches its tent. The one north of Saddam Hussein's home village of Tikrit was almost identical to the ones in the Hindu Kush. And they in turn were precisely the same as the ones in Pakistan's Swat Valley and further south in the tribal areas of Waziristan.

They consist of crude accommodation blocks, small unobtrusive buildings constructed of mud and rocks. There is invariably a shooting range and a much wider area to test explosives. There is usually a high wooden wall with primitive siege ladders for practice. There is always an obstacle course for training new recruits, but by Coronado standards of difficulty, these would be regarded as absurd.

In fact, military training for "warriors" who really only attack long-range, mostly with missiles and bombs, is a fairly steady waste of time. But it keeps them fit, focused, and single-minded. The trouble with this al-Qaeda/al-Shabaab alliance in the high wastelands of Somalia was a dire, life-threatening shortage of money.

And while the jihadists had made forays into the Somali pirate camps, demanding a share of the booty, they had not been very successful. The hard-eyed pirates risked their lives boarding ships and fighting for every last dollar of the ransoms, and they were not about to hand it over to the wild-eyed, bearded fanatics who came busting into their coastal villages asking for funds whenever they felt inclined. At least they were not about to do so without a fight. If necessary, to the death.

But in recent months things had worsened for the men in the training camp. With no more cash being funnelled to them from the bin Laden family, hardly a token payment from the pirates, and arsenals of weapons that seemed to shrink by the day, the situation was on the south side of desperate.

There was no longer a central command to which they could apply for cash. The hugely expensive war being waged against the slick, supremely well-provided forces of the Western world was draining every bank account al-Qaeda ever had.

The blast in Addis Ababa had wiped them out of ammonium nitrate, their ammunition boxes were low, and very soon they would have to steal to eat. And all the while there were astonishing tales of wealth beyond understanding in the tiny coastal town of Haradheere, two hundred miles to the east.

Sheikh Sharif el-Dahir, the forty-two-year-old Saudi-born commander-in-chief of the camp, called his fourth council of war in a week. He gathered around him his senior commanders. The camp, he declared, had become dysfunctional since they no longer had the wherewithal to mount another attack on anyone. To the north lay Ethiopia with its obdurate dislike of extremist Islam, and all around lay Somalia with its total disinclination to adopt the strict religious bonds of the Taliban, al-Shabaab, or al-Qaeda.

Sheikh Sharif understood he had to lead his troops somewhere. He needed funds, military hardware, and a new place to settle. There was no earthly point in remaining out in the wastelands, going broke and doing nothing. He felt the call of his hero, Saladin, and he felt, as ever, the urgent summons of the jihad.

With the entire camp of more than thirty warriors gathered around, he announced a plan that would lead them back to the promised land. They were moving out, heading east across the desert, through the scrubland and over gigantic sand dunes to the coast.

There they would once more experience the joy of conquest. Because Sheikh Sharif planned to attack and conquer Haradheere with all of its wealth and military supplies. The pirates' lair would quickly fall to the disciples of bin Laden, owing to the al-Qaeda army's huge reputation for merciless killing and mind-blowing bravery. Of that he was certain.

The sheikh, in his time, had established a personal reputation as a bloodthirsty warrior. He had taken part in both attacks against the US embassies in Nairobi and Dar es Salaam in 1998—no one disputed that both raids had been planned and mounted in Somalia.

But now al-Qaeda's little army was on the move, and there was not really much to pack up since there was hardly any food, they were down to the last sticks of TNT, a couple of old Russian medium mortars, and each man's personal Kalashnikov with ammunition belts. They were in possession of several very old SUVs, mostly stolen. And lashed to the roof of three of these vehicles were two of the twenty-foot high timber siege ladders, six altogether.

Flush with the triumph in Addis Ababa, they set off on the long journey to Haradheere. Sheikh Sharif did what he could along the way to recruit more troops, making a succession of cell phone calls to various contacts in Mogadishu.

All of them were very pleased to hear his plan. Every member of this ramshackle, fading brotherhood of quasi-religious militiamen looked forward to sharing in the fabled riches of the Somali pirates without having to do the actual fighting. But throughout the journey, Sheikh Sharif was able to find only a couple dozen young men prepared to go into battle on behalf of the jihadists.

They rolled through the scrubland, pooling their financial resources whenever they found a gas station. After a twenty-eight-hour journey, they finally reached a sheltered point four miles north of Haradheere, and there they circled the wagons, forming a defensive wall of the ten SUVs and pitching their tents in the clearing between the vehicles.

Sheikh Sharif dispatched two young braves in two SUVs to refill the water cans, either at an oasis or in the town where they might locate a communal pump or well. In the absence of that, they would have to buy from the village elders, a common practice in a land where fresh water is considerably more precious than roasted goat.

The plan that night was to check out the northern approaches to the town, to try to reach the center without attracting any attention. Sharif needed to decide on a point of attack, and speed was crucial since they could not survive much longer without an infusion of money.

Sheikh Sharif was anxious to find out precisely where the pirates' millions were stored. And then he needed to assess the strength of the guard. He had no knowledge of the Somali Marines, their leaders, their commanders, or how well they were equipped.

He was already disappointed in the size of his own force because there were, he knew, probably three hundred al-Qaeda operatives residing in Somalia, the majority of whom had infiltrated the country in the past five years. But thus far he would be fortunate to have fifty of them under his command.

He had no doubt that the superior war-fighting ability of his troops would win the day against the African tribesmen. The forthcoming raid would enable him to make a handsome contribution to the global movement of al-Qaeda by funding their ambitious plans to mount operations against their enemies.

He had everything to gain from this operation. Defeat, in the mind of the Saudi-born sheikh, was out of the question. But he had a problem the size of the Sahara Desert: The Haradheere Stock Exchange cash was stored in a fortress, the high-walled stronghold of Mohammed Salat. This was built along the lines of a small medieval castle—solid concrete with massive wooden gates leading out onto the central road to the "downtown" of tiny Haradheere.

Salat's house occupied the northwest corner and one hundred feet of the north wall. It was a 12,000-square-foot dwelling of unutterable luxury, with bomb-proof skylights throughout and windows on the south side only. The north wall ran for another 150 feet beyond the house and provided the back wall for the offices, operations center, and strong rooms for the cash. Set into the northeast corner was the armory, comprising ammunition and equipment stores.

Salat had six armed guards on duty at all times in the interior courtyard, which also contained an accommodation block for Salat's private army. There were high observation posts in the northeast and northwest corners equipped with mounted machine guns. Neither of them was ever unmanned.

On the south side, left and right of the main gate, two more observation posts were set atop the six-hundred-foot long side walls. Each post had an area that was eighty feet long, built high, with room for a six-man fighting force, one facing west and one east.

In addition to his personal fortress, Salat had on his payroll the local tribal warlord, who could produce a thirty-strong combat force on request within ten minutes. This cost the stock exchange boss $20,000 a month, which he considered a bargain. It worked out to $300 each for the bone-idle but aggressive tribesmen, with $10,000 for the chief, and a thousand for equipment.

Salat kept this tribal army on permanent standby. He had no doubt it might one day prove extremely useful. Besides, it kept the bloodthirsty warlord Colonel Patrick Zeppi onside at all times.

At this highly combustible East African redoubt, Sheikh Sharif intended to hurl his army. And in making his plans, guided by his desperation for success, he tended to ignore the military history and traditions of his own force, many of whom had come to Somalia to help in the 2006 wars against Ethiopia.

They were accomplished in bomb-making techniques and in the kind of sneak-attack expertise necessary to deliver IEDs of all shapes and sizes, including the big one that just knocked down a stretch of Churchill Avenue in Addis Ababa. They were also skilled in the ideology of martyrdom and the spiritual rewards awaiting suicide bombers.

They understood the strong international links between themselves and ambitious young Muslims in places like Great Britain who yearned to join the fight against the West.

There were four or five members of Sheikh Sharif's army who

had mounted a very successful attack against the Israeli-owned Paradise Hotel in Mombassa in November 2006, when a car bomb killed fifteen people. They had also been involved, minutes earlier, in the firing of two terrorist missiles at an Israeli-chartered aircraft as it was taking off from Mombassa Airport with 261 passengers on board.

However, the guidance systems may have been faulty because both missiles had missed and then failed to detonate when they hit the ground. In the tried and tested Arab way, they had spent about a zillion hours endlessly reliving that day of mixed fortunes with their new leader, Sheikh Sharif, in Somalia.

A more strategic military leader might have considered that their basic skills were in bombing, assassinating, and blowing up vehicles and buildings, staying as far away from their enemy as possible. They always relied on their more powerful, longer-range weapons, even in hot-firing battles against the Americans and, more often, against the undergunned British with their 5.56-caliber standard rounds.

Al-Qaeda troops were simply not used to being close to their target. Formal warfare was not their game. And their leader was about to commit them to an attack on an occupied armed fortress. However stealthily they made their approach, and however stealthily they launched their attack against an unsuspecting enemy, they still had to take Mohammed Salat's fortress by force of arms. And that might prove extremely challenging.

Sheikh Sharif's major decision was whether to attack by day or by night. But first he needed to insert men to conduct reconnaissance, critical to finding out where the treasure was kept. He knew of the existence of the mysterious Mohammed Salat, and he had heard of the Haradheere Stock Exchange. Everyone knew about the massive quantities of cash the pirates had stashed away.

But the geography of the thriving little outback town was unknown to him. He needed his troops to see for themselves. That first afternoon he dispatched three of his commanders into Harad-heere with orders to stay unobserved, separate, and watchful. He was certain that the pirates' stronghold would be more than obvious.

He was correct. The three al-Qaeda operatives walked the final two miles into town, split up, and then located Salat's garrison in-side the first hour. From the outside it was a fairly formidable sight: high grey walls, cast concrete, with obvious guards in two positions on the roof.

This did not faze the al-Qaeda killers. They merely assessed that it would be possible to climb the walls at night with the ladders and slit the throats of the guards. Then, somehow, they would open the gates. Their fifty-strong army would swarm in with their trusted Kalashnikovs, and the garrison would fall to them almost imme-diately.

And, of course, there were the Russian mortar bombs. Maybe they would fire a barrage into the courtyard beyond the walls to create a massive diversion before the attack on the guard posts. They would certainly make a good report to their leader when they returned to their new base.

However, they had grossly underestimated the sensitivity of the village of Haradheere, which, like most communities with far-reaching secrets to conceal, was ever-alert for intruders. The water boys had been most conspicuous, driving around the town until they located the central pump and then filling seven or eight stan-dard gas cans for each of their two sandblasted SUVs.

They had spoken to no one and then vanished into the semi-desert scrubland to the north of the main building. The three re-connaissance men had been more circumspect, operating far apart, and moving into the shadows to make notes while they assessed the strength of Mohammed Salat's garrison.

At no time did they raise a genuine suspicion among the tribes-men, except when one of them walked right around the building.

On the west wall, he went past the home of Admiral Ismael Wolde, who was sipping a beer in the forecourt beneath the questionable shade of a banana tree.

Wolde was alert, and he noted only that he had never seen the man in his life, which was a rare phenomenon in Haradheere, where there were no strangers. The pirate chief decided the guy could have been visiting anyone, and he watched the man disappear around the north corner. He thought no more about it until another ten minutes had passed, and the man showed up again, still examining the walls, and apparently on another circuit of the bastion where Salat kept the cash.

Wolde stood up and shouldered his AK-47. Then he walked a half block south to the home of Commodore Elmi Ahmed. Ismael asked him to bring his rifle because the two of them were going for a little stroll.

Together they walked up to the Salat stronghold and along the western wall, looking for the stranger. They stared along the north wall, and Ahmed waved to one of the guards. But there was no sign of the intruder, who could have been on the other two sides, out of their viewpoint.

"We should go back the other way," said Wolde. But then Elmi spotted a single figure walking away to the north across the scrubland. And, perhaps a half mile further on, there were two others. Far away, on the dusty horizon, Elmi could also see a parked vehicle, too far away to identify.

"Now, who are those people?" asked Wolde. "And what are they doing out there? There's not a building for miles."

"Perhaps just passing through, seeing the sights," suggested Elmi.

"Perhaps," replied Wolde, "but I think when we find a stranger walking in and out of town, examining the walls of our garrison with millions and millions of dollars inside, we should issue a military alert. At least inform the guards."

"I agree with that," said Elmi. They walked back to the main gate and whacked the door with a rifle butt, twice and then three times, the code for entry. The door was opened by Elmi's cousin, a huge black tribesman named Yanni who had accompanied them on a couple of missions.

He saluted both men and welcomed them with an enormous smile. Sensing the concerned look worn by Ismael Wolde, the local hero, he took them straight to the ops center, where they found the garrison CO discussing the appearance of the water boys and the number of gallons they had taken without saying a word to anyone. Yanni's boss had estimated fifteen cans, each holding four-and-a-half gallons, standard Russian military issue. That was almost seventy gallons.

He saluted the senior-ranking Somali Marine and listened carefully to his observations. At the conclusion of Wolde's informal report, he said, "Sir, seventy gallons may mean a group of forty to sixty people. It is possible the jackals of al-Qaeda may be preparing an attack.

"I see no reason to go out there and alert them to our strength. But tonight I will double the guard on the north wall. Every gun in the garrison will be primed. And I will inform Mr. Salat of my decisions. If you approve, of course."

"Excellent," replied Wolde. "It may be nothing. But the coincidences are there. And I think Mr. Salat should alert Colonel Zeppi because he'll make sure the whole town is aware of possible danger."

Thus it was that two very different fighting forces, stationed 9,000 miles apart, had effectively declared war on tiny Haradheere. One of them would attack that night. The other was starting the fourth day of intensive training in the massive sprawl of the 5,000-acre San Diego Naval Base.

The Delta Platoon had, so far, been in a submarine dry dock for the duration. Commander Bedford had located a sub up on the blocks, secured port and starboard by three one-foot-thick holding beams, set at right angles to the ship, stopping her from toppling sideways one way or the other. The beams were approximately thirty feet off the floor of the dock, and all day, every day, the personnel of Delta Force, including Mack himself, hurled their grappling irons up and over those beams.

Attached were knotted ropes, which provided easy footholds but made them heavier. Mack's maestros slowly became world experts in the deadly cunning and stealth required to toss those grapplers over a given target with minimum noise and zero chance of missing. Also, every member of the platoon could scoot up those ropes and straddle the beams without missing a beat. That was the easy part.

That morning they were leaving the three-hundred-acre submarine area and going out to sea, taking off in Zodiacs from one of San Diego's vast line of thirteen warship piers and tracking a guided missile destroyer out and under the bridge and then around the North Island Navy Air Station. Many of Mack's men found this especially agreeable since throughout their working lives they had been made to run around it. Seven miles.

The destroyer, by special request, would be travelling slowly, and throughout its journey to the open sea, Mack's SEALs would be alongside in the high-powered rubber inflatables, throwing the grapplers and trying to become expert at hooking the climbing ropes onto a moving target.

Within a few days, they would head into open water, where it was rougher and much more difficult to land the grapplers over the rails of a moving ship. It was hard enough swinging out of the Zodiac against the warship's hull, just a few inches above the waterline. But it was another matter when the ship was moving.

However, if they were to become proficient at boarding a ship going 12 knots, they needed to practice every hour available to them. And there would be no variation from every page of SEAL ethos they had ever learned: *We train and train and train, until nothing can withstand our onslaught on a chosen target.*

In the four decades since the SEALs had been inaugurated, you could count on the fingers of one hand how many times this approach had failed. And Mack's boys were good. They bore no resemblance to ordinary men.

They had their setbacks, mostly due to misjudgments and overconfidence, especially when moving at high speed. Guys did fall into the ocean, a few from high up the ship's hull. But there were highly trained US Naval personnel waiting in small boats to haul them out, ensuring they never strayed or were swept into the surging wake above the ship's huge propellers.

On one occasion Mack himself dived at the grappling rope, missed, slid down, and miraculously grabbed the end of the line as he crashed right under the water with full pack and rifle. Next thing anyone saw was the sight of Mack scrambling out of the Pacific Ocean without missing a beat and hauling himself up the rope, all the way to the rails next to the destroyer's helo pad on the stern.

It was an outrageous display of strength, born of error but sustained with granite discipline and a will of steel. No one laughed, but a few shook their heads in disbelief that anyone could possibly make such a recovery. And as if to remind them of what was expected, the half-frozen Mack refused to change into dry clothes for the rest of the day.

"Battlefield conditions at all times," he said. "I don't guess the fucking pirates are going to provide us with fresh underwear if we screw it up," he told them. "We're training to kick some very serious ass. Never forget that, and behave accordingly."

Everyone in the group he called "my guys" would have walked through fire for Mack Bedford. Thereafter no one took the opportunity to change clothes after a ducking. If the boss could stand it, they all could.

When the platoon finally went into combat, they would almost certainly go in wearing their frogmen suits. But the commander preferred to train in "cammies" and boots, which made it appreciably more difficult, especially in the ocean. The objective was always the same: that training should make combat seem easier.

The only member of the group consistently in his frog gear and big flippers was Petty Officer Barney Wilkes, the world-class swimmer, who acted as permanent swim-buddy to any member of the squad who fell in, instantly going over the side to stay with the SEAL until he was pulled out by the navy staff.

Barney missed some rope time in the beginning because he was always in the ocean. Navy SEAL philosophy—no man is ever left alone—was observed even in classified training sessions. If a man went over the side or fell off the hull of a ship, he would be joined immediately by the top swimmer in the group.

Day after day they went at it, learning the techniques, hurling the grapplers, clinging, climbing, boarding. And as they trained, the clumsiness vanished and the teamwork became flawless. Mack's guys could approach, hurl, climb, and board approximately four times faster than they could on the first day. Helmsmen hardly needed to slow the boats. Those hooks were up and over in the split second that the target was close enough.

No one hesitated. They were out and climbing before the Zodiacs were in prime position. In the beginning there was a tirade of yelling, cursing, laughing, and falling, with guys swinging on the sides of ships, trying to balance. Not any more. Now the training hits were carried out immaculately, in silence, with the SEALs up and climbing aboard with lightning speed.

Any boat sentry would have to be looking straight at them to detect the SEAL invasion, and in that case the sentry would most certainly be shot with a silenced rifle, probably by the Tar Heel Barney, who was always the last man to leave the attack boat, whichever team he was in.

The rumors about Delta Platoon reverberated around the

largest navy base on the West Coast. Everyone knew they were there, everyone saw them go out and return, but no one knew quite what they were doing. Even when it rained and squalls swept down San Diego Bay, those SEALs were out there, by day and often by night, all night.

A few destroyer captains had been informed of the special training and instructed to cooperate with any request from Commander Bedford. However, even they were not briefed on the SEALs' ultimate mission. A few guessed, but no one spoke. Delta proceeded under the highest classification. It was so secretive they hardly dared speak to each other, certainly not to their families.

After the boarding phase, they would move immediately to advanced helicopter attack operations—the technique of bringing in a big double-rotored troop carrier under the cover of a gunship swooping low, with fixed machine guns blazing—a form of air-to-ship assault generally believed to be unstoppable. Especially when conducted by this crowd.

Meanwhile they kept right on hurling and climbing, scaling the hulls of the Pacific fleet, twice as fast as climbing the wall at the Coronado O-Course. And all of them were outstanding at that.

▼

SHEIKH SHARIF HAD DECIDED on a night attack on Haradheere. His battle plan was detailed. Immediately after dark, he sent his two mortar teams forward to a position 1,000 yards from the north wall of the Salat redoubt. Up front he placed two forward observation officers with cell phones, men who would call back the range once the mortar bombs, each weighing 7.5 pounds, had launched and landed, probably too far, beyond the garrison.

The remaining members of the force were fanned out in formation, flat on their stomachs, and ordered to advance with all speed on that north wall once the mortars had found their range and softened up the target, exploding in Salat's courtyard.

Working in the dark, the mortar teams had a difficult task. Their medium-range Russian weapons had a simple but sensitive mechanism consisting of a barrel that could be raised and lowered by a bracket fixed to its tripod. Thus if the first bomb sailed clean over the town, the forward observation men would call back, "Overshot three hundred yards. Raise the barrel!"

The next shot would blast higher and steeper, and the bomb would hopefully travel less far and possibly land on-target. But even with very skilled men, it might take two or three tries. Sheikh Sharif's men were not very skilled, and when they finally unleashed their opening mortar shot, they nearly blew themselves up.

The time was 8:00 p.m. Inside the redoubt, Salat's machine gunners had their Russian-made night glasses trained on the scrubland north of the wall. Mustapha and Abdul, Yemen-born members of the al-Qaeda assault force, had the mortar barrel in position aimed straight at the garrison. Too low. A lot too low.

Sheikh Sharif yelled into his cell phone, "*BEGIN THE ATTACK!*" Mustapha shoved the shell into the barrel but forgot the speed with which the device explodes the moment the shell strikes the firing pin, which is, in effect the base of the barrel.

The Russian bomb launched out of the barrel with a blast and a *whoooosh!* It shot past Mustapha's head, singeing his hair and missing his face by about two inches, and rocketed fast and low straight at the garrison wall. Abdul nearly fainted with fright, hearing Mustapha's yell of terror.

The guards saw the bomb coming as it screamed through the night, flew overhead, over the garrison, over the town, and landed in the sand dunes, close to its maximum range of almost two miles.

Down in the sand, two hundred yards north of the wall, Sharif's forward observation man shouted into his phone: "Too far, hundreds of yards too far. *RAISE THE BARREL! GET A HIGHER ELEVATION! DON'T FIRE AGAIN UNTIL YOU'VE DONE IT.*"

By now, al-Qaeda's mortar-two was ready to go, but the barrel was raised very high and when it fired, the shell blew about 1,000 feet into the air and exploded in the desert, less than one hundred yards from the observation men, who were slashed with flying sand and gravel.

Up on the wall, the pirate helmsman, Abadula Sofian, ducked when the first mortar bomb ripped through the night air but was up and looking when the second one blasted skyward. His big twenty-pound Russian PK machine gun fired at the rate of 650 rounds per minute. Box-fed, 6.72 millimeter caliber. Range: 1,500 meters.

Abadula opened fire with short bursts straight at the point he thought the second mortar was sited. The bullets ripped past the al-Qaeda bombers lying flat in the sand. Two other Salat machine gunners also opened fire, and the ground was raked with deadly 6.72-millimeter shells.

Mustapha had never been this scared. Lying next to the Russian weapon, he knew it would betray his position if he dared fire it again. Mustapha fled, running through the desert, right into the guns of his own force, who, deciding he must be a crazed tribesman, opened fire and killed him stone dead.

By now all forms of secrecy or clandestine attacks were history. The guards on the wall knew they were facing a major attack, and the Islamists in the sand knew they had been spotted. Elmi Ahmed, the ex–brigade commander in the war-torn suburbs of Mogadishu, was also on duty on the north wall but held his fire until he had a target.

Moments later he had one. Abdul adjusted the range and slammed the next bomb down the barrel, hurling himself sideways as it hit home on the base firing pin. The missile blasted out on a much lower trajectory and dropped in the street, just outside the main gates to the compound, where it detonated with tremendous force.

Abdul stayed low, and Elmi Ahmed let fly with a short volley and then two more. A bullet ricocheted off the mortar itself, but nothing hit Abdul. He answered his phone to the forward observation officer, who yelled: "GREAT SHOT! May have damaged the main gate. Raise the barrel one tick, and fire again."

Abdul, who had fought the Americans in the backstreets of Kabul, wriggled forward, made the adjustment, and shoved another bomb down the barrel. This one ripped through the night down a perfect line and landed in the courtyard of Salat's garrison.

Like most mortars, this was a high-explosive fragment round, which had greater lethality the harder the ground on which it landed. The interior of the courtyard was solid concrete, and Abdul's mortar blew out the door to the accommodation block and injured three guards, one fatally.

Elmi, up on the ramparts, was again faced with total darkness and like the experienced street fighter he was, he ceased fire and called to his colleagues to do the same. "We'll see them soon enough," he snapped. "And we may need every round we have. Don't waste anything."

By now Sheikh Sharif's second mortar team had recovered their composure and fired two more bombs in quick succession. One flew wide but another hit the compound and bounced off the office block next to Salat's home, blasting two of his windows.

Mohammed rushed out of the house, where he had been speaking on the phone to Admiral Wolde on duty on the west wall observation post. "Is everyone okay up there?" he called, and Abadula shouted back, "Okay, sir. Elmi just gave the order to take out the mortar nests at all costs."

"Good idea!" exclaimed Salat, but his voice was drowned by the sound of both heavy machine guns on the north wall opening up and once again raking the ground in the dark. Even as they did so, another bomb flew overhead and detonated in the street beyond the gates.

Sheikh Sharif gathered his troops. The forward observation

guys had informed him they had hit and damaged the garrison, but the defensive fire was intense from off the north wall. Sharif, however, understood that a ground attack was his only objective— to break into the compound, take control, and then find the pirates' cash store. A standoff out here in the desert, firing long-range, was not an option.

What Sharif did not know about siege warfare would have filled the Great Mosque of Damascus. He had no idea of the strength of his enemies; it could have been a couple of dozen men, or less. Equally it could have been two hundred trained machine gunners.

In addition he hadn't the slightest idea of their arsenal, whether they owned RPGs or even mortars of their own. Neither did he know if there were troops outside the compound who would be called into action.

"*CHARGE!*" bellowed the Sheikh. "*LET'S GO! RIGHT NOW. FORWARD, MY BRAVE BROTHERS OF ISLAM!*"

He ordered his vehicles to fall in behind and his force to divide, with thirty men charging straight forward, firing at will, carrying the light siege ladders. The rest were to make a wide swing on his left flank and come at the garrison on the eastern side. His storm troopers would open the gates once they had scaled the walls.

Sharif's forward commanders were told to make their assault fast but silent, and they ran through the sand and brush with their courage high. They uttered war whoops of encouragement and shouts of joy for the victory to come and sometimes broke brittle twigs as they pounded over the ground, all of which was sufficient to alert Elmi Ahmed that his enemy was on its way.

"Stand firm," he snapped. "Don't fire until you can see something. And then fire at will. On my command." There were now two heavy machine guns on the north wall, plus four other guards armed with the lighter, more manageable AK-47s. They had more ammunition than the Red Army and a mortar that Hamdan Ougoure was man-handling in the courtyard, loading it with an illuminating-round with its time fuse set to eject a parachute-suspended flare. Seconds passed and Ougoure rammed in the shell, which blew skyward at a steep angle, about four hundred yards out over the battleground.

There was a sharp crack from the screaming missile, and then a bright-blue, flaring light burst into the sky, lighting up the area below like Yankee Stadium. Sheikh Sharif's running troops were suddenly out in the open. For thirty-five seconds, 300,000 candela (the military's basic unit of luminous intensity) floodlit the barren plain, with the main force of Sharif's men now only three to five hundred yards out, smack in the range of defending machine guns.

Night had briefly turned to day.

Elmi Ahmed, assuming a loose command on the ramparts, ordered: "*FIRE AT WILL!*"

The two high Russian machine guns opened up a withering field of fire, the barrels swivelling to and fro, across the vanguard of the enemy attack. In the first thirty seconds they poured more than six hundred rounds into the al-Qaeda force. The four other guards, selecting their targets with care, fired nonstop, cutting down the Arabs who would steal the pirate gold.

The attackers went down two and three at a time. As they fell, the flares above them died, and only the cries of the wounded could be heard. Ahmed's gunners kept going. With their ample supplies of ammunition, they fired steadily into the dark until the veteran pirate called it off. Sheikh Sharif himself had taken four bullets full in the chest and was dead before he hit the ground.

In less than a minute, every one of the thirty al-Qaeda attackers was dead or dying, although the full horror of the carnage would not be seen until first light. By then there would be no survivors, because each of these men had, without exception, taken an average of five or six machine-gun bullets.

Meanwhile, the second wave of Sharif's assault was swarming around to the east and was regrouping five hundred yards short of the wall. Their knowledge was limited. They knew their comrades had successfully bombed the courtyard, and they had seen the giant flare in the sky. But they were too far distant and running too fast to look back. The volleys from the machine guns had confused them and they had not known who was shooting whom. They were receiving no instructions because their CO's cell phone was dead, like its owner.

Unknown to any of them, Salat had summoned Colonel Patrick Zeppi at the very outset of the one-sided battle, and with supreme organization, he and fifteen of his warriors came charging around the corner of the west wall, from which Admiral Ismael Wolde and his men were already firing at the incoming al-Qaeda second army.

Colonel Zeppi's troops, many of them veterans of other Somali wars, stood back, close to the garrison, and let fly with their Kalashnikovs, coming at the raiders from their left flank.

The instant slaughter was, if anything, worse than that which Elmi and his men had inflicted. Some of the al-Qaeda men had gone down in the opening volleys; others had turned to run back to the east toward the coast. Others had kept going straight, racing for the town, trying to find cover from the merciless barrage being aimed at them with massively superior weaponry and huge volumes of ammunition.

No one made it. Mohammed Salat had been preparing for this day for many months. Sporadic raids by al-Qaeda forces and heavy-handed demands for a share of the pirates' prize money were commonplace in the north on the shores of the Gulf of Aden. But al-Qaeda was getting desperate, and Salat's view had long been: *They might be successful somewhere else, but they'll never break down Haradheere.*

The two wounded guardsmen were removed to the well-equipped Haradheere hospital, and at first light the village elders called in their two municipal bulldozers and JCB mechanical diggers to clear away the rubble outside the gates.

The workers were also tasked with digging a mass grave in the scrubland in order to bury the dead assault troops. This was not an act of respect toward Islam; it was standard cleansing and health procedure. To prevent the dead bodies from rotting in the burning sun, they would be immediately loaded into the pits with heavy quantities of lime.

Haradheere had its own health and sanitation officer, paid for by the pirate revenue. The entire cost of rebuilding and minor repairs would be taken care of by the office of Mohammed Salat. And that evening there would be a formal dinner at the house, whose blasted windows were already being repaired.

Salat's guard commanders would be there, along with the pirate leaders who had fought on the ramparts that night. Wives would not be invited. This was a military debriefing, a time to assess future dangers, a time to strengthen and improve.

And above all, from Mohammed's point of view, it was a time to congratulate his troops. Perhaps to promote the warlord Zeppi from colonel to brigadier. Yes, he would bestow that honor. The colonel would like that. Almost as much as Salat would enjoy his continuing role as god of all he surveyed.

▼

AL-QAEDA'S WORLD HEADQUARTERS tends to shift with the winds of war. There was of course a time when it was fixed in the high Hindu Kush on the Afghanistan-Pakistan border, bin Laden country. For a while it bloomed in Iraq, and then it returned to the Afghan lowlands, and then back to its beginnings in the Swat Valley north of Peshawar.

However, the carpet bombing of Tora-Bora by the US, the crushing defeats everywhere close to Baghdad, and the suddenly aggressive stance of the Pakistani government had effectively caused al-Qaeda to move on yet again. The professionals in the CIA, FBI, NSA, and MI6 were all inclined to believe its new headquarters was on its way to Africa.

But before that could be completed, al-Qaeda's senior commanders put down roots in Yemen, the Islamic stronghold that sits in a wilderness of sand dunes at the foot of the Arabian Peninsula on the Gulf of Aden. It's hot, swept twice-yearly by powerful monsoons, and the most heavily populated of all the countries on the peninsula. It's an arms-dealing mecca in the Middle East, and Mohammed Salat is one of its principal customers.

Communications have been excellent for many years in Yemen's inland capital city, Sana, which traces its roots back almost 2,000 years to a time when the country was already over 1,000 years old. The one exception to these smooth lines of contact was satellite calls into the Somali hinterlands, where everything was slow, difficult, and inefficient. It was a place battered almost to death by war.

For al-Qaeda commanders operating in remote areas of Somalia, trying to organize their own attacks on the West, it proved nearly impossible to report, brief, and debrief the high command in Sana's Old City. It took a day and a half to report the inside story of the magnificent blast in Addis Ababa, by which time it was already on the network news of Al Jazeera television.

The shocking report of the massacre outside Haradheere stood unreleased, behind a curtain of silence, made inevitable by the absence of survivors to call in with details of the ghastly defeat. In turn, Mohammed Salat had issued orders for a complete news blackout since he had no wish to inflame al-Qaeda into yet another unprovoked attack, with new and perhaps greater numbers of troops.

Which meant no one in Yemen had the slightest idea that anything had happened in the Haradheere area. It took more than a week for anything to leak out, and that came from a Mogadishu arms dealer, Kwesi Garoweh, who had a regular weekly conference with Sheikh Sharif and was mystified when the al-Qaeda commander failed to answer either call or text.

The man knew something was wrong. He had two other

numbers to try, and there was no response from either. So he sent two of his men to the old camp, two hundred miles up the Shebele River, and, when they called in, there was nothing to report. The sheikh had vanished and taken his entire army with him. Local herders had no idea where they had gone. However the arms dealers had come this far, and they saw no point in going home to Mogadishu without finding something.

So they pressed on to the town of Beledweyne, which was big enough to have its own airstrip. And there they spent hours trying to plug into an al-Qaeda network. They were just about to give up when they met a young woman working as a waitress in a bar. She had a friend who was going out with one of Sheikh Sharif's young warriors. Four hours later, just before midnight, they were told the "army" had decamped to Haradheere and was not expected back.

Kwesi took over from there. A strict businessman with no political or religious guidelines, he traded up and down the Somali coast and had a customer in Haradheere, the pirate ship captain Hassan Abdi, master of the *Mombassa*. And the ex–Puntland fisherman was delighted to recount the crushing defeat his men had inflicted on al-Qaeda.

The precise route of the communication was not clear. But from that point, the news travelled fast. And a day later, the al-Qaeda high command in Yemen was told that one of their top Somali forces had been wiped out.

This was greeted with enormous consternation, and warning was issued to al-Qaeda cells all over the continent that the Haradheere garrison of the Somali Marines was protected by probably the most heavily armed private military force on the Horn of Africa. According to Kwesi's well-sourced report, Sheikh Sharif's men had been cut down by superb weaponry and highly skilled modern tactics.

All al-Qaeda forces in the coming months should avoid direct contact with any operations, land-based or offshore, which emanated from Haradheere. Apparently they had killed without mercy, and, when the battle was won, they just went right on killing, ignoring signals to surrender, dismissing the pleas of Sheikh Sharif who was asking for terms ten minutes after the conflict ended.

By the time the al-Qaeda officers had finished, Mohammed Salat himself had started it and had torn into the heroes from the Arabian Peninsula while they were asleep.

The commanders, aided by a mullah, swore by the prophet that Allah had vowed revenge upon them all and had personally blessed the peace-loving martyrs of the Beledweyne camp. God would give them justice. And there was no other god but Allah. And Allah was great. And he awaited his sons on the other side of the bridge, where the three trumpets had already sounded a welcome when the martyrs approached the gates of paradise.

The recounting of the Islamic massacre at the hands of godless tribesmen in Somalia ripped through the Old City of Sana, gaining authenticity as it went. From the moment it reached the ears of the al-Qaeda C-in-C, it took one day, nine hours, and twenty-seven minutes to arrive in the office of Harrison Darrow, the CIA's Yemen bureau chief.

Harrison worked from three rooms behind an ancient basket shop for a rent that might be termed exorbitant but that bought him privacy and secrecy. It also had a secret passage out through the silversmith next door.

A forty-two-year-old native of upstate New York, the CIA bureau chief had started life with a scholarship to Cornell, where he completed a master's in criminology. His first job was in the police department in Washington, DC. His promotion was rapid, and he applied only twice to Langley before the CIA accepted him, with glowing references from the police.

Harrison was an intellectual by nature, and he missed very little that was happening in Yemen. He understood consequences and ramifications, and within five minutes of receiving news of the battle in Haradheere from his contacts in the Old City, he had flashed an e-mail to Bob Birmingham in Langley, who lost no time informing Admiral Andy Carlow at SPECWARCOM.

In these circles, in these troubled days, anything that involved Somalia or its pirate gangs counted as hot news. Because this quiet two weeks was an obvious calm before the bastards hit another oceangoing tanker corporation for another multimillion-dollar ransom.

# CHAPTER 7

▼

HARRISON DARROW MOVED OUT INTO THE CITY, MAKING calls, trying to discover precisely how the Somali pirates had crushed a recognizable al-Qaeda army. He did not know precise numbers, and for a while he thought Sheikh Sharif may have suffered perhaps one hundred casualties.

It quickly became clear that there were fifty dead Islamists. And what Harrison wanted to know was the content of the pirates' arsenal. If they could mow down a trained assault force, which had been hard-schooled in the al-Qaeda camps, they were a match for anyone. And right now that appeared to be any major oceangoing merchant vessel.

"These guys must have some serious gear," muttered Harrison, as he made his way to one of the biggest arms dealers in the city, Najib Saleh, a man he had befriended assiduously since arriving in Yemen eighteen months earlier.

Saleh looked nothing like the slick, impeccably dressed prototype of an arms dealer, who typically sported a Savile Row suit and fez. He was a hefty native of Aden, he always wore Arab clothing, and no one had ever seen him work in any form whatsoever, except on his cell phone, talking to his bookmaker in London.

His office appeared to be a coffee shop in the Old City, where he held court at an outside table, sipping special ginger-spiced *qahwa* coffee and tucking into a plate of *bint as-sahn*, egg-rich sweet pastry often dipped in a mixture of clarified butter and honey.

He was said to be the richest man in the city. And he did a lot of laughing. No one would ever have guessed that Mr. Najib was a widely travelled world expert on warfare. Or that he had regularly sold fighter jets and warships to Third World countries, not to mention vast supplies of brand-new Russian missiles and ammunition to anyone who wanted to buy.

He had never signed a contract or made a deal he did not honor. His financial terms were simple: half down, the rest on delivery. If there was a problem, he would absorb the loss. No one ever defaulted, and no one ever tried to defraud him. Except for one royally stupid African minister of defense, who was later found decapitated in the jungle.

From the biggest shipment to the smallest cache, Mr. Najib always gave the matter his personal attention. Rumor had it that he had once sold a submarine to a landlocked nation in Central Africa and refunded their money when they realized they needed an ocean in which to park it. One of his many clients in the gulf bailed him out and took the underwater warship off his hands for a profit believed to be close to $10 million.

Harrison Darrow knew with absolute certainty that if anyone in the country knew who had armed Haradheere, it was Najib Saleh. To his great relief, the great man was reading the newspaper in his usual outside chair, his trusty pot of *qahwa* well within reach.

The two had become fast friends and frequently dined together, except when Darrow's wife, Veronica, visited because she regarded the corpulent Arab as possibly the sleaziest man she had ever met and, owing to his chosen profession, a menace on the face of the earth.

Harrison found him, unfailingly, a fascination. "Aha," said the beaming Najib, "and how is my American friend today? Are you here to greet me and pass the time, or are you in search of information of such quality only I can provide it?"

"The latter," said Harrison. "And if you can help, I'll buy you dinner at Taj Sheba tonight."

Najib sighed. "You Americans," he said. "You think your money will buy you anything and everything. But here in the Middle East we have higher ideals. As you must by now have realized."

Harrison sat down. Najib poured him coffee and offered him one of the sweet breads and the honey dip. Harrison grinned and accepted both. "Pure indulgence," he said. "Do we have a deal?"

"Of course," replied Najib. "We always have a deal. What's on your mind?"

"Just a little place on the coast of Somalia," said Harrison. "It's called Haradheere."

"So it is," said the arms dealer. "I heard about it too. A very nasty little battle, I believe."

"When did you hear?"

"Sometime yesterday afternoon," he replied. "The al-Qaeda guys speak of nothing else. They are very shaken."

"Guess the tribesmen kicked some very major ass," said Harrison. "I heard there were no survivors."

"I heard the same. What specifically do you want to know? I'll tell you everything, but my knowledge is incomplete. Do I still get dinner if it's not enough for you?"

"Absolutely not," said Harrison. "Can I have another one of those pastries, while you still appear useful to me?"

"One only," chuckled Najib. "That might be all I get today."

"I doubt that, old buddy. And I'll try not to ask you direct and possibly incriminating questions."

"Thoughtful. I like that."

"Okay. I don't want to know if you sold weapons to Haradheere. But tell me if you'd like and, more importantly, tell me what they have."

"As you know, my dear Harrison, that little town has all the money in the world. All stolen, all stashed away."

"So I understand. Were the al-Qaeda guys trying to steal it?"

"Of course. There were fifty tribesmen armed with Kalashnikovs and mortars. They did some damage, but the Haradheere tribesmen were very superior, well led and well equipped."

"Any idea what they were firing?"

"Of course. I have always been their main weapons dealer, although they get some ammunition from Mogadishu. Certainly I have shipped them probably fifty brand-new Russian PK machine guns, twenty pounds, heavy and very effective—650 rounds per minute."

"Jesus," said Harrison. "They planning to start a war or something?"

"Probably not," said Najib. "But they seem to know precisely how to finish one. Those PKMs have enough of a bang to double as antiaircraft weapons, you know, fix-mounted on a Stepanov tripod, night-sights, anything your little heart desires."

"You mean they can knock a goddamned aircraft out of the sky?"

"No trouble. The modernized PKM is the finest weapon around at the moment. It plainly made short work of the al-Qaeda rabble."

"What else does Haradheere have?"

"Well, I have shipped them crates of Kalashnikov's best," said Najib. "All brand new. Current models: the RPK-74s, that's a hand-held, light machine gun, seventy-five-round drum magazines, selective fire. Plus the modern AK-47. I visit the factory a couple of times a year."

"You do? Where is it?"

"City called Izhevsk, way out there in the western Urals, about 650 miles east of Moscow. Mikhail Kalashnikov still lives there."

"Does he really?"

"Sure. He's an old friend of mine. I stay with him when I go there. It's got a lot of arms history. Mikhail designed his AK-47 assault rifle right there."

"Are these modern weapons vastly superior to the old stuff?"

"In the case of the Russians, yes. They're always improving, tweaking, redesigning. There's no comparison. The stuff I ship to Haradheere is the best there is, rifles personally guaranteed by the maker. They also have the most modern mortars and the purest forms of dynamite."

"Who runs the place?"

"Even I don't know that. But money is never an issue with them. They want the best and only the best—rifles with polished wooden stocks, precision weapons. And they pay in cash. We send stuff in by helicopter. A Chinook, if necessary. Our men land it ten miles north of the town, and they pay in one-hundred-dollar bills."

"Does all this make them a particularly dangerous opponent?"

"Absolutely. I guess Sheikh Sharif found that out the hard way."

"I suppose so," replied Harrison, thoughtfully. "You'd think a hard-trained army of seasoned al-Qaeda warriors, accustomed to attacking an unsuspecting foe, would have little trouble with African tribal guards."

"You would. But I've been hearing about these Somali pirates. They're something different. And you'd need to be very careful, if you were to go after them."

"I'm beginning to realize that, Najib, a lot better than I did at the start of the day."

"Harrison, I'll tell you something. There's an ops center in Haradheere. Kind of a garrison in the center of town. I'm told it has concrete walls three-feet thick. The guards are posted on the top ramparts, in all four corners.

"If it's attacked from the town, the locals will shoot you down like a dog. If you try to approach it from the north, like al-Qaeda did the other night, they'll spot you before you get inside the half-mile mark. Even in the pitch dark, the nearest anyone got was about three hundred yards from the north wall. And they're all dead. You wanna know why?"

"I sure do."

"Because I sold them the most expensive Russian night binoculars on the market. A crate of fifty. And I arranged for special night-sights to be fitted to all their heavy machine guns and some of the light ones. Latest technology."

"That's impressive."

"I'll tell you something even more impressive. They have the brand-new Russian RPG7—a rocket propelled grenade—but it really stands for *ruchnoy*, meaning handheld, *protivo-tankovyy*, antitank, *granatomyot*, grenade launcher. It's reloadable, weighs 15.4 pounds, and fires a gunpowder-boosted missile at 377 feet per second. Leaves a light grey-blue smoke trail. You can't miss them."

"Do you have time to get out of the way?"

"You jest, Harrison. When that RPG7 rocket motor kicks in after thirty-three feet, it accelerates to 968 feet per second and sustains flight to 1,640 feet. I'm telling you, it's the last word in small-rocket technology. It's got two sets of fins that deploy in flight, big ones to maintain direction, and a smaller front set to make the damn thing rotate."

"What's its full range?"

"Well, it will travel two-thirds of a mile, but it's only lethal up to a thousand feet. It has two types of missile, one designed to blow people up, one designed to knock out battlefield tanks, that's a HEAT missile: high-explosive anti-tank. But my professional code prevents me from telling you how many the Haradheere pirates have."

"Bullshit. How many? Or no dessert tonight."

"Forty-eight."

"Christ!"

"So there you have it. You want to attack these characters, go for it. But count me out."

"I never actually counted you in, fat boy," said Harrison, laughing.

Big Najib laughed, sampling another pastry with extra honey dip. "I'm looking forward to dinner," he confirmed.

▼

HARRISON DARROW'S next e-mail report was presented to Bob Birmingham at the CIA's Langley headquarters. He read it with mounting worry—accompanied by visions of American Special Forces being put to the sword by these supersonic tribesmen with their state-of-the-art weaponry and early-warning systems.

Harrison was not a man to exaggerate, and he had unearthed a lot of information. Nonetheless Bob had never before heard of an al-Qaeda battalion being totally wiped out, even by a Western force. The list of weapons in the Haradheere arsenal was chilling, and once more the CIA chief opened up the line to Admiral Carlow.

"Look, Andy," said Bob, "it's my obvious duty to inform the brotherhood: Bradfield, Lancaster, Andre, and Ramshawe at NSA. Because everyone's especially jumpy right now about Navy SEALs getting killed. I have to tell you, if they think the odds are heavily stacked against us, they'll call off the formation of Delta Platoon today."

"Are you planning a conference?"

"It'll happen. And you have to be there, Andy. And you better bring the Delta CO with you. He may not want to charge the Russian guns because it might be like the friggin' Light Brigade at Balaclava."

▼

ADMIRAL CARLOW, in company with Commander Mack Bedford, touched down at Andrews Air Force Base twenty-four hours later after a five-hour flight from Coronado. The US Marine helicopter awaited them, and they were flown directly to the Pentagon, where they were escorted immediately to the third-floor office of Secretary of Defense Simon Andre.

General Lancaster was there talking to Admiral Mark Bradfield, and Captain Jimmy Ramshawe was staring at some high satellite shots of the area around the East African town of Haradheere, in which Salat's heavyweight garrison could only just be picked out.

"Is that the most desolate-looking place you've ever seen?" said Simon Andre.

"Hell, no," said Jimmy. "There's places in Australia that make Haradheere look like Fifth Avenue. About 3,000 miles' worth, tell you the truth."

Bob Birmingham was the last to arrive from the CIA headquarters, eight miles up the parkway. Simon Andre led everyone into his conference room.

He began the meeting briskly. "Gentlemen, he said, "I think we all know why we are here, and we have all read Bob's memorandum listing the kind of modern arsenal they have in this pirates' lair. And we now know what a crushing defeat they inflicted on a small al-Qaeda army.

"I suppose one's natural instinct might be to take the darned place off the map. But I regret to say, that's not possible. There'd be lawyers swarming all over it if we did, claiming the pirates were unarmed, innocent, never been in trouble before, and deserving of damages big enough to pay the national debt.

"Not to mention that the unspeakable European Union is on the pirates' side, yammering on about their human rights. A big bomb in the middle of the town is not an option these days. Because it might bankrupt the insurance companies—and us."

Everyone nodded in assent, with obvious reluctance

"Gentlemen," said Secretary Andre, "we made our plans quite recently. And if I might remind you, it was to wait until the pirates were on board a US ship and then send in a specialist SEAL team to recapture the vessel, knock the hell out of the pirates, and very possibly smash their stronghold in Haradheere.

"Because that course of action had the overwhelming advantage of catching them in the act, rescuing our citizens, saving lives, and making darned sure nothing else happened in the future. We all know we may have to do it again, and perhaps even again. We also know that that way we must win. Because we'll demand a US court-room, produce terrified American witnesses to speak against a crime against the United States, and the European court can shove their human rights in the place where the sun does not shine."

Having spent a cloistered, intellectual, and scholarly life, Simon Andre was about four decades late with that particular cliché, and no one laughed, which was a fair measure of the serious nature of the meeting.

The drastic leftward swing of modern justice, leading to mad-ness like letting lethal terrorists out of Guantanamo Bay, had un-nerved the US armed forces and the security organizations. At the great, polished mahogany table sat perhaps the most concerned people in America.

"Since Commander Bedford will lead our troops into action," said Andre, "perhaps he might outline for us the readiness of the SEALs to move forward and what he now feels should happen in light of this new intelligence."

Mack Bedford frowned. "I have to admit," he said, "the strength of the pirate arsenal is a shock. And while I don't intend for any of my guys to get in the way of their fire, this illustrates the standard procedure for all SEAL attacks—the element of surprise, massive intimidation, and the advantage of showing up where we have no right to be. That's what wins out in the end."

Mack paused before adding, "Gentlemen, if I've got two men standing behind a pirate leader, with both barrels aimed at the back of his skull, it doesn't much matter if he's carrying an atom bomb. There's no chance he'll have time to let the thing explode. And that applies to every other weapon.

"We're not infantry. We don't stand fast and slug it out—al-though we would if we had to. Our game is the sudden devastating arrival, specifically designed to frighten and if necessary to kill whoever doesn't immediately surrender."

"Then you would not be advising that we pull back with the formation of Delta Platoon?" asked General Lancaster. "Despite everything we now know of their considerable strength?"

"Pull back? Hell, no. We haven't even got started yet."

"How about those heavy machine guns?" asked Andre. "The ones Bob's man says can be converted to antiaircraft, or those hand-held Russian missiles that can blow straight through a battlefield tank. Are you in any way, commander, concerned by those?"

"Negative," snapped Mack. "The machine guns are big and cumbersome, slow to aim. My guys will blow the brains out of ten pirate gunners before they can find the trigger."

This brought a smile to the faces of both Admiral Bradfield and General Lancaster. "Those rockets might be a pain in the ass," said Zack. "I mean if they got one away as you made your approach. By sea, I mean."

"Sir," said Mack, "if they have a heavy guard on duty, we'll come in underwater. We are the SEALs. And I don't recall any operation I've ever been on when anyone's found us before we were good and ready to be found."

"Do I not recall a sneak missile attack on four of our tanks along the Euphrates a year ago?" asked the general. "Several of our top men were killed."

Mack's face clouded. "Sir, I was not in command at that stage of the mission," he said. "But I was there before they fired a second time. And that took them about ten minutes to get the birds away. You have my assurance these pirates will not be given that much leeway."

"Nonetheless, a captured ship becomes a fortified garrison," replied General Lancaster. "Hard to get at without loss of life, which we are all trying to avoid."

"I understand, sir," replied the SEAL commander. "And I do accept that in certain rare circumstances a ship may be too well guarded for any approach. In which case we'll come at it by air. Two helos. A big one to land the guys. A gunship to provide intense covering fire."

"What about those antiaircraft machine guns?" suggested General Lancaster.

"Sir, if we have to switch to the air, we'll come at them so fast, so hard, and so unexpected, they'll never know what hit them."

"Hmm," said the general. "And if that's successful, do you intend to switch the attack immediately to Haradheere and complete the mission with a destruction of the pirate garrison?"

"Sir, I don't just want to kick his sorry ass into the Indian Ocean. I want the heel of my boot rammed across his throat. Just so he understands who he's fucking with."

The chairman of the Joint Chiefs leaned back and smiled. Then he slowly clapped, until all of the others joined in. "I've waited a while to hear some real fighting talk on this subject," said General Lancaster. "Sounded good, commander. Sounded real good."

"Mack," said Mark Bradfield, "what do you see as the single biggest problem with operations like these?"

"Distance, sir, always distance. It seems there is a pattern emerging. Pirates are going for targets farther and farther away from shore. Three years ago, they seemed restricted, never going near a foreign ship outside national waters, maybe a dozen miles off the coast.

"And ships were deliberately staying clear of all inshore waters. At that point, there were two things that could have happened: One, the pirates said, 'We can't operate out there, it's too far, and we'll have to find a new way to make a living.' Or two, they said, 'We'll have to find a way to operate out in deep water.'

"They took the second option. Which is why the last three

significant pirate hits, the Greek tanker, the *Niagara Falls*, and the *Queen Beatrix* were all attacked 800 to 1,000 miles off the coast of Africa. And a good, long way from Diego Garcia."

"I guess they used the ransom cash to improve their boats," said Admiral Carlow. "And I do think we need to examine the possibility of leaks. Someone must be tipping them off about certain ships. Because these villains keep showing up in the middle of absolutely nowhere."

"If you have enough bread, you can buy anything," said Jimmy Ramshawe. "And these guys are banking millions of dollars at a time. Everyone pays up because it's a hundred times quicker and cheaper than fighting and arguing. And it seems to me that the most efficient pirate asset is some $75,000-a-year shipping clerk, either here or in Rotterdam or one of the other tanker ports."

"I'd have to agree," interjected Mack Bedford. "Which brings us right back to where we were yesterday, and last week, and last month. We need to strike at them, take out the ringleaders, knock down their HQ, take their cash, and humiliate them.

"But most of all, we need to frighten them, and others like them. I know there's a theory about reasoning and doing deals, but sometimes you need a big stick—that's what will scare the living daylights out of them and get them to stop what they're doing, because it's just not worth it."

"And you're confident that can be done?" asked General Lancaster.

"Certainly, sir," replied Mack. "We can do it. But as I said, our biggest problem is distance. We need to come in and attack as soon as possible. And our main SEAL bases in the area are in Bahrain and Diego Garcia. And they're 3,000 miles apart. The pirates tend to strike somewhere in the middle of that line. And whether we come in by air or by sea, the operation requires a warship. That's our problem."

General Lancaster pondered the subject and then said quietly, "Mack, have you forgotten about Djibouti?"

"No, sir. But that place is always kinda secret. In my game, classified is classified. We don't even mention where we're going to our wives. Djibouti? Well, that's kinda like Casablanca in World War II. We know it's there, and we understand that God knows what happens there. But we don't say it."

General Lancaster chuckled. "Gentlemen, it is inconceivable to me that Delta Platoon will work out of any other base. We have a major presence in Djibouti, right there where the Red Sea meets the Gulf of Aden. It's home to our Combined Joint Task Force—Horn of Africa Command."

"According to my records," said Simon Andre, punching the keys of his laptop, "there are 2,000 US troops there, and the area is under the command of the United States Navy—used to be the Middle East Command Post, Second Marine Division. Now it's the US Naval Expeditionary Base."

"That's the place," replied General Lancaster. "And, somewhat quietly for a change, we seem to have the place sorted out. It now has the only deepwater seaport in the area and an international airport. We share that with civilian airlines, and our camp's right there, close to the runways. And they're big enough to land a Boeing 747. It's a big place now, five hundred acres."

"Can you get a decent sized warship in there?" asked Captain Ramshawe.

"Hell, yes," said Mark Bradfield. "When we first took over, we ran it off *Mount Whitney*, that command ship down in Norfolk. She weighs 20,000 tons full-load, and she's more than six hundred feet long, bigger than a destroyer. We can get into Djibouti with damn near anything."

"Where did we get the place?" asked Jimmy.

"From the French and the Djibouti government," said Simon

Andre. "Right after 9/11, President Bush wanted a secret ops center in the Middle East, and he pulled off a deal with the French military to share their old Foreign Legion base, Camp Lemonier."

"Did the French own the country before?" asked Captain Ramshawe.

"Oh, sure," said Andre. "It used to be French Somaliland. Anyway, for all intents and purposes it's American now. And it's a strategic masterpiece, stands right between Eritrea to the north, Ethiopia to the west, and Somalia to the southeast. Right across the water is Yemen. And we have very good relations with the Djibouti government. Can't beat that."

"Can't beat that," agreed General Lancaster. "Mack, will that make life any easier for you?"

"Certainly. If we're trying to get out to a ship from Bahrain, well, this would knock off more than 1,000 miles from the journey, minimum. That's important time. Probably critical."

Andre stared down at his map. "Closer to 1,200, Mack."

"That's even more important," replied the SEAL commander. "The trick is to be trained and ready to go—at a minute's notice. And I'm sure we can achieve that. Just need someone to start the engines and get us moving."

"I can arrange standard procedures in the seaport," said CNO Bradfield. "We want the entire SEAL inventory ready to load and leave. Boats and equipment. Pack down and gone. Also I think we'll keep a couple of destroyers offshore. The goddamned pirates are staging major hits every month or so. We just need to regard the whole area as a war zone and act accordingly."

"How long before you can deploy?" asked Mark Bradfield.

"Three weeks," replied Mack. "I have an excellent group of guys. I'd say we deploy for Djibouti twenty-four days from right now."

"Sounds good," said the general. "I just hope they don't strike again before that."

"If they do, we'll take 'em next time," said Mack. "But we will take them. That I promise."

There was a smile on the face of General Zack Lancaster as he asked Simon Andre to adjourn the meeting for lunch.

Before he did so, Andre mentioned, "Since the Brits might help us, I asked their Ambassador, Sir Archie Compton, to join us. He'll mark our card. Better if someone else comes with us. We might even escape the universal accusation of American bullying."

General Lancaster added, "I wouldn't be too hopeful. The Brits had a shocking decline under that last left-wing government. Also they're broke. Unsurprisingly."

A tall, grey-haired, distinguished-looking man, Sir Archie greeted the Chairman, who briefly outlined the purpose of the discussion. The piracy. The necessity of swift US action before it all got out of hand.

"Archie, my old buddy," said the General, "Do you think Great Britain would join us, I mean perhaps a couple of warships, a few SAS men, perhaps a battalion of Royal Marines?"

"I wonder, gentlemen," replied the ambassador, "If you remember March 2007, when a boatload of armed Royal Marines, and Navy personnel from the guided-missile frigate *HMS Cornwall*, were captured by Iran's Revolutionary Guards and taken into captivity without firing a shot at their enemy. It was a total disgrace."

For a few moments, no one spoke. Then Sir Archie said quietly, "Do you really want *them* to assist you, against a heavily armed Somali pirates? I may as well ask you."

No one said anything.

"And how about that British couple kidnapped off their yacht by Haradheere pirates?" said Admiral Bradfield. "Right in front of a Royal Navy ship."

"Correct," said Sir Archie. "The crew on board *Wave Knight* witnessed the action, and did nothing. They stood by, only fifty feet away, while the British couple were transferred to the pirate ship.

"Gentlemen, there were twenty-five Royal Navy sailors, with access to rifles, sub-machine guns, and pistols in the *Wave Knight*. And someone ordered them not to open fire!"

"Unbelievable," said General Lancaster. "And they scarcely covered themselves in glory in Basra . . . withdrew from the battlefield, in the face of the enemy. And when we finally poured thousands of US troops into the area to reclaim it alongside the Iraqi army, the British Army was not even invited to take part. They suffered a complete humiliation."

▼

ADMIRAL CARLOW and Commander Bedford flew back to Coronado that afternoon. They travelled mostly in silence, which made it pretty quiet on the Navy P-3C jet since they were the only passengers. Each of them had a lot on his mind.

Andy Carlow understood the danger of the forthcoming mission, and he, perhaps more than everyone else who had attended the meetings at the Pentagon, was unnerved by the sheer scale of the pirates' arsenal.

He dozed fitfully, and when he jolted awake, he was always thinking the same thing: *RPG7s, armor-piercing, tank-busting, antiaircraft guns, big, new, night sights, Jesus Christ!* Unthinkable thoughts surged through his mind: *What if the guys all got killed? What if Mack died in the action? What if it was the biggest SEAL disaster since June 2005 in the Hindu Kush? There would be a media uproar, and he would undoubtedly get the blame.*

Carlow didn't give a damn about that. It was only that he would have to live with it. The admiral knew the surviving SEAL from the Hindu Kush, Marcus Luttrell, one of the all-time great SEAL warriors. Carlow knew and admired him, but there was a sadness in Marcus's eyes that did not go away.

In the front of Luttrell's book, *Lone Survivor*, he wrote: "There is no waking hour when I do not remember them all with the deepest affection and the most profound, heartbreaking sadness."

Andy understood that would be his fate as well, if anything happened to the guys. And, let's face it, under his command, they were headed into the jaws of death against a brilliantly armed enemy.

Mack, too, was alone with his thoughts. The CIA report of the strength of the pirates had interested him but not to the extent it had engaged Admiral Carlow. Mack's equations involved people because that was his world, being one of a team of people, warriors, who took on other people. Essentially they had the same or similar weapons.

It was the people, their strength, training, fitness, endurance, skill, courage, and speed that swayed the battle. An English admiral had once told him that victory usually depends on the mind of the commander. *Darned thoughtful that. Because it does. The winner is always the guy who outthinks, outfights, and will not give up. The quality of the weapons used is a factor. But not THE factor.*

If there was a principal factor, it was that of the surprise attack, the pure shock of the enemy turning around and coming face to face with a half dozen of my guys, most of them huge men with black camouflage cream on their faces, wearing their green-and-brown bandanas, the drive-on rags, and holding machine guns and shouting.

Mack had seen the toughest looking Islamic cutthroats quake with fear at the mere sight of Navy SEALs coming through their front door with the aid of a sledgehammer and large hunk of high explosive. The technique is pure intimidation plus speed.

Sitting up at 30,000 feet flying over the great state of Missouri, Mack told himself over and over: *I never saw anyone who could outgun us. The issue is whether our enemy can shoot early enough, fast enough, and straight enough. And I've yet to meet that guy. He's certainly not some fucking tribesman holding a gun that's too big for his training.*

Someone brought them coffee as they flew over the Rocky Mountains above New Mexico, and they landed at North Island Naval Base, Coronado, late in the afternoon having picked up three hours. Mack went back to the officers' quarters, ordered a couple of cheeseburgers, and wrote to Anne and Tommy, who were still in Maine and not due to arrive for another month.

The following morning he rejoined the Delta team practicing with a helicopter over San Diego Bay. This was basically a straight-down and straight-up discipline, being perfected in case the team had to be either dropped in or hauled out of the ocean. Neither option was likely, but it was possible—if, for instance, the pirates managed to blow up a ship and the SEALs had to dive over the side.

They needed to hone their techniques, and Mack had laid on an ultrapowerful SH-60 Sikorsky Sea Hawk, the twin-gunned workhorse of the US carrier battle groups, to put everyone through their paces. Including him.

The helicopter is designed for Special Forces operations and can carry an eight-man SEAL team two hundred miles into their ops area. It was kicking up an unbelievable racket, its huge rotors whirring, beating the air, while the Delta team reached up from the water, one at a time, and grabbed the rope ladder, hauling themselves up thirty feet and climbing aboard.

The insertion drill was more spectacular: The Sea Hawk came in thirty feet above the water at 30 knots, at which point the lead SEAL dropped, holding on to his mask before crashing into the Pacific bay.

They did it over and over, dropping in and climbing out. The exercise would have killed most people, and even these iron men had to take care, judging the height and speed of the aircraft, because a fifty-foot drop at 50 knots can break your back. Everyone had to take it real steady. These wild men called it "helo-casting," and they had a sneaky pride that no other branch of the US Navy could do it. No other branch of anyone's navy could do it. It's a SEAL thing.

The other major exercise that week was fast-roping—far more serious than any other insertion technique—because it was more likely to come into play during an attack on a ship held by pirates.

Every member of Delta Platoon needed to hold the picture in his mind. Because they would almost certainly arrive in the ops area in a Sikorsky CH-53D Sea Stallion, the navy's mighty assault and support helicopter, built to transport up to forty US Marines to the battlefield.

The skill required to drive these things on and off ships is awe-inspiring. Navy pilots practice for months to perfect their technique. And the toughest call of all is to land combat troops on an enemy ship. The Sea Stallion is equipped with three 12.7-millimeter machine guns with which she can open fire while the insertion is in progress.

The pilot's task requires the delicacy of a mine-clearance task force, allied to the guts of a frontline gunner, bringing the helo down, sometimes to the level of a forest of ship masts and antennae, balancing, hovering, praying, trying to stay at ninety feet above the deck while the guys go in.

The two-inch-thick rope is always brand-new, so it's still rough for the SEALs' braking system. It's hooked on to the helicopter hoist bracket, and one by one they grab the rope and dive out of the door, virtually free-falling for sixty feet before clamping a powerful grip on the rough surface of the rope, slowing down, and hopefully coming to a halt just before their boots hit the deck.

This is something no one dares to misjudge because you can kill yourself coming in from such a height. And then the danger isn't over. Right above the man who just landed is another SEAL hurtling down the rope with the same fifty-pound weight on his back. And he too is desperately trying to slow down. Each man on the insertion needs to leap clear of the rope instantly to avoid being crushed by several tons of solid SEAL coming in fast.

To watch a SEAL team undergo this training is to watch clockwork, mostly without the slightest hitch. But that's what practice does, and it proves one thing: *The definition of professionalism is the total elimination of mistakes. It has nothing to do with money.*

And the speed with which they accomplish these insertions is breathtaking, split seconds rather than minutes. By the third day of helicopter practice, the Delta Platoon commander was putting thirty men on the deck of a ship in under a minute.

Then they practiced landing on a high roof, just to concentrate on precision and heighten the danger if anyone misjudged it. Then Mack split his force and put a dozen men in a destroyer playing the role of pirates, scattered around the warship, as the US helo came in toward them.

He needed to assess the element of surprise, the degree of panic each man experienced when the big guys came swarming down the rope with another US Navy gunship spraying the area with machine gun fire, swooping in from port or starboard, covering the SEALs at all times.

The brutal toughness of the attack was outstanding, but the speed was amazing. Mack Bedford would fight with a sensational advantage, and as he always had known, it wasn't the quality of the weapons and backup that would win the day; it was the brilliance and courage of the men who carried them into battle.

It was a very tough week's work, and Mack gave his exhausted men the weekend off to recover. They'd had their first two accidents, a broken ankle on the fast-roping to the stern deck of the destroyer. And then one man had dropped out too early on the he-locasting, too high and too fast, and knocked himself cold on impact with the water. They hauled him out very swiftly, but he needed hospital treatment, and navy doctors were still assessing whether he should deploy to Djibouti with the rest of them. The SEAL with the broken ankle was out of the game for six weeks.

Admiral Carlow came out to watch the action twice that week, but his main preoccupation was with the Djibouti transfer. SEALs traditionally live separately from other troops, principally because they are under a strict code of classification. Everything they do is top secret. From the moment they arrive in Coronado, they operate under a code that forbids them from speaking to any journalist or member of the media.

If news of their arrival in North Africa ever reached Harad-heere, their mission would be shockingly compromised, and it was Andy Carlow's task to insure the platoon was quartered in a separate area from the other 2,000 US troops. Certainly well away from the French Foreign Legion's Thirteenth Half-Brigade.

When the Americans first arrived in the opening years of the new century, the place was a complete wreck. The swimming pool had been used as a garbage dump, the buildings were uninhabitable, the water supply was suspect. Sanitation hardly existed. The US forces had to live in the *Mount Whitney* command ship for more than a year. They parked it outside the harbor, which needed dredging so badly there were places where a Zodiac could run aground.

With incredible speed the US military rebuilt the place, laying down concrete walkways and building apartment blocks for their personnel. They even cleaned out and then restored the swimming pool. Special ops teams were there often but rarely one as significant as the Delta Platoon.

It took hours of organization but within ten days of deployment the arrangements had been made. And with the exception of the base commanding officer, no one even knew they were coming. They would live in a separate block and train apart from the rest. Their new HQ was exactly twenty-four miles from Somalia's northwest border but over six hundred miles, across the desert and mountains of Ethiopia, to Haradheere.

▼

MEANWHILE IN THE PIRATES' LAIR there was considerable damage. The al-Qaeda assault troops may have perished, but they'd left their mark. An enormous amount of ammunition, thousands of rounds, had been fired into the scrubland. The newly promoted brigadier Patrick Zeppi needed ammunition boxes for his men, and a cache of dynamite had been soaked through when the guards had put out a fire caused by Sheikh Sharif's opening mortar attack.

They dried out the high explosives, but the veteran Elmi Ahmed was not certain whether the TNT could be relied upon in the future. This was considered an unacceptable risk. Also there was damage to the concrete courtyard, and windows had been blown out.

The building materials were ordered and came up by truck from Mogadishu. The ammunition and dynamite could only be acquired on a fast track from one source—Najib Saleh in faraway Yemen. As always he assured them that he could deliver Russian ammunition, machine-gun belts, and magazines. The dynamite was no problem.

He'd fly it down to the coast by helicopter—usual time, usual place—but subject of course to a $25,000 surcharge for the extra work required for the fast track. Otherwise there would be a two-month lead time. Mohammed Salat understood he was being hosed down financially, but he had no other options. His garrison needed to be at 100 percent efficiency at all times. Because no one knew when the next attack would come.

Three days later, as darkness fell over the long, sandy coastline, the garrison's 4 × 4 truck growled through the streets of Haradheere and set off along an ancient cart track, north across the sand dunes. It was a dreadful road, with deep holes and ruts all the way. There were ancient tribal records in Mogadishu suggesting that Egypt's legendary Queen Hatshepsut had travelled in these parts 1,500 years before Christ, which may have been the last time they'd fixed the road.

The truck driver was accompanied by four armed guards and behind them were two more SUVs, one with six guards and the other transporting Mohammed Salat and his personal bodyguard. The back of the truck also contained a pile of firewood, logs, and three old, wooden doors blown off in the battle. There were also axes and a can of gasoline for two bonfires, the traditional pirate landing lights for Najib Saleh's incoming shipments.

The journey was only ten miles but it was slow, and it seemed like a hundred miles as they bumped and jolted their way over one of the most desolate areas in Africa. It was a few miles inland, well out of sight-range of passing ships. It was actually out of sight-range of everyone. Salat believed no one since the Egyptian queen could possibly have found reason to visit.

It took them an hour, and Salat order the two bonfires to be lit, thirty yards apart. His guards sprinkled the firewood with gasoline and tossed a burning torch onto each pile. Five minutes later, with the flames shooting skyward, they smashed the three doors in half and added them to the blaze. At which point there was nothing to do except wait.

Najib's deliveries were always on time. This was something of a miracle since his cargo travelled over a difficult route with constant refuelling. He owned an old Russian Kamov-Helix assault helicopter, which flew at around 150 knots. And into this unusual freighter he loaded his cargoes of arms from his heavily guarded warehouse on the edge of the Yemen desert.

The helo still carried the single red star of the Soviet Navy on its tail and had proved reliable on a hundred different journeys. For this trip south from Yemen, the pilot flew across the Gulf of Aden and landed to refuel in the Somali coastal airport of Dabar.

The next leg of the trip was the least popular among Najib's

pilots because it took them due south from Dabar, across the frontier of the Federal Democratic Republic of Ethiopia, with its somewhat belligerent air force and its fifty fighter jets. They were fairly
relaxed about a Russian Navy helicopter heading south toward Somalia, 24,000 feet above their land. But when roused to action, they
would not be above shooting it down.

Najib's Kamov clattered its way very fast and very high before
coming in to land at the Ethiopian desert airport of Welwel, at
which point the danger passed. Because the one commodity the
locals really liked was money, and Hajib's corporate gold American
Express card, paying for hundreds of gallons of jet fuel, was very
attractive.

It was another two hundred miles from Welwel down to Galcao,
and from there a straight 160-mile run to the drop-off point, still
with sufficient gas to make it back to Galcao. Altogether it was a
long haul, around 1,000 miles from Yemen, and, with the four refuelling stops, took the biggest part of twelve hours.

The Yemeni pilot spotted the twin bonfires blazing in the dunes
with a half hour to spare on his ETA. It was a clear night and the
Kamov dropped swiftly to 1,000 feet for a low-level approach,
slowed, and put down on the soft sand.

He waited a minute and then cut the engine. This was the best
part of the trip because Salat's guards took over the unloading of
the ammunition and cases of TNT. Also they always brought out
warm roast goat made into sandwiches with Somali flatbread and
hot sauce. There was also a case of chilled fruit juices, bags of
cashew nuts, and hot coffee.

While the transfers were being made, the pilot and his two guards
sat and chatted with the men from Haradheere, who regaled them
with breathless tales of how they had wiped out al-Qaeda's army. The
military efficiency, the courage, the ruthlessness. This was the stuff
of tribal folklore.

When the boxes had all been counted, Salat handed to the

Yemeni crew a bag in which there was exactly $300,000 in cash, the agreed-upon price for the five hundred ammunition belts, the dynamite, the costs of transportation, and the surcharge.

The pirate warriors stood back in the sand dunes and waved as the Russian aircraft lifted off, swivelled to the north, before tilting forward and clattering away, rising higher with every beat of the rotors. Salat's convoy turned back toward the worst road in East Africa and braced themselves for the bumpy ride home, where they would refortify their tough, uncompromising little garrison.

It was almost 10:00 p.m. when they drove into town, where there was an atmosphere of high excitement. A message had come through informing the pirate commander that a very large Japanese factory ship was steaming slowly west of the Maldives, having almost filled its lockers with a gigantic catch of bluefin tuna, squid, shark, and sardines.

The information indicated that the Japanese were headed for a final trawl six hundred miles off the Somali coast, where fish had made a huge comeback since the polluted waters had cleared. This was the second or third time the Somalis had been told there was a fishing bonanza in their own ocean.

Japanese visits were extremely rare, but when they did show up anywhere south of the Gulf of Aden, they were the Somalis' favorite victims. Because the men from Kyushu and Yokohama worked for companies that only wanted the near-priceless catch, and if they had to, would pay any ransom to get these fishing leviathans freed up and sent home.

Fish commands enormous prices in Japanese restaurants and the profits are very high. The advent of a Japanese factory ship heading toward the Somali coast spelled big dollars to the pirates. And that night there was more activity on the dark Haradheere beach than in the Norfolk navy yards.

They had not yet worked out which pirate crew was going. The

*Mombassa* was ready and fuelled up, but another crew had a newer, faster boat and were requesting exclusivity. This was not a cutthroat business. Everyone shared in everything, and there were already shares available for purchase in the late-night stock exchange.

If the second crew won Mohammed Salat's approval, they could take on the job. He held counsel on the beach half an hour after returning from the ammunition drop. And he decided that for the moment Admiral Wolde and his men had done enough. He awarded each of them fifty shares in the forthcoming tuna expedition at the opening price of $5.00. It was entirely likely that the Japanese fishing corporation would pay up to $500,000 to reclaim its ship and its catch, and the stock exchange was issuing only 20,000 shares. These could easily go up to $20 and everyone would be happy. The fishing boat did not represent the massive fortunes that could be made from tankers and major international freighters, but they were solid little earners, and the men from Haradheere were extremely adroit at capturing busy working boats from the Land of the Rising Sun.

The phone number of the corporation and its president's private line were contained in the message from the biggest fish wholesaler in the Far East—a greedy Japanese buyer who had the ear of the chief of their international trading division.

He had long ago guessed the reason for his monthly check for $5,000 from Mohammed Salat-San. How he used the information was not his business. All he had ever done was to reveal the position, course, and speed of the biggest commercial fishing vessels in Japan.

Meanwhile, the new pirate team had its boat in the water, a fast, fifty-five-foot-long, former Yemeni customs boat they had stolen from outside the harbor in Mogadishu. From whom, they did not know or care. It had been riding at anchor and been empty of both people and fuel, probably the property of drug smugglers, and definitely stolen.

The pirates had seized it and towed it back to Haradheere. Now it was resting on its portside while local mechanics worked on its engine, fitting it with a new propeller, and bringing a tanker onto the hardtop at the top of the beach to refuel it. The name on the side was written in Arabic, and someone said it meant "Ocean Dart."

Salat's guards arrived with a dozen new Kalashnikovs, which they distributed among the new men. They also brought grappling hooks from the garrison quartermaster and a brand new radar system that needed to be fitted. By all accounts the fishing boat was riding low on her lines, now less than six hundred miles from the shores of Somalia.

Since the Japanese would never dream of taking part in a gun battle, they represented an extremely soft target. Certainly there were many other pirate crews who would have liked to join in the attack.

But no one else knew where the floating tuna factory was. Mohammed Salat's raiders had the operation to themselves in the open, desolate waters of the Indian Ocean.

# CHAPTER 8

▼

PETER KILIMO HAD BASICALLY LOST HIS NERVE. WELL, almost. In a sense, he may have only mislaid it. But for the moment, on the twentieth floor of the Olympic Tower above Fifth Avenue, he was closer to becoming a quivering wreck than an international master spy.

Peter had been visited by two CIA agents, men who had flown in from their headquarters in Langley, Virginia. They had been in contact with Constantine Livanos in Monte Carlo, and when they arrived they were taken into the offices of the president of Athena Shipping, Peter's boss.

Their question was simple: "How many people in this organization have access to the private numbers of Mr. Livanos in Monaco, London, and Athens?" Short answer: not many because that information was on a need-to-know basis.

The president himself had the numbers. So did his senior vice president in New York, who was often at the helm of the corporation when the president was travelling. The vice president in charge of finance also had the numbers because he often spoke to Mr. Livanos personally about the transfer of money.

The only other person in the organization who had the numbers was Peter Kilimo because the operations chief was the corporate troubleshooter, the one man who could be awakened at all hours of the day and night to deal with a crisis.

It went with the territory. Well-paid executives in his position the world over occasionally had to shoulder immense responsibility.

Peter's last line of defense if a ship was sinking or in the face of some other catastrophe was to phone Mr. Livanos. But that was only in the absence of his two immediate superiors. Thus far he had not once needed to call Monte Carlo.

He kept the European numbers on his cell, on his desktop, and in his personal contacts book, which he kept in his briefcase. The CIA men were perfectly pleasant and sat in his office sipping coffee. But they did wish to see the numbers on the computer, and the phone, and in the book.

They then asked him who had access—wife, girlfriend, children, secretary? Anyone who could, by fair means or foul, end up with the private phone number of Constantine Livanos.

Peter could not help them. He did not think his secretary could access the computer file that housed the numbers. He always kept his cell in his pocket. She did not have a key to his locked briefcase. And then they stepped up the heat.

"Who else can get into this computer? Fellow workers in ops? Someone in this office must be able to get into it, right? What would happen if you dropped dead or got hit by a truck? The whole place wouldn't grind to a halt, would it? Who else, Mr. Kilimo?

They wanted to know about his wife. "Can she access the phone numbers on your cell? Does she ever look into or share your contacts book? We noticed there were personal numbers in there— surely friends of both you and your wife? Mrs. Kilimo must have had access, yes?"

Peter had started the meeting feeling safe and confident. Twenty minutes later he felt under siege. Did they suspect him? Did these two hard-eyed government agents believe that he had a connection to the pirates in Somalia?

He tried to control himself. The agents told him they would be looking into everyone's phone records—everyone, that is, with Livanos's numbers. He did not mind that, since all of his contacts with Mohammed Salat were conducted by e-mail and even that was one-way. The Somali pirate leader never responded.

And here was Peter Kilimo's masterstroke. Everything he sent to Haradheere was done on a laptop computer he had purchased especially for these weekly messages. He never brought it to his office, keeping it instead in the trunk of his car, under the floor on top of the spare tire. The only e-mails sent from that machine were to Haradheere.

Peter's blood ran cold when he thought that these two investigators might go to his home to talk to his wife and somehow discover the hidden laptop. He must have had a sixth sense that this day would come, because he never even had an e-mail account of his own.

For his communiqué to Mohammed Salat, Peter always drove to the nearby suburb of New Rochelle, parked the car in the main street, and sent his message on any Internet hookup he could locate. The men from the CIA might find the computer, but they'd never find the evidence of communications. And they'd have to hurry. Tonight he would destroy that laptop with an axe and drop the pieces in the Hudson River.

Eventually they left. But Peter knew they were unconvinced of his innocence. He'd heard them talking to the president and he'd heard his boss say, "Peter? Never. He's been here for more than thirty years. He's probably the most reliable man in the entire place."

Peter understood such a response could only have been elicited by someone who had made an accusatory remark against him. Jesus! What if someone found out about the secret bank account? And then traced the $20,000 payments to their source?

He needed to get out and clean house. Give up the money and forget all about Somalia and everyone in it. Tonight he would begin doing precisely that.

Somewhat forlornly, he looked down at his desk where there were downloaded schedules—sailing dates and times for several ships. And one of them he'd intended to relay to Mohammed Salat. She was an 80,000-ton deadweight LNG vessel named *Global Mustang*, and she was currently moored at the gigantic Ras Laffan Industrial City on the north coast of the Qatar Peninsula in the Persian Gulf.

Ras Laffan is the largest liquid natural gas operation on earth, sprawling over forty square miles, fifty miles north of Dohar. The heavily dredged, deepwater port loading facility covers a total area of more than three square miles. Ras Laffan moves 40 million metric tons of liquefied gas every year.

And what a sight the *Mustang* made. She was nine hundred feet long and drew thirty feet below the waterline. Along her deck were four enormous golden domes, independent spherical holding tanks, 130 feet in diameter. They carried 140,000 cubic meters of liquefied gas. Half of each dome was visible above the deck, and the other half was concealed below in the hull. She looked like a floating commercial for the University of Notre Dame. Her 23,000 horsepower turbines drove her through the water at 20 knots, much faster than any VLCC.

The giant holding tanks carried gas that was frozen to $-160°C$, the temperature at which the gas changes to liquid, and requires .06 of its original volume. The *Mustang* was owned by a Houston corporation, Texas Global Ships, whose president was Robert J. Heseltine III.

In partnership with three US banks, Heseltine owned seven other oil industry vessels, but this was his only LNG carrier. He operated from an office on the thirty-second floor of his Travis Street headquarters. His international agents, who were responsible for keeping those ruinously expensive energy giants filled with oil and gas at all times, was Athena Shipping of New York in conjunction with their friends at Inchcape Shipping of Tokyo.

The *Global Mustang* was scheduled to leave Ras Laffan in four hours bound for Japan. Her client was the largest corporation in that country, Tokyo Electric Power, and she would dock at its LNG port of Futtsu, forty miles down the bay from the great city itself.

All the Japanese corporations that imported liquefied gas were fantastically reliable. They paid on time, and they could not take delivery fast enough since almost every household in the country cooks on propane. Japan guzzles up 43 percent of the world's LNG trading volume. And use of propane is on the increase, owing to the closing of several nuclear plants. Nine of the world's twelve LNG exporters sell to Japan.

The *Global Mustang* had actually been built by the Japanese, Mitsubishi Heavy Industry in Nagasaki, and she headed back to the imperial empire twice a month—back and forth from Qatar to Tokyo Bay. She'd never even been to Houston. Bob Heseltine had never even seen her. The crew was changed and airlifted both in and out at various points along the route.

A spike in world natural gas prices to $20 for twenty-eight cubic meters made *Mustang*'s cargo worth a fortune—she carried 140,000 cubic meters of liquid gas, which flashes off into a gaseous product six hundred times over. The math was dazzling, and Peter was not absolutely certain of the accurate format for assessing the value of the cargo to Tokyo Electric.

But he knew that Mohammed Salat would kill for information about her route. He could always gauge the pirate chief's demeanor by the speed at which his payment arrived in Westchester County.

But now it was plainly over. The CIA was all over it, and the only thing that mattered was to get rid of that laptop and forget all about his Somali connection. He was gratified the president of Athena did not even bother to mention the visit of the agents, so unlikely did he consider the possibility they were harboring some kind of spy.

Peter left early that afternoon and walked to Grand Central Station for his daily homeward journey, fifteen miles to Bronxville on the Harlem line. He lived close to the station and walked home, knowing his wife would be out for the next couple of hours.

He walked into the garage, checked the trunk for the laptop, and placed it on the passenger seat. He knew he should smash it and then dump the remnants in the river. But he also knew a few sentences on that keyboard were worth $20,000 minimum. He might even ask for $30,000 for a vessel that was carrying cargo worth an astronomical sum. Then he could dump it.

Peter drove the familiar route to New Rochelle, parked in his usual spot, and searched for an Internet connection. He found it quickly and sent an e-mail to Mohammed Salat:

> LNG carrier *Global Mustang* clears Ras Laffan Qatar 0300 (local) today, Wednesday, bound for Tokyo. She carries four domed holding tanks, gold in color, and full of liquefied gas. She will make 20 knots down the Persian Gulf and is expected to enter the Arabian Sea Thursday 0900. She turns south off Muscat and runs 1500 miles. She makes her turn east Sunday at 1200 hours, 2.05N 60.00E—approx 700 miles off Somali coast.
>
> Her master is Captain Jack Pitman. Her cargo priceless: delivery to Tokyo Electric. *Global Mustang* sails under an American flag.

Peter concluded his note with the name and cell phone number of the president of Tokyo Electric, the home number in Houston of Bob Heseltine, and that of Constantine Livanos in Monte Carlo. Customer, owner, and agent, the men who made the biggest decisions.

His action, he knew, was the function of boundless greed. Every instinct he had told him this was a very bad idea. But $20,000 was too tempting, and if he heard the *Global Mustang* had been hijacked, he would ask for another $10,000 or $20,000 as a bonus.

Mr. Salat, he knew, was not a man to shirk a generous payment to reward a major informer.

He arrived home to find the house still empty and he took an axe to the laptop, obliterated it, and then, wearing gardening gloves, put the pieces back in the computer carrying case. Then he went out again and dropped the pieces into a succession of trash cans throughout the outskirts of town. He estimated it would take about twelve men four hundred years to find all the pieces if they started right now. Even then the tiny shards would mean nothing. The Haradheere link was down.

▼

APPROXIMATELY ONE HOUR BEFORE the *Global Mustang* pulled out of Ras Laffan, steaming into the Arabian night, the *Ocean Dart* was manhandled out through the gentle surf of the dark but calm Indian Ocean. The beach was crowded with those who had helped her on her way, heaving on the ropes behind the horsepower of four SUVs and the clatter of the winch.

The Japanese factory ship they were speeding out to intercept was a minute objective compared with the LNG carrier, and navigation for the new pirate team was much simpler. The Indian Ocean was deep and deserted. The route of the *Mustang* carried her huge cargo past Qatar's north gas field, the biggest on earth.

She would steam three hundred miles to the rugged point of the Musandam Peninsula, which juts into the Strait of Hormuz. And all along there is a jungle of oil and gas fields, pipelines, warnings, sandbanks, shoals, and restricted areas. Also the *Mustang* needed to run north for thirty miles and east for three hundred.

That route would take her ever closer to the glowering coastline of Iran with its hostile navy, which exercised endlessly on the edge of these vital free-trading waters. The master of the *Mustang* would stay well south of the Iranian big guns.

Her journey from Ras Laffan started on a latitude of 25.90N and she would sail around the Musandam headland on 26.20N before coming 90 degrees right, southeast down the Gulf of Oman, and into the open ocean.

In general terms, the *Ocean Dart* tuna boat had little in common with the gargantuan gas vessel. But the citizens of Haradheere would, in time, hope fervently that fate would, in a sense, hurl the two ships together. And that the big bucks represented by the respective cargoes would somehow end up in their stock exchange, bringing joy, happiness, and prosperity to the community.

Meanwhile Mohammed Salat's chief of staff had downloaded the communiqué from Peter Kilimo. It was getting light and he knew the chairman was asleep, so he left it on the desk in the private office.

It was thus almost ten o'clock in the morning before Mr. Salat read it. And when he did, he felt the victorious surge of a conqueror. The mighty cargo must certainly be worth the thick end of $10 million.

Life had rarely, if ever, looked better. He picked up the telephone and called Ismael Wolde, who was sitting across the street under a banana tree, sipping fruit juice and cleaning his AK-47, the way modern-day pirates do.

Five minutes later he was in the garrison office sitting next to Mohammed Salat, reading the unsigned message from New York and pulling up Internet pictures of the world's biggest LNG tankers, including the *Global Mustang*.

When the four-domed giant popped out of the ether, Ismael whistled through his teeth as he scanned the picture for the best place to board the vessel. Again, he suggested it must be the stern, but it would not be easy, and he considered it too dangerous to persuade the captain to slow down with an RPG7.

"Mr. Salat!" he said. "If we accidentally put one of those Russian rocket grenades through one of those domes, she'd go up like an atom bomb. Wouldn't be no survivors inside a five-mile radius. Sir, I'll do what's possible, but I don't want to get fried by no Arab gas bomb."

"No, I don't want that to happen. And I think we agree we cannot attack this giant from the water. Our only chance is to take her by stealth. We need to board her in complete secrecy. And then plant four bombs at the base of each one of those holding tanks. We then capture the crew and tell them what we've done, mined their ship from the inside."

"Okay, and what's our threat?"

"Ten million dollars, cash, delivered on deck; otherwise we'll blow the *Global Mustang* to high heaven."

"And where will we be at the time of this disaster?"

"In the *Mombassa*, five miles off."

"And the crew of the tanker?"

"We'll have to escort them off. There'll be about thirty of them in two lifeboats. We don't leave until the deadline is approaching. Then we all leave and wait for the drop."

"And how do we get the cash?"

"We keep the crew at gunpoint. Then we have four of our guys go in, collect the cash, and disarm the bombs. At that point the crew can go back and continue their journey."

Wolde should have been smiling. But instead he was frowning, still staring at the close-up shots of the LNG tanker. "The issue is," he said, "can we get on board? Because this ship, according to these photographs, rides higher in the water than a regular crude-oil tanker."

"She does in these pictures, which were taken as she left Tokyo Bay. We should assume she was empty. Loaded, she's got to be a lot lower, carrying thousands of tons of liquid."

"I think so," said Admiral Wolde. "The good news is that rail that seems to run right around the deck. If the grapplers go high enough, they'll grip anywhere."

"The rail's lowest at the stern," said Salat. "Drops down at least twelve feet to a kind of transom—that undercover area, like a quarterdeck, under the helicopter landing area."

"How high do you think that is, under a full load?"

"I'd say about thirty to thirty-five feet. No more.

"Then we can get the hooks on. Because we don't need accuracy. Just height. To get 'em up and over that rail."

"Are you concerned about her speed?"

"Sure I am. A ship that size moving through the water at 20 knots is a very difficult target. But I doubt there'll be guards. And we got good drivers; they'll put us right on the hull moving at zero relative speed. We'll use knotted ropes and then rope ladders. And it's a night attack. But if the water's rough, we cannot do it."

"I accept that," said Salat. "And I also accept that we cannot open fire on this ship. Because if we hit and punctured one of those tanks, she would blow up."

"Sir, I've never heard of anyone trying to capture an LNG vessel—I suppose for those very reasons. She's too dangerous to hit, and too big and too fast to board, except for very skilled men. Like ours."

Mohammed Salat was pulling up information on the Internet, and he said suddenly, "You know something, Ismael? These things have sailed 100 million miles around the world without a shipboard death or a major accident of any kind. Says it right here."

"We'll be the first, ha?" laughed Admiral Wolde. "We make naval history. Remember us in many books. Maybe get Somali Marines on television worldwide. Frighten our enemies!"

"I'm not sure about any of that," said Salat, thoughtfully. "It's much better if we stay very private."

"If we hit the *Global Mustang*, we will be very public," replied Ismael. "And very rich I think."

"That's the part I like most," said the chairman.

▼

WITH EIGHTEEN DAYS LEFT from deployment, Commander Bedford gathered his platoon to prepare them for the critical part of the forthcoming missions: the SEALs' arrival at the mission headquarters, which would be some kind of a warship, out in the Indian Ocean.

"However we decide to attack these maniacs," he said, "we're almost certainly going to start off on a destroyer or even a carrier. Every scenario involves launching from one of our own ships.

"If the pirates are in command, we have to come in by air or by sea, maybe in helicopters, probably in little boats. But whatever it is, we kick off from a navy vessel.

"The most likely event is a signal to our Djibouti base instructing us to head out to an area where a US merchant ship has been captured. They'll need to fly us to the warship immediately, possibly in a helicopter, but more likely in a fast, fixed-wing aircraft.

"As you all know, our Djibouti posting cuts hundreds of miles off our journey. But speed is everything. And to get on the goddamned ship we'll probably have to drop in by parachute."

"Is that into the water, sir?"

"You got it, kid. And because we'll have a lot of equipment with us, probably a HAHO jump—high altitude, high opening. That way we got a good chance of staying together in the stack. Low man, that'll be me, guides us in with the compass. Warship personnel will be in the Zodiacs waiting to hook us out as we drop in."

"We going out around 10,000 feet, sir?"

"Well, that might have been the case. But the new information we have about the pirate weapons suggests they have heavier guns than we first thought. All Russian and capable of antiaircraft action, so we'll probably fly in at 25,000 feet, and that's where we'll jump."

"Any chance of an aircraft carrier, sir?"

"If there's one anywhere near the pirates, we'll use it, maybe even fly directly in and launch from her flight deck. But we can't count on that. Because in the Indian Ocean we have many more destroyers and that'll be our way in."

Mack Bedford told them to have lunch and then report back for the ride out to the North Island Naval Air Base, where they would begin practice for the parachute jumps. "Matter of fact, guys, we'll be there probably 'til midnight," he said. "The mission will definitely involve a night jump, so we might as well start off the way we're gonna finish. The whole course will be in our frog-suits."

"How long are we out there, sir? A week?"

"Minimum. Most of you have not jumped much since Fort Benning, where we all trained second week. Everyone's a trained parachutist, but you need to get used to this stuff. Diving out of an aircraft at that height needs to be like second nature to us. Straight out, straight down, and straight into the ocean. No sweat. But we gotta be experts. That's the way to stay alive."

"I'm in favor of that," someone shouted.

"Have a good lunch," snapped Mack. "Right here 1430 hours."

When they returned, everything was ready, including the Lockheed C-130 Hercules, engines running moments from takeoff, pilots and navigator already in place. The SEALs disembarked their three trucks at the end of the runway and filed into the aircraft led by Lieutenant Josh Malone and his swim buddy Brad Charlton.

Each man would make his first ocean jump under full pack and rifle, but they wore special SEAL hooded frog-suits with flippers clipped on to their thighs. Mack Bedford was last man in, and the moment he was seated, the doors were closed and the aircraft rumbled forward, down the west-running runway, and climbed into the blue skies above Southern California.

At the Fort Benning Jump School in Georgia, they had concentrated on technique and familiarizing themselves with standard procedures. This new course of intensive training was geared strictly for the Pacific Ocean and the SEAL techniques of landing in the water.

The aircraft headed out over the vast military cemetery on the Point Loma peninsula, gaining altitude as it cleared the headland

and roared out over the Pacific. Up ahead the pilot could see the US warship making a racetrack pattern in the water, tracked by four Zodiac inflatables, which he could just make out against the deep-blue of the afternoon water.

The SEALs began to file up toward the exit, gripping the static line as the dispatcher opened the aircraft door on the port side. Everyone felt the aircraft throttle back, and the dispatcher called out: "*Approaching the drop zone. Action stations!*"

Assembled in the area right in front of the opening, the SEAL team could no longer hear themselves think in the rush of the wind through the door. The aircraft was still making 150 knots, and once more Delta Platoon checked their static lines.

"*Stand in the door, number one!*"

The dispatcher was yelling at the top of his lungs to make himself heard. And Commander Mack Bedford stepped into the doorway watching for the light to glow above his head, the signal that the mission was a go.

"*RED ON!*"

Mack knew they were over the drop zone and he braced himself, sensing the guys moving forward behind him.

"*GREEN ON! GO! GO! GO!*"

The dispatcher slapped him on the shoulder, and Mack Bedford plunged out of the aircraft. He swept clear in the slipstream, and then dropped fast, sideways. He clamped his knees together, and he could feel the sensation of rolling backward. And he found himself staring up, watching for the canopy to billow out.

Somewhere above him was Barney Wilkes, followed by Cody Sharp and then Shane Cannel. But he couldn't see them, and his parachute suddenly billowed, which prevented him seeing anything.

By this time, all fifteen chutes in the opening stack were blooming white against the azure, cloudless sky. And the ocean from 1,000 feet looked markedly less like a soft, blue carpet. Mack could see the white caps rolling on the surface, meaning there was a good bit of wind.

At 150 feet he could see the four inflatables circling right below him, and he could see the little boats rolling around as they waited for their airborne cargo to land. He pulled the harness forward under his backside, banged the release button on his chest, and freed the straps to fall away beneath his feet. Mack was just hanging there now, gripping the lift-webs above his head, the water rushing up to meet him.

He was hurtling toward the ocean, and he thrust his legs downward until he was standing upright. Ten feet above the surface, he let go and crashed straight into the Pacific, submerging at least ten feet. He kicked hard and the flippers drove him to the surface, no longer encumbered by the parachute.

He glanced up just in time to see Barney and Shane plummet into the water, not fifteen yards away, but before he could get his bearings, he felt two pairs of hands grabbing him and hauling him up over the gunwales into the rigid-deck inflatable. He noticed Barney was breathing normally but Shane was coughing and spluttering all over the place.

"Guess you better get right back up there and do it again," said Mack. "I don't want a lot of this spitting and farting when I'm about to blow the brains out of the Somali pirates. Christ, man, get a grip, will you?"

In fact Mack was laughing. But Shane was embarrassed. They had all been shown how to clamp up and hold their breath just before they hit the water. And Shane could hardly blame the temperature of the ocean for having opened his mouth on impact, because the frog-suit protected all of them from the remotest sensation of cold, except on the hands and face. He'd just screwed up, that was all. And far from feeling admonished by his CO, he wanted to get back up there and do it right.

"Just imagine what it would be like if we all did that after a ducking. There'd be chaos," said Mack. "We gotta conquer it, get the breathing right. Don't worry, kid, we're all going to do it again. Just as soon as the first stack gets aboard. There's a helo on the ship to fly us back to North Island. The Hercules will be down before we get there."

Trained to have the strength and reactions of mountain lions, as fit as Olympic athletes, Delta Platoon entered the final days of their program. They'd mastered the techniques of boarding a moving ship, and they'd hauled in and out of navy helicopters until they knew more about them than the pilots. And they could hurl a grappling hook over a moonbeam and heave it tight.

Every attack strategy in the vast playbook of the US Navy SEALs was like the Twenty-third Psalm to them. They knew the stuff backward and forward. In a matter of days they would leave for the Horn of Africa, taking off in deadly secret at 0100 hours from the North Island base.

The only technique left to polish was the ocean drop. And they would dive out of the Hercules sixteen more times each before Commander Bedford was perfectly satisfied that he could send two stacks of SEALs directly into the Indian Ocean from 25,000 feet with a minimum of fuss and zero possibility of a screwup.

Under his command, the SEALs could mount a death-defying, world-changing assault on the pirates.

In the favorite words of these princes among elite combat troops: *God bless America, and God help the enemy.*

▼

BACK IN HARADHEERE, a signal was in from the new pirates confirming that they were in possession of the Japanese factory ship *Ocean Dart*. The crew had surrendered, offering no resistance to the Somali attack.

But Mohammed Salat had decided not to trust them with the critical information they needed to contact the president of the

Kyushu Ocean Fishing Corporation, and now the latest assault group commander wanted further instructions.

Salat ordered them to stand by and keep the crew at gunpoint while he telephoned Mr. Nobataka Orita at his home in Kagoshima at the southernmost tip of the Japanese islands. It was 4:00 p.m. in Somalia and 10:00 p.m. in Japan, but Mohammed had Orita's cell phone number.

This was the third time Mohammed Salat had used the number, and it would be the third time he had asked the south island fishing boss for a huge sum of money. The previous two were for $250,000, which had been paid immediately. This time Salat decided that a pay raise was in order, and he asked for $500,000 or else he would order his men to scuttle the ship and send the cargo and the crew to the bottom of the Indian Ocean.

Orita was furious. This African tribesman was holding his corporation for ransom once a month. If he paid this time it would mean he had given away one million dollars to the international gangster.

He longed to tell Salat to get lost, to go and do his worst. But that huge catch, deep-freeze refrigerated, was ready for market as soon as it landed in Japan. And it was worth $10 million. Wearily he asked the pirate king how he wanted the money and was told to make a beach drop on the ocean sands of Somalia.

Orita was becoming good at this. He had all of his African accounts at the Dashen Bank in downtown Addis Ababa, right down the street from De Gaulle Square. The Dashen president understood the Somali pirate menace and did all he could to facilitate the payment of ransoms.

For customers like Nobataka Orita, he even arranged transport, lending the corporate jet to fly over the beach and drop the money on to the sand. He charged fees for this service but nothing exorbitant, which was probably why his bank was one of the most successful in Africa.

Salat handed over the GPS numbers to Orita and told him he had twenty-four hours or else. His men would be on the beach starting from 7:30 the following evening, and he had a two-and-a-half-hour window to make the drop. The customary two bonfires would be lit to guide the aircraft in.

Orita silently offered a polite bow, the traditional domo, in this case a double domo, of particular thanks and respect. The news was bad, but it could have been a lot worse. This son of a palsied dragon could have asked for $2 million.

Like many a big businessman with work in the Indian Ocean, Orita was very thankful for getting off so lightly, and the double domo for Salat was the least he could offer. For a handful of lotus blossoms he'd have thrown him a triple, right there in the empty room. But he decided that would have been overkill.

Salat terminated the call. And while Orita opened up the line to his Ethiopian banker, the pirate king called in Ismael Wolde to strategize the hit on the LNG tanker. Before them they had a large map of the Indian Ocean, and Ismael carefully marked with a cross the convergence of the 2.05N line of latitude with the sixty degree line of longitude, the spot where the *Global Mustang* would make her easterly turn at noon on Sunday.

"I suppose we must allow for the possibility that the tanker's master might cut the corner," said Wolde. "So it would probably be better if we waited for her somewhere south along her easterly course."

"Right," replied Salat. "When you have a big modern ship moving easily at 20 knots through the water, you don't want the *Mombassa* trying to play catch-up. Hassan says she really shakes and shudders at that speed."

"That's true," said Wolde. "She's an old boat, even with her new engine. Our policy has to be like always, sir. Let's get out in front of this target and then close in on her port quarter."

"Okay. When do you want to leave?"

"We got seven hundred miles to cover. And we don't want to run her at more than 15 knots. Hit the calculator, sir. How many hours?"

"Forty-six."

"So we need to leave at noon on Friday. She's fuelled but we need to start loading her. We'll have a full crew, twelve, plus Captain Hassan. So we'd better take a lot of sandwiches, bottled water, and fruit juice. There's no stove, but we might get lucky if we take the tanker."

"*When* you take the tanker."

"That's what I said," grinned Admiral Wolde.

"You'll be gone for a week," said Salat. "Two days out, two back, and three on station while we organize the ransom."

"Yessir. The *Mombassa* has a big refrigerator on board, so the food and juice will be fine. But we need to be careful about our armaments, especially if you want an on-deck drop for the cash. We have to cover a lot of ocean by ourselves, and if we get attacked, with all that money on board, we will have to destroy our enemies, right?"

"I had thought about that," said Salat, "and for this very important mission, we will have a special cache of arms that will be used to defend the ship if necessary. We will store the stuff separately from the weapons we use for the mission."

"What do you suggest, sir?"

"I'd say one spare crate of six Kalashnikovs loaded with a couple of dozen spare magazines. We should have a box of twelve RPG7 grenades. A half dozen hand grenades and a heavy machine gun in case we're attacked by superior numbers. We might need to cut them down to size."

Ismael Wolde nodded in agreement. "And for the mission?"

"Each man will be issued an AK-47. There will be three more on the *Mombassa*'s bridge, with ammunition magazines. To be used, if necessary, by Captain Hassan and anyone of the assault party who loses a weapon."

"You'll need four packs of dynamite, that's twelve sticks taped together for each one. Plus five radio-link detonators. You'll need det cord plus spare tape, and you'll need RPG7s, I guess three or four, though you almost certainly will not use them. The initial assault group will carry four hand grenades, just in case you meet stiff resistance. There had better be one heavy machine gun. How many grappling hooks?"

"I'd say six, plus four rope ladders, the ones with the brass rungs. This boarding will be the fastest we've ever done. I don't want people hanging around waiting for a spot on the ladders. We need to climb up onto the deck four at a time."

"How about mooring lines for the skiffs?"

"We have them, sir. On board the *Mombassa*. I already checked."

"Are the skiffs gassed up?"

"Yessir."

"Anything else?"

"Just the medical box in case anyone gets badly hurt. Make sure there's morphine."

"Okay, Ismael. What time at the beach?"

"Two hours from now, 1900 hours. We'll start loading."

The admiral left the garrison and walked around the town gathering up his men. He called on his missile director Elmi Ahmed, who would be at the beach for the loading. Kifle Zenawi, second in command of the boat, was told to join the forward planning group, and the skiff drivers, Abadula Sofian and Hamdan Ougoure, were instructed to report for duty at 10:00 a.m. the following morning.

The evening passed slowly. Almost everyone in the town drifted down to the beach on the warm equatorial night. They loaded the boat and stowed the hardware under the direction of Hassan and the head of ordnance, Hamdan Ougoure. The moon was high and the sea calm when Hassan made his decision to launch the boat, tow her down to the surf, and then manhandle her out into deeper water and drop anchor for the night, four hundred yards offshore on the ebbing tide. Hassan, along with two guards, would sleep there and be ready to go before noon.

The monsoon season was approaching and the weather could change very quickly. Hassan wanted to avoid a general panic if the sea got up and it became difficult to launch the *Mombassa* in the rolling surf and perhaps even rain squalls. He much preferred to float her tonight on the calm evening tide.

And so once more they gathered, the citizens of Haradheere, manning the lines behind the revving SUVs inching the *Mombassa* across the sand, all 1,500 tons of her plus fuel. The winch howled as it wound in the long steel painter attached with a ringbolt to the stem of the boat, the foremost steel member forming the bow and joined to the keel.

The *Mombassa* was a relatively unprepossessing vessel, but she had been built of tough stuff and she was strong enough to take the strain as she was hauled back to the water, like an aged, slightly rusty walrus.

Shortly after 10:30 the tide began to splash against her hull. The SUVs could do no more and the winch was silent, and the people had to push. They waited for the waves to raise her, especially the ninth one, and as it broke they all heaved together. The *Mombassa* began to twist around, her bow striving to aim seaward.

Everyone was up to his knees in the ocean. The biggest wave so far lifted the boat, and more than sixty of the strongest men in town rammed their shoulders into the hull and that deep African chant, haunting but joyous, echoed rhythmically on the moonlit water . . . *O-O-O-O-H! HOW SHE FLOATS! . . . H-E-E-E-E-Y WHOMBA!*

The *Mombassa* flopped over from her starboard side to port, and as the water caught her, they heaved once more. The pirate boat was afloat, bumping on the sandy bottom, but definitely floating. On board young Kifle Zenawi hauled the rudder over, trying to back the stern into the deepest water.

He started the engines, and on the next wave he jumped her into gear and the propellers spun her out into the surf into the second line of waves, with five feet now under her keel.

*Mombassa*'s bow rose up, and Kifle gave a quick burst on the throttle. His ship was under way. He gave two long blasts on the horn like a maestro before the assembly of his musicians. And the Haradheere throng, still in the water, clapped in unison, uttering one of those long, lonely cries of the dark continent . . . *O-O-O-O-H SOMALIA . . . GOD BLESS YOUR SONS . . . H-E-E-E-Y WHOMBA!*

Zenawi gave them another short blast, and Mohammed Salat, back in the garrison, heard it. He raised a glass of chateau-bottled French claret and addressed his people through his very beautiful wife, "Thank you, everyone, we are on our way."

The intonation was that of the royal "we" utilized for hundreds of years by Great Britain's monarchs. And Salat, in his own way, was a monarch, an African chief over all the land as far as the eye could see. And right now he was looking at another enormous payoff.

Back on the beach, Abadula and Hamdan were hauling one of the skiffs into the water assisted by Captain Hassan. They slowly chugged out to the pirate ship and climbed aboard. It was still very warm, and the captain poured everyone fresh fruit juice, and they talked for a while about the mission. Hassan, for the first time, seemed concerned that they might become targets for a rival gang, and he confessed that he was afraid they were becoming too famous.

"I hope the Battle of Haradheere sent a message that we are not to be interrupted in our lawful business. But some people may feel they want a share of our success. The *Mombassa* might become too well known, and I accept I have to change her soon. I have a feeling we must stay on our guard, night and day."

"We have enough heavy weapons on this ship to attack Pearl Harbor," laughed Hamdan, the head of ordnance for the Somali Marines. "And everyone in this crew knows how to use them."

"I understand that," replied Captain Hassan. "But I do intend to step up our watches, night and day. I believe we can destroy any enemy, but we must be alert. I'm putting two or three lookouts on duty at all times. These have become very dangerous waters, and we have more to lose than most people."

"Especially on our way home," chuckled Hamdan. "Don't worry, boss. We can handle anything. I never heard any group had better weapons than us."

"Stay alert," said the captain. "That's our motto. And if you take a look through the night glasses, you will see there are three armed guards right there on the beach. Three guards. One task. To keep us safe. That's the way Mr. Salat and I want it. Nothing left to chance."

"That's good," said Hamdan. But two hours later he learned a sharp lesson. All three men were dozing under the moon in the deck chairs Hassan had loaded. They were awakened by a soft bump as one of the skiffs came alongside, bringing a large jar of coffee they could drink iced, a present from Mr. Salat.

Captain Hassan thanked the two guards who had made the short journey, and they watched as the boat putt-putt-putted back to shore. As soon as it was beyond range, the skipper turned on both Hamdan and Abadula.

"You see?" he snapped. "See how easy it is for someone to creep up on us in the night. That guard could have been an enemy, and he was practically on board the ship before we came awake. And remember, the guard was not even trying to keep quiet. Our enemy would not have made that bump that woke us."

Hamdan was forced to agree. "If he'd been our enemy, we'd be dead." Abadula shuddered involuntarily. It was a good lesson. Both men would have that incident in their minds throughout the forthcoming voyage.

The following morning the crew began to arrive, ferrying out by skiff. At ten o'clock, Captain Hassan took them through his plan to defend the ship in case of an encounter with an enemy. At the first sign of an intruder, however far away, everyone would disappear below the gunwales, weapons would be primed at all times, and the heavy machine gun would be operational from the stern area. The RPG7s would be launched from the raised cockpit of the bridge, straight through the door where Hamdan would be stationed.

No vessel of any description would be permitted closer than twenty-five yards. If anyone dared come nearer, the Somali Marines would open fire with everything they had. Captain Hassan expected the intruding ship to be sunk. There would be no prisoners, no survivors.

"Our business is private," he said. "No one lives to tell the tale of an encounter with us."

In a way it was quite inspiring. Captain Hassan was not in command of the pirate operations in capturing an enemy ship. But he was in command of the *Mombassa*, and he alone had the authority to order its defense.

A few people walked down to the beach to wave good-bye to the *Mombassa*. They were mostly relatives of the crew, the main population of the town having bid farewell last night. At noon Captain Hassan ordered the anchor hauled.

He gave two sharp blasts on the horn and headed out to sea, adjusting the helm to course one-three-five, southeast, aiming for the second parallel, which ran east-west 160 miles due south. According to Salat's contact, the *Global Mustang* would make her easterly journey three miles to the north of that second-degree line, and Hassan wanted the *Mombassa* to come up under her to the south.

They ran before a light southwesterly breeze, which wafted over the *Mombassa*'s starboard quarter. The sea was long but the swells were gradual, and conditions could scarcely have been more pleasant. There was barely any traffic, and aside from a large tanker heading south, ten miles up ahead, they saw only one other vessel in the first three hours, a local Somali fishing boat hauling heavy nets.

Shortly before 4:00 p.m. they spotted a new boat on the horizon. She was dark red and looked like a converted trawler without the familiar outriggers, the booms that swing out port and starboard to tow the trawl. She was bigger than the *Mombassa*, maybe seventy feet overall, with a forward superstructure housing the wheelhouse and accommodation and an aft working deck. She was probably seven miles away and travelling fast on a diametric course. If she kept going on that bearing, she would cross the *Mombassa*'s bow in thirty minutes.

"Keep an eye on her," said Captain Hassan. "She's not a fishing boat and she's not naval, so she rates as a mystery. And she's bigger and faster than us."

Fifteen minutes later, the other boat had not changed course and she was running more or less neck and neck, two miles off *Mombassa*'s starboard beam. Unless Captain Hassan made a course change, the boats would come together in the next ten minutes. Thus far there had been no signal or contact between them, but Hassan did not like what he was seeing.

Five minutes later, with the dark-red boat less than a half-mile distant and closing in, he roared, "*ACTION STATIONS!*" In the opinion of *Mombassa*'s master, the other boat had increased her speed and come 12 degrees red. Unless someone throttled back, the two boats were on a collision course.

Captain Hassan throttled back. Ismael Wolde was in the wheelhouse with him, and Elmi Ahmed was loading an RPG7 into the launcher. Omar Ali was flat on the deck below the portside gunwales holding a hand grenade. Everyone was holding a loaded AK-47, and the oncoming intruder could not see a thing. Wolde was holding the heavy machine gun.

As the other boat began to converge, Captain Hassan could see the name on her bow, *Somali Star*. She flew no flag but her captain, a powerfully built black-skinned Somali seaman wearing a US Navy baseball cap, was on the high, sloping foredeck, and he was holding a bullhorn. And some kind of light machine gun. An older model, not a top-of-the-range Kalashnikov.

"*Ahoy, Mombassa! You are the famous pirate ship from Harad-heere, ha?*"

Hassan called back, "*No. Wrong ship. We're just fishermen.*"

"*I know who you are, Mombassa. And we want a deal. A share of your wealth. In return we give you protection. My men are all well armed. Very good fighters.*"

"*I told you,*" yelled Hassan. "*I'm out here fishing. Just with my assistant here. We're not pirates. You got the wrong boat.*"

"*Not wrong boat. You pirates. I'm Major Marro. And we want to take over your operation. We're a bigger boat, faster, more experienced people. You cooperate now. We're coming aboard.*"

"*I don't want that,*" yelled Hassan. "*Get away from me. We're just unarmed fishermen.*"

"*You lie to me, Cap,*" shouted the major, and he turned around and signalled for his crew to show themselves. There were twenty of them, all carrying various rifles. "*We're coming aboard. If you don't cooperate we kill you and your mate. Take all your money.*"

There were only twenty yards between them, hull to hull, and closing. "*GET AWAY FROM ME!*" bellowed Hassan.

"*STAND BY TO BOARD!*" shouted the major to his crew.

Captain Hassan snapped, "*Fire at will. Take them. AND TAKE THEM RIGHT NOW!*"

Ismael Wolde opened up the heavy machine gun and fired a volley straight through the doorway that hit Major Marro with such force it shot him ten feet backward, blood pouring from his shattered head and chest.

Wolde sprayed the deck, cutting down six of the astounded crew of the *Somali Star*. Elmi Ahmed launched one of his Russian RPG7s, which smashed into the wheelhouse and almost blew the superstructure off its mountings, detonating in a violent blast of fire and smoke.

Up from the deck rose Captain Hassan's gunners led by Abadula Sofian in company with Abdul Mesfin and the ex–army sergeant Ibrahim Yacin. They fired their superbly accurate AK-47s at the now fleeing crew members of the *Somali Star*.

They fired steadily, hitting them in the back, head, legs, even blowing the brains out of three who tried to jump into the water. The noise was deafening and the fire was beginning to rage. The only two crew members still alive climbed onto the portside gun-wale and tried to jump clear, but Ibrahim shot them both dead before they could leap into the water.

And into this uproar of fire, death, and carnage, stepped Omar Ali Farah, ripping the pin out of his hand grenade and hurling it across the narrow stretch of water and onto the deck, where it landed with a clatter, rolled, and nearly blew the *Somali Star* in half.

The blast split the deck asunder, flattened the main bulkhead, blew out the stern, tore the mast off its mountings, and smashed a gaping hole into the hull, which ripped downward below the water line. The force of the explosion hurled the former trawler into an upward spasm and broke her back.

In a hail of sparks, hissing steam, flames, and cordite, the *Somali Star* sank in three minutes. One dying crew member pathetically raised his old Kalashnikov out of the water, like a grotesque scene from Tennyson's *Morte d'Arthur*, when the king's sword, Excalibur, rose from the lake. Except this had less nobility. Ibrahim blew his brains out with a burst of machine gun fire.

As Captain Hassan had instructed, there were no survivors. There was almost no trace, except for a few patches of burning oil on the surface, a shredded life-belt, and a pall of gun-smoke and blood. And soon there would be nothing. Like the shattered, lime-soaked buried corpses of Sheikh Sharif's broken army, the sunken wreck of the *Somali Star* would be a silent, unseen testament to the blind stupidity of attacking Mohammed Salat's highly trained pirate brigade.

They had achieved their victory in less than three minutes. They had sustained no casualties. No one was even wounded. In fact not one of Major Marro's men had managed to fire a return shot.

Captain Hassan was about to ask his crew to clear up the ship after the battle, but there was nothing to clear up. So each man just shouldered his rifle and stowed the ammunition and armament boxes. Kifle Zenawi took the helm, opened the throttle, and headed southeast.

▼

AT 8:00 P.M. ON THAT FRIDAY NIGHT, Captain Jack Pitman sat down for dinner with two of his senior officers. The *Global Mustang* had an excellent dining room for the senior command, and the three men who ordered New York sirloin steaks were old friends, having sailed together ever since the ship had been commissioned three years previously.

Jack Pitman, along with a fellow native of Washington State, First Officer Dominic Rayforth, and the navigator, Ray Kiley, had brought the *Mustang* directly to the Persian Gulf on her maiden voyage from Nagasaki. It took a crew of thirty-two to drive her, including the four specialists who monitored the freezing, round tanks full of liquid natural gas.

At that time, the three officers had been with Bob Heseltine for many years but saw him only rarely. They were highly paid due to the enormous responsibilities each man carried, not to mention the four-month tours of duty they endured, four months when the only land they saw was the loading docks of Qatar and the unloading piers of Japan.

All three of them had passed their forty-sixth birthdays. And the great ship had obliterated two of their marriages. Mary Pitman and Sarah Kiley had tired of the long absences and filed for divorce.

Which left Jack and Ray owning small apartments in the Northwest and running through a list of totally unsuitable girlfriends, who at first thought it glamorous to be with wealthy international mariners, until they thought better of it.

Dominic Rayforth was still married. Barely. His wife and four children lived in the suburbs of Seattle and had reached the point where no one cared whether or not he came home. He provided for his family generously, but he kept a couple of girlfriends on either side of the world and had convinced his wife that his tours of duty were six months, rather than four. The previous year had seen him home for five weeks total.

All three of them were married to the *Global Mustang*. Every month their salaries were wired to their respective bank accounts: Pitman earned $300,000 a year; the other two got $250,000. And every six months they received $200,000 bonuses for their role in transporting hundreds of millions of dollars' worth of gas safely around the world.

It was a lonely but also carefree existence. No bills to pay for their own living, plenty of money, and no worries for the rest of their lives. Kiley and Rayforth were fine with it. Jack Pitman, in his more reflective moments, understood he had paid one hell of a price for financial independence.

That night, staring out of the dining room's portside windows, Jack could see the moonlight on the water. They were cutting through a black, calm sea and the ship was quiet. He had two watchmen on the bridge who occasionally scanned the radar screen, but essentially the *Mustang* was sailing herself on automatic.

If anything showed up that might impede them in the water, a couple of alarms would sound immediately, but the fact was that other vessels could pick up the colossal bulk of the LNG carrier in ample time to stay out of the way. For a skilled navigator, sailing the *Mustang* was relaxing, even boring. Jack, Ray, and Dominic could not remember a time when anything truly interesting had happened.

Everything was operated from the control panel on the bridge. Course and speed were set: They were through the Strait of Hormuz, down the Arabian Gulf, and heading south across the Indian Ocean, and the water was deep all the way. No rocks, no sandbanks, hardly any traffic. They were 760 miles from the point where they would make a hard easterly turn and head for the wide channel that cuts through the Maldives south of Male.

They finished dinner at 10:00 p.m. and sat chatting over coffee. Dominic had spent time browsing the Internet and noticed a breaking story about a big Japanese factory ship being taken by pirates some four hundred miles to the southwest.

"Have they asked for a ransom?" wondered Jack Pitman.

"I guess so," replied Dominic. "But it doesn't say anything definite. I did see that Reuters was quoting the president of a fishing outfit way south on Kyushu."

"Didn't say whether they were paying up, did it?"

"Not really. But it'll be the same as always—the cargo's worth a bundle of money and the pirates only want about 5 percent of its value to send it on its way. Otherwise they'll shoot everyone, scuttle the ship, and vanish into the night. It's always easier, and a lot cheaper, to pay."

"It's the goddamned insurance companies that make the rules these days," said Jack. "Because if a bad scenario takes place, like death or loss of ship or cargo, they end up footing a huge bill.

"And there's the threat of heavy increases in premiums, which nobody wants but can't afford not to pay. Seems to me the insurance outfits run the shipping lines. We're getting to the point where we can't live with them, but can't live without them."

"Well," said Dominic, "you know one thing. They are always going to urge the owners to pay up. When Bob had that problem with the VLCC off Sumatra a couple of years ago, they said they'd share the cost of the ransom with him. They're making it financially beneficial for themselves in the short term but encouraging the goddamned pirates to keep at it because they're getting goddamned rich. Every time, seems to me."

"I wonder what we'd do if they boarded us?"

"They seem to be boarding everyone," said Jack. "But they've never boarded one of these things."

"If they did, we couldn't do much," said Ray. "We have no weapons on board, nothing to shoot 'em with."

"And you know why we don't have anything to defend ourselves?" asked the captain sternly.

"Not really."

"Because Bob's insurers have threatened not to cover any ship that has guns of any type on board."

"You wouldn't think they'd care. And it would save a lot of ransom money if we had a couple of armed guards who could shoot the pirates."

"Easier in one way, not in another," said Jack. "Because there are lawyers out there just waiting to represent some poor Somali family whose pirate son got shot while he was climbing aboard. Poor kid, unarmed, just trying to hitch a ride, meant no harm to anyone . . . "

"Just get that weeping mother into the European court of human rights," chuckled Dominic. "And give her 5 million bucks for the loss of her innocent son."

"Jesus Christ," said Captain Pitman. "How about a glass of brandy?"

# CHAPTER 9

▼

THE *MOMBASSA* RAN EAST ACROSS THE INDIAN OCEAN FOR forty more hours after the attempt on its crew and wealth. Her new engines ran flawlessly, never slowing below 15 knots on a calm sea with little wind. By 10:00 a.m. on Sunday morning, they had put six hundred miles between them and the spot where the *Somali Star* had gone down.

Captain Hassan had adjusted the radar to its long-distance mode and stood in front of the screen with Wolde and Ahmed while Kifle Zenawi drove the boat. And they watched the seas to the north for the paint of a really big oceangoing tanker, which, with its huge golden domes above deck, was almost certainly sixty or seventy feet higher in the water than a regular VLCC.

When the *Global Mustang* showed, it would be unmistakable and almost certainly travelling very fast, both through the water and, comparatively, on the screen. The crew ate cold goat sandwiches and drank iced coffee in the heat of the wheelhouse. They watched the green radar arm make its endless revolutions, pinging its findings, electronically relayed from the all-seeing dish that swung on the roof.

The message from New York had suggested that the *Mustang* was steaming straight down the sixtieth line of longitude and would make her left turn when she reached a point three miles short of the second northern parallel. The *Mombassa*'s GPS showed her three miles south of that line, positioned exactly at 60E, and everyone was hoping they had not missed their quarry.

If they had, they could hardly be blamed. They had arrived at their rendezvous on time and were set to track the *Mustang* until after dark. Captain Hassan believed the hours after 10:00 p.m. were most favorable for their attack because on a long voyage, many of the crew would be asleep. Ismael and Elmi went along with that. But first they had to find the ship.

Eleven o'clock came and went. There was not a sign of anything in this lonely part of the Indian Ocean, southwest of Cape Comorin, the southernmost tip of the Indian subcontinent.

They passed the time taping the grappling hooks with thick, black electrical insulator. The hooks had no need to be sharp enough to dig into the ground. They just had to be bent hard to grab and hook the ship's rail. The thick tape would almost eliminate the clatter on the steel deck, muffling it to a dull thud, hopefully too dull to be heard by anyone.

When they had boarded the *Niagara Falls*, the metallic clatter had basically cost the ship's first mate his life. Wolde had shot him, and he understood the ramifications. Stealth was the key, and the absence of metal clashing with metal would help.

But at fifteen minutes before noon on that Sunday morning, there was still no sign of the *Mustang*, and Captain Hassan decided to move further east. He would run at flank speed for a half hour, just in case the LNG tanker had cut the corner and begun to beat southeast a couple of hours early.

At 12:30 the *Mombassa* was still south of the second parallel, but there was no sign of the *Mustang* anywhere to its north. And the radar was set to twenty-five miles. Admiral Wolde debated calling home base and maybe checking with Mr. Salat's source. But Elmi Ahmed advised against it because if the *Mustang* suddenly showed, they'd look jumpy and unprofessional.

At 1:00 p.m. the *Global Mustang* hit the screen. It was a big paint, bright and sharp. No chance that it was weather or a small fishing boat or even a medium-sized freighter. This was one of the ocean's giants.

"It's gotta be her," breathed Ismael. "She's heading southeast and she's going fast."

"She would be," grumbled Elmi, who would probably be the first man up the hull of the great ship, right next to Wolde.

"We'll stay well south of her," said Hassan. "But we can't let her get away. We'd never catch her."

Once more they headed east, running miles out of sight but somehow in tandem with their target.

"You planning to close in on her during daylight hours?" asked Admiral Wolde.

"No, sir," said Hassan. "There isn't any point. We have a much better chance of staying invisible in the dark. And this is a hell of a good radar."

All through the afternoon they ran fast along the horizon from the *Mustang*. One of the Filipino watchkeepers on the bridge saw the pirate ship far away to the south, but he never gave it a thought. The sheer size of his tanker inevitably induced a feeling of mild contempt among its crew.

When darkness finally fell, before 7:30, the *Mustang* became an even more splendid sight. Her deck lights went on and floodlit the four massive golden orbs that shaped her almost nine-hundred-foot profile. She was cutting through the night waters glowing golden bright, a Liberace jewel of the deep, hauling a near-priceless cargo directly to the Orient.

Captain Hassan changed course shortly before 9:00 p.m. He was still moving east and still had the throttles open, in order to lay up with the *Mustang*. But the *Mombassa* had come fifteen degrees north to zero-seven-five, and she was running dark, with her red-and-green navigation lights switched off.

Captain Hassan understood he could not catch up and overtake the *Mustang*. The most he could do was drive the *Mombassa* directly into her wake and follow her dead astern. He'd then let the skiffs flash over the last two miles at 30 knots and move in port and starboard, right below the aft rails, for the boarding.

It was a little after 10:00 p.m., and he had the *Mombassa* running absolutely flat out, close to 22 knots. His biggest problem was the *Mustang*'s speed. The huge tanker made 530 yards every minute, so if they stopped for four minutes to launch the skiffs, get aboard, and take off, the *Mustang* would be a mile and a quarter farther away.

That made every second count. Because even the *Mustang*'s idle bridge crew might notice that she was being hotly pursued by a couple of speedboats making 30 knots in the middle of the Indian Ocean.

Captain Hassan understood this was a very vulnerable part of their mission. If someone sounded the alarm, the stern deck would be swarming with sailors, and they might be armed. Also there would be zero chance of hurling the grappling irons without having them thrown right back, probably killing someone.

The *Mombassa* was shuddering with the demands being made on her engines, and at 10:23 p.m. the captain suddenly throttled right back and shouted, "*STAND BY TO LAUNCH!*"

Immediately the two drivers, Abadula Sofian and Hamdan Ougoure, climbed into the already loaded skiffs, one on the portside, one on starboard. The four juniors began to lower away, with Wolde and Ahmed hanging on to the painters attached to the bows of the skiffs, playing out the two lines that slipped though their hands.

By the time the assault boats splashed down in the water, the *Mombassa* was stopped. Both Yamaha engines on the skiffs, finely tuned by the mechanics on the Haradheere beach, fired first go. For the moment, Wolde and Ahmed made them fast on the stern fishing-net cleats, and everyone climbed over the gunwales, their gleaming AK-47s slung over their backs.

The junior pirates went first, then Kifle Zenawi, followed by Omar Ali Farah, Ibrahim Yacin, and Abdul Mesfin. Ismael Wolde and Elmi Ahmed, each carrying taped bundles of dynamite, were the last to jump down into separate boats.

Everything else was loaded, the hand grenades, the grappling irons already lashed to the knotted ropes, the brass-rung ladders, the heavy machine gun, and, in case of dire emergency, the launcher for the RPG7 missiles, which were stored in a wooden box, one in each boat.

Captain Hassan, expertly trained by the Somali Marines missile director, Elmi Ahmed, had the other launcher on board the *Mombassa*, plus four missiles. On the word of command over the phone from Admiral Wolde, he would slam one of them straight into the *Mustang*'s high bridge and hope to hell it didn't blow up half the world.

Wolde thought it could be done without penetrating the stern holding dome, but Hassan better be as accurate as any missile man had ever been. This last move was one of desperation and would not be implemented unless something shocking had occurred— either the assault team was suddenly in a life-or-death situation or was about to go over the side into the water.

With the engines chugging slowly, but out of gear, Hassan raced to the stern and released both skiffs, throwing the lines skillfully inboard, as the two small boats backed away and then roared forward, their bows arching upward and quickly flattening out as the Yamahas settled into a high-speed mode.

The launch of the skiffs had taken only two and a half minutes, which put the *Mustang* two miles ahead, plus only three-quarters of a mile. The pirates would close the gap at the rate of 10 knots an hour in about seventeen minutes.

The megawatt illumination of the LNG tanker cast its brightness all over the place. What should have been a fast approach over black water suddenly felt as though they were flying over a Hollywood film set. The skiffs and their crews were actually casting shadows on the water as they raced in.

There was no escape. Everything around the tanker was in a light field. Wolde and his teams were like prisoners under the Nazi lights, trying to make the wire in *Stalag 17*. The scene lacked only Billy Wilder standing on the bow with a bullhorn.

Ismael Wolde had never been so scared. The whine of the motors was so loud in the night, and the floodlighting so penetrating, he was counting the seconds, preparing to tell Abadula to peel away left, back into the dark.

There was only one place on the entire ocean surface where there was shadow. And that was hard against the hull of the tanker, where the light could not reach. Whether or not they could make it to that doubtful haven without being spotted was, in Ismael's opinion, about ten-to-one against.

In truth, Wolde had no concept of life on these ships, the impersonal nature of the men who sailed them from so high up, one hundred feet above the water. Whatever else, this remoteness from the sailors' traditional element instilled in them all a complete loss of intimacy with the sea.

Modern-day tanker men had practically nothing in common with any mariners from other ages. Because these ocean giants give the impression of being shore-bound. Because they need almost no seamanship while in transit between ports. Somewhere down below the decks, there are humming caves propelling her forward, providing every possible requirement for power. There is a permanent emptiness about the gigantic main deck. Hardly anyone ever goes out there.

The crew, like its sea-borne home, performs automatic duties. There are cooks, mostly foreign, laundrymen, and cleaners, and the ship follows a predictable pattern, which scarcely varies on the bridge. The gigantic bulk of the gas carrier slows everything down. Her solidity on the waves removes the feeling of possible danger. Ships like a fully laden *Global Mustang* can smash their way forward, however bad the sea. They can shove aside the very worst that nature hurls at her, and hardly anyone even notices she has done so.

Driving through the tropical night above the unfathomably deep waters of the Indian Ocean accentuates a crew's indifference to its element. They can play table tennis, watch movies in the ship's cinema, watch television, play cards, send e-mail.

Up on the bridge, the watchkeepers chat and sip coffee, checking the radar screen every hour. Nothing happens for hours, days, weeks on end. There is only the impression of unassailable steadiness.

The thought that the *Global Mustang* was a minute away from a murderous, multimillion dollar, life-threatening pirate attack was nothing less than outlandish—as if the White House butler were about to kick the president straight in the ass.

Admiral Wolde and his men reached the shadow of the hull without anyone on the *Global Mustang* having the remotest idea they were there. Abadula and Hamdan were in direct phone contact as they steered left and right out of the wake and made their way to separate sides of the ship's stern. Both helmsmen cut their engines back, trying to fix zero relative speed to the monster they had almost grabbed.

However the sheer bulk of the *Mustang* had caused her bow wave to roll almost her entire length, and the skiffs were riding up and then down six to eight feet, almost being sucked into the steel hull plates.

Wolde and Elmi Ahmed, on different sides of the ship, stared up and gasped. The hull towered above them. It may have been no more than thirty feet to that stern rail, but when the skiffs rode down on the wave, it looked like two hundred feet.

Wolde grabbed his helmsman's open phone line and snapped to Hamdan in the other boat, "Can Elmi throw the grappler on the rise?"

"He thinks he can," replied Hamdan. "And he's ready to go if you are."

"Ready," said Wolde. "Let's go right now. One grappler either side. I don't want the damned things clattering around everywhere. Tell him to meet me up there."

And with that, he began to whirl the big, heavily taped hook on the end of the knotted rope. One, two, three times he completed a full circle, and the sound of the rope sang on the light wind. On the fourth swing he let go, and in the searing lights of the great ship, the exposed tips of the hook glinted as the grappler flew upward about twenty degrees off the perpendicular. Wolde thought it might not reach, but somehow it snaked over the rail, landing with a clump but no clatter.

On the other side, Elmi hurled and missed. The grappler hit the top of the rail and fell back down the side of the hull and into the sea. Elmi cursed and began to haul it out; meanwhile, on the starboard side, Wolde grabbed the knotted rope and swung out over the side of the skiff and onto the side of the ship.

Ramming the soft soles of his combat boots onto the large knot in the rope, he pushed hard, pulling upward with his arms, covering around two feet at a time. It was a gruelling climb, but Ismael was built like a whip-thin mountaineer. He carried not one ounce of excess weight, and he made it thirty-three feet to the top, exhausted but safe.

He dropped a much lighter rope and hook down to the skiff, and Omar Ali fixed two rope ladders onto it for the admiral to pull up.

Ismael was halfway through the exercise when Elmi tried again, but his rope was soaking wet and much heavier, and this time it never reached the rail. It hit the side of the ship, hard. In the night silence even Wolde heard it, and he was all of 150 feet away on the far side.

Instinct told him that Elmi was in trouble, but his commander's brain told him that before he did anything else, he needed to get his two rope ladders fixed and dropped down to the skiff. He hooked them both over the rails, grabbed his Kalashnikov, and then rushed the width of the huge ship to the portside to help Elmi. At which point one of the lower doors to the upper-works came open and flooded the area with light.

Two crewmen, both Panamanians, walked out and looked around quizzically. At precisely that moment, Elmi tried again and, with a supreme effort, flung his grappler up and over the rails. It landed with a thump, right at the feet of the first crewman, who almost had a heart attack as he jumped clear of the three-pronged hook. He yelled loudly once, but not again because Admiral Wolde shot him dead at point-blank range, then swung his rifle left and shot the other man as well.

By now the heavily armed Kifle Zenawi and Ibrahim Yacin were up the rope ladders and over the rail onto the starboard side of the stern deck. Elmi Ahmed had hauled his grappler tight and was on his way up the rope, climbing fast.

Wolde rushed over and shut the door to the upper-works too late. Another door opened and a uniformed engineering officer stepped onto the deck, spotted Wolde lurking in the shadows, and demanded, "Who the hell are you?"

Kifle Zenawi gunned him down in cold blood. Ahmed clambered over the rail in time to see the uproar, but he stuck to his task, dropped down his hook and line, and hauled the starboard-side rope ladders up and fixed them firmly, same as Wolde's.

This allowed the teenage pirates, two on either side, to climb aboard, then Omar Ali and Abdul Mesfin with the heavy machine gun on his back. With all ten members of his assault force on board, Wolde opted for housekeeping before the main attack, and he ordered his troops to clear the three bodies and throw them off the stern of the ship.

While they did, Ougoure lashed his skiff to the stern of Sofian's boat and then followed his team up the rope ladder, while the other helmsman stood off to starboard and kept steering alongside the *Mustang*, which was moving at 20 knots.

Ougoure, the ordnance chief, was involved in the most difficult task of all—laying the dynamite bombs at the foot of each of the four holding domes without blowing up the ship and without being seen. On the plans of the ship, Wolde and Salat had seen only one definite entrance from the main deck down to the holding tank area—a large hatch, starboard side, between the stern dome and the third one, counting backward from the bow.

The picture showed it just aft of the massive loading and discharging manifold, which helpfully cast a deep shadow over that section of the ship. Through a magnifying glass, they could also make out the words in heavy red lettering: DANGER—NO ENTRY.

From what Wolde had seen, there was a long companionway going down beneath the hatch, and it was the only one, except for three entrances inside the upper-works, through which the engineering staff could enter.

Somehow they had to get that on-deck hatch open, and then Ahmed and Ougoure could go below with two bodyguards and place their bombs under the domes. Only then would Admiral Wolde attempt to take over the ship.

For the moment, he ordered no more shooting and instructed the remaining five members of the assault party to stay out of sight with him, deep in the shadows until the bomb group returned.

Ahmed, Ougoure, and three armed junior bodyguards dropped to their knees and began the long, one-hundred-yard crawl along the steel deck to the hatch that led down to the bottom halves of the four domed holding tanks. In Elmi's view this was a potentially fatal maneuver because for at least eighty of the hundred yards, there was no chance of concealment. They would be floodlit, moving along a part of the ship where no one had the right to trespass except senior officers and engineers.

Elmi thought their only hope was that the crew was almost certainly unarmed, like most other tankers. But this one was American, and they took instruction from no one. If they were seen, someone would open fire on them, and their only chance of escape was to dive over the side and trust that Admiral Wolde was watching and that Captain Hassan or the skiffs were not far away.

As the senior man, Elmi set the pace: dead slow, trying to make the journey without moving, or at least being seen to move. It took them ten minutes to get there and when they did, they found the hatch was not locked. Elmi opened it with a twist and a heave. He immediately detailed one of his guards to remain on duty in the shadows next to the hatch. The other two would go with him.

The gap led directly onto a yellow-painted steel staircase. There were lights on and Elmi could see the steep flight of steps that led down to a steel gantry situated perhaps ten feet off the ground and running the entire length of the ship. Every twenty yards there were steps down to the enormous floor area on which one of the massive domes rested on great support girders.

Each dome apparently had its own steel room, each about the size of Carnegie Hall. This suited Elmi, being out of sight, one from the other. They moved swiftly into action, running down the short flight of steps from the gantry and taking up positions at the base of the tank. It was like kneeling in the shadow of Mount Rushmore.

Elmi hauled off his rucksack and took out the first taped pack of dynamite, twenty-four sticks, Russian-made, a foot long with enough explosives to blast a hole in the walls of Fort Knox. Ougoure handed him the spliced det cord and the electronic detonator, which would react to a remote-controlled device they would, if they had to, operate from the starboard side of the ship.

Elmi connected the battery and tightened the terminals on the wire. He then slid the device hard under the girders, touching the dome. If that thing blew, the cascading liquefied gas would flood through the massive hole blasted through the single hull and freeze the ocean solid around the ship. Then it would vaporize back into gas before it exploded, probably causing a chain reaction and blowing apart the three other tanks. The scene would likely resemble a cross between the destruction on the Ross Ice Shelf, west of the South Pole, and Hiroshima on August 6, 1945.

Swiftly, tracked by their bodyguards, Elmi and Hamdan moved across the floor space and went through the archway leading to Dome Three and repeated the process. Their preparation had been so thorough that each area took only five minutes.

By the time they had completed Dome One, just aft of the foredeck above, they were five hundred feet and twenty minutes from their start point. They had seen no one. In peace and quiet they had set the explosive devices, which were capable of laying waste to one of the most valuable cargo vessels on earth. Captain Jack Pitman might have been in command of the *Global Mustang*, but her fate was entirely in the hands of Ismael Wolde.

Carefully, their soft boots making no sound on the steel floor, they moved aft down the ship and scooted up to the gantry and then the stairs. Ismael shoved open the hatch and his "sentry" pulled it open, dropping it closed when the four pirates were out.

At this point the need for stealth was over. They were now going to take the ship and it did not matter who saw them. They were armed to the teeth going into combat against an almost certainly unarmed and helpless opposing force.

They ran down the starboard side and back to the base bulkheads of the upper-works. Wolde could still see Abadula off the port side charging along at 20 knots, level with the ship, and towing the second skiff. He assembled his men and positioned three on each of the three deck-level doors.

He opened the door from which the now-dead Panamanian crew members had emerged. He and Elmi rushed in, Kalashnikovs held in the firing position, and blasted one short burst into the interior wall. There were two Ping-Pong tables inside, and the four players dropped their paddles in terror.

"Hands high, everyone," said Wolde sharply. "Back over there against the wall." Four other crew members who had been sitting in the wide recreation room also raised their hands and joined the line of prisoners, which the Somali Marine admiral now addressed.

"Right now no one is going to get hurt," he said. "Is anyone armed?"

No one responded and Wolde added encouragingly, "My men will now search all eight of you. Should we find a firearm, we will shoot two of you and throw the bodies overboard. Let me ask once more: Does anyone have a firearm or a knife?"

Everyone shook his head. "Okay, start the search. And meanwhile you and you," said Wolde, nodded toward two men who were dressed in light engineer's overalls. "You will accompany me to the bridge." He beckoned to Abdul Mesfin to join him, along with two of the bodyguards who had kept watch while he had set the explosives at the base of the domes.

"Round up the ship," he told Elmi. "Go room to room. Take the prisoners with you and get everyone back in the recreation room inside a half hour. Anyone who resists, shoot to kill. In this ship a prisoner is an obedient, privileged person. Anyone who steps out of line dies."

"Get us to the elevator, directly to the bridge," he told the engineers. "Nobody gets hurt so long as you obey my instructions."

All five men stepped inside and the elevator took them seven floors above the deck. They walked out into a carpeted area, and the engineers indicated a wooden double door with gold letters that proclaimed: CONTROL ROOM GLOBAL MUSTANG. And in smaller lettering: *Authorized Personnel Only*.

Wolde waved everyone back and told Abdul to fire a burst from the heavy gun, straight down the length of the door on the line where the handle and lock were located. The staccato noise of the big gun pulverizing the wood, splitting the door from end to end, shattered the calm of the evening.

Wolde kicked it open and rampaged into the room with Abdul and his assistant right behind him, guns levelled. Captain Pitman could not believe his eyes. Faced with the obliterated door, the pirate king, and three machine guns, one of which clearly worked, he just stood there, gaping.

"*HANDS HIGH!*" yelled Wolde. "All of you! Right now."

Dominic Rayforth, first officer, flung his arms skyward. The navigation officer, Ray Kiley, was slower but hopped to it when Ismael mentioned that he'd probably blow his head off if he didn't obey his orders.

There were two other members of the *Mustang*'s crew on the bridge, a watchkeeper and a cargo technician who had been standing in front of a long bank of instruments. They all had their hands high, and Ismael told the captain to slow the ship down to 3 knots. The others, all six of them, were told to back up against the interior wall of the bridge.

"This ship takes a long while to slow down," said Jack Pitman. "I should tell you that."

"Just make sure the engines throttle back right now," said Wolde. "And then stand over there with everyone else."

They felt the huge turbines cut and slow. And Captain Pitman walked over and stood against the wall with his hands raised.

"Anyone armed, please hand over your weapons. My men will then search you, and if anyone has lied to me, I will shoot him stone dead. Is that clear?"

It was so clear that no one even needed to answer. And it dawned on them all that this was about as serious as anything could ever be.

"Let me introduce myself," said Ismael. "My name is not important, but I'm the field commander of the Royal Somali Marines." He'd been contemplating giving his platoon a slightly grander name for some time, and being in this empress of an ocean freighter seemed an excellent time to start.

"So far as anyone here is concerned, my troops have taken command of the ship," he said. "There are eleven of us armed with automatic rifles and hand grenades. Within the next few minutes, every last member of your crew will be my prisoner. In your position, I should not even consider resisting my commands because I will not hesitate to shoot anyone who defies us."

Wolde paused. Just to let his words hit home. And then he continued, "Captain Pitman, now that the ship has slowed, I would like it turned around to face Somalia. When you have done that, I want you to show me your communications system.

"I will be making three phone calls: one to the ship's owner, one to the cargo's buyer, Tokyo Electric, and finally to the shipping agents in New York. My price is 10 million US dollars, to be dropped on the main deck in cash. At which point you can have the ship back and continue on your way."

"And what if my people refuse?"

"Then I shall blow up the ship with the entire crew on board, leave in our very fast boat, and no one will ever know we were here. Our loss will be nothing. To Tokyo Electric and the agents, the losses will be enormous. And the insurance companies will probably double your premiums."

Captain Pitman asked, "May I know how you intend to blow up the ship?"

"Not yet. No." replied Wolde. "Just lead me to the phones and remember: My men will shoot on sight if anyone tries anything unusual. Also you must dim the deck lights on the ship."

The captain led Admiral Wolde to the telephone desk and pointed out which ones had access to overseas communications.

The pirate chief ordered him to join the other prisoners and then he picked up the phone and dialled the number of the Haradheere garrison.

The operator put him through immediately to Mohammed Salat, who listened with undisguised glee as his operations admiral said simply, "The *Global Mustang* is now seven hundred miles off the Somali shore and under our command. I am on the bridge and the ship has slowed. I have ordered it turned around to face west, and I am now ready to call the relevant parties. I have informed the captain that we require 10 million US dollars for his freedom to proceed to Tokyo Bay."

"Excellent, Ismael. Couldn't be better," said Salat. "I will take care of Tokyo Electric from here. You call this man Heseltine in Houston. And then try your old friend Livanos in Monte Carlo. But be flexible. Advise them both to share in the ransom, and I'll do the same in Japan."

"Roger that," said Admiral Wolde. "I'll get back to you when the calls are made."

▼

OUT IN THE SKIFF, Abadula could see the golden tanker slowing down, so he cut his speed to stay level. It was obvious to him that Ismael Wolde had captured the *Global Mustang*. He had thought he heard gunfire but nothing prolonged. And he'd watched the guys swarm up the side of the ship.

Now she was stopping. And there could be only one reason for that. The Somali Marines had done it again, and Abadula grinned broadly as he throttled back and called Captain Hassan on his cell phone.

*Mombassa*'s master was glad for the call—he was staring directly ahead, and he could see the *Mustang*'s red-and-green running lights, which signalled to any seaman that she was coming dead toward. For a few moments he'd thought Wolde had been beaten and that the tanker was trying to run the pirate ship down.

"She's stopping, Hassan," Abadula said. "I think she's coming to a complete halt. The marines have taken her."

▼

THERE WAS A FRENZY of activity in Haradheere. Wolde's news has sent the $10 shares in the *Mustang* mission to $20. Then $25. And there was still heavy buying. Salat himself had walked down to the main office and drafted the dramatic bulletin for the electronic board:

BREAKING NEWS—BREAKING NEWS!
*The world's largest carrier of*
*liquid natural gas, the* Global
Mustang, *was captured by the*
*Somali Marines 700 miles offshore*
*at 11:00 p.m. this Sunday night.*

When the words began to flash inside the main trading area, there was a stampede among the tribesmen to invest. It was a license to print dollar bills. A license to double their money and then some.

Several people had bought $1,000 worth of $10 shares at issue, and their money was now worth $2,500. Salat personally doubled his stake and then bought some more for his wife. He liked to be seen trading in his own stock market because it gave people a sense of confidence.

Shortly after midnight he returned home, accompanied by a squad of his guards, and opened up the phone line to Japan, which was six hours ahead. Masaki Tanigaki, president of the giant Tokyo

Electric Power, the fourth-largest energy company in the world, was awakened at 6:00 a.m. as he slumbered peacefully in a private room at the glorious Bristol Hill Golf and Residential Club.

In the middle of this 6,947-yard paradise, the president nearly jumped out of his skin when his cell phone jangled on the bedside table. Mr. Tanigaki was unused to being disturbed without giving specific instructions to do so.

"This is Masaki Tanigaki speaking," he said. "Who calls me at this hour on my personal phone?"

"My name is not important," replied the voice, "but I am the commander of the most important ocean pirate operation in the world. My men have just taken over the *Global Mustang* in the middle of the Indian Ocean. I believe you own the cargo, several hundred thousand tons of liquid gas?"

Never had Mr. Tanigaki come awake so swiftly. "*You've done what?!*" he exclaimed.

"We have taken command of the American LNG tanker *Global Mustang*. Right now she is heading west at two miles per hour, and my troops have planted massive, high-explosive bombs under each of her domed holding tanks.

"I expect you want to know our price. It's $10 million US, and when we receive it, we will send the ship on its way as we always do. Most people are happy to do business with us. We are men of our word."

Tanigaki sat back down on the bed. "You want my corporation to give you $10 million or you will blow up the ship?" he said.

"And its crew," said Salat. "Everyone dies. And you probably don't want that on your conscience."

"*Are you some kind of a madman?!*" roared Tanigaki. "How do I know you have the ship? And why me? It's not even our ship. We only own half the cargo. We don't pay the rest until the *Mustang* docks."

"Mr. Tanigaki, listen to me very carefully." Salat was the soul of reason. "We are not asking you for the $10 million. We are asking you to share in the $10 million. And we suggest $2.5 from the owners, $2.5 from you, same from the agents, Athena in New York, and the balance from the insurance company. My staff is talking to the others."

"*How am I supposed to verify all of this?*" yelled Tanigaki.

"Well," said Salat, "since the time is three o'clock yesterday afternoon in Houston, I'd start off by phoning Robert Heseltine if I were you. It's his ship and your oil. Then you can both put the squeeze on Athena in New York. Phone Livanos in Monte Carlo and make the shipping agents share. They can also take care of the insurance company."

"This is the most disgraceful telephone call I have ever received," said Mr. Tanigaki. "But give me the number of Texas Global Ships. Do they know what's happened?"

"By now, probably," said Salat.

"Do they realize I will be asking them to help pay a ransom? This is most embarrassing."

"I shouldn't worry about it if I were you," retorted Salat.

He terminated the call, mostly to stop himself from laughing.

▼

ADMIRAL WOLDE SIGNALLED for his prisoners to be escorted onto the private promenade deck, which ran around three sides of the bridge. When Abdul finally closed the door behind him, Ismael dialled the number of Texas Global Ships in Houston.

He was told that Robert Heseltine was not in that afternoon.

But Wolde had already rung off and was dialling the private line at the Heseltine home on the outskirts of the city. When the butler answered, the Somali admiral said, "Sir, I am calling from the bridge of Mr. Heseltine's *Global Mustang*. I have captured the ship, and in the next five minutes I will blow it up with everyone on board. Put Mr. Heseltine on the line immediately."

Forty-five seconds later, Robert J. Heseltine III was on the line. And he sounded furious. "Just exactly who is this?" he demanded. "And what's this bullshit you've been telling my staff?"

"My name is not important. But I am the commander of the Somali Marines. We have taken possession of your ship the *Global Mustang*. The purpose of my call is to settle a final figure on the ransom . . . "

"A final figure on *WHAT?*" bellowed the six-foot-five-inch, Texan shipowner.

"*Now you listen to me, boy,*" he snapped. "I don't take instructions from fucking pirates. I want to make that real clear. If I have to, I'll call the president of the United States, and we'll send in the goddamned navy, so you better quit even mentioning the word 'ransom.' *You hear me, boy?*"

"I hear you, sir," said Ismael softly. "The disturbing thing is, I don't think you hear me, Mr. Heseltine. And I want this to be very simple. So let me finish . . .

"My men have just placed a massive dynamite charge under each of the four domed holding tanks in the *Mustang*. Should we not reach agreement in the next few minutes, I will leave the ship and make my getaway in a very fast boat. From precisely one mile out, I intend to blast the *Mustang* out of existence with your entire crew on board."

"*I don't have any proof, you black bastard,*" yelled Heseltine. "You have any idea who you're talking to?"

"Sir," interrupted Ismael, "would you like to check my credentials with your captain, Jack Pitman? I'll put him on the line for two minutes only."

So far as the blustering but canny shipping boss was concerned, that was probably game, set, and match to the pirates. Christ! He had Jack captive.

"Hello, Bob," said the *Mustang*'s captain. "I'm afraid this is for real. This character nearly blew the door off the bridge with a heavy machine gun, and he says he'll blow up the goddamned ship. My advice is to listen to his terms. Everyone says the Somali pirates are usually reasonable. They just want to get paid and leave."

"Then there's no doubt in your mind he can do what he says he'll do?"

"No doubt whatsoever, Bob. There's apparently eleven in his gang, and they're holding everyone at gunpoint. We're in the middle of nowhere, way out in the Indian Ocean. There's no help in sight, and if he has set bombs under the holding tanks, there's not much we can do anyway."

"Thanks, Jack. Put that black bastard back on the line; let's hear what he has to say."

"Mr. Heseltine," said Admiral Wolde, "my price is $10 million. I'm suggesting you pay $2.5 million, and my colleague is negotiating with the president of Tokyo Electric Power for them to pay the same. My next call will be to the owner of Athena Shipping in New York; that's Mr. Livanos in Monte Carlo, and I will ask him for another $2.5 million."

"*What about the last installment?*" rasped Heseltine. "*Who pays that?*"

"I will suggest to Mr. Livanos that the insurance company pay it," replied Wolde. "Let's face it, this is a bargain for everyone. If or when I blow the ship, there will probably be 200 million dollars' worth of natural gas obliterated. The ship must have cost you something like 200 million . . . "

"*Three hundred, asshole!*" bellowed the Texan.

Wolde ignored him. "So my little price of $10 million, $2.5 each, is a bargain. Not a lot of money for your corporations. A fortune for my poor people, many of whom have nothing, not even anywhere to live or fresh water. My people die of malnutrition every day. Damn your ship and your oil. I'll blast it all to hell and never think of any of you again."

Heseltine knew he was being offered a bargain he could not refuse.

"I'll call you back on the captain's line inside fifteen minutes," he told the admiral.

"Make it ten," said Wolde. "I don't have much time, and you have even less."

Heseltine slammed down the phone. "*Black bastard!*" he confirmed. And then he dialled the cell phone of his friend Masaki Tanigaki, startling the electricity tycoon for the second time that early morning. Their conversation was brief.

▼

MEANWHILE, ISMAEL WOLDE called the private line of Constantine Livanos in Monaco. He opened the conversation with a breathtakingly insolent remark: "Mr. Livanos, we are old friends. And I am afraid I have just captured another one of your ships."

The Greek shipping magnate exploded: "Christ! Not you again! What have you done this time?"

"My men have captured the LNG tanker *Global Mustang*," he replied. "As you know, she is fully laden with liquid gas. My price is $10 million for her release. Otherwise I will blow her up. I have dynamite charges set under all four of the holding tanks."

Constantine did not need reminding that the ship would go up like an atom bomb if someone detonated those charges. But the prospect of paying out $10 million was a serious shaker. He had an enormous amount of money, but it wasn't even his ship, or his gas.

Wolde stepped in to prevent the Greek going into a total decline. "Don't worry, Constantine," he said, smiling at his audacity to use his first name. "I have already suggested to Mr. Heseltine in Houston that each of you pay $2.5 million—that's Texas Ships, Tokyo Electric Power, Athena, and the insurance company.

"Mr. Heseltine and Mr. Tanigaki are speaking right now. I suggest you talk to the insurers, who stand to lose more than anyone. They will certainly agree that $2.5 million is far better than a payout totalling hundreds of millions for the ship and the gas cargo."

"Not to mention stupendous claims for damages from the families of personnel who are killed in the blast," said Livanos. So far as he was concerned, the $2.5 million was beginning to sound like small change. Like Heseltine and Tanigaki, he was beginning to think this sweet-talking desperado from East Africa represented the very essence of rational argument.

Livanos was not involved in the heavy-hitting end of the financial conundrum, but Athena was in for perhaps a $20-million commission as shipping agent, sales agent, and loading agent. In a choice between blowing the vessel sky high and destroying the cargo, and cutting the commission to $17.5 million from the full $20 million, there was no discussion.

"I will speak to Bob Heseltine and then to the insurance broker in London," he said. "And I have the captain's phone number on the bridge. I will be back on the line very soon with our offer for the ship's freedom."

"No offers," replied the pirate. "It's $10 million. Or nothing. Fifteen minutes from now, the *Global Mustang* will not exist." Wolde hung up the phone.

Constantine Livanos called Nigel Pembroke, the Athena insurance broker, at his home in West London. News of the hijack both shocked and horrified him. The shipping market had been poor for his company in the past year, but this threatened to be one of the biggest maritime losses they had ever underwritten.

"Christ!" said Nigel. "That bloody pirate blows the *Mustang*, they'll ring the Lutine Bell for the first time since 9/11."

This was banter between two scions of long-established shipping and insurance families. And the bell to which Nigel referred was the ancient one-hundred-pound ship's bell from the French frigate *La Lutine*, which went down off the Dutch coast in 1793 with 150 million dollars' worth of cargo in gold and silver. The Lloyds brokers paid up.

The *Lutine*'s bell had been salvaged off the ship and had hung ever since in the Lloyds underwriting room at their London headquarters. Traditionally it was rung for breaking news—one stroke for bad, two for good. But in recent years, it was used mostly for ceremonial occasions.

It did, however, ring at the news of the 9/11 terrorist attack on the World Trade Center. And in Nigel Pembroke's opinion, it would be rung again when news of the *Mustang* broke. "Any way out of it?" he asked Livanos. "I mean, can this fucker be stopped?"

"Well," replied the Greek tycoon, "he wants $10 million for the release of the ship, its cargo, and its crew. But he's asked $2.5 million from both the owners and the purchasers of the cargo. He wants the same from us as the agents and suggests the same from you."

"Two and a half mill—what's that in real money?"

"About 1.6 million British pounds."

"One point six to get us off the hook for a half-billion dollars! Hell, Constantine, that doesn't want much looking at it, does it? I can tell you, we'll pay it and so will the others. I imagine you wouldn't have made this call, not if you'd thought any differently."

"Look, Nigel, this bastard sounded like he was going to blow up the ship in the next ten minutes. So I'd better get off the line and call someone back. It's Bob Heseltine's ship, so I guess he'll make the running."

▼

IN THE MEANTIME, back on board the *Mustang*, Admiral Wolde and two guards had marched Captain Pitman and First Officer Dominic Rayforth down to the bowels of the ship to assess his threat.

Wolde told them he would take them to the base of each of the holding domes so they could see the bundles of dynamite taped together and attached to an electronic timer. Just so that everyone understood the Royal Somali Marines were not joking.

Jack Pitman was totally astounded that these maniacs had somehow boarded his ship, right under the eyes of the lookouts and the rest of the crew, taken command of this gigantic floating edifice, in floodlit conditions, and then calmly placed explosives precisely where they wished.

There they were, tucked right against the steel casing of the domes. There was no doubt in Jack's mind: If the dynamite in just one of the bundles blew, it would park his ship in tiny pieces on the bottom of the Indian Ocean.

They walked back in single file, Pitman in the lead, a guard between him and Rayforth, followed by another guard and Wolde bringing up the rear, holding his AK-47 in firing position.

They took the elevator up to the bridge floor, through the shattered wooden door and back into the control room. As they entered, the phone was ringing and Heseltine was on the line, asking to speak once more to the captain. Wolde permitted this contact but listened in on a phone hookup.

Heseltine's question was basic: "Jack, have you actually seen the explosives this guy says are planted around the gas domes?"

"I have now. They just took me and First Officer Rayforth down to see their work. And it's genuine. A big bundle of dynamite under each one, wired up, battery-operated detonator with a remote control fixture. He says he could blow the ship to pieces in under five minutes from the moment he leaves. I believe him, Bob. And so should you."

"Have there been any casualties?"

"I cannot be certain. The entire crew is being held captive in the recreation room. But I have not been allowed a head count."

"Have you seen the assault crew? I mean, aside from the leader?"

"Yessir. I've seen about six of them. All armed. But there's more in the rec room. I saw them but not close-up."

"Okay, here's what I need. I have an agreement with Japan Electric. And Livanos called and left a message that he's willing to pay his $2.5 mill and so are the insurers. Put the leader on again. I need instructions for the payment method."

Wolde came on the line and said the $10 million must be paid in cash. "We require an aerial drop," he said, "preferably on the deck of this ship. I'm talking big mailbags roped together with a float device and a luminous marker that we can see."

"Okay," said Heseltine. "But this will take a few days. Not many banks have $10 million lying around in hundred-dollar bills."

"Then you'll have to fly it in from a bank that does. Since you represent three very large international corporations, it should not be beyond your capability."

"Okay, okay. We'll get it done somehow. Gimme a drop time."

"Since we now have a deal, I'm canceling my ten-minute threat and changing it to twenty-four hours. We work on Somali time, and on our coast it's now 2:00 a.m. That'll be 5:00 p.m. in Houston, correct?"

"You got the time right—as well as a lot of other things," said Heseltine. "Okay. You want the money dropped on the ship from an aircraft at 2:00 a.m. your time tomorrow?"

"Make that 1:45 a.m. I'll need two boats in the water, port and starboard, in case they miss the deck. If nothing's happened by 2:00 a.m., I will assume you have changed your mind. At that point, the Royal Somali Marines will leave the ship, and five minutes later my four bombs will detonate."

"Will my crew still be on board?" asked Heseltine.

"That will no longer be my concern," replied the admiral.

"How can you be sure the crew will not race for the bombs the minute you leave and deactivate them?"

"That will be an interesting race against time," said Wolde. "It took us twenty minutes to set them, not including travel time to the far end of the ship.

"By the time they get out of the locked recreation room, they'll have about four minutes to de-fuse. Impossible. Especially as we need only one to explode. I'd assume the *Mustang* will be destroyed if you don't make the drop."

Rarely had Robert Heseltine III felt such an overpowering sense of frustration. And the entire nightmare was heightened by the fact that the *Global Mustang* was his most treasured possession.

"Okay. You better give me the ship's GPS numbers. I assume she's stationary. Put the captain on again."

"Bob, where the hell are you? We need good numbers for the ransom drop."

"There's a problem with the GPS right now; a few wires got damaged when these guys blasted their way in."

"But right now we are 712 miles off the Somali coat, about three miles north of 2.00 North. We were on 60 East longitude about an hour before we were stopped, heading east. Guess we're at 60.10 East and stationary."

"Can you have the problem fixed for the rest of the journey?"

"Yes. We have a computer technician on board, all the way to Japan."

"Good boy, Jack. Hang in there. Put the fucking wild man back on."

"Mr. Heseltine," said Wolde, "I assume we have an agreement."

"We do. The money will be there at 1:45 a.m. your time tomorrow. God knows how but we'll get it delivered. And I need your assurance that the bombs will be disconnected the moment you receive it."

"You have that assurance. I'll send a disposal team to the base of all four domes at 1:30 a.m. If you check our record, you will find we have never reneged on an agreement. We are businessmen and we only want the money. Play your part, and the *Mustang* will be back in service."

▼

IT WAS 6:00 P.M. IN NEW YORK, and Jerry Jackson, president of Athena Shipping, was still on the phone to Constantine Livanos. Neither man was as concerned with this latest hijacking as they were when the VLCC *Queen Beatrix* was captured. Because that had been an Athena charter.

This latest outrage involved someone else's ship and someone else's cargo. Nonetheless, the Athena chief found himself in the middle of the ransom problem, trying to piece together the four components and organize them for the drop.

Constantine Livanos had arranged for the insurance money. Nigel Pembroke in London was wiring $2.5 million to the Athena account in New York the following morning. Heseltine was wiring the same amount to the same account in the next ten minutes.

Tanigaki would be wiring his $2.5 million in one hour when his bank opened. At which point Jerry Jackson would have the whole $10 million safely deposited—but 8,000 miles from the action. He'd heard about the ransom money for the *Queen Beatrix*, and he knew the transaction had been put together by Barclays Bank International via Nairobi.

Athena had always banked with JP Morgan and had no doubt that their friends there could organize the transfer of funds to Barclays. The problem was, he needed to have the cash bagged up and flown out to the ship.

And while he thought the bagging would not be a difficulty, he had not the slightest idea how to get hold of an aircraft with a sufficiently long range to make the flight. Or where the money should originate. There were Barclays locations everywhere, but Jerry was not keen on doing business in Africa.

There was a large, illuminated map of the Middle East in the Athena operations room, and Jerry stood staring at it, looking for a friendly port of call. He wrote off Africa, south of the Blue Nile. And north as well, for that matter.

He wanted somewhere relatively close, which more or less ruled out Europe, and after some study he decided the answer was the hugely wealthy United Arab Emirates. In particular he liked the trading port of Dubai, where Athena conducted a lot of business.

For Jerry, Dubai had significant advantages. Barclays Bank sponsored the important Dubai International Tennis Championship. So Jerry knew for certain that they must have a major banking operation in the ruling Maktoum family's glittering city. He also knew they had a substantial air force, and Jerry understood the cash to the *Mustang* would need to be flown out in a military aircraft. The bizarre prospect of a bunch of air stewardesses trying to heave 10 million bucks out of an aircraft door flying over a gas tanker was out of the question.

This was, in all but name, a military operation. The cash needed to be dropped by people who knew precisely what they were doing. Jerry sent an e-mail to his clients in Dubai, the biggest seaport in the Middle East, asking for urgent help. He knew it was probably three o'clock in the morning in the emirates and did not expect a reply right away.

But he got one. The night duty officer in Dubai's global seaport corporation, DP World, was at his post and sensed that the tone of the e-mail bordered on desperation. He immediately picked up the phone and called Jerry Jackson in New York.

The two men talked for ten minutes, and the night officer promised to call the sheikh in four hours when he would be awake and inform him of the problem. Meanwhile, he would insure that the air force had a Hercules on standby to make the drop that evening.

Jerry called Athena's bankers on the night-line for major international clients, and ten minutes later an officer from Barclays International called back. They could arrange for a cash sum of 10 million dollars to be available at Barclays' downtown branch on Dubai's Sheikh Zayed Road any time after 3:00 p.m.

Jerry called back the seaport officer who was in touch with the UAE Air Force. He assured the Athena boss that an air marshal, a senior member of the Maktoum family, would stand guard at the bank while the cash was prepared. And then supervise its transfer to the Dubai International Airport and the loading on to the aircraft.

The Hercules, crewed by two air force colonels and their staff, would fly south across the Rub' al-Khali, the vast "Empty Quarter" of the Arabian Peninsula. They would cross the Gulf of Aden and land at the US base in Djibouti to refuel. The aircraft would then set off on its eight-hundred-mile journey to the *Mustang* with full tanks.

The plan was to leave at 11:00 p.m. and arrive in the drop zone a little more than two hours later. The officer added that he very much doubted there would be any charge for the operation since he was perfectly certain Sheikh Mohammed bin Rashid al-Maktoum and his brother Hamdan would wish to extend the hand of friendship to help rescue this enormous American cargo ship in its hour of need.

Jerry Jackson had not informed any of the US security agencies about the kidnap of the *Global Mustang*. As the agent, he did not feel that Athena should step in and start handing out information. That should be the responsibility of the ship's owner, Bob Heseltine.

He called the Texan back and was quite surprised to learn that Heseltine had already contacted his Houston buddy General Hack Ryecart in the Pentagon and informed him of what was going on.

According to Bob, General Ryecart had gone to see the chief of naval operations and gained an assurance that at least one US warship would be deployed to the area around the *Mustang*, mostly to insure that the crew was protected.

There was, however, the massive problem of the bombs placed under the gas tanks. The US Navy felt completely powerless under these circumstances. Certainly they could not attack the ship or the pirates. The most they could do would be to sail out to the datum and park there, glowering at the group of savages, try to keep them in line, and make sure they evacuated the ship the instant the cash was dropped.

One of the warships, probably the destroyer *Chaffee*, would let them know that if the *Mustang* went up in flames, there was absolutely no possibility that any of the Somali pirates would get out alive. All three of their boats would be sunk by US Navy guns.

Peter Kilimo, with a couple of colleagues, was working late in the Athena operations center. He had picked up on some of Jerry Jackson's conversations. And to say his blood had run cold would have been an understatement. Peter's blood was around the same temperature as the gas tanks on the *Mustang*: −160°C.

He knew what he'd done; knew how he'd betrayed the precise course and position of the LNG carrier; and he understood that he'd done it knowingly, fully aware of the likely effect his actions would have on his own firm. Peter was not proud of this activity.

The ransom would run into the millions, and Athena would obviously have to share some of the enormous cost. And all to give him, Peter, an extra $20,000 this month. He tried to rationalize it but couldn't. He felt an entirely new chill of stark and awful dread when he heard Jerry Jackson yell to a secretary to connect him to the CIA.

At that point, the boss walked over and closed his office door. Moments later, Jerry was connected to the chief of the investigation, the senior of the two CIA men who had visited him a couple of weeks ago.

The agent had not yet heard about the *Mustang*; in fact, he did not think anyone at Langley had yet been informed that a major American cargo ship was being held by Somali pirates with the crew still on board and obviously in very grave danger.

"I guess it will come out sooner or later," said Jerry.

"It will come out tonight," said the government agent. "By the way, is there a complete record of its sailing and docking in your office?"

"Hell, yes," replied Jerry. "We're the agents, shipping, sales, and loading . . . the *Mustang*'s complete details are all in here. The owner's an old and trusted customer of ours."

"And how about that old and trusted employee of yours, Peter Kilimo?" he said. "Would he have been party to this information?"

"Of course."

"Well, that really narrows it down. Because someone told the Somali pirates exactly where to find that ship. And if it wasn't you, it must have been him. He's part of it. Jerry, you got a pirate on your staff."

# CHAPTER 10

▼

B OB BIRMINGHAM, DEEP IN THE CIA OFFICES IN LANGLEY, could not believe what he was hearing. It was as if he were addressing someone who did not speak a word of English.

He hung up the telephone and asked someone to connect him to the chairman of the Joint Chiefs, General Zack Lancaster. He then informed the most senior serving officer in the United States armed forces that a gang of Somali pirates had captured a fully laden American-owned LNG tanker bound for Tokyo and was holding the ship and its crew hostage for $10 million.

"Worse yet," said Bob, "she's sailing under an American flag, crewed by senior American officers. Even worse, the ship's owners have agreed to pay the money."

Like Bob, General Lancaster could not believe it either. "Any idea why they agreed to pay so quickly?" he asked.

"The pirates have placed loaded dynamite charges under each one of the four holding tanks. Apparently they took the captain down to see them—big bombs, all on a remote control."

"Lousy timing from our point of view. Delta Platoon's only about three days away from deployment to Djibouti."

"Could they go early?"

"Well, I suppose they could rush out there. But then what? If the pirate bombs are correctly placed, that ship is the touch of a goddamned button away from extinction."

"Kinda ties your hands," replied the CIA director.

"Sure does. If your enemy is ruthless enough. We assume their leader means what he says?"

"Zack, these guys boarded a huge ship, climbed up the hull on ropes and grapplers, took the entire crew prisoner, set their four bombs, blew the door off the control room with a heavy machine gun, and then phoned the three principal executives at their homes asking for 10 million bucks."

"Bobby, that sounds to me a lot like guys who mean precisely what they say."

"I thought so. Right now I'm still gathering data. I've got a lot of people on it. Can I suggest a meeting at your place in, say, a couple of hours? We better call in Ramshawe and Mark Bradfield, right? Even if we are powerless to do anything."

"I'll get people assembled. But Jesus," said the general, "it's just so goddamned frustrating."

"I'll bring the case officer, Karl Ryland. He's been investigating the information leaks from the shipping companies. Right now he's our best source."

▼

TWO HOURS LATER, a small group of the most exasperated men in Washington assembled in the chairman's private conference room on the second floor of the Pentagon. General Zack Lancaster looked several degrees more exasperated than the rest of them put together.

"I've said it before, and I'm darned certain to say it again," he began, "but this pirate bullshit has to stop. Somebody has to do something."

"In this latest case," said Bob Birmingham, "we are slightly hampered by the fact that the friggin' pirates have placed four enormous dynamite charges under each of the holding tanks in the LNG carrier."

"It seems to me," said the general, "that we have also lost our major card: that we do not negotiate with terrorists. When we paid up for the *Beatrix*, we sent a signal that if push comes to shove, we will negotiate like every other sonofabitch. I know we were all aware of it, and I know we did it reluctantly, but we still did it. And when something like this latest bullshit happens, you can't help thinking that we should have let that first ship go. Because now they think they have us by the shorts."

Bob Birmingham asked how far advanced the Delta Platoon was, and Admiral Mark Bradfield told him that so far as he knew they were three days from deployment to Djibouti. But, he added, it would hardly matter if they were already there. Since the ship was dynamited, and the US did not have a warship within several hundred miles of the datum, there was little they could do.

"Anyone makes a move, I guess they'll just blow the damn thing," said the general. "What a goddamned mess this is."

"It's the wrong ship, at the wrong time," said Mark Bradfield. "They've chosen a vessel that will go up like an atom bomb, and they've done it within days of our being ready to attack."

Bob Birmingham then introduced Karl Ryland, who had been working on the US end ever since the *Queen Beatrix* had been seized.

"Gentlemen," said Karl, "it will not have escaped you that these tribesmen from the least civilized nation in Africa show up with uncanny accuracy, hundreds of miles from shore in the middle of nowhere and immediately start calling the private numbers of the ship's owners.

"And that's not all," he went on. "For the second time in a month, the pirate chief went straight through to the private line of Constantine Livanos in Monte Carlo. And here's the kicker: Livanos had changed his phone number after the *Queen Beatrix*, and this pirate guy had the new one! Sonofabitch was only three weeks old."

"This is unbelievable," said Admiral Bradfield.

"Only, sir," said Ryland, "if you have difficulty with the obvious fact that these Somali villains have some kind of a network here in the US. Now I know the same guy filled them in about the *Beatrix* and the *Mustang*. Because the same shipping corporation, Athena, was involved with both of them.

"But the *Niagara Falls* was betrayed right here in Washington, DC—almost certainly by a guy from USAID over there in the Reagan Building."

"Can we arrest them?" asked General Lancaster hopefully.

"Not yet. I've located one of them. But he's a very clever character. There is not one trace of a single phone call or e-mail from him to anyone in East Africa."

"Probably a go-between somewhere, and it could be anywhere," said Bob.

"I guess so," replied Ryland. "But I have been in close contact with Jerry Jackson, the president of Athena Shipping. He's the right-hand man to the Livanos family, and he's been heavily involved with these latest negotiations.

"Do you know that this pirate spoke to Heseltine, Tanigaki, and Livanos and suggested they each pay $2.5 million and that Athena, as the agents, should persuade the insurers, Lloyds of London, to pay the same, making a round total of $10 million? And that's what they're going to do."

"Well, the only American ship they took in three years was the one where the SEALs shot the pirates dead," said General Lancaster. "And now, thanks to our new policy of paying them what they ask, they've hit three in a few weeks—that's if you count the *Niagara Falls*, the tanker under charter to a New York shipping corporation. I guess we can look forward to more of the same."

"There's one thing we do have to accept," said Admiral Bradfield. "There are certain circumstances that make it impossible to do anything. And this is one of them.

"The only fast way out to the *Mustang* is in a fixed-wing aircraft, and since we have no warship anywhere near her, the guys couldn't get in. Not with the ship dynamited. Even now, there's no point going out to her. You need the two prongs of your attack to dovetail—the cruising warship and the Delta guys out there fast.

"That way you got a chance. But even then you need two helicopters, one big and one fast gunship. You can't fly them out there. It's too far. You gotta get them out there on the flight deck of a warship. And then you gotta get the guys out there in a major hurry. And if for any reason an air attack is not feasible, you gotta have fast rigid-deck inflatables ready to go. I'm telling you, we need all the luck and organization in the world to hit these Somalis."

"Tell you what," said General Lancaster, "when we do catch up with them, and we do hit them, I want them to stay hit, okay?"

"Roger that, boss," said Mark Bradfield. "But if we're going to take this seriously, I need to have some powerful hardware out there. Mack Bedford and his team will smash up any pirate attack, but we have to get them out there, and the distances are vast."

"Right at this minute, there is no greater priority," said Zack Lancaster. "Because these fucking maniacs are inflicting not only defeat and financial pain; they're also inflicting a worldwide humiliation on us.

"How many fourth-rate banana republics do you think are out there laughing their balls off at us? The almighty Uncle Sam being given the goddamned runaround by a bunch of tribesmen."

"Not to mention the Russians and the Chinese," said Simon Andre. "And I personally find that especially irritating. We're making a few disapproving noises toward the Chinese and their aggressive moves all over Africa. And now they can smile at us with shit-eating grins."

"Listen," Mark Bradfield said, "do you guys want me to station four warships out there, maybe a cruiser, coupla destroyers, and a frigate? Because there's no other way to do it. Mack Bedford and his guys must have a platform—both to land and then to launch their attack."

"I don't see a way around it," said General Lancaster. "If we want to stop this crap, we need to put some real muscle behind it. Otherwise it's going to drag on for months. I understand this *Global Mustang* bullshit is obviously impossible since the shipping guys are going to pay up right away. Anyone know how?"

"Yessir," said Karl Ryland. "This pirate has persuaded Heseltine, the owner, and Tokyo Electric Power to get the cash to Athena's bank, JP Morgan, in New York. That's a transaction they are both well accustomed to making.

"The Athena owner, Livanos, has told the insurance company in London that if they don't come up with their $2.5 million share, it will probably cost them several hundred million dollars if the pirates blow up the *Mustang*. Anyway they're all agreed."

"How're they moving the cash?" asked the general.

"Through the Arab Emirates. Barclays Bank is consolidating the money in Dubai. Then it's being flown out by the UAE Air Force, straight down to our base in Djibouti to refuel, then straight out to the ship for an ocean drop. They'll be trying to put it right on the deck. It's military all the way."

"What are the overheads?" asked Zack Lancaster. "Is Dubai asking an arm and a leg for their help?"

"Quite the contrary," replied Karl Ryland. "Sheikh Mohammed has been very generous, apparently charging nothing for the services of his Air Force. Says he's glad to help a US tanker at this time. Gesture of friendship."

"Okay, I guess that just leaves us to wait for the next attack and to trust we have Mack Bedford's platoon on station by the time it happens."

The general stood up and fiddled with the controls of the illuminated world map on the opposite wall. He zoomed in on the

Indian Ocean and then zoomed in some more on the area between longitudes 56 and 66, from one degree latitude south of the equator to five north. "It looks as if the main pirate gangs, the big-ship guys, have settled on a new ops area," he said. "Right inside this square."

"They've moved offshore alright," said Mark Bradfield. "Probably because they know ships are less suspicious of attack way out there. But also because it's hard to get assistance. That European mercy fleet, or whatever the hell it's called, has proven more or less useless, mostly because it's always in the wrong place."

"So," said the general, "if we're going to make a serious impact, we need warships patrolling inside that square. It's 360 miles by 736 miles. What's that? 265,000 square miles. I guess that sounds like a lot. But you can look at it another way. North/south we can have a ship every seventy miles, and lengthwise we can have them each 140 miles apart, forming a diagonal across the datum."

Mark Bradfield, a former surface-ship commanding officer, had been following the general's numbers on a writing pad in front of him, translating the words into a picture. He now had a rectangle longer than its height. And across the middle he drew a diagonal line of four small crosses, the four US warships.

"The fact is, sir," he mused, "if an atrocity occurred at the farthest point from our nearest ship, there would still be a maximum of only three hundred miles to steam. These things make a comfortable 30 knots through the water, so the most it could take us to get on station would be less than nine hours."

"Right!" said the general triumphantly. "They hit after dark at 2100 hours, and we're on the scene before dawn a little after 0530, with Mack and his boys flying out for the drop. That's beautiful. Four warships it is, Mark. Get 'em out there, with the helos, right in that little box with the crosses."

"Let's get these bastards," he added. "Let's show them who they're really dealing with."

▼

FOR THE FIRST TIME for several months, the office of the CNO looked like the engine room of a nation at war. Somehow the words of General Zack Lancaster had added a new dimension to America's view of piracy on the high seas, and it was a battlefield mentality. Anyone within thirty yards of Admiral Mark Bradfield's suite of offices on the fourth floor of the Pentagon could sense the urgency in the air.

There were navy personnel coming and going. Phones were ringing, computers humming, lights flashing, and staff calling out data. The lines to the Norfolk yards were open. Lt. Com. Jay Souchak was trying to locate the 10,000-ton guided missile cruiser *Port Royal*.

This was normally a ten-minute task. But Admiral Bradfield wanted to know right away. So far as Jay could tell, the warship should have cleared the Malacca Straits, running north, and ought to be fifty miles southwest of the Nicobar Islands.

But "should have" and "ought to be" were not acceptable. The *Port Royal* was probably 1,400 miles from Diego Garcia, and Admiral Bradfield wanted to know precisely when she was expected to dock. Before the evening was over, the admiral would organize the deployment of four ships: the *Port Royal*; the guided missile destroyer *Chafee*; a second destroyer, USS *Momsen*; and the Harpoon missile frigate *Reuben James*.

All four of them would head directly to the US Navy base at Diego Garcia for resupplying and then head out in convoy to the 265,000-square-mile stretch of ocean where the next Somali pirate attack was expected to occur. Lt. Com. Jay Souchak also needed to check for helicopters and their availability.

So far as he knew, the four selected ships were already equipped with helos. But Admiral Bradfield wanted to insure that the *Port Royal* could carry a Sikorsky CH-53D Sea Stallion. If not, he'd have to start thinking aircraft carrier. And that put his back to the wall time-wise because the US Navy did not have a flattop within striking range of Diego Garcia, and it would take three days for the *Harry S. Truman* to get there from the South China Sea.

Also, a Nimitz-class carrier was a very hefty piece of gear to deploy against a group of pirates. But the chairman of the Joint Chiefs himself had decreed that this was a priority, and if the CNO had to move a carrier to help clear up the problem, then that carrier would swiftly be on its way.

There was no doubt in Jay Souchak's mind that there were unusual forces at work. The pure frustration of the apparently unsolvable pirate problem was profoundly irritating the best minds in the US Navy. This latest seizing of an unarmed ship, the *Global Mustang*, had injected anger, short tempers, and an element of overkill into the equation.

It was as if everyone understood that the US was wielding a sledgehammer to crack a nut. But that's how it was. And these goddamned tribesmen from East Africa were about to be severely slammed by the sledgehammer of the United States Navy—Special Forces, aircraft carriers, destroyers, missiles, and whatever the hell else it might take, to quote General Lancaster. It was, in a sense, a formal announcement that Uncle Sam was done with this piracy bullshit, so hang on to your hats.

Meanwhile millions of dollars were flying not only through the banking ether but also in the face of every instinct the US military possessed. On Fifth Avenue in New York, preparations were being completed to pay off these goddamned hooligans. And from Zack Lancaster down, no one in the Pentagon approved of the system.

Because there was only one surefire method . . . *NEVER pay off these bastards because they will come straight out and do it again. They have to be stopped, slammed, and obliterated. That way no one's in any doubt about the consequences of attacking the United States or its allies or its possessions. That's anything or anyone operating under the American flag.*

▼

THE $10 MILLION REQUIRED to free Captain Pitman's ship was, thanks to the miracle of interbank wire transfers, safely in the ground-floor vault of Building Six, Barclays of Dubai, at the downtown end of Sheikh Zayed Road.

Five tellers were counting, stacking, and packing the $100 bills into ten heavy-duty mailbags. The UAE Air Force would strap them together and fit the huge package with four luminous flares, which would fire on impact with water should the drop from the aircraft miss the deck of the *Mustang*. Sheikh Mohammed's air force personnel would also take care of the flotation device, which would prevent the bags from sinking.

At 6:00 p.m. (local), the bank was closed, but waiting for the mailbags outside was a Dubai military truck and six armed guards, ready to deliver the money to the airport.

At 6:15 the guards lifted the bags into the truck and drove out to Dubai International. Its $10 million cargo was swiftly loaded and the Hercules took off, flying southwest, deep into the Arabian Desert toward the burning sands of the Rub' al-Khali.

It was a long, 1,200-mile haul down to Djibouti, across the widest part of the Arabian Peninsula, and then over the southern mountains of Yemen to the narrow waterway where the Red Sea flows into the Gulf of Aden. Djibouti lies right on the coast, and the Hercules touched down at 10:00 p.m.

The Americans were waiting to refuel her, and two members of the catering staff were at the end of the runway, together with the tanker, to serve Sheikh Mohammed's pilots and crew hot coffee and sweet pastries. On the return journey they would land here again, probably close to 2:30 a.m. and spend the rest of the night at the US Navy base before flying home across the Empty Quarter.

The Hercules took off on the last leg of her journey to the *Global Mustang* at 11:00 p.m. She hurtled down the sand-swept runway into a cool southwest wind directly off the Ethiopian highlands and then banked hard around to the southeast, climbing toward the Somali coastline, and out over the dark waters of the Indian Ocean.

By midnight they were at the halfway point, having covered almost four hundred miles over the ocean.

▼

ON BOARD THE *Global Mustang*, Admiral Wolde was in conference with the captain. Abdul Mesfin was still wielding the heavy machine gun, and there were lookouts posted on the promenade deck that almost surrounded the bridge.

Elmi Ahmed was in command of the imprisoned crew, and he had them divided between the dining area and the recreation room. They had been permitted to return to their regular sleeping quarters immediately after dinner. Somali guards patrolled every area, and the ship was still more or less stationary.

Captain Hassan had the *Mombassa* running slowly about three hundred yards off the *Mustang*'s port beam, and Abadula Sofian was back in his skiff, while the veteran Somali army sergeant Ibrahim Yacin had the helm of the second skiff. Both were making their way to different sides of the *Mustang* in readiness for the drop, just in case it missed the deck and tumbled into the ocean.

As the time ticked slowly past midnight, the tensions grew. Ismael Wolde appeared on the high walkway above the stern and peered through his Russian night-glasses up into the dark, moon-lit sky, searching for the navigation lights of an incoming military aircraft.

Back on the bridge, after he returned, Wolde said to the captain, "Perhaps they have let you down, sir. Perhaps they're not coming. Perhaps they are prepared to sacrifice this ship and its crew, trying to discourage us from this kind of naval conquest."

It was as if he thought threatening the captain would somehow push the shipowners to greater efforts, even though they could not hear his words.

But Jack Pitman, who privately believed the phrase "naval conquest" was a bit extravagant, just grunted. "They're coming, admiral. Keep watching. Those men do not want a loss on this scale. They like profits, not catastrophe. They'll be here."

Wolde was by now very tired. He and his men had been aboard the *Mustang* for more than twenty-four hours. Sleep was impossible for the dozen men involved in holding the ship captive, especially as a well-lit US warship had just appeared over the horizon and was steaming slowly toward them.

Wolde was confident that the four bombs under the gas tanks would preclude any kind of aggressive action from the Americans. But he was aware of the warning he had been given: If anything went wrong with the operation, none of the Somalis would get out alive.

He understood the benefit of having a dozen men with Kalashnikovs holding an unarmed crew captive, but the approaching US destroyer could probably start and end World War III all on its own. Wolde needed everything to go smoothly, and he prayed silently for the aircraft bearing the readies to show up ASAP.

Another half hour went by, and there was a sudden yell from one of the lookouts: "*Aircraft approaching from the west, about seven miles out. It's losing height—STAND BY!*"

Admiral Wolde rushed out of the door to see for himself. He raised his glasses, spotted the lights, and knew in that moment that the $10 million ransom was about to be paid. He picked up his cell phone and called Elmi Ahmed, telling his missile director and explosives chief to start making his way down to the floor of the tanker to disconnect the bombs.

The moment the cash was in Wolde's hands, the bombs would be disarmed, packed up, and removed. Captain Hassan would bring the *Mombassa* in close, and the pirates would scramble down the rope ladders and pile into the skiffs.

The journey home would be in the nature of a stampede because this was the point where they were most vulnerable. The ship would no longer be at their mercy, and worse yet, there was a 10,000-ton US destroyer watching them make off with an enormous amount of blackmail money. They understood full well that the warship could put them all on the bottom of the Indian Ocean.

The answer was speed—the speed of the getaway, roaring away into the night, reaching *Mombassa*'s maximum of 20 knots. Of course the destroyer could, if it wished, cut them down and sink them. But Wolde was counting on the fact that a deal was a deal. The shipowners were about to fulfill their side of the bargain, and he did not believe they wanted any more strife.

Ismael Wolde instructed Captain Pitman to turn the deck lights on, until the entire forward area, three hundred yards down to the bow, was floodlit. As he did so, the Arab air force pilot and co-pilot in the Hercules, howling through the night sky, suddenly spotted their drop target, about six miles up ahead, gleaming golden on the dark water.

The captain decided to make the drop from a stern approach, the mailbags and the floater set to fall from the dispatch ramp. They were making a little less than 200 knots and losing height fast. In not much short of a powered dive, the pilot came down to 200 feet, then 150 above sea level.

With a minute and three miles left, he levelled out, and the navigator checked the GPS numbers. They had a direct bead on the *Mustang* and would run straight down the length of the deck, about fifty feet above the domes. Everything was *GO!* And with Admiral Wolde standing outside the bridge watching the approach, the Hercules came roaring overhead right above him.

Ismael watched someone jettison the mailbags, which blew out sideways into the slipstream, then tumbled down, hitting the top of Dome Three and then sliding down the right-hand side, landing on the starboard-deck loading manifold.

By any standards it was a supremely accurate drop. And two of

Wolde's men were already racing down the deck to grab the bags and haul them back to the stern area. At this time, the crew was incarcerated in the recreation room, locked and bolted. Only the captain was on the bridge with Wolde, who was on the line to Elmi Ahmed, telling him to stand by to disarm the bombs.

Without a word, the admiral left the bridge and raced to the elevator, which one of his guards had waiting for him. Down on the stern deck, Wolde and three of his men opened and inspected the delivery. They had no time to count, but they were becoming accustomed to the size and weight of a million bucks packed into a single mailbag.

"*DISARM THE BOMBS!*" yelled Wolde into his cell phone. "*ELMI! WE'RE LEAVING . . . LET'S GO, EVERYONE!*"

He hit the buttons on his cell phone and immediately told Captain Hassan to close in to one hundred yards. The Somali Marines were evacuating the ship, down the ladders and into the skiffs. It was the ex–Puntland fisherman's task to mastermind the loading of the little fleet and to have the helmsmen right on station, ferrying the cash and the assault troops back to the *Mombassa* with all speed. They'd dump the grapplers and ropes in the skiffs and they'd drop the rope ladders down from the tanker's rails, but the last one they would have to leave behind.

Already the pirates were up and over, climbing down to the boats, the first four men somehow hanging on to the mailbags and heaving them into the first skiff, which Ibrahim Yacin held steady, and then raced out to Captain Hassan who hauled the pirates' bounty aboard.

Admiral Wolde stood right next to the rope ladders supervising the getaway, his machine gun in the firing position. Deep in the cellar of the tanker, Elmi Ahmed, working with two guards, was already disarming the second bomb. He wasted no time unfastening the electric connections—cutting the critical wires with garden shears.

The moment the bomb was made safe, they pushed forward to the base of the next dome and repeated the operation. The plan was to render each bomb harmless and then, on the return journey, gather up the electronics and the stacks of dynamite, moving everything back to the stern end for the evacuation. Wolde's men never left behind anything that could be used again. And right now, flushed with their biggest triumph ever, no one was in any mood to retire anytime soon.

Elmi worked fast, clipping and separating, urging his guards to stay alert and to treat the components of the bombs with unwavering respect. They were in a lethal environment. Out to port there was a deadly US warship that could renege and come after them at any moment. The slightest mistake in this operation could cause a catastrophe.

Even the mildest explosion down in the gloom could blow millions of gallons of the world's most combustible cargo to high heaven. And with every clip of the garden shears, the bargaining tool that had thus far kept them safe was diminished.

When the fourth bomb had finally been dismantled, they began the return journey, jogging through these vast steel caverns, scooping up the high explosives, cramming the electronic detonating parts into a large rucksack. They left the area the way they'd entered, via the steel staircase up to the starboard side of the main deck.

Further astern they could see Wolde, waving at them, beckoning them to get moving, lower their bomb bags over the side into the skiffs, and get on board themselves. There was desperation in the air. The dark glowering shape of the US warship was inching closer and closer. Ismael Wolde knew with all of his considerable brain that they had to get the hell out of here, as fast as anything he had ever done.

The pirates scrambled over the rail, slipping, grabbing, and clambering down the ladders and into the skiffs. It was plain that the crew was still locked in the rec room, still fearful of Wolde's last threat: *Anyone even thinks of coming through that door, I'll personally blow his head off.*

Sofian and Yacin were jockeying for position, revving their engines, trying to get the evacuation complete in just one more journey to the *Mombassa*. But there was just too much gear, with the bombs, the rifles, the ladders, and grappling irons. Also no one felt much like trampling over tightly stacked sticks of dynamite.

Sofian eased away from the *Global Mustang*'s hull and called out, "I'll be back!" which was just as well because Elmi and Ismael were still up on deck, working by the rope ladders, lowering the heavy machine gun and ammunition belts down to the remaining skiff. Yacin grabbed it and immediately took off. By now Sofian was back, and he grabbed Elmi's waist, hauling him off the ladder and into the boat. They both grabbed Wolde and the skiff took off, back to the *Mombassa*.

For the moment, they didn't bother to attach the davit lines to the skiffs. They just unloaded the cargo and lashed them to the stern of the ex–fishing boat, and Hassan opened the throttle. They roared off into the night, towing the skiffs, standing on the deck, and watching the US warship close in on the *Global Mustang*.

Ismael Wolde, ever the admiral in his own mind, shook hands formally with every member of his crew and with Captain Hassan.

"Thank you, gentlemen," he said, quietly. "Nicely done." And beside him, as he spoke, was the dark pile of mailbags.

The night was hot, and Wolde sipped a glass of iced coffee before taking out his cell phone and sending a text message to Mohammed Salat, who was wide awake with the rest of the town.

Wolde transmitted: *10 million safely delivered. No casualties. Coming home. Long live the Somali Marines!*

▼

IN THE DARK OF THE INDIAN OCEAN NIGHT, the *Mombassa* vanished. She carried no running lights and roared away into the endless blackness during the small hours of Tuesday morning.

The crew of the US guided missile destroyer *Chafee* watched her leave and immediately dispatched their helicopter bearing the executive officer, Lieutenant Commander Revson, and four naval guards to the *Mustang*.

By the time they landed on board the tanker, several of Captain Jack Pitman's senior command team had made their way down from the bridge and released the *Mustang*'s crew from the recreation room. The visiting US Navy XO assumed a loose command and ordered an immediate roll call, during which it became apparent that two Panamanian orderlies and the ship's engineering officer, Sam McLean, from Brockton, Massachusetts, were missing.

No one had seen them since the pirates had boarded the tanker late on Sunday night. But three people remembered hearing two short bursts of gunfire just as the Somali assault team were climbing the rails. It seemed obvious that the missing men had been killed and thrown overboard.

Lieutenant Commander Revson ordered everyone to take part in searching the ship, but he did not expect the three men to be found. He was right. There were no traces. The Panamanians and Sam McLean were gone, and First Officer Dominic Rayforth was tasked with informing the next of kin.

Captain Jack Pitman warned that nothing be made public without first consulting the Pentagon, and XO Revson agreed. Indeed, he and the commander of *Chafee* were under strict orders to conduct a personnel news blackout until further notice. All of the oceangoing executives understood the strong opposition of the American security forces against revealing that another huge ransom had been paid out to the East African outlaws.

And so, the lines of communication were opened very carefully, first to the office of the chief of Naval Operations, Admiral

Mark Bradfield, and then to the office of General Lancaster. The first part of the message was simple: The *Global Mustang* had been freed to continue her journey to Japan.

The second part was cringe-making: An enormous ransom had been paid to the Somali pirates. The third part was absolutely diabolical: $10 million had been paid to a group of gangsters who had murdered the ship's chief engineering officer.

There was no way the lid could be kept on that piece of information. Murder tends to be a public business. Nothing can prevent the news from leaking out, and if the authorities are hesitant and the truth comes from a grieving family member, the media is inclined to scream foul—implying a cover-up or a screw-up. Either way everyone looks bad—which is why it's always better to move fast and release the truth immediately.

The *Global Mustang* was freed in the middle of the western end of the Indian Ocean near 3:00 a.m. in the morning, 6:00 p.m. on the East Coast of the United States. The Department of Defense's press office needed first to inform the CIA, the FBI, the National Security Agency, and then SPECWARCOM in Coronado. Two hours later, they issued a general release, angling the announcement to the role played by the US Navy and the close proximity of the destroyer USS *Chafee* and playing down the ransom payment, the amount of cash involved, and how the money had been delivered.

The Pentagon's public relations writers understood that the following morning's newspapers would have a completely different tone. But they'd done their best to play it down and keep the incident low-key—only one American death, the ransom shared, and the sheer impossibility of negotiating in the face of four bombs, which would have blown the ship to high heaven.

Nonetheless everyone was prepared for an uproar when the news finally hit the airwaves. And their preparation was well founded. The media went straight for the murder of the ship's engineering officer. Never mind the gigantic sums of money and the ship's vast and valuable cargo. It was the death of a Massachusetts-based US citizen that overshadowed all.

The television news stations jumped on the murder story, sending reporters from their Boston offices to the leafy suburb of Brockton, Massachusetts, to 1472 Honeypot Drive, where a heartbroken Cassie McLean and her two young sons were under siege in their own home, stunned by the death of a beloved husband and father.

By the time the 10:00 p.m. bulletins aired, the media had fastened on its themes for the night: (1) This was the second US ship to be hijacked for ransom in a very few weeks; and (2) It was the first time the Somali pirates had killed an unarmed merchant seaman. The death of Sam McLean was not comparable to that of Charlie Wyatt in the US aid ship *Niagara Falls* because that had occurred during a full-blown gunfight in which the American captain Fred Corcoran had indisputably opened fire first.

The death of Sam McLean, however, had changed everything. The black Robin Hoods of the Indian Ocean were a lot blacker now, prepared to shoot down unarmed men in cold blood, their only motive being money. Ruthless, tribal, armed robbers killing Americans was not acceptable to the general public. Fanned by the media, the mood had become plain: The Somali killers had to be stopped. And what precisely were the government and the military planning to do about it?

On that very first day there were newspaper editorials criticizing the US Navy. And they were mostly written by journalists who knew nothing of the procedures required to retake a captured ship that had been turned into an "armed enemy stronghold."

The DOD press office did its best to hit back. Admiral Hudson, a former carrier battle group commanding officer, was brought in to elaborate on the difficulties of retaking a captured vessel when the brigands were heavily armed and there were hostages and explosives in the hands of desperadoes who would stop at nothing.

With great care Admiral Hudson pointed out the lethal nature of the propane gas cargo. He pointed out the necessity for an attack platform from which US Special Forces could work—a warship in close proximity, from which assault boats or helicopters can be launched. Guided missiles were of course out of the question because just one of them might have blown the *Mustang* to smithereens.

"There's only two ways to board and retake a captured ship," insisted the admiral, "one, from the sea, and two, from the air. If the pirates are guarding the ship with even light machine guns, we could expect to lose perhaps half of our force just trying to climb aboard.

"Bringing a helicopter to within thirty feet of the deck in order to get the guys in is fraught with peril in the face of sustained fire from a heavy Russian machine gun, which the pirates did have. And they always have rocket grenades, which are capable of knocking a helicopter straight out of the sky."

For excitement, none of this compared even remotely with: SENATORS TO QUESTION US NAVY BRASS ON 'CRASS FAILURE TO ACT' IN THE FACE OF THE ENEMY. Never mind that the nearest US warship, the *Chaffee*, steaming at flank speed, was almost a day away from the datum when the initial assault on the *Mustang* had taken place.

The one thing the Pentagon chiefs could not be seen to do was indulge in arguments with journalists. They had issued an answer for their conduct, and there was a ton of information, mostly involving the Delta Platoon, which would not be released under any circumstances.

Even the press release had done considerable damage, alerting the entire East African coastline to the achievement of the Somali Marines. Every hostile pirate crew in the area now knew there was a fishing boat stacked to the gunwales with $100 bills, and even if they could not attack and grab it, they could sure as hell copy it and make their own assault on the next big tanker that came steaming through their turbulent waters.

But when there's been a murder, there needs to be an official announcement. The press release was unavoidable, but that did not stop Admiral Mark Bradfield and General Lancaster from being absolutely hopping mad about the way the military was being portrayed in the media.

The issue was and always had been speed, the US Navy's ability to steam out to the problem and tackle it with a level of ruthlessness that would make any pirate's eyes water.

In Commander Bedford they had the right man for that. But even he could not easily solve the problem of the speed required to establish an attack platform hundreds of miles from anywhere and then crash into battle, guns blazing.

There was nothing the navy could do to prevent commercial corporations from paying off the pirates in order to reclaim their property. But when the right time came, the Pentagon understood that it would need to hit as hard and fast as anything it had ever done.

General Lancaster crashed his fist down on his enormous desk and snapped, "Mark, do you get the feeling everyone is against us? The public, the media, the pirates, the shipowners, insurers?"

"Well, they are," said the admiral. "All they want is peace and quiet. And their profits restored. They're not emotionally geared up for a battle or for the bloodshed and death that goes with it."

"No," added Zack Lancaster. "And they do not know or care that by paying off these bandits, it will just continue on and on until world trade in that area grinds to a standstill, and a lot of people end up getting killed."

"Not to mention that the media will want to close down the powerless US Navy."

"I wonder if poor Mack Bedford realizes the level of responsibility he has right now," said General Lancaster. "Because right now he's just about our last hope. We need a victory, and we need a big one. How soon does Delta Platoon leave for the Middle East?"

▼

COMMANDER BEDFORD'S pack-down was a major deployment of troops and supplies. The SEALs never travel light, and for this they travelled heavy. When any US Special Forces platoon moves its operational base to a foreign country, they take everything with them. When they leave, it's as if they have left forever.

Aside from each man's gear, which includes clothes, uniforms, training gear, wetsuits, flippers, personal weapons, camouflage cream, battle harness, and sundry boots and jackets, the SEALs load every conceivable requirement on board the aircraft. They travel as if they were setting up camp in a desert, bereft of everything.

Each man carried his own light machine gun and combat knife. But they loaded the heavy machine guns, boxes and boxes of ammunition, and separate boxes for the magazines that went with their 9-millimeter Sig Sauer automatic pistols. Of course there could be equipment for them at the other end of the journey, but they assumed nothing. Which meant they loaded two dozen grappling irons with long, knotted ropes in case they needed to scale the hull of a ship.

That was only two fewer than second battalion rangers used to fight their way up to the heights of Pointe du Hoc on D-Day. But the SEALs, in common with Great Britain's SAS, leave nothing to chance.

There were boxes of welder's gloves in case the whole platoon needed to fast-rope from a helo down to the deck of a captured ship. It was likely that any US Navy assault helo carrying SEALs into combat would be amply supplied with heavy ropes for the landing. But it was not certain. And that meant Delta Platoon took their own. Just in case.

They loaded cases of hand grenades, RPGs, missiles that could be fired from handheld launchers. They also loaded long-range sniper rifles, binoculars, long-range night-glasses, boxes of GPS systems, compasses, charts, rulers, pens and pencils, callipers, and laptop computers.

They took dynamite, det cord, detonators, four boxes of electrical wiring, batteries, and sundry electronics. Not to mention screwdrivers, pliers, tape, and fuses. They loaded tents, camouflaged sleeping bags, and about a half ton of medical supplies, especially Ibuprofen, bandages, morphine, and malaria and dysentery tablets. Wherever SEALs were deployed, they assumed it was a Third World tropical swamp, and they could not afford to get sick.

The four SEAL medics, who were part of the assault team, also packed supplies for battlefield operations in case any of the guys got seriously hurt, and time was running out. These included canisters of oxygen and anesthetics, plus supplies for blood transfusions, the vials of blood corresponding to each man's blood type.

The US Navy, perhaps above all other fighting forces in the world, understands that if you send a man into the gravest possible danger, you owe him every chance of help that you can provide.

It was 2030 hours in San Diego when the aircraft was finally loaded. The SEALs were driven back to Coronado for dinner. After that, they sat around and watched television, and, typical on the eve of a deployment, nerves were beginning to tighten.

Even PO2 Barney Wilkes, the wisecracking Tar Heel from the salt marshes of North Carolina, was quiet. Chief Cody Sharp from North Dakota was subdued. He'd been officially appointed Commander Bedford's personal bodyguard. But there was something unusual about this mission, whenever it started. Every one of these seasoned veterans of Baghdad and Afghanistan knew they would end up attacking a ship, which had been commandeered by heavily armed pirates.

The chances of getting hit by gunfire during the mission were high in Cody's opinion. All they could do was obey their combat rules, remember their training, and trust in the iron-clad reputation of their near-legendary commanding officer.

At three minutes after midnight, Commander Mackenzie Bedford himself walked into the SEAL team's recreation room and said sharply, "Okay, guys. This is it. We're going."

▼

CAPTAIN HASSAN RAN the *Mombassa* hard through the night, heading due west, with eleven hundred fathoms below the keel. He kept two watchkeepers on duty at all times, and they used their Russian night-glasses to check the sweep of the radar. The *Mombassa* carried no running lights.

News that a heavy ransom had been paid to free the *Global Mustang* had been transmitted worldwide. In the opinion of Ismael Wolde, there were probably a half dozen pirate ships out there searching for them, anxious to bully their way into a piece of the action.

No one, of course, in his right mind would dream of taking on the Somali Marines, not if he had any idea how heavily armed and skilled the warriors were on board the *Mombassa*. And the twenty men who had a better idea than most were lying dead on the ocean floor, close to the blasted *Somali Star*.

One of the night duty guards was Elmi Ahmed. He sat in the cockpit with Captain Hassan, his two loaded grenade launchers resting three feet from his right hand. If the boss called, "Action stations!" Elmi was approximately twelve seconds from depositing any intruder on the ocean floor. Unsurprisingly, he never missed with that launcher, which was, like all of their gear, state-of-the-art.

By dawn, still running at flank speed, they were eighty miles from the last known position of the *Global Mustang* and her warship escort. The engines were humming sweetly, and Captain Hassan had posted ETA Haradheere at 6:00 p.m. the following day, which meant another thirty-six hours of hard running.

They had plenty of fuel but were light on food. The roast goat had almost run out before they hit the *Mustang*, and they were down to a couple of large cans of ham and some moderately stale flatbread. They had plenty of fruit juice, but in the general panic to get clear of the tanker, no one had thought to raid the heavily stocked galley and storeroom.

Fortunately the cans of ham were industrial size, and Omar Ali Farah, who would have been the cook had there been a stove, estimated there was sufficient meat for four sandwiches for each man on the return journey.

Hungry pirates are inclined to sulk, something to do with risking your life and still feeling like a pauper despite 10 million bucks lying on the floor. Everyone was sitting around on deck midway through the burning hot afternoon wishing there was a spare ham sandwich and paying not the slightest attention to anything except their boredom.

However they all snapped to it when the captain suddenly shouted: *GIVE ME SOME POSIDENT—THAT SHIP OUT THERE 'BOUT SIX MILES OFF OUR STARBOARD BOW!*

Hands fumbled for the glasses and keen eyes focused on a sizeable fishing boat way out on the horizon—

*She's a dragger . . .*

*Twice the size of the* Mombassa *. . .*

*Coming toward but she's not as fast as we are . . .*

*She might be—can't tell if she's running hard or just cruising . . .*

Ismael Wolde spoke next. "Men," he said, "with this cash cargo on board, we cannot take any chances. Can't let that ship anywhere near us. She's not official, is she? Coast guard or Indian Navy?"

"No sign of that," called Hassan. "She's not even flying a flag and she's dark green in color. If she was official she'd be grey with national markings all over the place."

"Well, whatever she is, she just changed course as if she wants to cross our bow. But she may not be fast enough. I'm not seeing an increase in her speed." Abadula Sofian, a former Haradheere fisherman, loved the maritime aspect of his pirate job. And instantly he called again, "She's raising some kind of a flag—can't see what it is, but it's white on black."

"Looks like she's closing but not gaining," said Hassan. "ELMI! Stand by. The rest of you go to *ACTION STATIONS!*"

"You want me to sink her?" asked the missile director.

"I do," replied Captain Hassan.

"So do I," added Wolde. "And be darn quick about it."

"I can hit her twice at one hundred yards," replied Elmi.

"Don't miss," said Ismael. "Let's slow down a bit to let her catch up."

"Don't let her get one inch closer than that hundred yards," yelled the captain. "Because she might have missiles as well. I don't want to get sunk."

Elmi Ahmed carried his two launchers out from the cockpit and set up two of his four tripods on the starboard side. He screwed the launchers on and studied the range finders, focusing on the oncoming fishing boat, which was now two miles away off their starboard quarter and gaining.

These were ultramodern launchers, complete with telescopic crosshairs. Elmi, who had fought for the Somali government in the backstreets of Mogadishu with primitive, twenty-five-year-old RPGs, would find it almost impossible to miss with them.

So far as he was concerned this was a case of "fire and forget."

"Who's giving the order?" he shouted.

"No one," answered Wolde. "It's up to you. Fire at will."

Elmi stood up and stared at the fishing boat as it came speeding in toward them, making around 15 knots. There was little more than a half mile between them, and the boat was not slowing. It looked as if she might ram them.

Elmi went back to his launch and stared once more through the range finder. He could see his quarry clearly, especially the four armed men on the foredeck. Seconds passed and then Elmi rammed back the launch trigger and the missile screamed out of the tube, a fiery tail behind it, which soon turned white.

Carefully, he moved to the second launcher, focused, and fired. As he did so, the first missile flashed across the foredeck of the oncoming boat and blasted straight through the cockpit window, obliterating the glass. It almost blew the upper works clean off the deck.

Instantly the ship's operations structure burst into flames, which enveloped the entire working deck. And into this maelstrom of fire ripped Elmi's second RPG, detonating much nearer the waterline with a force that very nearly cleaved the ship in two.

She began to sink. Ahmed could see men burning alive on the deck, but only two of them. The rest of the crew could not possibly have survived a blast of such magnitude, and within moments, the ship had turned turtle, and with a huge hiss and giant plume of steam, she was gone. No one would ever know for sure what she had wanted with the *Mombassa*. But Ismael Wolde and his men were able to hazard a pretty good guess.

With evening closing in, everyone was extremely tired, and Wolde changed their night duties to two-hour watches instead of four. Captain Hassan had an old ship's clock, which was rarely wound, but the pirate admiral went below to retrieve it and prepare it for a night's work like everyone else.

Throughout the long evening homeward and then through the blackest of rain-swept nights, the clock tolled out the bells of the watch, four quick strikes and then eight for the changes. It was a kind of ghostly requiem for the forty-three men who had perished during the course of the $10 million mission against the giant LNG carrier.

# CHAPTER 11

▼

R EAR ADMIRAL ANDREW MACPHERSON CARLOW, C-IN-C
SPECWARCOM, was born with the distant thunder of navy
guns echoing through his soul. His father, Tom Carlow, was a retired US Navy admiral, and his grandfather, Admiral James Carlow,
fought the entire span of World War II on board the greatest of all
US warships, the 30,000-ton carrier *Enterprise*.

Of course, Navy SEALs fight on land and sea, and in Andy's case
this was possible because of his mother's side of the family. Miranda
Stuart Carlow, as svelte and beautiful at the age of seventy as any
woman could hope to be, was a direct descendant of the swash-
buckling Confederate major general Jeb Stuart, the cavalry commander who fought shoulder to shoulder with Stonewall in the
valley.

Andrew was brought up listening to his grandfather's tales of
the Second World War. And he never tired of hearing James Carlow's account of the Battle of Midway, when the *Enterprise* and
*Yorktown* sent their dive bombers lancing down out of the sun like
a silver waterfall blasting the decks of the Japanese carriers, sending
four of the ships that had devastated Pearl Harbor to the bottom
of the Pacific Ocean.

Lieutenant Commander Carlow, who had been a landing signals officer at the battle, had never had a better audience, and
young Andy, fists clenched with excitement, would sit enraptured
at the feet of his grandpa. Even then he could hear the shouts and
commands of the LSOs as they desperately tried to get the shot-up

US aircraft back on the flight deck: *Too low . . . nose too high . . . lie up too far left . . . rate of descent off the mark . . . power control erratic!*

At the age of eleven, Andy Carlow understood the hammer-locked relationship between the fliers and the officers who fought to bring home their aircraft—sometimes shot or malfunctioning, sometimes in the dark, sometimes in a big sea that caused the carrier to lurch upward on the rise of the wave, multiplying the danger a thousand times.

Never had landing officers represented such a stark delineation between life and death as in those terrible hours at Midway, when the embattled US pilots came screaming in to home base, out of the fire and carnage, with the Pacific war hanging in the balance.

James Carlow made it all the way up the ladder to vice admiral. His son, Tom, fell short by family standards, retiring as a rear admiral during the years when his own son, Andy, was commanding a SEAL platoon with Mack Bedford in the backstreets of Baghdad.

Whichever way you looked at it, Tom Carlow had groomed Andy for a career in dark blue, insisting he attend the United States Naval Academy at Annapolis and uttering no objection when the young officer demanded to become a SEAL, just as soon as he completed his first tour of duty on a surface ship.

They were all from Virginia, and indeed Admiral Tom and Admiral James both concluded their naval careers at the navy's Norfolk HQ. Family reunions always took place in Virginia, nowhere near the ocean. The Carlows traditionally gathered in the picturesque Blue Ridge Mountains at a white colonial mansion, Laurel Heights, owned for almost two hundred years by the family of Admiral Tom's wife, Miranda Stuart Carlow.

Miranda Carlow had inherited the house after the death of her father when Andy was five. Years later, when Admiral Tom retired from the navy, they turned away from the sea for the first time since they were married and retired to the mountains.

Andy and his wife visited when they could but his SPECWAR-COM command had, for the past three years, kept him tightly anchored in Coronado. He could remember no other family home, and his own room, set to the rear of the house, had a spectacular view of the Blue Ridge Mountains sweeping away to the north.

In the late afternoon of southern Virginia's mild winters, the endless stretch of the softly shaped peaks were swathed in lilac-blue mist and shadow. And you had to be on station at the precise right time to catch it. Then, and only then, could you understand firsthand how the mountains had acquired their name. The blue haze that hangs in the air is sufficiently thick for the sun to play games with it—sometimes turning it a fiery aquamarine and then, at sunset, turning the sapphire peaks to deep purple.

There is no great height to the Blue Ridge range, mostly only a couple of thousand feet above sea level. But its alma mater, the 2,000-mile long Appalachian chain of mountains, is a billion years old and its ancient peaks are long and rounded. Down in southern Virginia they seem to stretch forever, triumphant in their old age, protected by a thick and generous cloak of misty-blue trees.

Inside the house, there were large portraits of the still revered Confederate generals with whom Jeb Stuart had fought. Stuart's portrait dominated the vast entrance hall and was flanked by another oil painting depicting one of the South's most fearless and brilliant battlefield commanders, Lt. Gen. Ambrose Powell Hill, another Virginian, cut down by sniper fire when Petersburg fell on April 2, 1865.

"Remember, Andy," said his father, "great victories are invariably born in the mind of the general. And remember always, whenever you go into combat, the blood of General Jeb Stuart runs through your veins."

Andy Carlow loved his father and admired him above all other men. And when, at the age of twenty-four, he finally lined up on the grinder to receive his SEAL Trident, his mind was locked onto the admiral who pinned it upon his chest. But he could see his father, Admiral Tom Carlow, who sat watching in a seat of honor. And he clearly heard the words of the SEAL base commander, who told him quietly, "Well done, Andrew. Always remember you must earn this every day of your life."

Despite Miranda's love of the Virginian mountains, she allowed her occasionally irascible husband one major triumph every year. She agreed to accompany him on a vacation cruise so that once more he could hear the slash of the bow wave down the ship's hull, listen to the boom of the ship's horn, and stare out over the ocean through his sea-blue eyes.

Whenever he stood on a ship, even a cruise ship, his bearing was still upright and his white hair framed his permanent deepwater tan. Tom Carlow looked as if he ought to be in command of any ship he boarded. All year long, he would look forward to his cruise, and sometimes on a moonlit tropical night, he would leave their stateroom and walk outside, where he would lean on the rail and listen to the sounds of the ocean.

▼

LIEUTENANT COMMANDER BEDFORD and the Delta Platoon drove out to the North Island Naval Air Station in the middle of San Diego Bay and boarded the giant turbo-prop C-130 Hercules at 0045. This great leviathan of the skies is a purpose-built warehouse, the workhorse of the US armed forces. It's like travelling in an echoing steel cave, noisy as all hell with not enough seats, and catering facilities that would certainly have been rejected by the San Diego Zoo.

Many of the SEALs, vastly experienced at this level of discomfort, rigged up hammocks and crashed out among the crates and packing cases. The rest settled into seats made of rough netting. There were a lot of head sets, a lot of iPods, and a stupendous amount of smart-ass remarks.

They flew east across southern California, Arizona, and New Mexico before heading slightly north toward the East Coast almost 3,000 miles away. They landed in the sprawling Norfolk Navy base a little after 0700 and disembarked. While the aircraft refuelled, they were grateful for a ride down to the chow hall where an excellent breakfast had been prepared for them.

By 0900 the Hercules was on its way back down the runway for the transatlantic flight to Germany. They took off into a stiff south-wester, banked left over the other major US Navy SEAL training grounds at Virginia Beach, and headed northeast over the ocean for 4,000 miles to the base at Landstuhl, fifty-five miles southwest of Frankfurt.

It was nighttime when they landed in Germany, six hours ahead of Norfolk. Once more they were grateful for a hearty supper laid out for them, and once more they could feel the ripples of curiosity at their presence. The entire base seemed aware that this was a major SEAL operation; the guys were "going in."

Refuelled, they took off at 0100 (local) and headed southeast, the new navy pilot gunning the giant aircraft across the Alps and straight down the Adriatic Sea past Italy and Greece to the Mediter-ranean. From there they swerved high above Egypt and headed all the way down the Red Sea to Djibouti.

The 2,400-mile journey from Landstuhl took them seven hours and the sleeping SEALs touched down on the desert runway at 10:00 a.m. There were six trucks, two military buses, and a large staff car to meet them. They'd been travelling for twenty-five hours. The temperature beyond the enormous hull of the Hercules was 100°F without a breath of wind.

The commanding officer of the base came out to greet them, and he and Mack Bedford rode back together, finalizing arrange-ments for their potentially lengthy stay. Right now the lives of the Delta Platoon were irrevocably bound up with those of Admiral Wolde, Mohammed Salat, Elmi Ahmed, and the rest.

If the Somali Marines made a major move, the Delta Platoon would be right there with them. If the Somalis stayed home and did nothing, Commander Bedford's men might get bored, parked in the sweltering North African desert with nothing to do except train and hone their standards of fitness.

The base commander, General Jeremy Offiah, known locally as "Chariots," had no such doubts. "Those friggin' pirates are on a roll," he told Mack. "No chance they'll retire. I'd give it three days max, and they'll be out there again. Right now they have a license to print money. Everyone's paying them because no one's worked out a better way to get their goddamned ships back."

He added that he had an aircraft on standby, fuelled and ready to fly the SEALs out to the ops area at a half-hour's notice. "Tomorrow morning we'll get the loading guys out there and start transferring the gear out of that Hercules and into the barracks.

"Phase two will be for each man to separate his own equipment for the mission, and we'll load that onto the ops aircraft, along with the heavy weapons and the rest of the explosives and ammunition you guys need. I'm flying that direct to Diego Garcia. USS *Chafee* is waiting there, and the CO has been instructed to set up a complete SEAL base on board, ready for when you arrive."

"Beautiful," said Mack. "It's kind of amazing what this navy can do when someone gets mad enough. I'm planning to recapture whatever ship they grab, and when we've freed it, I'm switching our attack immediately to their land headquarters, which I intend to destroy."

"That's fighting talk, sailor," grinned the general.

"Guess so," replied Mack. "You don't think we just flew close to 10,000 miles to fuck it up, do you?"

▼

THE GRATITUDE OF MOHAMMED SALAT was reflected in the size of Peter Kilimo's secret bank account in Westchester County. The

Pirate King of Somalia had sent $40,000 by wire transfer the day after the *Global Mustang*'s connections had paid the enormous ransom. Without Peter, there would have been no mission, and Mohammed Salat, like some tribal godfather, loved having friends. But more than that, he liked keeping them.

Peter was thrilled by his reward. But he had smashed the laptop computer, and he had vowed never to provide further information, not with the CIA investigators burning with suspicion.

If the payment had been the normal $20,000, he would have stared it down and stuck to his personal vow, ending his involvement. But $40,000! And tucked right up near the forefront of his memory, Peter Kilimo had a major piece of information. Information that had been in his possession for four months. And Peter never forgot nor mislaid anything in the shipping world.

It involved the Athena president, Jerry Jackson, and Jerry was in hot and heavy with the CIA guys. Essentially this potential project was absolutely fraught with danger. And it was driving Peter nuts.

Not on its own account. It was the thought of another $40,000— just for sending an itinerary to Salat. Who could resist that? Not Peter.

The issue didn't really have anything to do with Athena, but Jerry Jackson had asked Peter to help him organize a winter cruise for his sister Janice and her husband. Jerry had asked him because Peter Kilimo's contacts were as widely spread as his own, and he was capable of getting a great deal on a good ship with a reliable company.

He had done so, to the letter, calling in a favor from a well-respected US cruise company called Southern Islander, which was based in New Orleans but had a big operation in the Indian Ocean, cruising to Madagascar, the Seychelles, and the Maldives. They owned jetties in Mombassa and Kenya and made Kilindini Port their headquarters in East Africa.

Peter negotiated a half-price tariff for a first-class fare, a beautiful cabin on the starboard side of the Riviera Deck. The ship was the elderly but superbly refurbished *Ocean Princess*. He knew the date and time of departure and the date and time of every port of call from Zanzibar up to the Seychelles and then the Maldives. Jerry had requested that Peter tune in to this itinerary because he wanted to keep a distant but close eye on his little sister whose overbearing husband he detested.

The *Ocean Princess* was certainly a fitting place for the Athena president's relations. Refitted to a near-perfect degree, she was a white-painted, air-conditioned masterpiece in teak, brass, and polished mahogany, with deep-pile carpets, antique clocks, tables, and chandeliers. Her brand-new turbines were warship-standard, and she ran with massive stabilizers. The *Princess* possessed the elegance of a nineteenth-century New York Yacht Club committee boat and, in a big sea, the punching power of an Arleigh Burke destroyer.

She ran under an American flag and carried only two hundred passengers, eighty less than in her former life when, for many years, she cruised the Mediterranean. She had only 102 cabins on three decks, and her American officers commanded a crew of 140, most of whom were Vietnamese or Filipino. The *Princess* displaced 5,800 tons and measured 360 feet overall. She was almost fifty feet wide and drew 170 feet. Her cruising speed was approximately 16 knots.

Expensive cruise liners have become rare in the western Indian Ocean principally because of the pirate threat. The large operators have been frightened off by the threat of boarding, capture, and ransom by ruthless Somali brigands.

But the problem is the number of ships that sail under a flag of convenience, like Panama, Liberia, or the Bahamas. The pirates would rather go for them than a ship flying a Russian or an American flag, because those nations have made it clear that they will attack the pirates if given even half a chance.

The board of directors that controlled Southern Islander, however, decided to keep running throughout the northern hemisphere's winter months. It had cost a vast amount of money to refurbish their Indian Ocean flagship, and she had become a major moneymaker. Passengers loved her, and many of them came back for another cruise.

The *Ocean Princess* had a big reputation in an industry where brand loyalty is traditionally hard to acquire. And she flew the American flag, which gave her some sort of immunity, considering the regular proximity of US warships.

And while reluctant to run any further north than the main Maldives archipelago, the masters of the *Ocean Princess* were more than happy to run the ship at a very substantial profit a few hundred miles off the coast of Somalia.

She was not in significant danger because she was owned by a private corporation and her itinerary was never published. There were often groups of VIPs on board who appreciated anonymity and, as a consequence, hardly anyone knew where the *Ocean Princess* was or where she was going.

Peter Kilimo, however, knew precisely where she was and precisely where she was going. That evening, after he finished work on Fifth Avenue, he took a cab to an Internet café he knew west of Broadway, and there he utilized, for the last time, the e-mail address of Mohammed Salat. His communiqué read:

Chairman Salat: The 5,800-ton cruise ship *Ocean Princess*, American flag out of Mombassa, with 200 embarked passengers, will run west-east dead center through the One and a Half Degree Channel south of the Haddumati Atoll in the Maldives between 0230 and 0430 on Monday morning, the 22nd of this month. ETA Male, Maldives, 1700 same day. GPS checkpoint in the channel: 1.5N 73.20E. Speed: 16 knots cruising (approx). Her owners are Southern Islander

(New Orleans). Phone 504-661-2000. Chairman Brad Hyland: 504-761-9916 (home); New York: 212-555-6300.

No more was expected of Peter Kilimo. Just accurate numbers fixing the course and forthcoming position of the ship. And the contact. He deleted the message from the café's computer screen, picked up his briefcase, and left, making his way back to Grand Central Station for the train home.

On the other side of the world it was 0100 in the morning. The Somali Marines had landed at around 7:00 p.m. the previous evening and there had been great rejoicing on the beach when the *Mombassa* came home bearing the $10 million ransom.

Ismael Wolde and Elmi Ahmed were carried shoulder high across the sand and then driven with an armed escort into the village, where both they and Captain Hassan dined at the home of Mohammed Salat. The pirates were extremely tired but the feeling of pure exhilaration kept them running the rest of the evening on adrenalin alone.

Salat had arranged long trestle tables and a grand feast for all of the pirates in the courtyard of the garrison, and there was champagne and red wine for everyone—wives, girlfriends, and anyone claiming a relationship to the heroes of the hour. During the evening, the village elders and officials called to pay their respects, and Mohammed handed out special cash bonuses to all of the heroes who had captured the *Global Mustang*.

The assault crew received an extra $5,000 each, Hassan and Ahmed were given an extra $8,000, and Wolde was given an envelope that contained $12,000. Down the road at the stock exchange, shares in the mission were worth $100 and settlement day was tomorrow, when cash certificates would be issued to all investors—locals who had put up the original $10 bonds to finance the mission.

There were at least twenty people in Haradheere who had purchased five hundred shares and they saw their money multiply ten-fold. Wolde's total reward, when the 10 percent cut for the crew had been divided up, came to $110,000.

Mohammed Salat's personal wealth increased by at least $2 million. But he was the brains, he had organized the intelligence, and he had backed the mission with hard cash, provided the equipment and the firepower, without which the operation may well have floundered. No one begrudged Mr. Salat one dollar of his earnings. It was the biggest payout in the history of the Haradheere Stock Exchange.

The weary warriors of "Mission Mustang" had retired to bed. Only the new guards were wide awake on the ramparts of the garrison. But Salat, ever the 24/7 chief executive, elected to take one final look at his e-mail for the evening. All communications from Europe and the East Coast of the United States came in late, and tonight there was only one.

It was unsigned but Mohammed knew who had sent it—the contact who'd been given a $40,000 reward for the *Mustang*, a man who needed to be continually nurtured. And here he was again, transmitting priceless information about a rich cruise ship that would be sailing into the range of the Somali Marines in the very near future.

▼

ADMIRAL TOM CARLOW and Miranda were about as far away, metaphorically, from the high and windy, late-autumn slopes of the Blue Ridge Mountains as it was possible to be and still remain on planet earth. Tom was at sea level, sipping a local version of Planter's Punch, the ice-cold, fruity and spicy rum cocktail beloved by the colonial rulers in the former British East Africa.

Miranda was slightly below sea level, swimming in the warm Indian Ocean, forty yards off glorious Shanzu Beach, twenty miles from Mombassa. A five-day break at the luxurious Serena Beach

Hotel, shaded by coconut palms in an exotic corner of the Swahili coastline, was everything their travel agent had promised.

They were not scheduled to join the *Ocean Princess* for another couple of days. Tom was looking forward to the cruise, steaming south to Zanzibar and then east to the Seychelles for a few days before heading northeast to the Maldives, inadvertently cutting the corner of a vast square of naval operations as designated by the CNO in Washington.

The admiral did not, of course, know this, only that this vast and ancient ocean was 13,000 feet deep all the way to the Maldives and that the remote One and a Half Degree Channel was a place where nothing could be seen on the surface for miles and miles.

He'd been through there before, as a US Navy gunnery officer, but he remembered little beyond its vast expanse. Except that once the navigation officer, in the destroyer in which Tom served, had told him there was a "goddamned sandbank" in the middle of that channel, which rose up from the ocean floor to a depth of only six fathoms.

To understand the romance of that piece of navigational minutiae, it helps to have been a serving admiral. And Admiral Tom Carlow had enough of that in his soul to have come completely equipped for the journey, almost as if he were commanding the *Ocean Princess*. In his luggage, he had a photocopy of the original charts of that Maldive channel drawn by the British captain Robert Moresby, the first man to chart the region back in the 1830s.

His work was so exemplary that the charts were in regular use until the 1990s, when the first satellite improvements were made. But many captains still would not go through the rough, treacherous waters south of the Haddumati Atoll without copies of Moresby's originals in the chart drawer. If the master of the *Princess* had been in any way remiss, Admiral Tom Carlow would whip him sharply into line—much as he had been treating lower ranks for most of his working life.

The other eccentricity Tom maintained from his days as a combat sailor was using his old seaman's leather duffel bag, a battered dark-blue navy hold-all that still bore the faint golden insignia of the embattled destroyer USS *Maddox*.

Hidden deep in the dark recesses of the bag was a small pouch in which Tom had always kept a vial of cyanide pills, in case of capture and torture by the Vietcong. He never went on a cruise without the bag, but the vial of pills was long gone—replaced by his cell phone and GPS unit.

Sipping a cocktail beside the pool in the late-afternoon sun, Tom Carlow had his life under control. Miranda, looking at least twenty-five years younger than her seventy summers, was walking elegantly toward him. The only aspect of the vacation of which he would not have approved had been put in place without his knowledge.

A discreet phone call had been made from Lt. Com. Jay Souchak in the Pentagon informing the president of Southern Islander that they had a VIP on board the *Princess* and that the chairman of the Joint Chiefs would consider it a personal favor if the parents of the SEAL C-in-C, Admiral Andrew Carlow, were treated like royalty. Nothing less.

▼

MOHAMMED SALAT checked his computerized charts before retiring. He pulled up the pages on the *Ocean Princess* and noted her size and height from the water at the stern end. He estimated that she was a little taller than the *Global Mustang* but still well within the range of Ismael Wolde's grappling hooks.

This was plainly a ship for which someone would pay a great deal of money to free from the clutches of pirates. Salat checked the rates for cabins, staterooms, and suites. The first thing that struck him was the absence of any inexpensive fares.

This was first-class all the way. There would be no one on board who was worried about the next hot meal. In fact the rates for the top cabins, those on the Promenade Deck both port and starboard, were more than $1,000 per day. The cost of the Presidential Suite on the upper deck would have refurbished the entire road system of Haradheere.

Salat's assault teams had never hit a passenger ship. His antennae told him that it might be the way to ruin—attracting the firepower and anger of the whole maritime world, especially if someone was hurt or killed.

Mohammed always stressed to his commandoes that killing people was a very bad idea. "You can get away with darn near anything," he told them, "except murder. Because that makes people very mad at you."

Thus it was that the Somali Marines had never killed anyone, until the gunfight on board the *Niagara Falls*, which had not been their fault. And then the three men on the *Mustang* who had unwittingly shown up when the pirates were climbing in, trapped on ropes down the ship's hull, their most vulnerable point.

Aside from those unfortunate incidents, there had been no killing in more than twenty-five operations launched from the Haradheere base. Mohammed was proud of that. It was part of a CEO's job to issue the warnings, identify the potential problems, and avoid trouble wherever possible.

The only other serious warning he had tried to follow was to avoid American ships because of the natural arrogance and power of their armed services. Salat believed that the men in the Pentagon were capable of the most vicious reprisals against the pirates. If there was any way to hit another nation's ships instead, that would always be his plan. Dutch, British, French, Spanish, Japanese, Greek—all fine but not Russian and definitely not American.

The trouble was, so far as Mohammed was concerned, his information out of New York and Washington was so outstanding that he had little choice these days. Kilimo provided impeccable data: times, dates, positions, and speeds. Pirate attacks were safer when conducted far out to sea, and the precise quality of Kilimo's work consistently made it safer and easier to hit an American ship than waste time roaring around the ocean, burning fuel, and looking for poorly charted Dutch or Greek vessels.

Salat stared at the image of the *Ocean Princess*. She was not a freighter, and she would have many, many more crew, hopefully none of them armed. Of course most of the two hundred passengers would be asleep, but nonetheless, a gunfight on this ship might result in the deaths of dozens of people, and the owners were American. If this went wrong, it would probably be the end of the Somali Marines.

And yet . . . the *Ocean Princess* had to be extremely vulnerable, almost certainly without armed guards for the very reason Mohammed had just outlined. No one could afford a gunfight with the marines.

From the charts, it seemed to Mohammed that this channel was hundreds of miles from nowhere. He didn't even know whether US warships ever went through there. Certainly he had no such record. The warships were always farther west. So here it was, a totally vulnerable passenger ship, miles from anywhere, almost certainly unarmed with a couple of hundred wealthy people on board, some of them perhaps hugely important.

Salat reached for his calculator. At first he worked on a per-head system. What would one of these wealthy families pay to get their loved ones back—perhaps $100,000? How much would the shipowners come up with to get this beautiful moneymaker back—$5 million? And how much would the insurers pay to avoid a massive payout if someone were hurt—$3 million?

The numbers looked good to him. They looked very good. And Ismael Wolde's men had been so successful lately, they were so confident; it would be a shame to miss such an opportunity.

He guessed there would be a lot of valuable trinkets on board the ship: jewelry, gold, precious stones, watches, not to mention cash. Could be a tremendous haul. And the same rules still applied: You can steal to your heart's content. What you cannot do is shoot people.

Mohammed Salat went to bed very happy, reminding himself to wire $20,000 to Peter Kilimo's Westchester bank account, win, lose, or draw, with a $30,000 bonus to come if the mission was accomplished. As usual, he made the transfer by e-mail from his account in Nairobi.

▼

BART MEINHOFF was his real name, East German by birth and a member of perhaps the most feared secret police organization in old Europe, the Stasi. He was one of the most naturally suspicious policemen in the free world, which he was damned lucky to be in. Meinhoff had been "turned" just in time by one of the CIA's top operators behind the iron curtain, the present director at Langley, Bob Birmingham.

Bart Meinhoff made it to the West with about six months to spare, but not before he had smashed the lives of countless East German families suspected of disloyalty to the Soviet regime. Fifteen times he had personally discovered individuals with wives and children trying to make a break for freedom over the Berlin Wall. And fifteen times, instead of having them arrested, he let them proceed. He saw to it that every last one of them was shot dead by the guards as they struggled across the narrow, floodlit no-man's-land between East and West.

When he was finally called into Langley, two months after President Reagan's iron will had removed the hated concrete barrier across the city, Bart had betrayed every single one of his former colleagues to the CIA, supplying their names and addresses, their crimes against humanity.

He was a man with scarcely a friend in the world. Bob Birmingham loathed Meinhoff for everything that he was, but he recognized his value and considered he was forcing the ex-Stasi man to pay penance for his evil on behalf of the Central Intelligence Agency.

The former Bart Meinhoff, fifty-five and living on the outskirts of Washington under the name of Bart Merritt, was the agent investigating the US end of the Somali pirate operation. And as he had with every aspect of his duties in East Germany, he was consumed by a single fact. In this case, the new Monte Carlo phone number of Constantine Livanos, which no one in America knew except for Jerry Jackson, Athena's president, and his chief of operations, Peter Kilimo. Someone had given it to the villains of Haradheere.

Bart Merritt was as certain as he had ever been that Kilimo was the man tipping off the pirate organization to the exact position of certain ships. He was unsure of how illegal this was and he certainly could not have the shipping exec gunned down. Not here in the US. But he was going to nail him. That was for certain.

Bart's line of attack was through the banks, all of which were prepared to jump to it when the CIA came calling. He reasoned that if Kilimo was transmitting intricate details of the voyages of big tankers in the Indian Ocean, someone must be paying him.

He would have trouble finding access to Kilimo's account since Athena's head of operations had not been found guilty of any wrongdoing. But the money must have been sent to him somehow, and since the capture of the *Global Mustang* had been extremely recent, the cash must have either just arrived or be on its way.

Bart doubted whether any bank in Mogadishu was capable of such sophistication. So he searched for the nearest point of contact in a neighboring country, the obvious one being Kenya. He checked with MI6 in London whether there were obvious links between Kenya and Somalia, and to his surprise the Brits came up with a good one.

They described an unusual suburb east of Nairobi, a bustling former slum called Eastleigh, which for the past couple of years had been burgeoning with new high-rise apartment blocks that were springing up all over the place. The area had a strange atmosphere of prosperity: new vehicles, lavishly decorated homes, even some expensive bars and restaurants.

But there was nothing that resembled town planning. Buildings were springing up in a haphazard and often garish way, and, according to the Brits, the local Kenyans did not like it. The exceptions were the Nairobi builders who were constructing wildly overpriced real estate with somebody else's money.

And it was not just expensive homes. There were at least two major shopping malls going up in Eastleigh. This was more than a real estate bubble. This was heavily backed development with no signs of a slowdown.

The MI6 guys had taken a closer look and discovered that the place was known as "Little Mogadishu" because the cash being used was unquestionably pirate money from that benighted land north of the Kenyan border. It had to be. There was no other money worth talking about in the whole of Somalia.

This rapid development was being bankrolled by some very heavy hitters. No one knew precisely who. What everyone did know, however, was that Swahili had ceased to be spoken in this affluent suburb. The native language of Eastleigh was Somali. And somewhere beyond the new high-rise walls there must have been a clue to the identity of the main backers, but the Brits had yet to find it.

Mohammed Salat was very careful about that sort of thing. But his Swiss bank account was no longer adequate for the enormous sums of money that he and his chief executives were earning. The funds needed to be invested somewhere outside of Somalia. The far more urbane capital of Kenya was ideal: not too far away, with a stable, Westernized banking system, and very few questions asked.

Not surprisingly, the frenzy of economic activity attracted new branches of established banks. Barclays had so far refrained but the East African National was there. And so was the Mercantile Bank of South Africa. The Chinese-owned Africa and Shanghai Banking Corporation was on its way.

Bart Merritt would be able to summon up substantial help, if necessary, from US banking institutions, acting as he was in the national interest on behalf of the Central Intelligence Agency. Armed with his new knowledge, he went in search of important-looking wire transfers from the Dark Continent to New York.

A week ago, the search would have been broad, Africa wide. But now it could be narrowed down to East Africa. Better still it could almost certainly be narrowed down to a transfer from Kenya, though Switzerland was still a possibility.

But Bart had a hunch, honed from an instinct forged in the brutal communist regime. He believed that the money, if it existed, must have been wired not just from Nairobi but from the suburb of Eastleigh, Little Mogadishu. And there were only two international banks there: the East African National and the Mercantile Bank of South Africa.

Bart put four of his agents on the case. They were to search for a sum of money between $5,000 and $50,000 wired from one of those banks to an account either in New York City or in the suburb of Bronxville, where he knew that Peter Kilimo lived.

Initially they found nothing. In fact there had been just one dollar transfer to anywhere beyond the regular trading corporations that dealt with coffee, tea, horticultural products, and cotton garments. The previous day there had been a $20,000 cash transfer from the East African National in Eastleigh directly to an account in Westchester County, not Bronxville. No one, but no one, was going to provide the name of that particular client, not without some powerful political clout behind the request.

The contact being used by the CIA agents had, however, ascertained the name of the account from which the payment had come:

Haradheere Ocean Enterprises, c/o East African National Bank, Eastleigh, Nairobi. Fat lot of good that did anyone, except the word *Haradheere*. Pirate Central, Somalia.

Bart Merritt sent an e-mail to Bob Birmingham informing him that he was well on the way to locating the spy in Athena shipping who was tipping off the Somali Marines. He requested the name on the bank account in Westchester County that had accepted $20,000 in cash the previous day from a source in Nairobi, Kenya.

It took ninety minutes. Birmingham never even acknowledged the e-mail. But an unsigned reply landed in Bart's laptop: Mrs. Marlene Kilimo, PO Box 4833, Bronxville, New York.

At precisely 6:30 p.m. that evening, Peter Kilimo was arrested at his home by two officers from the Bronxville Police Department. He was immediately charged with conspiracy, actively assisting known criminal gangs in acts of robbery on the high seas, and warned that he could be implicated in the murder of engineering officer Sam McLean of Brockton, Massachusetts, who had been shot dead on the US-owned LNG tanker *Global Mustang*.

Wearing handcuffs, Peter Kilimo was led to a police cruiser, blue lights flashing, and driven to the local police precinct, where he was transferred to an unmarked car and driven on to Manhattan. His last stop was the FBI's New York headquarters at the gigantic Federal Plaza Building, adjacent to the Brooklyn Bridge.

They entered by a side door and went immediately to the twenty-sixth floor, where two officers from the NYPD were waiting with three FBI special agents and two field officers from the CIA, including Bart Merritt.

This was no ordinary arrest; the case of Peter Kilimo would have the most severe ramifications, not to mention overtones of counterterrorism and counterintelligence. One of the FBI men was a member of the Joint Terrorism Task Force. The CIA was leading the investigation and had requested partnership with the FBI in the event that anyone was arrested for involvement with the Somali Marines.

Peter Kilimo had never been this afraid in his entire life. His wife, Marlene, was left sobbing at the door as they marched her husband away. With considerable presence of mind, she had called Jerry Jackson at his home and tried to explain what had happened. She had no idea where Peter had been taken and left it to Jerry to trace him.

This was a two-minute exercise since he had the cell phone number of Bart Merritt, who had conducted the original inquiries at the Athena offices. For the record, Jerry did not believe that Peter Kilimo could possibly have done anything wrong, and he told Bart that he would be sending the Athena corporate lawyer to FBI headquarters immediately.

The lawyer, who lived on the Upper East Side, took a half hour to get there, and they held the questioning in abeyance until he arrived. But as soon as he had been briefed, they threw the book at Peter Kilimo, demanding answers, demanding confessions, and above all demanding to know the name of his contact in the pirates' lair.

For an amateur, Peter Kilimo found his nerve very quickly. He pointed out that he was a Somali by birth, like his father before him. And that although he had become a US citizen, he had close family ties to the old country. There were ancient real-estate deals that had been concluded and he was owed a share of the money. He had not informed the IRS of the transactions and for that he was sorry.

But that did not make him an accessory to murder or a member of a notorious network of international pirates. And no, he was not a mole in the Athena offices supplying information to men who went out and held oceangoing ships for ransom.

Bart Merritt did not believe him. He could not remove from his mind the new phone number for Livanos. Someone who knew it had passed it on to the pirates. And that someone was the same person who had blown the information about the tanker *Queen Beatrix*.

Bart was certain that given time he could punch holes straight through Kilimo's story. But right now it was two o'clock in the morning, and there was not much punching left for him to do. The FBI guys were, in any event, wary of the potential charges. Even if Kilimo was guilty as hell, what had he really done? He'd offered the precise whereabouts of a few, massive oceangoing ships to someone who apparently valued the information.

Was this a criminal offense? Well, it might have been but the FBI team thought a good lawyer could blast the case apart. The position and direction of long-distance freighters and tankers on the world's oceans was surely knowledge anyone could have. And whatever had happened most definitely took place in international waters.

Everyone wanted to go home to bed. Bart Merritt was becoming the most unpopular man in the vast Manhattan building. Only he, brooding at the interrogation table, was looking to the future. He glared at Kilimo, wondering what the hell the Athena "mole" was planning next.

Merritt had asked him a dozen times if he had offered any further information to the Somalis regarding the sailing of major freighters and tankers. But Kilimo had merely shaken his head and conferred with his lawyer, who insisted there was no evidence that his client had ever given anyone any information about anything, never mind pirates.

In the lawyer's opinion, it was nothing short of bullying to continue holding Mr. Kilimo. The questioning so far had not uncovered anything. The lawyer formally asked that Mr. Merritt desist.

Bart was uncertain who was actually winning the contest but knew it was not him. With immense reluctance, he agreed that the questioning should be postponed for the night, and that the NYPD would proceed with further investigation the next day.

Before he left, the CIA agent warned everyone: "These pirate operations are becoming extremely dangerous, and they are being masterminded by a very shrewd operator. The pirate leadership has access to information. And that information is coming from New York as well as Washington. I just hope the time does not come when we all look very stupid—when the next assault occurs and people get killed.

"I recommend that we undertake a very careful investigation of the main ships sailing under the auspices of Athena Shipping. Because I think Mr. Kilimo may very well have supplied the data for yet another pirate attack. Time alone will show whether I am right or wrong."

The gathering broke up in an atmosphere of latent suspicion, unproven facts, and overwhelming speculation. Peter Kilimo was driven home in a police cruiser. But there was nothing definite against his name. Yet.

▼

FIRST THING IN THE MORNING, Mohammed Salat called in his senior marine commanders, Wolde, Ahmed, and Hassan. He outlined the new intelligence he had received and pulled up an ocean chart on his desktop computer, pointing to the layout of the Maldives and in particular the wide and turbulent waters of the One and a Half Degree Channel.

Captain Hassan offered an explanation for the roughness of the waters—citing the flow of the Indian Ocean currents that surged across the central reaches but then swirled, collided, and split into riptides when the main flow of the water hit the long, uneven group of mid-ocean atolls.

They were really just vast sandbank mountains rising from the ocean floor. "But it can be very rough in there," he added. "Not ideal for boarding a ship moving at 12 knots."

Admiral Wolde was concentrating more on the size of the *Ocean Princess*, staring at the stern deck, which looked high and somewhat old-fashioned. There was, however, an obvious pair of private decks directly below, under cover, and Captain Hassan thought these might be exclusive to a couple of the very expensive royal suites.

There was ample room to hurl the grappling hooks straight through the openings to these decks, and they were positioned quite low on the hull, certainly not as high as the rails on the *Global Mustang*.

"We'd need to be very careful boarding," said Wolde. "Probably timing the throw on the rising wave."

"That's how the old gun-decks worked in the eighteenth century," said Captain Hassan. "The British always fired their first salvo on the rising wave. And then another as it subsided."

"That must be our aim," said Wolde. "We hurl the grapplers at the top of the wave and then hang on to the lines. We'd need leather gloves for this, even though we can have the skiffs making zero relative speed against the hull."

"I'm seeing the pictures," said Hassan, "and I think Ismael and his guys can board the ship. My biggest problem is the distance. It's more than 1,200 miles from here to the Maldives. That's way beyond any distance we've ever taken the *Mombassa*. It's 450 miles further offshore than any previous pirate attack.

"And we can't run at top speed all the way. If we did we'd be there in a little over three days. But I wouldn't want to push her that hard. We'd run at maybe 15 knots and that would take us over four days. Three days on station, and four back. It's all too long, Mr. Salat. Much too long."

"Precisely what worries you the most?" asked Salat.

"Four things. Food, water, fuel, and then the biggest worry: We'd be vulnerable for such a long time, running hard trying to get home, knowing that a US warship could catch us easily and sink us out of pure revenge. I just don't think the *Mombassa* is man enough for the job."

"I agree," said Wolde. "We could pull this off. But not in the *Mombassa*. I doubt we'd get home alive."

"Gentlemen," said Salat, "are you saying we ought not to try this, or are you saying we need a different attack boat?"

"Second option," said Wolde. "Different attack boat."

"Gimme the stats," said Salat.

"She'll want to be at least sixty-five feet long, 2,500 tons, twin-shafted, fast, maybe up to 35 knots max, running real easy at 25. Big gas tanks, range around 3,500 miles. Spare tanks."

"What kind of a boat—fishing vessel, motor yacht?

"I'm not sure a fishing boat would be fast enough for a project like this," said Captain Hassan. "I wanna say a motor yacht, something with a real good engine. But I don't know where we're going to get one."

"I'll get one," replied Salat.

"From where? We have nothing like that," said Hassan.

"I'm going to charter one," said Salat.

"You're gonna what?!"

"Charter one," repeated Salat. "Hire a big motor yacht for a month."

"What? To rob and then ransom a luxury US cruise ship?" Wolde was incredulous.

"Sure."

"You can't do that," said Hassan.

"I've got the money, and in my experience you can buy anything if you want it badly enough," said Salat. "The *Ocean Princess* does not even leave Mombassa for another two days. And it doesn't reach the channel for another twelve days after that. We need to be out there to meet her. That gives me at least a week to get us a good boat and bring it here."

"But where are we going to get it?" asked Wolde. "There's not a boat like that in the entire country."

"I don't know where I'll get it—but I will get it," said Salat. "You can count on that."

"If you get it, we'll take the *Ocean Princess*," said Wolde. "You can count on that."

▼

COMMANDER BEDFORD made the Delta Platoon's opening day in Djibouti a full study session—maps and charts, a familiarizing process for every one of the SEALs, and quality time taken to understand and digest exactly where they all were on the map and exactly where they were going.

Each man was issued personal charts, hand-marked by the SPECWARCOM cartographers, drawing in the theater of operations, the big square in which the four patrolling US warships were already on standby. Rolling in from the southeast was the carrier *Harry S. Truman*. In addition to its normal complement of eighty fighter/bombers and Black Hawks, the flattop carried two extra helicopters, one of them a Sikorsky Sea Stallion, assault troop delivery.

The next two days were spent once more practicing parachute operations. They were accomplished at the first phase of their arrival in the ops area, the ocean drop from high altitude, and then the pickup by navy crews.

The second phase, which might require them to perform a HALO drop, the 26,000-foot free fall, and low opening for a ground landing was their least practiced area of expertise. And Commander Bedford was happy that there was ample opportunity in Djibouti to spend time honing this.

They were all expert parachutists and they could land in the ocean in their sleep. But Mack and the service chiefs at the Pentagon wanted this Haradheere garrison taken out. And the Delta boss could see no alternative but to land by air along the beach from the garrison itself and attack from the ground with helicopter cover.

That would mean a carrier coming inshore with a complement of Black Hawks. It would be a big, costly operation, but the top brass, Lancaster, Bradfield, and Andre, wanted it dealt with. And if that's what it would take, so be it. That was all that mattered. *Just get it done*, he was told. And that's exactly what he was doing.

Mack Bedford was more than pleased with his team. Their marksmanship was impeccable; they were trained to the minute either for an ocean, ground, or air attack. Either way they were geared to take a moving or stationary target, no matter how big or well-armed their enemy was.

For now all they could do was train on the Djibouti base, perfect their freefall parachuting, and retain their sensational fitness. Other than that, there was nothing more to do except wait for the pirates to strike again.

▼

Tom and Miranda Carlow boarded the *Ocean Princess* early in the evening and settled into their fabulous suite on the Promenade Deck. The ship was due to sail on the tide at 0100 the following morning, and that first evening Andy Carlow's parents had been invited to dine with the captain, Hugh MacColl, a lifelong seaman from Cape Cod.

After dinner, Miranda retired to bed but the admiral went out onto their small private deck and took with him a brandy and ginger ale, a sailor's drink he had learned from the Royal Navy during an official visit to the Faslane submarine base in Scotland, soon after receiving his first command.

He drank in the atmosphere of the jetties and soaked up the general buzz of a ship scheduled to leave. It wasn't much different from the departure of a US warship—except a bit sloppier with ropes and lines all over the place. And there was a lot more yelling as various African shore-hands went missing or showed up late or in the wrong place.

But the basic procedure was the same: lines cast off, signals from the foredeck and stern, the wash of the giant engines as she eased away from dry land. And finally the short blast on the ship's horn as the *Ocean Princess* pulled out into the harbor and set a course southeast down the channel and out into the broad waters of the Indian Ocean.

▼

SITTING IN HIS REGULAR SPOT in the middle of the Old City of Sana, the capital of Yemen, was the secretive Middle Eastern arms dealer Najib Saleh. For the third time that day he was talking on the phone to Mohammed Salat and this time the news was agreeable to both of them.

"She's lying at anchor in the harbor on Socotra Island," he said. "The owners are Saudis. They only use her a couple of times a year. I'm empowered to charter but I never have."

"What the hell's she doing in Socotra?" asked Mohammed. "I thought that place was prehistoric."

"Twenty years ago you might have been right," laughed Najib. "Not anymore."

The island to which the hefty Yemeni referred was about 80 miles long and located 240 miles off the Arabian Peninsula but only 160 miles off the Horn of Africa. It is probably the most remote, unspoiled place in all the world, the largest island in the ancient Land of Sheba.

Socotra has a small native population and is a place of unspoiled natural beauty, unchanged since the Middle Ages. In recent years, however, the march of civilization has been encroaching. There are paved roads, one hotel, an airport, and a harbor located four miles from the main town of Hadibo.

The president of Yemen has a beautiful residence there, as do two Saudi princes. The boat that Hajib was discussing was a powerful seventy-foot oceangoing motor yacht that belonged to one of the princes.

"Is she fast enough?" asked Mohammed.

"Hell, yes. She makes 35 knots if you ask her. Big range, too. She'll go more than 3,000 miles and after that she has a 1,000-gallon spare tank."

"What's her name?"

"*Desert Shark*. She's painted white and sails under a Saudi flag. She's just been fully serviced. The prince won't be back for three months."

"How come he trusts you to guard his boat?"

"I don't guard it. I charter it if anyone is rich enough."

"You ever been to Socotra?"

"Are you crazy?" laughed Najib. "I only leave the casbah to go to Russia and Riyadh. The prince and I do a lot of business."

"How long?"

"A month."

"How much?"

"Normally a boat like this would cost you $300,000—$10,000 a day in the Indian Ocean. She'll carry fourteen people easily. I'll let you have her for $200,000—cash, payable on delivery."

Salat had not the slightest doubt that the Saudi prince would not see a dollar of that money. And in his mind, there was only one question: "How do I get her?"

"No problem, old friend," replied Najib. "I'll have her delivered to Haradheere. By sea, she can bring that merchandise you ordered."

"I need it now."

"She'll leave tonight."

"Who pays the freight?"

"I'll cover the journey to Haradheere. You fly my guys back. Three of them."

"Done," said Mohammed with a self-satisfied smile on his face.

# CHAPTER 12

▼

THE *DESERT SHARK*, CRUISING AT 30 KNOTS THROUGH calm seas, took exactly one day to run down the six-hundred-mile coastline of Somalia and sound her horn off the village of Haradheere.

Her captain, one of Najib Saleh's employees, brought her inshore and dropped anchor into the sandy ocean bottom about fifty yards off the beach. Mohammed Salat and Captain Hassan came out in one of the skiffs to board her and inspect their latest pirate attack ship.

There was no doubt she was a beautiful boat, and her Saudi flag kept her safe from attack by other Somali gangs. No one fools with the property of the Saudi princes since most of them have the power to call in the entire Saudi Navy to help them out. The ruling family maintains an iron grip on the vast area surrounding the Arabian Peninsula.

The biggest problem was refuelling. There were no jetties, and the operation had to be done by one of Salat's tankers, which was driven down the beach. They'd done this before and it was not easy, eight boats positioned every few yards, all the way out to the *Shark*.

Across this pontoon they would run the long diesel line and couple it to the new arrival's tanks. They then pumped the gas until she was full, and the little boats hauled the line back inshore. The whole operation took about fifty minutes, and Captain Hassan stayed on board until it was completed.

They unloaded the merchandise the following morning—a

shipment of Kalashnikov machine guns, RPGs, and ammunition. Then Salat's guards took the *Shark*'s crew to their regular helicopter landing site, from where they were flown home to Yemen.

The remainder of the day was spent with the entire village helping to restock the boat in readiness for what Salat believed might be the biggest operation they'd ever mounted—the attack on the *Ocean Princess*, crammed as she was with wealthy Americans without a gun between them.

Ismael Wolde did not pretend this would be easy. He was certain it was possible, but no more than that. The truth was that no pirate gang had ever gone for a passenger ship, for the very obvious reason that they always carried large crews. Also there was the danger of a shoot-out involving innocent civilians. The whole operation would be fraught with unforeseen danger.

The capture of the *Ocean Princess*, if successful, would be a first. Wolde studied online photographs of the ship, trying to imagine what she would look like from the water, close-up. The boarding problem would be, as ever, the most difficult part, and there was no doubt this had to be done from the stern.

With so many people aboard, the attack would need to be highly coordinated; companionways would need to be taken and held immediately, making movement through the decks impossible for anyone except the pirates. The assault on the bridge, probably at three o'clock in the morning, would need to be swift and brutal. In Wolde's experience, masters of big ocean liners were reluctant to give up without resistance.

That meant he and his men must attack suddenly, with all the advantages of surprise, and perhaps blow the door to the bridge off its hinges and then charge forward. Ideally he would like to secure the ship in secret, with none of the passengers aware of what had happened. But that could be hoping for too much.

Down on the beach the residents of Haradheere were ferrying the equipment out to the *Desert Shark* in small boats. Stocking sufficient food would be less of a problem because the luxury yacht had a big galley with plenty of storage space, all of it refrigerated. There was a huge, fresh-water tank, both for drinking and washing.

They loaded six cases of bottled water. Captain Hassan's ban on any open flame was still in force, which more or less ruled out cooking—but the boat had a microwave, which was agreeable to the boss and would go far in quieting the crew's discontent.

For this longer voyage, Wolde appointed a village cook who had not served with them before. He was a twenty-four-year-old local named Elijah Sarami, who had worked as an assistant chef in two restaurants in Cape Town but had left the last one suspiciously fast after the head chef had been found murdered.

Elijah was plainly "wanted" in South Africa and had escaped to seek refuge in his homeland. He had not been found guilty of anything yet, but when Wolde interviewed him, the commander of the Somali Marines was left with a distinct impression that Elijah might prove just as handy with a machine gun as he would with a frying pan.

Elijah fitted right in, stationed himself in the galley, and supervised the provisioning of the new pirate boat. He ordered frozen food from the only local store in Haradheere, ready-cooked stuff that he could heat in the microwave, which was a gigantic step up from the usual cold, roast goat sandwiches on stale pita bread.

He was a tall, good-natured man with an athletic build. He quickly pleased the captain by how he finished storing the food and then moved immediately onto the starboard deck to help load the ammunition boxes.

Brand-new guns for the voyage came out in three cases—light Kalashnikovs, six-packed together. For this mission they also brought three heavy machine guns and four thousand rounds of ammunition. No one had forgotten that they had twice come under attack on the *Mustang* mission and everyone agreed they needed major firepower.

They also had a box of RPGs, a stack of dynamite, and three boxes of hand grenades. They had a dozen pairs of night-glasses and big leather gloves for the boarding: strictly for that moment when the grapplers held, and they might need to hold fast to the knotted climbing ropes if the ocean liner tried to pull away from them.

They took four grappling irons and six rope ladders with the brass rungs. It took hours to transport the boxes from the garrison, down the beach, and out to the *Desert Shark* in the skiffs, and then lift the heavy cases up and over the side and into the dry lockers.

In the mid-afternoon, Salat's stock market launched the new issue of shares for "Operation Princess." He offered 10,000 shares at $20 each, and the wealthy citizens of Haradheere snapped up the first 5,000 in about twenty minutes, many people going in for one hundred at a time. Salat himself bought 1,000, and Wolde's wife took 500 for herself. Elmi Ahmed's father also went for 500.

At least their investment covered the cost of the boat charter, and Salat was planning to issue 10,000 more, just as soon as Admiral Wolde informed him he had the *Ocean Princess* in his sights. Once the ship had been captured, he'd issue another 10,000 at 30 each. The buzz around the stock exchange was that these stocks would go to 120 if the mission was successful. And right now the good folk of Haradheere were used to nothing but success.

That night, Salat posted six of his most trusted guard commanders on the *Desert Shark* as she rode her anchor off the beach. The crew were all permitted to sleep ashore until it was time to depart.

While most of the town gathered excitedly in the local bars, Salat concentrated on tracking down their target. He called the local hotel in Mahe in the Seychelles and found the number of the harbormaster, who confirmed that the *Ocean Princess* had arrived that afternoon for a two-day stay.

It was 960 miles from Mahe to the One and a Half Degree Channel, which meant the *Princess* was two-and-a-half-days' running time from the pirates' ops area. It was Tuesday, and if she left Mahe on Thursday afternoon she'd be on station in the channel around midnight on Saturday.

Captain Hassan planned to cruise out there at an easy 20 knots, but it was 1,250 miles from Haradheere, and that was also around sixty hours' running time or two and a half days. The *Desert Shark* would pull out at first light on Thursday morning. For the moment she would remain offshore with her generators gently running.

Mohammed Salat kept a regular check on the *Ocean Princess* and put in a call every six hours to make certain she was still at her berth. The assault team went down to the skiffs late on Wednesday afternoon and began to ferry out to the new ship. All of the regular men were there: In addition to Ismael and Elmi, there was the ex–army sergeant Ibrahim Yacin, Omar Ali Farah, Abadula Sofian, Hamdan Ougoure, Abdul Mesfin, and Kifle Zenawi, the man who shot Sam McLean. They were joined by the new gastro-killer Elijah Sarami.

The four junior pirates who had served so professionally on the *Mustang* mission were there, driving the skiffs back and forth. No pirate attack had ever been so well prepared.

They slept on the boat that night, two or three of them in each of the carpeted cabins, with a four-man guard patrol on watch at all times. Wolde and Hassan shared the stateroom.

Dawn came very suddenly. The sun rose out of the eastern horizon in a great blood-red ball, and Captain Hassan blew two short blasts on the *Desert Shark*'s horn. He revved the engines quietly and then slipped into gear, hauling the wheel over and turning the boat away from the shores of Somalia.

He set course one-zero-five coming fractionally south of due east and ran for two miles at a careful 8 knots just to allow the big turbines to run easily before their marathon journey. He was an old-fashioned captain and believed that engines should be allowed time to warm up before the throttles were opened.

Elmi Ahmed was the next man on the bridge and took the seat next to Hassan. Wolde followed and turned on the navigation aids, radar, GPS, and computer. The time was 0610, and the *Shark* was cutting smoothly through a calm sea. A couple of miles offshore, Captain Hassan opened the throttle, and the boat increased speed.

Little by little he worked it up to a steady 20 knots, which allowed her to cruise effortlessly, well within herself, running quietly with a sure and sympathetic hand on the controls.

At 7:00 a.m. three plates of scrambled eggs and toast were delivered to the bridge, and down below, the crew was clustered around the galley, where Elijah was on his way to becoming the most popular man on board.

He made fresh coffee and cleared everything away before he went to help rig the tripod for the heavy machine gun on the foredeck. The Somali Marines understood how quickly an enemy could appear, and though they hoped the Saudi flag flying from the stern would discourage intruders, Wolde insisted they take no chances. Anyone who came near the *Shark* on this outward leg of the mission would not live to tell the tale.

The sea got up around noon, not in a short, choppy way, but in long ocean swells that required careful steering. It's necessary to proceed at just the right speed, maybe a little faster, maybe a little slower, because all good helmsmen hate thumping a vessel into the oncoming trough. They try to ride the waves, crest to crest, but never to put her bow down into the approaching wall of water.

Hassan was a master. He kicked the *Shark* up a few notches and made her just too fast for the ocean, smiling as the expensive motor yacht sliced over the tops of the rollers, ripping along at 25 knots without even straining.

Elijah produced dinner just as they approached the Chain Ridge, where the Indian Ocean floor rises up to a depth of a thousand fathoms instead of the 3,000-fathom depth of the central areas. The cook served a mixture of frozen meals that had been reheated in the microwave: roast beef, roast lamb, steak, and sausages. It was a steaming-hot culinary mishmash, but it tasted very good, all mixed together with a pile of garden peas. Admiral Wolde's masterstroke was undoubtedly Elijah Sarami, and the pirates drank a fruit juice toast to the chef as they sat around the stern promenade deck, watching the sun set behind them.

At the same time, the *Ocean Princess* was clearing the jetties at Port Victoria on the island of Mahe. This old seat of British colonial government had provided a fascinating couple of days for Tom Carlow.

He sat outside watching the island slide away astern, and he felt the warm, tropical wind on his face as the *Princess* shouldered her way into a rising sea, heading northeast across deep, lonely waters, up to the wide channel that divides the northern and central Maldives from the southern atolls.

Miranda Carlow could very easily have lived without this 960-mile journey between the islands. Like most people she found an endless sea voyage with no land in sight for hundreds of miles a tiresome exercise. But she knew that her husband loved it, everything about it, the rise of the ship on the waves, the gusting blue-water breeze, the swish of the bow wave, the familiar motion of the deck.

Because for him, it brought back a thousand memories, a thousand adventures, and a thousand lost friends, shipmates he had once known but would very likely never see again. War and the passage of time do that—they heighten the best moments, making old friendships seem more poignant than they were and, above all, recalling far-lost triumphs as if they were yesterday.

Sometimes Miranda joined her husband gazing out over the ocean as they made their way to the northeast, and when she did, she knew it would not be long before he transported her again to the shattering noise of the gun deck of the USS *Maddox* under attack in the Gulf of Tonkin. She'd heard it so many times she almost believed she had been there, and she smiled as an unmistakable light of battle gleamed once more in Admiral Tom Carlow's eyes as he crossed the mighty waters.

▼

THE *DESERT SHARK* was going for her life, running at close to 30 knots across a flat-calm Friday afternoon sea. They were 850 miles into their journey—four hundred to go—and they had seen only a couple of fishing boats all the way from Haradheere.

They were passing the top right-hand corner of the square Mark Bradfield had mapped out for the four anti-pirate US warships, all of which were deep into that area: the guided missile cruiser *Port Royal*, the destroyers USS *Chafee* and USS *Momsen*, and the Harpoon missile frigate USS *Reuben James*.

In addition, the aircraft carrier the *Harry S. Truman*, was due to reach the square that night, bearing the huge insertion helicopter the Sikorsky CH-53D Sea Stallion, which could transport up to forty marines.

The level of ignorance on the Indian Ocean was at an all-time high: The pirates knew nothing of the presence of US warships, and the high command of the warships had no idea that the smooth-looking Saudi motor yacht was chock-full of armed brigands, although the *Chafee* had logged its presence on the ocean surface. And the captain of the oncoming *Ocean Princess* had not the slightest idea of what would be waiting for them in the One and a Half Degree Channel—or that help was at hand.

But the biggest secret of all was in the US naval base in Djibouti, a thousand miles west of the square.

Friday evening on the *Desert Shark* passed without incident as they ran through the night, although a sudden squall had blown up and the sea had become more difficult. Captain Hassan cut the speed back to 20 knots and pressed on while most of the crew sat watching a movie and eating ham-and-cheese omelettes, which Elijah had managed to make, four at a time, in the microwave.

The captain went to bed around 11:00 p.m. and Elmi Ahmed took over the helm, with Ibrahim Yacin assisting and checking the navigation. They were still right on course heading almost due east, and when the sun rose in the morning they'd be within 120 miles of their ops area.

Elijah's considerable skills did not compare with the gastronomic splendor of the *Ocean Princess*, where Admiral and Mrs. Carlow once more dined with Captain Parker Lansdale, an ex–US Navy commander who had served with considerable distinction in the second Gulf War.

Dinner at the captain's table consisted of oysters and smoked salmon followed by baby lamb chops with new potatoes and leaf spinach. They were treated to a selection of French cheeses before being presented with a dessert trolley resplendent with pastries and cakes.

Miranda called a halt after the lamb chops but the admiral enjoyed every course, concluding the evening by sitting up with the captain and swapping naval stories. At one point Tom asked Captain Lansdale if he had any concern about the known pirate activity in the surrounding waters, and the master of the *Ocean Princess* was dismissive.

"It almost always happens to the north of here," he said, "and for whatever reason, they do not seem to favor cruise ships. Especially American ones. They have never attacked one."

"Do you have a contingency plan should they change their minds?" asked Tom.

"Well, I always have guards on duty on my ship, although we do not identify them as such. They are professional security people, but we disguise them as deckhands or engineers. Don't really want the paying customers to be alarmed when there's no need."

"Are they armed?"

"Not officially. But they wouldn't be much good if they weren't, eh? These friggin' pirates attack with Kalashnikovs. And we have one other thing that might discourage them: This is a high-sided ship, hard to board. If we caught them in the act, they'd be at a bad disadvantage."

"Yes," replied Tom, "I guess they would. By the way, do you keep firearms on the bridge, just in case?"

"Again, not officially because firearms are banned by the insurance companies. But between you and me, sir, my first mate and I have immediate access to a couple of machine guns if it became necessary."

"Does he know how to use one?"

"Oh, sure. Johnny's ex–US Navy, like us."

▼

As THEY APPROACHED THE CHANNEL, the water became even choppier, and Captain Hassan throttled back to 15 knots. It was a little after noon when they arrived at the western end, and they guessed the *Ocean Princess* would probably edge over to the northern half of the throughway.

Wolde had insisted on a thorough recce before they placed themselves out in the middle, and he picked up the cruise liner on the radar as soon as she came within range. As usual, they would come in on her stern with the skiffs primed, loaded, crewed, and ready for action. The *Shark* would tow them in before releasing them to make a dash for the hull.

They were all surprised by the heavy swells they encountered in the channel, but since none of the pirates were surfers, they had no way of knowing they were among some of the world's most spectacular shoreline waves, great rollers caused by the so-called Roaring Forties that form in the southern reaches of the Indian Ocean. Surfers regard the distant shores of the One and a Half De-

gree Channel as the best waves in the Maldives. The pirates, however, did not share their admiration.

The *Desert Shark* was riding the crests but it was not comfortable and a couple of the juniors felt seasick. Captain Hassan promised he would look for flatter water, but out in the middle of the
channel he was not going to find it.

He headed north, seeking shelter on the far side, and to make
matters worse, it began to rain, and the wind blew hard out of the
southwest. Hassan put the boat right before the breeze and surfed
his way across the channel. It wasn't perfect, but it was much
smoother. As it grew dark, both the weather and the seasickness
subsided.

All they had to do was calm down, have a light supper, and wait
for the *Ocean Princess* to come rolling through the channel.

At midnight, everyone came on watch. Every sharp eye on the
ship was trained on the black, southwestern horizon. The moon
was high and the sky bright, but there was not a paint on the radar,
not even out on the twenty-five-mile circle.

At 0100 they spotted something, a sizeable paint from an incoming ship, too big to be weather, much too big to be a shoal of
fish or even a sperm whale, which had lived and bred in the area
for centuries.

No, this was a real boat, moving quite fast. And if it were the
*Princess*, she was right on time. It would take her a little over ninety
minutes to reach the precise spot where Mohammed Salat's contact
said she would be: south of Haddumati Atoll at 0230 on the GPS
1.5N 73.20E. Exactly where the *Desert Shark* was making a racetrack pattern in the water.

Wolde never took his eye off the screen and at 0200, with the
ship only eight miles away, Hassan, peering through night-glasses,
declared it was without question the *Princess*, running easily
through the swells. She was lit up like a Christmas tree.

"Soon she'll pass due south of us," said Hassan. "Extinguish all lights, transmit nothing, and we'll close in on her stern. Right now we'll lower the skiffs and make them fast, and we'll tow in."

"I'll give the order to board the skiffs two miles from the ship," said Wolde. "Everything's loaded. Carry only your personal weapons."

By now they could see the lights of the *Princess* without night-glasses. She was a good-sized ship but nothing close to the *Queen Beatrix* or the *Global Mustang*.

Hassan waited until the bow of the *Desert Shark* was pointing directly at the beam of the *Ocean Princess*, and only then did he move forward, still with no lights, still transmitting nothing. He wanted to chug in slowly but the liner was going at a real clip through the water and, whether he liked it or not, the master of the *Shark* had to get moving.

It was 0230, the middle of the night, and unless someone had been staring at the radar screen on the bridge of the cruise ship, it was unlikely that anyone would notice their approach. Captain Hassan edged his way into the wake of the ship, running hard astern at the same speed, about 16 knots, a mile behind.

In the pitch dark they slowed down for the pirate assault team to board the skiffs. One by one they climbed down into the attack vessels, one on the portside of the *Shark*, the other to starboard.

"We're boarding on the starboard quarter," Wolde told his men. "Sofian drives the lead boat; Kifle and me throw the grapplers and climb on board immediately. I'll carry one rope ladder. When it drops, two more of you will board, bringing up two more ladders as we discussed. Bu we must get aboard fast. The ship's asleep. Let's get in front of the problems."

And now the skiffs were up and running, leaving the *Desert Shark* in their wake. Elijah stayed on board with the captain and would join the others only if there was trouble. Hassan dropped further and further behind because the skiffs were under the radar and could not be seen unless someone was out on the deck looking, and no one was.

Sofian maneuvered into position but it was damn tricky at this speed. Finally he had his little boat travelling at exactly the same 16 knots as the liner, almost bumping her but working his way along, fighting an eight-foot rise on the wave.

"Okay, Kifle, *LET'S GO!*" snapped Wolde. And the two began to rotate the grapplers in underarm clockwise arcs . . . *one, two, three, and NOW!* Both the steel hooks flew upward, about ten degrees off the vertical. The rail that protected the private decks was about twenty-four feet above the water, and both hooks sailed over, landing with a *clump*, the noise deadened by the heavy tape around the prongs.

The lines attached to the hooks were knotted and fixed onto the seats in the skiffs, which now lurched around as the big ship towed them along, Sofian revving, trying to stay at zero relative. But the grapplers had grabbed and held, and Ismael and Kifle grabbed their ropes as high as possible and swung out over the side, clinging on powerfully, before making the critical but perilous climb up to the decks of the *Ocean Princess*.

The speed of the ship was a nightmare. When the lead skiff slipped off a wave, it pulled the line out tight, and the two climbers were forced to the underside, clinging on like monkeys and fighting their way upward from knot to knot. The weight of the rope ladder Ismael was carrying was very tough on him, but he kept going, finally flinging his right leg over the rail and hauling himself aboard.

He was very glad to have the ladder because he did not think everyone could have made that climb. He attached it to the grappler and then dropped it down to the skiff, where grasping hands dragged it inboard. By now Kifle was up and over, standing next to his commander, grateful that he had somehow cheated death on that climbing rope above the surging sea.

The next two men up Wolde's ladder brought ladders of their own and dropped them down. And now the pirates were in full cry, climbing up with practiced dexterity—Ibrahim Yacin, Elmi

Ahmed, Omar Ali, Hamdan Ougoure, and Abdul Mesfin. Two of
the juniors were next and then Abadula Sofian. Each of them
brought attack equipment and spare grenades. Yacin and Elmi,
working side by side on the ladders, hauled up one of the heavy
machine guns, and then went back down for a second. The other
two junior marines held onto the helms of the skiffs.

The entire operation had taken a total of twelve minutes from
the moment Wolde had cleared the rail. And now Admiral Wolde
stood on the deck of the *Ocean Princess* at the head of a band of
nine pirates, all with AK-47s slung over their shoulders. Four of
them were holding the two heavy machine guns, slung between
them on lifting straps.

These four had hefty ammunition belts around their necks, and
Wolde ordered them off the small decks below the main stern
promenade. Their instructions were ironclad: *Get into the main
throughways of the ship and seal them off. There's no need to shoot
or round people up. Just get into control. Make it impossible for people
to move around. Shout and threaten but do not open fire unless you
are personally fired upon.*

Meanwhile, Ismael, with Elmi and the ex–army sergeant Yacin,
would head to the bridge and take it by force if necessary. The pirates would move up to the main deck, which would become their
center of operation, but it was only one floor up to the bridge, although, unlike in the tankers, it was sited much further forward.

Kifle Zenawi assumed a loose command on the main deck and
began deploying men to the public rooms, the two juniors detailed
to the dining room and main lounge. On the bridge, meanwhile,
Wolde and his cohorts had reached the main door. As they did, a
security guard down on the main deck hit the interior line to the
bridge to report, "Sir, this ship has been boarded by a group of
armed men. They are on the main deck right now. I am trying to
assemble the guards."

Captain Lansdale ordered his second in command and the

young bosun on duty on the bridge to grab the guns out of the locker and to bring one to him. Just then, Admiral Wolde tried the handle and found it locked. He raised his boot and kicked it, but the big teak door held. Elmi opened fire, blasted the lock asunder, and charged in shooting.

Lansdale fired back and hit Sergeant Yacin full in the chest. Elmi blew the captain away with a short burst from his AK-47, and Wolde shot the bosun dead. The first officer dropped his gun and raised his hands. Wolde raised his right hand, palm extended, and bellowed, "*STOP SHOOTING!*" But it was already too late. The bridge was a bloodbath, and three men were dead, including the pirates' beloved veteran Ibrahim Yacin.

Again the voice of the main deck security guard could be heard on the intercom: "I'm having trouble assembling the team, sir. Most of the guys are asleep. And the corridors are under the control of the pirates. No one dare leave a cabin."

Wolde spoke to the first officer, Johnny Barrow, and instructed him to inform the guard that both the captain and the bosun were dead. That he was to gather his men and surrender immediately. There was to be no more bloodshed. The staff of the ship was no match for professional killers.

Barrow did as he was told, and then Wolde told him to slow the ship to a couple of knots. After that, on behalf of the captain, he was to broadcast to the crew and inform them what had happened, ordering both passengers and crew to throw any firearms out into the corridors.

Twenty minutes later, passengers on board the *Ocean Princess* were being ordered to dress and prepare for the pirates to round them up at gun- point and march them to the main assembly areas, the lounge and dining room.

There was a terrible incident up on the Riviera Deck, where three of the ship's guards managed to gain entrance to the communications center and form some kind of a stronghold. They shot one of the junior pirates, an eighteen-year-old from Haradheere, through the head. Hamdan Ougoure, stationed at the base of the stairway and an uncle of the boy, immediately opened fire with the heavy machine gun.

He pumped bullets into the comms area and all three of the guards were hit and killed. Most of the electronics were smashed beyond hope by the murderous heavy-duty salvo fired by Ougoure. The *Ocean Princess* was not only held captive; she was also incommunicado by normal channels.

Again, under instructions from the pirates, the first officer broadcast on the ship's internal system, requesting there be no more gunfire. He assured passengers there was no need to panic, that the pirates would be making their demands of the ship's owners, and that arrangements would be made.

He reminded them that the Somalis had never killed innocent passengers knowingly and that all five of the dead on the ship were employees of Southern Islander in New Orleans, professional men who had died trying to defend the *Ocean Princess*.

Up on the bridge, Wolde and Ahmed had seized control. That left six gunmen to rule the ship and intimidate the passengers and crew. At this point, using the captain's private line, Wolde dialled the number for Brad Hyland, the chairman of Southern Islander. There was no reply from Houston, and Wolde redialled, this time using the Hylands' number in New York, where Brad answered the phone.

"Mr. Hyland? I am the commander of the Somali Marines First Assault Group," explained Wolde. "Twenty minutes ago, my men took command of the *Ocean Princess*. As we speak, your captain and bosun are dead, and I have been assembling the passengers and crew in the dining area."

"*WHO THE HELL ARE YOU?*" yelled Brad Hyland. "*IS THIS SOME KIND OF A GODDAMNED JOKE?*"

"No joke, Mr. Hyland," said Wolde. "We are in the One and a

Half Degree Channel in the southern part of the Maldives, approximately 73.20E, Indian Ocean. I am using Captain Lansdale's phone, which unfortunately he will no longer need."

Brad Hyland's mind was in overdrive. It seemed this character was not joking but neither had he made any demands.

"Well," he said slowly, "what do you want from me? You already have my ship and apparently have no qualms about killing members of my crew."

"A very easy question," replied Wolde. "I require 10 million dollars from you. If you get it here within thirty-six hours, that sum of money will remain in operation. If we cannot agree, it immediately increases to $12 million. And then every two hours, I shall take out two passengers and shoot them publicly, before throwing their bodies over the side.

"You have two hundred passengers, so the process will continue for several days. When all the passengers have been killed, I will blow up your ship, with your crew still on board, and accept that my mission has not gone according to plan. Except that my men are currently stripping every one of your passengers of their valuables, jewelry, gold, watches, cash. So it will not have been entirely without reward. You, of course, will have the deaths of more than three hundred people on your conscience."

Hyland needed time. If this joker was not bluffing, he needed to give the $10 million serious thought and he needed to talk to his insurers, who stood to lose more money than the rest of the pirate victims put together. Two hundred very rich but very dead American passengers represented a financial catastrophe for the Lloyds shipping brokers in London.

"Okay, tell you what," said Brad, "it's a bad time here. Offices are closed and people aren't home yet. I can't raise $10 million right now on my own, but I don't want to lose my ship. I'll need help, so you better give me some time."

"How long?"

"Six hours. I'll try to get my insurance company involved. Plainly the ransom is a whole hell of a lot better than everyone dying and the ship being scuttled. But I expect you have already considered that."

"I have. But I do not have six hours to give you. I'll give you four, at which point the first two passengers die, unless I get assurances."

"Will you call me, on this line?"

"I will. That will be 0700 my time."

"Eleven in the evening mine."

Both men hung up without the courtesy of a good-bye. Brad Hyland went to work, immediately telephoning the FBI in New York and requesting a link to the antiterrorist unit. From there, in the space of five minutes, a report of the capture of the *Ocean Princess* in the Maldives islands was relayed to every possible branch of the United States armed forces.

The FBI alerted the CIA, and Bob Birmingham called General Lancaster at the Pentagon, where two assistants telephoned Admiral Mark Bradfield and Simon Andre. The CNO personally called Admiral Andrew Carlow at SPECWARCOM, and Andre, the secretary of defense, called the Oval Office to inform the president.

Every recipient of every call was shocked at the brass neck of the pirates—an American passenger ship sailing under an American flag, members of the crew gunned down, and a chilling threat issued against the United States by brigands. These guys were criminals of the worst type.

General Lancaster sent out a signal to all the relevant departments. It read succinctly: "Capture of the *Ocean Princess* unacceptable to this office. Fire at will." No one was in any doubt about what he meant.

But the man who would issue the crucial command was in greater shock than all the rest when Mark Bradfield called.

"Jesus Christ," said Admiral Carlow, "the *Ocean Princess* in the Maldives! My parents are on that ship."

"They're what?"

"They're on the goddamned ship—a cruise from Mombassa up through the Seychelles to the Maldives."

"Admiral Tom?" gasped Mark Bradfield.

"I'm afraid he's the only dad I've got," replied Andy. "And you're telling me this bunch of fucking savages have taken him prisoner?!"

"That's not all I'm doing, bro," said the CNO, slipping into the idiom of the SEALs. "I'm telling you, this is it. No more options. I'm ordering you to send in Mack Bedford's Delta Platoon and recapture that ship. No holds barred. Take it by force, and let's go right now."

Andy Carlow checked his e-mails and right there was the precise position of the *Ocean Princess* in the western regions of the One and a Half Degree Channel, Maldives 1.5N 73.20E.

The destroyer *Chafee* had already been ordered to leave her station in the northeast corner of the operations box, make flank speed four hundred miles to the datum, and be prepared to take on board the entire Delta Platoon, ocean drop, Indian Ocean, in the next three hours. The Sikorsky Sea Stallion, which would carry in the SEALs team, was on board the *Chafee*.

The cruiser *Port Royal* was also headed directly for the *Ocean Princess*, and she carried another critical component of the near-certain air attack on the *Ocean Princess*—the AH-1 Cobra helicopter gunship, especially requested by Commander Bedford.

Admiral Carlow, appalled by the news of his parents' capture, was in a daze as his assistant opened up his phone line to the Djibouti base and told them to put Commander Bedford on the line immediately.

One minute later, when Mack came on, it was almost 3:30 in the morning on the Horn of Africa. But the SEAL leader sounded alert and listened carefully as his friend recounted the shocking news of the *Ocean Princess*.

Before the Delta boss could reply, Andy told him that his

mother and father were on board the ship. "They're quite elderly now," said Andy. "Mack, promise me, bro, you'll get them out of there."

"I'll get 'em. Admiral Tom, right?"

"That's the man, bro. I'm counting on you."

Mack Bedford came out of bed like a bullet. He opened his door and stood in the corridor and yelled, "*CHIEF SHARP! CHIEF CHARLTON!* Get dressed and get in here right now. *WE'RE GOING!*"

He grabbed the base intercom and ordered the mission aircraft to be ready to leave in thirty minutes maximum. He then called General Offiah, briefed him on the situation, and requested hard copy from the comms center, providing the latest movements of the *Chafee* and *Port Royal*, information expected to be transmitted directly, hour by hour.

Chief Sharp was the first into his stride and toured the SEAL rooms, bellowing at the top of his lungs and ordering the men out of bed and into action. "*WE'RE GOING!*" he yelled, "*We're going right now. Check your personal weapons. This is SEAL Team 10, Delta Platoon going to ACTION STATIONS! RIGHT NOW!*"

It may have looked like pandemonium in the SEAL section of the living quarters as they stampeded for their lockers, hauling on their wet suits, but it was not. These were the ultimate professional troops, men who knew full well that the ship to which they were headed, USS *Chafee*, was a floating SEAL base, already loaded with two crates of their personal stuff, plus heavy weaponry and essential battlefield gear.

This would be an obvious ocean drop, which none of them looked forward to. But they were world-class exponents of the most difficult entry method in the book. Each man would make the parachute jump with only two items strapped to his back: a light, waterproof rucksack and a machine gun, carried in a sealed holster. Everything else they needed was already onboard the *Chafee*.

Every hour of their training both at Coronado and on the Horn of Africa had been geared for this moment. In fifteen minutes the men were in one of the trucks transporting them to the end of the runway. Five minutes later they were piling into a Lockheed C-130, one of two kept permanently at the Djibouti base. Its engines were already running, well . . . howling.

As the last man climbed on board, the big doors slammed shut, and the SEALs got down on the floor for takeoff. They faced a two-and-a-half-hour flight to the rendezvous point with the *Chafee*. Most of the journey would be dedicated to preparing for the jump. Limited seating would be organized, but the main part was to fix the parachutes on forty men, check them, and check them again.

The loadmaster and the dispatcher worked with Mack Bedford while he briefed and talked to his team. In the cockpit of the aircraft there were two pilots, a navigation officer and a special communications operator, whose task was to make contact with the *Chafee* ASAP.

The huge aircraft hurtled down the runway in a cloud of drifting sand and screamed into the night sky, banking left over the coastline of northern Somalia and out over the Indian Ocean, heading east.

It took an hour to make contact with the American destroyer DDG-90, but both the aircraft and the ops room of the *Chafee* were receiving satellite signals advising each on the other's position. The warship's journey from the northeast corner of the box took twelve hours and she was running through the night for three of them when the C-130, flying low, came through: *Delta SEALs on time making 400 knots . . . ETA Chafee 0630.*

*Chafee*'s ops room picked them up instantly: *Low-flying contact 5,000 feet . . . speed 250 . . . course zero-nine-zero . . . range sixty miles . . . IFF transponder code correlates Delta SEALs.*

"*LAUNCH THE INFLATABLES!*"

Up on deck the crews began to lower away, easing four rubber

Zodiacs down to the water. Within moments the two-man crews were aboard, the engines running, moving away from the ship, out to the designated landing area 1,000 yards off the portside beam.

In the C-130 the dispatcher assumed command: *Okay, get ready now—we're heading right toward the zone . . . another four minutes . . .*

The SEALs, hoods up, flippers clipped to their thighs, began to move toward the aircraft doors, port and starboard. Each man was struggling aft, hauling his backpack and rifle and the parachute pack. Commander Bedford took the lead and would exit the aircraft first at the head of his team.

*Coming to the drop zone now, right on our nose . . . action stations . . .*

The dispatcher opened the aircraft door on the starboard side, and the sudden roar of the wind was a shock even to those who were prepared for it. The SEALs grabbed for the static line, and Mack looked down at the ocean gleaming far below in the early dawn light.

Again they checked their lines and pushed forward to the area immediately in front of the opening.

*ONE MINUTE!*

Mack braced himself for the next command.

*STAND IN THE DOOR, NUMBER ONE!*

He was trained for this and he was ready. A feeling of exhilaration swept over him as he gritted his teeth and the light above him flickered.

*Red on!!*

Mack knew they were just about over the zone and the dispatcher confirmed it:

*Green on . . . GO, GO, GO!*

The dispatcher slapped him on the shoulder, and Mack Bedford plunged out of the aircraft, sweeping clear in the slipstream and then dropping swiftly sideways.

Back in the aircraft the radio operator snapped into the secure VHF encrypted: *Delta SEALs go.*

*Chafee* came back on: *Roger and out.*

Suddenly there were two sticks of eighteen parachuting SEALs swaying thousands of feet above the Indian Ocean, remembering their hundreds of hours of training and realizing at last what it had all been for.

Mack stared down from about two hundred feet and prepared for splash down. At 150 feet he could see the Zodiacs circling around a wide area, deliberately left clear, he knew, in case one of the SEALs crashed straight down and landed in the boat.

He pulled the harness forward under his backside and banged the release button on his chest, which allowed the straps to fall away, leaving him in a sitting position holding on to the lift webs above his head. If he let go, he'd fall out of the chute and drop straight down.

He realized there was a light southwesterly blowing across the water, and he was literally hurtling across it, coming down fast. At fifty feet Mack was gripping the chute with all of his strength: At twenty he was ready, and at ten feet he let go and crashed into the ocean.

The Zodiac was on him in seconds, and big, friendly hands grabbed him under the armpits and hauled him aboard.

"Hello, sir," said one of the seamen. "Nice jump."

At which point Barney Wilkes landed in his lap as they dragged him over the wide, inflatable sides of the Zodiac.

"Morning, boss," said the ace swimmer of the platoon. "Think they might give us some breakfast?"

The helmsman answered for him. "You guys can have any darned thing you want."

And then Chief Brad Charlton came tumbling aboard, followed by Shane Cannell. The other three Zodiacs were revving and seamen were grabbing and hauling, and the SEALs were being rescued hand over fist. It took little more than eight minutes to land them all in the boats, and Chief Cody Sharp, in charge of the final roll call, yelled over to Mack, "All thirty-six men assigned on board, sir. Ready to leave."

The little convoy of inflatables set off over the last half mile of the SEALs' journey out to the *Chafee*, and up ahead they could see the destroyer cruising slowly, waiting for them to climb aboard. On her stern helicopter deck, they could see the huge Sikorsky Sea Stallion, which would land them on the captured *Ocean Princess*, the cruise liner that held the parents of Admiral Andy Carlow, the hugely popular SPECWARCOM C-in-C, the Emperor SEAL.

They reached the *Chafee* and split, two boats port and starboard. Fixed to the hull there were rope ladders and cargo nets. The SEALs were up and into the warship in five minutes flat, greeted by the commanding officer, Captain Tyron Marks.

Marks was all business. "We unloaded everything from the aircraft in DG and stowed it below," he said. "Everything you need is in an area designated for your operation. Right now we're about eight-and-a-half hours from the *Ocean Princess*. We'll be there by 1530. *Port Royal*, with the gunship aboard, is catching up fast. She's probably only fifty miles behind right now and making 40 knots. We'll probably get there together."

"Thank you very much, sir," said Commander Bedford, deferring to Marks's rank. "We really appreciate everything you've done. It's a highly dangerous mission as you know. And I expect you also know it's very important to all of us."

"I do know, commander. Andy Carlow's parents, right?"

"Yessir."

▼

ON BOARD THE *OCEAN PRINCESS*, Wolde laid down the ground rules. All passengers would surrender their cell phones. There would be no contact with the outside world. Anyone indulging in any form of communication, or carrying a firearm, would be executed immediately. All passengers, no exceptions, would be escorted to the lower deck lounges next to the dining room. Meals would be served as usual, and anyone not moving toward the assembly areas would wait in their cabins for his men to collect them. No passengers or crew would be allowed to move about the ship without escort.

Wolde said he was continuing negotiations for the ship's release and would be speaking to the ship's owners in the next twenty minutes. He repeated: Cell phones must be surrendered. Anyone found in possession of one would be shot. This was not an empty threat. It was a promise.

Admiral Tom Carlow heard the instructions on the ship's intercom system, and he spoke very sternly to Miranda, telling her that when the knock on the door came, she was to go with the pirate escort while he hid in the big wardrobe—with his cell phone sealed in a hidden pocket in his old navy bag.

Miranda protested, telling him not to be a damn fool. But the blood of a seafaring commander coursed through Admiral Tom Carlow's veins, and he told her quietly, "That's an order."

Two minutes later, there was a sharp bang on the door and someone called out, "Anyone in there?"

"Yes, I'm here," replied Mrs. Carlow, as she opened the door to Kifle Zenawi, the man who had slain Sam McLean.

"Cell phone?" he asked.

Miranda, trembling, handed over her phone.

"Anyone else in here?" asked Abdul.

"No. My husband was picked up outside and taken to the dining room. I was getting dressed."

"Okay, ma'am," said Kifle. "I need to search your handbag."

Miranda handed it over and the pirate, slightly intimidated by this very important American lady, rummaged for a moment and then handed the bag back without even taking her money or her watch.

Deep inside the wardrobe, Tom heard the cabin door slam shut, and he muttered, "That's my girl."

Then he climbed out, locked and bolted the cabin door, and rummaged in his bag for his state-of-the-art satellite cell phone. He dialled his son's private number at SPECWARCOM Coronado and heard the familiar tones of the younger Admiral Carlow.

"Jesus Christ, Dad, where the hell are you?"

"Right now I'm in my cabin on board the *Ocean Princess*. How much do you know?"

"I know more or less everything," he replied. "Are you in danger? Where's Mom?"

"She's with the other passengers. Now listen. At least five crew members have been shot, the ship is almost stationary, but every passenger except me is in the lounges. I'm telling you she's definitely susceptible to attack. Especially the bridge area and the offices below. The passengers are far away at the stern end of the Riviera Deck, main-deck level."

"Delta's on its way in."

"Mack Bedford's guys, right?"

"You got it, Dad. Can I have your number?"

"Sure. I'm staying right here; there's a big wardrobe. Nobody knows where I am."

"I'll have Delta make contact as soon as possible. Keep your eyes and ears open. You're our advance man!"

Tom cleared the line and hid the cell phone back in the bag, muffling any sound with a couple of big sweaters. He placed it in the wardrobe, unlocked the cabin door, and sat in an armchair reading a book. If the pirates should look in, he was a picture of uninformed innocence.

▼

MACK BEDFORD SAT with the captain marvelling at the rate the *Port Royal* was catching them. They'd be level by 3:00 p.m.

"The Zodiacs are serviced and fuelled if you should decide on a sea attack," said Tyron Marks. "But I was told by the Djibouti command that you favored a strike from the air."

"I've decided the air is better. Mostly because it's quicker and we can assess the risk much better. Coming in from the ocean in broad daylight we are completely dependent on no one seeing us. And that's something we can't control. If some fucking tribesman spotted us incoming, we would certainly face sustained machine-gunfire and take losses. I guess you know how well-armed they are, especially out of Haradheere."

"What time do you want to go in?"

"Just as soon as the *Port Royal* gets here, soon as they can fire up the gunship. I'd like to embark my guys in the Sikorsky no later than 1530."

"No problem," said Captain Marks. "The helicopter will be ready as soon as you are."

By 1430 Commander Bedford was in communication with the cruiser, speaking to the commander of the AH-1 Cobra, one of the most lethal attack weapons in the United States armed forces. The helicopter packed FEAR rockets and antitank missiles on the stub wing pylons, with a twenty-millimeter cannon in the gun pod beneath the nose.

The Cobra was only lightly armored, but she had a very slim profile head-on. She was thus a tough target to track and even tougher to hit. Her cockpit panels were made of bulletproof glass. With her back to the wall, the Cobra could fire up to fifty-two rockets, and her three-barrel M197 Gatling gun blazed seven hundred rounds per minute. She carried a two-man crew, with the pilot above and behind the gunner. Her 1,400-horsepower engines rattled her along at 165 miles per hour. She was fourteen feet high with a wingspan of only ten feet. The Cobra's range was almost three hundred miles, and that afternoon she would stand guard over Mack Bedford's SEALs as they made their treacherous descent, probably under fire, onto the deck of the *Ocean Princess*.

The operation was standard SEAL air-attack procedure. The commander of the Cobra had trained for such a mission for years. His gunner, CPO Billy Ray Conners, a native of Alabama, was a Gulf War veteran who had also flown gunships in Afghanistan. He was known locally as the Helo Squadron's top gun.

By 1445 they could see the *Port Royal* steaming over the horizon. They were thirty miles north of the *Ocean Princess*, tucked in behind one of the atolls. When Delta Platoon took off, they would come unseen across the islands, running due south, and then fly into the open waters of the ops area, with maximum surprise to the pirates.

Commander Bedford was still in conference with the Cobra crew when the SEALs began piling into the Sea Stallion, and loading two heavy machine guns, which would be lowered onto the deck when the assault force was aboard.

By 1520 they were embarked and ready to go. They had the signal from the *Port Royal*: The Cobra had no more questions and was ready for immediate takeoff. Commander Fritz Halliday, who would pilot the Sea Stallion, already had Admiral Tom Carlow's cell phone number for a final check on the whereabouts of the passengers and any other behind-the-lines information.

At 1525 the Delta SEALs, sitting in lines inside the huge helo, lifted off from the stern deck of the USS *Chafee*. They were less than ten minutes from their target, and way out off their left side, they could see the Cobra flying lower. Even in a nonurgent situation, the heavily armed gunship looked nothing short of menacing.

Commander Bedford had elected to fly south across the Maldives' western atolls for the approach, and Fritz Halliday came in low over both North and South Nilandu and then came rocketing over the Kudahuvadhoo Channel directly to the north side of Haddumati Atoll.

Approaching the southern shoreline, they got their first glimpse of the *Ocean Princess* in the choppy waters of the One and a Half Degree Channel, and the radio operator opened up the line to Admiral Tom Carlow.

Deep inside the wardrobe, the cell phone played its ring tone, "Anchors Aweigh," and the admiral swiftly locked the cabin door. Mack Bedford's voice greeted him but there was no chitchat: "Tom, do you favor a stern or bow landing for Delta?"

"Definitely bow," said the veteran admiral. "The stern's full of staterooms, and every one of the passengers is in the aft lounge. I'm assessing there are four pirates on guard in there. The rest are on the bridge. If you have to fight your way in, the bridge makes a proper target. The stern area of this ship is a goddamned mess. Stay away from it."

"Roger that!" shouted Mack. "Over and out."

The Sea Stallion hurtled toward the cruise liner. Mack Bedford yelled above the din: *"GO FOR THE STERN, THEN MAKE A LAST-MINUTE SWING TO THE BOW END!"*

"Roger that!" shouted the pilot.

The SEALs immediately went to action stations and lined up at the doors, port and starboard. Chief Sharp checked the ropes while the enormous helo made its descent to fifty feet, then forty. With both rotors pounding the hot ocean air, the doors were opened and the thick ropes dropped down to the deck.

Mack Bedford scanned the wide bridge that stretched the entire width of the ship, right in front of the enormous yellow funnel. It was probably eighty feet from the point of the bow, white-painted and glass-fronted.

There was no sign of life on the foredeck of the *Princess*, and Mack ordered the SEALs, *"DESCEND TO TARGET!"*

One by one they gripped the rope, leapt out of the doorway, and started down. There were three of them on each rope when Mack spotted the portside bridge window smash, and the barrel of a heavy machine gun come jutting out. Wolde's defenses, not surprisingly, were up, and the pirate chief had ordered the gun to open fire on the SEALs at their most vulnerable point.

"FUCK!" yelled Mack as he viewed an assault commander's nightmare—they'd been spotted and would be fired upon by the enemy as they made their descent. Instinctively, he raised his rifle and sent a volley through the door, straight over the heads of the SEALs and into the bridge.

But he was too late, way too late. With two sirens blaring loud enough to frighten the bejesus out of a passing school of porpoise, the Cobra came swooping in from the port side, thirty feet above the deck, as subtle as a train crash, and ripped a pair of antitank missiles straight at the bridge windows of the *Ocean Princess.*

Chief Conners watched them fly, slashing through the air with a white tail behind, before slamming through the glass and instantly killing Ismael Wolde and Elmi Ahmed and blasting the control room to smithereens, blowing out the entire front end.

The lead SEALs were pouring out of the Sikorsky. And down the ropes they came, sliding, shouting, and gripping with their leather gloves but landing like snowflakes, moving deftly away from the landing square and grabbing for their rifles.

Mack Bedford and Chief Sharp came last, one on each rope holding their heavy gun in a sling between them in an outrageous display of strength. There was no return fire from anywhere on the ship, not after Billy Ray's rockets, and Mack ordered the advance, two teams of eighteen moving down the deck, port and starboard.

No one knew where the pirates were. There was, apparently, no one in the upper works of the ship. Everyone must have been at deck level or below.

"Okay, guys," ordered Mack, "fan out in teams of three and take the corridors one by one, usual house-to-house procedures. Any door doesn't open, blast it. We assault the big room together. Order the passengers to hit the deck and then take out the terrorists. Shoot to kill."

"Is that no prisoners, sir?" asked Lt. Josh Malone.

"Can't risk prisoners, bro," said the boss. "They booby-trapped their last ship, and they might have done the same to this one too."

"Dead men can't press detonators, right, sir?" said Josh.

"You got it, kid. In our business you don't have time to fuck about."

A short ripple of suppressed laughter ran through the SEAL ranks as they moved aft down each side of the ship. None of them knew there were seven pirates left or that the two leaders and the veteran combat trooper Ibrahim Yacin were dead.

Down below Omar Ali Farah and his buddy Abadula Sofian had been detailed to hold the corridor running inside down the starboard side of the main deck. They'd heard the roar of the arriving helos but had not dared go outside, and they'd heard the blast of the rockets on the bridge and not dared even to look.

But now the silence of the SEALs unnerved them even more. The sound of the rotors had gone and the intercom was dead. There was no reply from Wolde's cell phone, and they debated throwing down their rifles and surrendering to whoever the hell had come on board.

They could smell smoke wafting through the air-conditioning system, and they decided to get out from the stifling corridor into the fresh air, where they would have the chance to jump overboard and make it back to the *Desert Shark*.

They pushed open the double doors and there was an immediate bellow of "*HOLD IT RIGHT THERE, PAL! AND DROP YOUR FUCKING RIFLE RIGHT WHERE YOU ARE.*"

Omar Ali and Abadula had not a clue about military precision, and Omar swung around to see who was yelling. But he had failed to drop his rifle, and in a split second it was pointing directly at Mack Bedford and Lieutenant Malone.

Mack and Josh's rifles spat fire and two of the youngest pirates were each hit eight times, crumpling dead to the floor. The SEALs never broke stride.

# CHAPTER 13

▼

O N CAME THE SEALS IN A FORMIDABLE HALF CROUCH, half run through the decks of the *Ocean Princess*. They were watched by one terrified junior pirate who had been sent up from the dining hall to reconnoiter the ship and try to find out who precisely was there.

But the kid was only eighteen, and he was too afraid to hang around when he saw the seemingly giant Americans advancing in menacing formation. He simply fled back to his boss, Kifle Zenawi, who was in command of the entire complement of passengers in the dining room. The boy was so frightened, he could only report, "They comin', boss. They . . . they . . . they're most certainly comin'. Yessir. They comin' alright."

Zenawi's worst fears were crowding in on him. He stared at the kid, and he gazed around the room at his prisoners. He too had heard the muffled explosions high on the bridge, and he knew that every line of communication he had was down. In addition to the two kids, he knew Abdul Mesfin was still alive, but he had the gravest doubts about the rest. It was possible that Wolde was as dead as his cell phone.

Kifle's instincts told him to surrender to whomever was in charge. But that was as scary as death. What if the military force was Russian and they took the remaining Somali Marines prisoner and transported them back to Moscow, like those other guys from Puntland? That could mean a lifetime incarcerated in the Lubyanka or somewhere worse. Out of the question. Kifle and his men would fight to the death because there was still a chance they could make it back to the *Desert Shark* and make a getaway. The chances of completing the mission and raising a ransom from the ship's owners were somewhere between remote and out of the question.

Abdul Mesfin, on roving guard duty, knew something really bad had happened, but he was uncertain precisely what it was. Hamdan Ougoure, manning the second heavy machine gun just above deck level portside, was completely in the dark. From his vantage point he could not see the advancing SEALs led by Chief Sharp.

But he heard them and, using his best judgment, opened fire before he saw them, hoping to frighten them to death. The bullets hit nothing worthwhile, but they prompted Cody to send Barney Wilkes around to the starboard blind side to take the hapless gunner Ougoure from the rear.

Barney shot him dead with two bullets to the head. Hamdan died slumped over his heavy Kalashnikov, the long ammunition belt dangling around his neck.

"That got the easy part done," said Mack Bedford. "Now let's drop down a deck and take control of the ship."

But just then, Chief Charlton came skidding around the corner, yelling, "Sir, sir, the fucking bridge is on fire! . . . Really burning . . . we need to get it out!"

"Take four guys and find the crew," snapped the commander. "There are 140 of them somewhere. Then send 'em up there with the firefighting gear."

The speed with which Brad Charlton charged back down the companionway demonstrated just how concerned he was about the fire on the bridge. And Abdul Mesfin's half-crazed dash for freedom, straight for the starboard rail and over the side, showed much the same state of mind.

If he'd dumped his rifle and charged for the ocean, he might have made it. But when an enemy's running hard down a corridor, directly at an advancing SEAL assault squad, with his rifle in firing position, that's suicide. With coldhearted certainty, Shane Cannell shot him dead.

Kifle Zenawi, flanked by two teenaged rookies, knew the ball was in his court. Before him were close to two hundred prisoners, unarmed but growing angry. The last of the pirates understood they were on their own and that a trained military force was aboard, a force that would not hesitate to gun down the three of them.

He had no appetite for this fight, but he desperately wanted to avoid being taken prisoner. He'd heard the short bursts of gunfire, the last from the starboard side of the ship. He signalled to the two kids to follow him out of the door and up the wide staircase to the portside throughway.

They made it to the outside deck and found themselves about twenty yards behind the SEAL team led by Chief Sharp.

"*JUMP!*" yelled Kifle, "*JUMP OVERBOARD!*"

Everyone heard him and, as the SEALs spun around, the three Somali Marines cleared the rails and hurled themselves into the ocean thirty feet below.

"*HOLD YOUR FIRE!*" shouted Chief Sharp. "*WE'RE NOT SHOOTING FISH IN A GODDAMNED BARREL!* . . . Two of those guys looked like they shoulda been in school."

Thus ended the siege of the *Ocean Princess*. Brad Charlton raised the firefighting team, and it took about an hour to bring the blaze on the bridge under control, by which time the *Chafee* was alongside. A special team from the American warship was dispatched to take charge of the cruise liner since she no longer had a captain.

Her engines, propulsion systems, generators, and electronics were intact, but there was no way to control her since the steering and acceleration gear had been blown apart. The situation was, however, not as bad as it looked. Two of *Chafee*'s engineers masterminded a kind of jury-rigged steering, and three others fixed temporary speed controls.

She would head under escort with the *Port Royal* to Diego Garcia, from where the United States Air Force would fly the passengers back to Mombassa to await flights home.

Delta Platoon meanwhile was making a helicopter transfer back to the SEAL base aboard the *Chafee*. They had suffered no casualties, but they had several days more of this mission ahead of them.

Commander Bedford spoke on the phone to Andy Carlow and reported that no passengers had been injured and that he knew his parents were safe. So far as Mack could tell, Admiral Tom Carlow had more or less directed the entire operation from his closet.

Admiral Andy Carlow confirmed the procedures the navy would follow over the next few days. A press release would be issued stating only that a pirate attack on a US cruise liner in the Maldives had failed. Nothing more. No details of the SEAL attack.

Commander Bedford was to proceed with the mission as agreed by Mark Bradfield and General Lancaster. The commanding officer of the USS *Chafee* was under orders to transport Delta Platoon to her next theater of operations. Any further supplies the team needed would be air-dropped from a Djibouti-based aircraft.

"Mack, how much equipment did you use?"

"Nothing much. Couple dozen rounds of ammunition. Cobra launched a coupla missiles. That's all. Everything else was either unused or recovered, including the fast-rope gloves."

"Great job, bro," said the SEAL C-in-C. "Any of the pirates survive?"

"Coupla kids and some weird-looking black fucker. Crazy pricks jumped overboard."

"You didn't intimidate anyone, did you?" laughed the admiral. "You know, contrary to section 189, part 10, sections C, D, and M, paragraph 6,073?"

"Never," joshed Mack. "Fuck that."

"See you, bro," said Andy as he hung up the phone.

▼

WITH ALMOST ALL OF HIS MEN airlifted over to the *Chafee,* Commander Bedford was watching a luxury motor yacht, about seventy feet long, moving slowly in about a half mile off the stern of the *Ocean Princess.* And then, to his amazement, he saw the boat slow down and pick up the three swimmers, the pirates who had just jumped ship into the Indian Ocean.

"Who the hell are they?" he muttered to Cody, who was staring at the rescue through powerful SEAL binoculars.

"God knows," replied the chief. "I got a coupla black guys hauling the two kids aboard and that weird-looking prick climbing in last, up a ladder."

"Is that the goddamned pirate mother ship?" said Mack.

"I don't know," said Chief Sharp. "But there's a couple of long, narrow skiffs towing off her aft end."

"It has to be the pirate command ship—these guys are together."

"Pirate command ship!" exclaimed Cody. "Steady, boss. That sonofabitch cost the fat end of ten million bucks. Anyone owned that, he sure wouldn't need to be a pirate."

"Could be a couple of merciful towel-head princes, right?" chuckled Mack.

"With a couple of native canoes hanging off the stern? But maybe they found 'em just floating around."

"And maybe they didn't," said Mack. "Remember one thing, Cody. These bastards have stolen a couple of giant oil tankers plus this cruise liner in the last month. I'm guessing they stole that motor yacht and are about to make their getaway with the only survivors from their mission."

"Well, we better find out, right? I believe our policy is to leave no trace of our activities."

"Correct, chief. That's our policy. Hop up that gangway and ask the captain to close in on them. We'll board and find out exactly who they are."

"Okay, boss. Be right back."

Cody made his way up to the bridge and explained the problem to *Chafee*'s Captain Marks, who immediately turned the wheel hard to starboard and headed out toward the stationary *Desert Shark*.

First thing Mack saw was the Saudi flag flying off the stern. Then he saw the name. Someone handed him a bullhorn and he yelled for the master of the *Desert Shark* to identify his boat and its passengers, none of whom were visible.

Captain Hassan, who was in the wheelhouse, completely ignored the request, which was an unusual thing to do given that he had one of the most powerful warships in the world, armed with heavy navy guns and missiles, standing off about forty feet from his hull.

Mack yelled again. "*DESERT SHARK!* You are flying the flag of the Islamic kingdom of Saudi Arabia. This is a United Sates naval destroyer. We are your country's principal ally. Please identify yourselves. There has been a fatal act of terrorism here, and you have taken on board three of the perpetrators. You must identify yourselves."

Captain Hassan was terrified. He had no idea what to say to this American officer. Elijah was below with the three soaking-wet pirates who had escaped. Hassan was alone in the wheelhouse. He said nothing but began to turn his sleek and very fast craft away from the *Chafee*. He'd outrun it; that was the game.

"If you do not comply with my request," bellowed Mack, "my men will board the *Desert Shark* and arrest all of you on suspicion of piracy on the high seas . . . in the name of the government of the United States of America."

Hassan hit the throttle and rammed it open with such force that the *Desert Shark* almost lurched up on her rear end. But she flattened out and blasted clear of the US warship, making 30 knots plus, heading west, with the three pirates rolling around on the floor of the stateroom, trying to regain their balance.

"*Jesus Christ!*" shouted Mack. "Captain Marks, sink that ship! And stay well clear. She's probably loaded with high explosives."

Captain Marks ordered an antiship action. The *Desert Shark* was racing away so quickly they would need to make decisions fast—like gunfire or missile—and by warship standards the *Shark* was not much of a target.

The *Chafee*'s missile director called to the bridge: "*Taking* Desert Shark *out with a SLAMMER*"—navy-speak for Standoff Land Attack Missile Expanded Response. A Boeing Harpoon guided missile: an all-weather, over-the-horizon, sea-skimming, low-level, 570 miles per hour ship-killer with a five-hundred-pound-blast warhead, one of the destroyer's many steel-cased angels of death.

The *Desert Shark* was ten minutes and six miles away on the horizon when the Harpoon launched, lancing out of the tube with a fiery blast and hurtling toward the fleeing Hassan. Within twenty-eight seconds it had switched on its seeker, swerved, and then smashed into the port quarter of the elegant white-hulled yacht.

Designed to knock over a full-sized enemy warship, it practically blew the stern off the *Shark* and reduced the rest of the vessel to burning matchwood. The explosion was, however, not in scale to the size of the boat, which was, as Mack Bedford had feared, packed with high explosives: hand grenades, RPGs, dynamite, and ammunition.

It was a spectacular display of pure combustion, flames and black smoke billowing three hundred feet in the air. One of the trailing skiffs did a passable imitation of the space shuttle as it blew skyward, 250 vertical feet, totally engulfed in flame.

A passerby would have assumed that someone had hit and sunk an aircraft carrier. And long after she had slipped beneath the waves, there were deep, muffled sounds of explosions, and great, oily bubbles broke on the surface. No luxurious motor yacht, in all of maritime history, ever went to the bottom with a greater roar of belching rage and protest.

The sailors watching from the deck of the *Chafee*, even from a six-mile distance, could not believe the volume of the explosion that signalled the end of the pirate ship.

If Hassan and Kifle were on their way to hell, they must surely have made a grand entrance.

The *Ocean Princess* mission had been a disaster for Haradheere. There were no survivors, not one pirate left to tell the tale. Everything they had brought with them was gone, their food and equipment had vanished, and there was no trace of the boat or the men who had sailed with her.

Mohammed Salat, worried out of his mind, still could not reach Wolde or Ahmed. The last message he received had been six hours earlier: "*Somali pirates control the* Ocean Princess. *Speaking to owner Hyland shortly. Ten million asked and agreement expected. Ismael.*"

At that point Salat had issued the secondary tranche of "Operation Princess" stocks, 10,000 more at $30, and there had been a buying stampede. The market had waited with immense patience for news that a ransom had been agreed upon.

But since then, the silence had been endless. Salat was in possession of several numbers: Ismael's cell, Elmi's cell, Captain Hassan's cell, the fixed cell on board the *Desert Shark*. But all lines had been dead for two hours. And there was only one possible conclusion left. Somehow, his Somali Marines had been stopped in their tracks. Only death or capture could have prevented them from taking a call from pirate HQ, Haradheere, the garrison to which their personal fortunes were so irrevocably bound.

There was the slightest possibility that a band of pirates could receive ransom money and then flee across the ocean with ten sacks of one-hundred-dollar bills to live happily ever after.

But that was not the character of Wolde and his men. Most of the Somali Marines had left their entire families in Haradheere—wives, children, fathers, mothers, and other relatives. Even more importantly, the shipowners and insurers had not had time to pay a ransom. No, in Salat's opinion something had gone catastrophically wrong. At 6:00 p.m. that evening, the Haradheere Stock Market crashed.

Salat's despondency was infectious. He was being bombarded with questions by his investors. He'd been in the stock exchange for several hours, and in a twenty-minute period, the price of the bonds issued for Operation Princess had crashed from $30 to $4. Everyone was trying to bail out, to preserve some of their money, and there was a desperation about the investors who had gone in at $30.

Guards had already gone back to the garrison and returned with cash to pay off the bondholders. Even the pirates' relatives were trying to get out. There were the local big hitters who'd gone in for 1,000 shares at the original $20, and they were getting out for between $4,000 and $6,000.

Out in the street, a throng of Africans was spreading over the entire town, and their mournful cry echoed in the morning air. It was at once a sound of loss, sadness, and an unmistakable expression of tribal melancholy . . . *O-O-O-O-H-H CRY FOR THE SO-MALI WARRIOR!! DEATH HAS TAKEN OUR HEROES . . . O-O-O-O-H WHOMBA!!*

Deep in the garrison, Salat's staff tried to make contact with the outside world, tuning the television to the satellites and searching out the twenty-four-hour news channels from the Western world. This was never easy, but now, even when they managed to get connected, there was no news of any mayhem in the Indian Ocean.

They even tried e-mailing their New York agent, Peter Kilimo, but there was no Internet connection. Salat tried a phone call to Najib Saleh in Yemen, but the arms dealer knew nothing, and

Salat's news about a possible disaster practically gave him palpitations since he might need to explain the disappearance of the *Desert Shark* to her Saudi owners.

Late in the afternoon, the first breach in the mystery appeared. American radio stations were announcing that a pirate attempt on a US cruise ship in the Indian Ocean, close to the Maldives, had failed. Nothing else. No details. The press release appeared to have emanated from the Pentagon, an organization that does not respond to questions from outsiders.

Salat's radio operators picked it up, and Haradheere shares in Operation Princess crashed to zero. The only remaining question was whether any of the pirates had made it out alive. No one knew the answer.

▼

EVERY US WARSHIP either actively involved or standing by during the effort to free the *Ocean Princess* was bound by the navy's highest rules of classification. There was a complete communications blackout. No one, repeat no one, was permitted to utter one word about the operation.

And that included the recently arrived aircraft carrier CVN-75, the 100,000-ton *Harry S. Truman*, with eighty fighter/bombers embarked. In this instance, the United States Navy was sworn to secrecy. And the reason had shades of Robin Hood written all over it.

Zack Lancaster, Mark Bradfield, and Andy Carlow had heard the stories of the $78 million stashed away in Haradheere. They wanted the pirate operation and all of its finances smashed. In addition they wanted the money back. They planned to return it to the shipping organizations that had paid it, with the rest going to US Navy charities.

Their biggest fear was if the main players in this all-African enterprise heard the Americans were coming, they would pack up the money and flee to Kenya or somewhere else, never to be heard from again. Hence the highly classified nature of the operation, with a total news blackout, worldwide, every shutter slammed tight, essentially to prevent Salat Mohammed from finding out what had happened on board the *Ocean Princess*.

At this point, there were about a dozen men who understood the plan, and the leader was the SEAL commander Mack Bedford. He'd been closeted in the captain's office for almost a half hour on a conference call to General Lancaster and Admiral Bradfield. And he was ready to outline the strategy for the SEALs' next attack.

They were steaming slowly west, directly toward the coast of Somalia eight hundred miles away. Captain Marks ordered an immediate increase in speed, up to 30 knots, which would get them to within ten miles of Haradheere in twenty-seven hours, around 2100 the following night.

Marks sat at a table with Commander Bedford and the two SEAL chief petty officers, Cody Sharp and Brad Charlton. Lt. Josh Malone was also in attendance. Out on the horizon was the *Harry S. Truman*, falling into step with the *Chafee*, which had been designated her official escort.

At the captain's invitation, Mack sat at the head of the table and told the select gathering that he had been tasked by the Pentagon to destroy the pirate stronghold in the town of Haradheere. He mentioned that the long-range plans for this operation were somewhat in disarray.

"We had always assumed we would launch from Djibouti in a C-130 Hercules and deploy at 26,000 feet, landing close to our target, HALO in the middle of the night.

"That," he added, "is no longer possible since we are floating around in the middle of the Indian Ocean, where C-130 Hercules transporters are a bit thin on the ground. But we're still going in."

He outlined the new operation, which had been finalized with the Pentagon in time to fly a squad of helicopters on board the carrier while she was in Diego Garcia—four Black Hawks and an Army Apache gunship.

"Anyway," he said, "we're going to hit Haradheere tomorrow night. We're going to land on the beach four miles to the north in the Black Hawks. I preferred them to the Sikorsky that landed us on the cruise ship because this garrison is well armed and they have antiaircraft missiles. Couldn't risk one of them hitting the big guy with all of us on board, wiping out the entire mission."

"Do we have data on their arsenal?" asked Cody Sharp.

"The CIA is listing that Russian heavy PKM. It's a heck of a weapon, easily doubles as an antiaircraft gun. But they also have the latest Russian rocket grenades, the RPG7s, handheld, reloadable, antitank. Aside from those they have brand-new state-of-the-art Kalashnikovs."

"We just hitting the town?" asked Josh.

"Not really," said Mack. "They have a fortified garrison. I have satellite photos, which I'll show you in a minute. The walls are about three feet thick, and the only way in is through a massive wooden door."

"You expecting someone to open it for us?" asked Cody.

"No need," replied Mack.

"How come?"

"We're gonna blow the sonofabitch off, that's why."

"Jesus," said Cody.

"Funny, I'd always understood we would deal with the ship, return to base, regroup, and then fly back and deal with the town," said Josh Malone.

"We were," said the commander, "when I wasn't thinking properly. But now it's more obvious. If you were the pirate money guys sitting there in Haradheere, and you found out what had taken place on the *Ocean Princess*, and you had close to $80 million tucked away in the garrison, what would you do?"

"Outtahere," said the lieutenant. "I'd gather that huge bundle of cash and hightail it right out of Haradheere and get myself into a foreign land with the speed of 10,000 antelopes."

"That's right," said Mack. "Because when you hear that the *Princess* fell to a mighty armed force, which came out of the sky in a helicopter the size of Mount Kilimanjaro and nearly blew the bridge off the ship, you're calculating that force is coming right after you, probably sooner rather then later."

"So that's why we're attacking Haradheere tomorrow night?"

"Correct. The best decisions tend to make themselves. And right now the pirate bosses do not know what happened out here. There were no survivors, not even their mother ship. There's no one they can call to get the full scoop on the operation. I'd say that buys us the day and a half it will take us to get in there."

"Guess that means the carrier will come all the way with us?" asked Chief Charlton.

"Sure does. Tomorrow morning we'll make a ship-to-ship transfer of all our gear. Tomorrow night we'll fly off the *Truman* about ten miles offshore. The Black Hawks will take us in."

Commander Bedford produced copies of the satellite photographs of the Haradheere garrison. He also distributed diagrams of the compound, which clearly showed the position of doors and windows. It looked as if there was a residence in the northwest corner. According to the CIA dossier, the office building next-door was the likely location of the strong room, where the millions of dollars were kept.

The diagrams marked the location of the guard posts, which gave even the SEALs cause for concern. Normally the intentions of the enemy are regarded as irrelevant, but this crowd was obviously armed with up-to-date weaponry, plus rockets and missiles. The issue was never how to avoid being hit and killed but how to destroy the guards and their arsenal before they knew what had hit them.

Commander Bedford had a plan, which they refined until the meeting broke for dinner. Unsurprisingly, the SEALs were far more tired than they realized, and they passed out immediately. No one stirred until the sun was long above the horizon.

They made the ship-to-ship transfer of their gear by helicopter to the carrier. Right after lunch they said good-bye to the crew of *Chafee* and flew over to CVN-75, where several members of the crew turned out on the flight deck to welcome them aboard.

This took place while the two ships were thundering through the water at more than 30 knots, the carrier powered by two nuclear reactors driving four screws, each with four blades, twenty-one feet across and weighing 66,000 pounds.

They were already six hundred miles closer to the shores of Somalia than when they started, after a twenty-hour voyage from the place where they had destroyed Wolde and his gang. There were still a couple of hundred miles to go, but the two ultramodern warships ate up that kind of distance without breaking stride.

They'd arrive in their ops area on time at 9:00 p.m. and embark the Black Hawks after a final briefing with the four pilots plus the aviators, who would bring in the Apache gunship to pave the way for the opening attack on the garrison.

The latest satellite pictures showed Mack that there was absolutely nothing along the beach immediately north of Haradheere. In fact there was hardly anything along the beach north of Haradheere for six hundred miles. Except sand.

In consultation with his two senior chiefs, Cody Sharp and Brad Charlton, Mack had already decided that the helos would come in from the north against a southwest offshore wind, which would deaden the sound. They would land two miles from the town, then walk in to the target. Since there would plainly be some kind of a battle, the walk should be as short as possible.

The SEALs slept most of the afternoon and had dinner together at 1800. As usual, they stayed separate from the rest of the crew, since this remained a highly classified Black Ops mission, and cell phones were still banned.

Shortly before 2100 the huge carrier began to slow down, and Mack ordered everyone to ready their battle harnesses, combat knives, pistols, machine guns, ammunition magazines, hand grenades, rocket grenades, camouflage cream, and their green-and-brown drive-on bandanas.

The combat medics stuffed supplies into their harnesses, morphine and bandages tucked in with the ammunition and night-glasses. They gathered in a large, private recreation room for their final brief. Up on deck the pilots were firing up the Black Hawks.

The only non-SEAL outsiders in the room were the Apache's pilot and gunner.

"If we get a chance, I'd like to take the pirate chiefs alive," said Mack. "But I'm not hopeful. Most of you have read the report of that battle several weeks ago when the Haradheere guards wiped out an entire al-Qaeda army, which had been taking a shot at stealing all the pirates' bread.

"These guys are so well-equipped we cannot take chances. Tonight we go in firing, right behind Jimmy's opening attack." Jimmy Shand, the Apache gunner and rocket man, nodded sagely and left the room before everyone else to make his way to the gunship.

"Okay, guys," concluded Commander Bedford, "there's a couple of things I want you to have in mind before we go in. These pirate characters are not some band of well-meaning buccaneers just trying to provide for their families. And their propaganda that they never kill anyone is bullshit.

"We think they're the same guys who took the *Niagara Falls* and murdered the first mate Charlie Wyatt from Baltimore. They also took the *Global Mustang* and shot dead two crewmen plus the engineering officer Sam McLean from Brockton, Massachusetts. Remember, when they took the *Ocean Princess* they shot and killed five Americans, including Captain Lansdale and his bosun.

"These men are ruthless cutthroats. And they've turned some of the most popular cruising waters in the world into no-go areas. Not to mention the main tanker routes, which have been altered in order to transport the world's oil supply.

"These guys have fucked up people's lives. They're fucking up half the world, they're murderers, and our ultimate bosses at the Pentagon want the situation dealt with just as brutally as necessary. Some of the biggest brains in the US military have been wrestling with this problem for months, just looking for a solution.

"And we are that solution—the delta solution, the guys entrusted with sorting this out. And I know darned well you will not let anyone down. Okay, gentlemen, let's go."

Delta Platoon set off through the giant carrier: big men making their way up to the flight deck, carrying their packs, machine guns over their shoulders, faces black with cammy cream, the outriders of American frontline muscle.

All the way through the mighty warship, people just stood and watched them in obvious awe. No one knew quite where or what their mission was. But everyone knew that tonight the SEALs were going in.

Occasionally one of the more senior officers would offer a handshake, an expression of goodwill, the goodwill of the 5,000 men on board. Twenty minutes later they were embarked in the four Black Hawks, and shortly after 2230 hours, they took off, one by one, setting course two-seven-zero straight for the coast of Somalia ten miles to the west.

It was a cloudy night and there was a gusty headwind. Mack Bedford sat in the lead helicopter, right behind the pilot, watching the GPS numbers. The journey took less than ten minutes flying at half speed, low level, a hundred feet above the water, line astern.

Up ahead Mack could see the long, white lines of the surf as they neared the beach. The pilot chose a spot behind the sand, where the dunes looked flat and green with eelgrass, suggesting a firm surface, and the Black Hawk put down in a maelstrom of flying sand. The ground was firm, but the pilot nevertheless ran a few stress tests before lowering the full weight of the helo onto terra firma.

Mack Bedford led the nine SEALs out and behind them they could see the other three aircraft coming in to land. One by one, the men and their gear left the helos, which immediately took off again, back to the carrier, where they would become a part of the SEAL home base, ready at a moment's notice to fly in and either assist or rescue the men who would take the pirate stronghold.

Once they were alone, Commander Bedford assembled the men and took a roll call, insuring every man was right where he was supposed to be, armed, fit, and ready to move. This completed, he signalled the whole platoon to begin the two-mile walk across the dunes. Midnight was H-hour (H for hit). The SEALs would walk in four columns at four miles per hour, allowing time to traverse the soft, sandy ground.

The night was hot and muggy, but the breeze off the land made the air slightly more tolerable to the troops carrying their heavy packs and weapons. Four of them were lifting a couple of big machine guns. Everyone knew they may need to fight heavy fire with similar weapons.

They walked as if Mack Bedford had ordered a Trappist vow of silence. No one spoke; they just gripped their gear and kept going, across the dunes and through the grasses, with the Indian Ocean rolling gently in to their left.

They could see the lights of the town in the distance, but in the all-enveloping darkness and the barren landscape, it was hard to judge the precise yardage left. Mack kept pausing to check through the glasses and eventually signalled the platoon to make a right-hand swing and come in from the west, a couple of hundred yards from the wall of the garrison.

He relayed this information to Chiefs Sharp and Charlton, who moved among the SEALs keeping them informed and answering their whispered questions. Finally Mack signalled for total silence and for the guys to go into their crouch as they moved around the fortified garrison without making a sound.

Through the glasses it was just possible to make out the guard stations on the high walls, and Mack could see they were manned. But apparently there had been only one attack on the place in a year, and for the moment he did not detect any sense of urgency or high alert.

Two hundred yards from the west wall, Mack set up the first SEAL RV point, where two of his team would man the communications equipment. This was the vital link for all information between the assault force, the support helicopters, and home base on the carrier. The two comms experts hunkered down in the desert brush, fixed the aerial, and checked cell phones and connections to Mack and the chiefs. Then the whole platoon left them and moved off, travelling parallel to the west wall, well out of sight of the high garrison guards.

Softly they moved across the sand until they reached a point seventy-five yards from the southwest corner of the compound, within sight of the enormous timber gates. Mack could see no guards on the outside in the street, but there was a light on the high wall on the corner. He designated two of his team to slam that corner with a couple of RPGs as soon as they opened their attack.

Mack split the force, placing himself at the head of a group of eighteen SEALs, who were lying flat and ready to charge through the main gate as soon as it was opened. The other eighteen, under Chief Charlton, took their position further south of the compound from where they could deliver vicious covering fire as Mack's team stormed in and breached the garrison defenses.

Also from that half-hidden position, they could nail down any attack from the town, where it was possible that a reserve force was stationed, in the event of a major attack against them. According to Bob Birmingham, the whole place was involved in piracy on the high seas.

It was fifteen minutes to the midnight H-hour. The SEAL teams fixed the heavy machine guns, one with each of the two groups, both weapons ready to lay down withering fire either toward the garrison entrance or the guard posts.

The minutes ticked slowly by as they lay motionless in the sparse desert brush. With five minutes to go, Mack's phone vibrated in his harness and he took a call from RV Point One, the SEALs around the other side of the compound.

*Apache's taken off, sir. Heading in right now. ETA four minutes. Over . . .*

*Roger that, out.*

Its rotors beating low over the water, the AH64D Boeing gunship came clattering into the area where the Black Hawks had landed. Then it made a long swing to the south, avoiding the town, before finally turning back up the beach and screaming straight toward the garrison.

Jimmy Shand opened fire approximately two hundred yards from the south wall with two Hellfire missiles—antiarmor HEAT (high explosion anti-tank with a shaped charge). They blew out of the pods and rocketed above the head of the SEALs before blasting into the huge garrison gates with a stupendous explosion that obliterated the entire entrance, flattened both gates into burning matchwood, and knocked down half the wall.

The Apache streaked above the garrison and then made a hard left-hand turn down by the ocean before coming in at speed for a second run. Shand opened up with his nose-mounted M230 chain gun, hammering thirty-millimeter cannon rounds into the entire compound, blasting windows and doors, and mowing down the panic-stricken guard platoon on the main southwest corner wall.

Anyone inside the garrison was rushing for cover. And as they did, Commander Bedford stood up and roared, *"LET'S GO, GUYS, RIGHT NOW! . . . GO! GO! GO!"*

All eighteen SEALs sprang to their feet and charged forward, machine guns drawn, running hard behind the boss. Through the gaping hole of the gateway they came, four of them peeling right and heading for what looked like a guardroom. Barney Wilkes threw two hand grenades straight through the open window and reduced the entire place to rubble.

Four more SEALs performed exactly the same task on the west side of the courtyard, and the massive blast brought down the building and the wall above it, where the high lookout position had once been. By now the only operational guard post still standing was the one on the northeast corner, where they were struggling to assemble the launch post for the RPGs and desperately trying to knock the Apache out of the sky.

But it was dark with billowing, black smoke everywhere, and many of their colleagues were either dead or wounded. There was an atmosphere of mass confusion. No one knew who had attacked them. Half the compound was on fire, and the Apache was making one last steep turn, incoming again, guns blazing away with the last of Jimmy's 1,200 rounds, going for the high walls, sustaining fire above the heads of the SEALs.

One final staccato burst finished the last, high guard post. No survivors. They never even got a shot away, so sudden and deadly was the onslaught of the Apache from Delta Platoon. The SEALs watched their helicopter bank away to the left and, as suddenly as it had arrived, head back toward the ocean where the *Harry S. Truman* awaited.

Mack Bedford now sensed the first resistance since they had entered the compound. He called in to RV-1 and told them he was inside the garrison with his team, but the place was not secured and the second team led by Lieutenant Malone was to stay right on station in case a new force was regrouping in the town.

There was sporadic fire coming down on them from the glass-fronted building in the northwest corner. The SEALs were in a safe position behind the rubble of the guardhouse, and the enemy was behind a twelve-foot wall built across the front of the big house. No one knew it, but they were looking at the first line of defense built for Mohammed Salat's palace guard.

Armed to the teeth, the tribesmen formed a recognizable line of battle, facing south, staring directly at their unknown assailants, the men from Coronado, the men who wore the Trident. The palace guard had no trouble with their launch post, and through the drifting smoke the tribesmen unleashed two Russian-built rockets, aimed roughly in the direction of the invaders.

One of them lanced across the courtyard and shot through the gateway, down the main street, and ended up on the beach. The next hit the pile of concrete rubble behind which the SEALs were crouching. It blew with a thunderous bang, shook the ground and the SEALs, but injured no one.

Barney immediately suggested he take three guys and attack the house, getting some high explosive to work in there.

But Mack overruled on the basis that anything they wanted out of this exercise, including personnel and material assets to the tune of millions of dollars, was likely to be in that house. The last thing anyone needed was for Barney and his buddies to knock it down and kill everyone.

"There's no way we can accomplish this mission," said Mack, "unless we can get some goddamned prisoners and find that cash. And I sure as hell don't want to blow it all up before we've even located it. We need to be a bit more subtle and careful," he added.

"But isn't that against our religion?" asked Barney.

"Usually," replied the boss, "but we gotta be clever here. We must overwhelm the guard and take the house. That's how we take prisoners. Those are the facts. So let's not screw it up before we start."

"Okay, sir, what next?"

"We can't storm it because we'd be running directly into heavy fire. I'm guessing there's a half dozen guards behind that wall, and we need to take them out. They can't see us, but they may realize there's another group of invaders hidden on the far side of the compound.

"Either way, we need to get two or three grenades behind the wall and take everyone out. Just treat it like an enemy machine-gun nest."

"Okay, sir," snapped Barney. "We'll run in, take cover under the wall, and then hurl the grenades over the top, right?"

"Correct. Cody will provide heavy covering fire and you and I will charge in."

"Okay, sir, just give me the word."

"Get the grenades ready. We need two each in case one of us gets hit. I'll talk to Cody."

Moments later, Mack was back. "Barney," he said, "when Cody's machine gun opens up, we charge straight for the wall, dive in head first, right along the ground."

"Kinda like second base."

"You got it, bro. We don't move until the guns start. Then we go in hard."

Four minutes later, Cody Sharp, the cattle rancher's son from North Dakota, hit the trigger on the heavy gun, opening up a withering volume of gunfire, all along the top of the wall, the bullets studding into the plate glass windows of the grand residence behind it.

Four more SEALs joined in firing at the same target. Anyone behind that wall must have thought he was facing one hundred armed warriors as the huge volume of bullets screamed, ricocheted, whined, and spat over their heads.

Mack Bedford and Barney Wilkes rushed forward and pounded across the ground and dived into the base of the wall, covered in dust and sand but unharmed. Cody and his men stopped firing as suddenly as they had started, and that's when Mack and Cody ripped the pins out of their grenades and tossed them over the wall.

All four of them had landed on the ground when the first two exploded with mind-numbing force, shaking the compound to its foundations, shuddering the wall, and sending raking cracks across the spectacular glass-fronted south elevation of Mohammed Salat's beautiful home.

"Holy shit," said Barney. "You could probably hurt someone real bad with one of these things."

What he meant was, "If anyone happened to be behind that wall right there, those boys are outstandingly dead. Yessir."

Mack Bedford summoned his SEALs, standing in the courtyard and beckoning them forward. "*LET'S GO!*" he yelled, "*RIGHT NOW!*"

Like a swarm of angry wasps, Delta Platoon raced to his side en masse and followed him straight into the Salat residence, fanning out as they went, kicking open doors, machine guns raised, and conducting a routine house search just as if they were back on the side streets of North Baghdad.

They found Salat in the basement with his wife, both unarmed. There were various other "officials," secretaries, and computer operators, and the Delta team rounded them up in short order.

Commander Bedford had his senior men conduct interviews to try to work out who was who, but he already assumed that Mohammed Salat was the owner of the house and therefore the kingpin of the Somali pirates.

He posted a four-man team outside the house and made contact with the RV guys outside the compound's main wall. But just as he was attempting to speak, there was an incoming call from Brad Charlton: "*There's an entire fucking army moving through the town, heading right toward the garrison.*"

Mack was unsurprised. He'd anticipated an uprising in the town, which was why he'd put Chief Charlton at the head of an eighteen-man SEAL assault team in the first case.

"Drive 'em back, Brad," he said. "They'll be well armed. So let 'em get close and then open fire. But shoot to kill only if you're being overwhelmed. They'll be civilians mostly, and they scare easily. Keep them under sustained fire until they retreat.

"I'll send extra men. And I'm calling in the Black Hawks. If you get under pressure I'll have the Apache back here in ten minutes. Stay in touch."

"Roger that, sir," replied Chief Charlton, who was now flat down in the grass, next to Shane Cannel, watching a highly unusual sight. Marching four abreast was a tribal army, possibly 150 people, all carrying a rifle of some kind.

At their head was a uniformed character. They could not know this was the fabled Commodore Patrick Zeppi, the $10,000-a-month Somali warlord who was paid to protect Mohammed Salat if the garrison ever came under a major attack.

When Patrick had started over to the Salat residence a half hour ago, he'd thought he was witnessing World War III. The helicopter had scared him, and the concrete-ripping explosions had unnerved him. But he knew one thing: The wealth of the entire town was tied up in that compound, and he, Commodore Zeppi, was tasked with saving the cash.

He'd raced from house to house, summoning people and calling on every man who owned a rifle to fall into formation outside his house. They would march to the garrison and fight, if necessary, to the death.

Commodore Zeppi did not believe this would be necessary since he had driven off marauders trying to steal the pirate money many times before. What he did not know was that he was marching directly into the guns of one of the most highly trained platoons of Special Forces the world had ever seen.

Chief Charlton had Shane Cannel pass the word among the eighteen-strong force that he would give the word and then they would open fire, sustained for thirty seconds, to see if the enemy would turn and run. If it didn't, then shoot to kill and drive them back into the town. Mack plainly did not want them inside the compound.

With all the advantage of surprise, the iron-souled US Navy SEALs remained flat in the dusty scrubland and watched the Haradheere militia advance into what might prove to be certain death.

No one was comfortable gunning down armed civilians. But SEALs were not trained to be comfortable; they were trained to do whatever it took to save their lives and execute their mission. Suddenly there was a strange lull. Commodore Zeppi had turned around and was facing his army, shouting instructions.

"Christ! Have they seen us?" muttered Brad.

"Not possible," replied Shane, his black cammy-creamed face making him almost invisible from a distance of six feet.

Already the Delta men were preparing to open fire. "Hold it, hold it," muttered Brad. "They've stopped."

At that moment the game changed. Commodore Zeppi spun around and let out a bloodcurdling war whoop, raised his Kalashnikov, and charged forward straight at the hidden SEALs. There were no more than 150 yards between them and Brad Charlton.

Falling in line behind Zeppi, the chaotic-looking army charged. They all raised their rifles and began firing into the sky, shouting and laughing maniacally, high excitement mingling with mass hysteria, as they came bounding across the ground going for the garrison, determined to reinforce Salat's guard.

There were bullets flying everywhere, into the dark sky, straight at the garrison walls, into the ground high and low. Two young SEALs in the back line were hit, though not seriously, and then a volley spat into the ground between Brad and Shane, covering them in dust.

"*FUCK ME!*" bellowed Chief Charlton. "*This is it! Open fire right now . . . Drive these crazy bastards back!*"

The SEALs let fly with their deadly M-4 machine guns straight at Commodore Zeppi's front rank, which was now only seventy yards away. Four tribesmen went down, then four more. They shot the commodore dead in his tracks. No one could live in the face of the steel-curtain of machine-gun fire being unleashed by the men from Coronado. It was partly in self-defense but mostly to make these wild men turn around and head back the way they came.

Thirty-two Somalis were down, eight dead, before someone yelled the retreat. And then they all began running, stampeding back down the dusty main street, shouting and wailing, disappearing into houses and side alleys.

Brad Charlton, too, ordered a cease fire, and Shane Cannel went to check on the two walking wounded, both of whom had been hit in the upper arm. Then the chief ordered the entire force to move back into the garrison and report to the boss. He did not expect the tribesmen to bother them again.

The entire force, once commanded by Commodore Zeppi, re-grouped outside their soccer field. Once more they began to advance up the central street toward the garrison.

Chief Charlton had his SEAL team inside the battered walls with an eight-man guard patrol taking up position at the gateway. Commander Bedford came out to meet him and they deployed the troops sparingly while the boss spoke again to RV-1, instructing them to hold the helos for fifteen minutes.

He then returned to the house while six men searched the next-door building, the one that held the offices, ops center, and strong room. By this time Mohammed Salat had been handcuffed along with two of his main henchmen. The three women in the house, one of them Salat's wife, were being held under lock and key in the basement.

Mack Bedford told the pirate financier that he wanted all cash held in the garrison located because it had been taken illegally following numerous acts of piracy. Salat himself was being transferred immediately, with his executives, to the US interrogation camp in Guantanamo Bay, Cuba.

They had discovered a massive vault inside the strong room, and Mack was perfectly happy to blow the sonofabitch in half. But he hoped for an easier way. And for the third time he asked Salat to open it. Salat just shook his head, and Mack Bedford kicked him sharply in the balls to see if that might change his mind.

Salat's eyes almost popped out of his head and he fell writhing onto the floor, grasping his wedding equipment, which he plainly would not need for some time. Slowly he struggled to his feet, and with a look of utter loathing on his face, he led the American commander to a total of $78 million dollars in one-hundred-dollar bills, neatly packed and stacked in mailbags.

Salat spun the combination lock, the door swung open, and Mack sent four SEALs in to start bringing them outside so they'd be ready for the helicopters. Then he hit his comms receiver and told the guys out on RV-1 to whistle up all four Black Hawks from the carrier right away.

At which point the rag-tag-and-bobtail civilian rabble, still heavily armed and still numbering well over one hundred, was approaching the rough ground in front of the main entrance to the compound. Again they opened fire, aiming their Kalashnikovs every which way and rushing forward with shouts and taunts.

The SEAL guard patrol ducked back inside and returned fire. The oncoming army hit the ground and then opened up with their heavy machine gun.

"*WHAT THE FUCKING HELL'S HAPPENING NOW?!*" bellowed Mack, who could see none of the action.

Someone yelled back, "It's Salat's second army, about a hundred strong! They got us pinned down at the gateway. But they're not advancing."

Mack grabbed the phone and told RV-1 to instruct the Black Hawks to come in to the compound from the south, two at a time, in battle mode.

*Roger that, sir.*

Meanwhile out at the gate there was heavy gunfire, most of it from the tribesmen. The SEALs steadily aimed and fired, more slowly, but more deadly. Essentially the armed citizens of Haradheere were unable to stand up, never mind move forward.

With both sides pinned down, Mack Bedford spoke again to RV-1, ordering them to contact the Black Hawk pilots once more and to ensure they were in full attack mode when they came in, the first two to fly over the beach and land in the compound. Not firing, just making a ton of noise.

For ten more minutes the stalemate at the gate continued because Commander Bedford did not wish to wipe out half the population of the little town. He had what he came for and now he wanted to leave with his prizes intact, with no one much the wiser about who had smashed the Somali Marines.

Everyone heard the helos coming in over the water, but just before they reached the shore, both pilots switched on the heavy warning gear—searchlights, arc lights, and God knows what else. Then they hit the frighteners on the lead helo—two sirens that howled into the night like four police cruisers.

The second Black Hawk, fitted with two loudspeakers right below the fuselage, unleashed Wagner's *Ride of the Valkyries* at top decibel level. The palm trees swayed. The hot sand blew into a swirling cloud. And more than one hundred Haradheere residents nearly died of fright.

The noise was shattering as the Black Hawks came slowly down toward the garrison, sirens and music blaring. It very nearly drowned out the thunderous noise of the rotors. No one could hear anything above the din, except perhaps Mack Bedford's laughing as people covered their ears.

Outside, lying in the dust, possibly praying to Allah or some lesser tribal idol, the terrified people of Haradheere cut and ran for their lives, dropping rifles, shoes, and any other encumbrances, and fleeing across the rough ground, running through the fallen warriors for the cover of their homes.

Commander Bedford rushed for the helicopters and signalled for the SEALs to start loading the sacks into the ample space behind the cockpit. The first one took off immediately, stuffed with cash and carrying the two wounded SEALs, and headed straight back to the carrier.

The second one waited for the SEALs to load Salat and his two cohorts, plus two SEAL guards, and then rose into the air and headed back to the *Truman*.

By this time, the other two Black Hawks were on their way in and, not having been given further instructions, landed in the courtyard.

With the principal captives and all the money on its way out, Commander Bedford ordered twenty more SEALs to embark the helos and head back to base. At which point he began a general cleanup before the first two Black Hawks were back again.

He brought the two RV-1 guys in and thanked them for their efforts. He then toured the compound until he found the armory and ordered the complete destruction of the place and everything in it. Out in the street he found an SUV with the keys in the ignition and ordered a couple of the guys to take him down to the beach and to bring grenades.

There he found several fishing boats, including the *Mombassa*, which he knew was the name of the mother ship that had attacked the *Queen Beatrix*. There were two other sizeable crafts, which he guessed had been used in pirate operations, and he blew up all three of them.

"Guess these guys can still go fishing," he muttered, "but not for expensive oil tankers and US cruise ships."

They drove him back to the compound just as the two Black Hawks showed up again. Mack counted out the rest of the SEALs to ensure that everyone was present and then he ordered the final evacuation. And leaving behind a scene of impossible destruction and general carnage, he ordered the helos straight back to the carrier.

In just a couple of days Delta Platoon had brought an end to piracy in the southern part of Somalia. No other gangs of brigands would push off from that benighted Haradheere beach to rob, steal, and petrify seafarers and tourists.

Haradheere was finished. And there was a discernable sense of fear and unrest throughout southern Somalia. If Uncle Sam was capable of smashing into an operation as well-financed, well-armed, and well-organized as Salat's most certainly had been, then Uncle Sam could come blasting into the attack against anyone.

Politically it created a hot potato. Russia immediately declared that any Russian ship, naval or civilian, was perfectly at liberty to strike back against piracy any way it wished. Moscow stated that pirates, when captured, would be transported back to Russia, where they would face life sentences, probably to be served in Siberia.

The Brits were plainly ashamed of themselves and, with equal urgency, proposed a new set of laws concerning British citizens attacked by pirates.

Even Westminster, battered by thirteen years of half-crazed, left-wing doctrine, muscled up under a new and more right-wing government. And in the mother of Parliaments, the squeals of the liberal European Union would no longer be heeded in the matter of piracy.

The Royal Navy was informed that henceforth they must be prepared to attack enemies of the people, precisely as citizens of the UK expected. And fraudulent lawsuits citing the human rights of the international villains of the high seas would be dismissed as derisive.

Uncle Sam had shown the way, and Mack Bedford had taken the lead, ripping a line out of his all-time favorite country-and-western song, Kenny Rogers's "Coward of the County" . . . *Sometimes you gotta fight when you're a man.*

# EPILOGUE

▼

UNDER THE PERMANENTLY CLASSIFIED RULES OF US MILITARY Black Operations, the Pentagon never released details of the two naval actions off the Maldives and on the Somali mainland. In response to media inquiries, the press office stonewalled with a slightly mischievous bewilderment.

> I'm sorry, sir, but you know perfectly well we cannot disclose details of any activities by Special Forces . . . Yes, I do understand that your readers have a right to know, but I am afraid this office has not been told anything about the subject of your inquiry.

The mystery went on for several weeks, if not months, even when passengers from the *Ocean Princess* regaled their local newspapers with stories of the sensational smash-and-grab raid of the Navy SEALs on that sunlit late afternoon in the One and a Half Degree Channel.

The shipping companies were reluctant to disclose the story of the rescue. Thus nothing was ever confirmed or denied. And every senior naval officer, when questioned, replied in the same monotone, "Sorry. Can't help. No one's told me anything about it. Sounds pretty unlikely to me."

It was a frustrating time for the media, seething with the certain knowledge that something big had broken out but equally certain that no one was ever going to tell them anything official.

And there were no hard clues. The CIA never even prosecuted Peter Kilimo for his alleged role in the Somali pirate operation.

There was not a solid truth upon which to base a major national story. Nothing confirmed. Nothing in writing except for one short official letter from the US Navy. It was a private letter. And would remain private since SEALs are permitted no public recognition of their work. But this letter had a special glory of its own.

> Dear Mack,
>
> On March 2nd next, I will personally accompany you to the White House, where you will be awarded the Navy Cross for combat heroism. This is, as you know, the highest honor the Service can bestow on anyone. It's a fabled decoration, its dark blue ribbon slashed down the center with a white stripe, signifying selflessness.
>
> In my long naval career, I have not met anyone who deserved it more.
>
> With kindest personal regards,
>
> *Andy*
> Rear Admiral Andrew M. Carlow
> C-in-C SPECWARCOM, Coronado

The envelope was stamped with the seal of the United States of America and was addressed in big, red letters:

> FOR YOUR EYES ONLY:
> CAPTAIN MACKENZIE BEDFORD
> Commanding Officer
> Team 10
> United States Navy SEALs

Following is an excerpt from

# TOPGUN on Wall Street
*Why the United States Military
Should Run Corporate America*

by
**Lieutenant Commander Jeffery Lay
with Patrick Robinson**

ON SALE MAY 2012

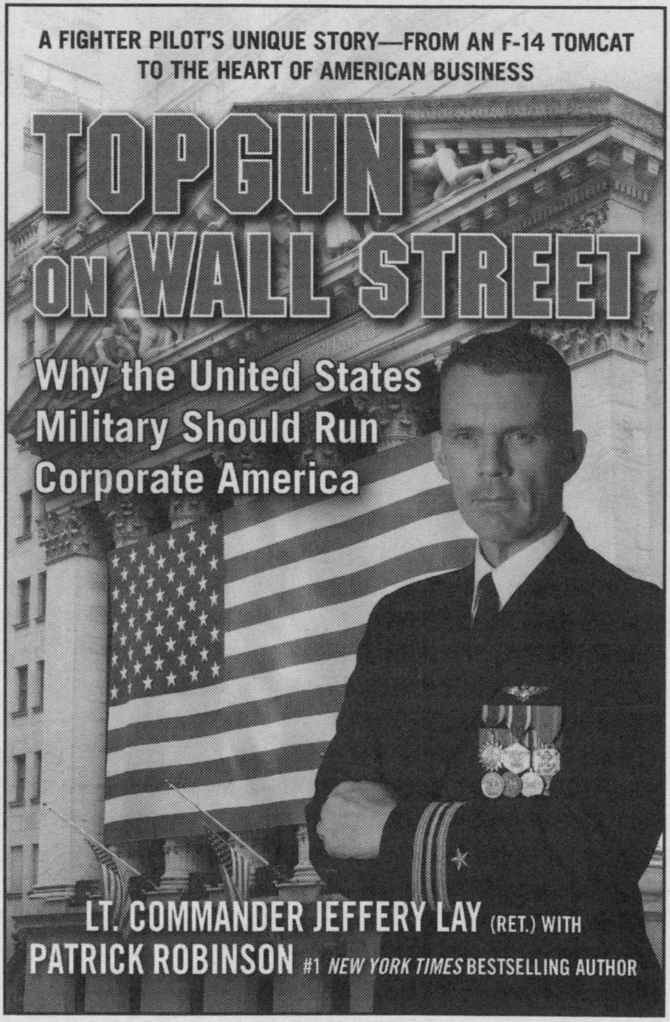
A FIGHTER PILOT'S UNIQUE STORY—FROM AN F-14 TOMCAT TO THE HEART OF AMERICAN BUSINESS
TOPGUN ON WALL STREET
Why the United States Military Should Run Corporate America
LT. COMMANDER JEFFERY LAY (RET.) WITH
PATRICK ROBINSON #1 NEW YORK TIMES BESTSELLING AUTHOR

# AUTHOR'S NOTE

*TOPGUN on Wall Street,* while loosely autobiographical, has one driving force behind its narrative: the demarcation line between military and civilian management philosophies. The majority of this story inevitably concentrates on the significant gulf between military beliefs, training, demands, and honor, and the diametrically opposed civilian dog-eat-dog ethos, breathtaking personal greed and susceptibility to convenient lies, frequently on a Wagnerian scale.

My first experience of this military-civilian clash involved my service as a Naval Aviator flying strike fighter combat missions from a giant US aircraft carrier parked in the middle of the Gulf of Iran at the turn of the twenty-first century. We were flanked to the east by the menacing shores of the Islamic Republic of Iran, while we in turn glared hard west toward the distant shores of the Republic of Iraq. Because there, the half-crazed Lion of Babylon, Saddam Hussein, swore by all that was holy to blow the US air patrols out of the sky.

We could, of course, have dealt with this quasi-Iraqi "warrior" in about twelve minutes, except for one thing. The White House had decided to assume command of America's front-line muscle, the 1,000 mph TOPGUN fighter pilots. For the first time, the guys at the Tip of the Spear were under their direct civilian "command" while operating in a war zone.

The result was a "phony war," right out there in the vaunted no-fly zone. It was a hideous situation, and it resulted in shocking mistakes, which had inevitably catastrophic and bloody consequences. Worse yet, it drove some of the finest United States Naval Aviators out of the service we all loved. I was personally tortured mentally by all this. How could these clever, accomplished presidential advisors possibly demonstrate such foolishness? A better question might have been, how could they ever be so uncompromisingly arrogant as to dismiss entirely the considered views of the best brains in the US military? I actually thought it might be some kind of aberration. But I spent the next dozen years finding out there was nothing unusual about these apparently eccentric civilian decisions. They make them all the time, in politics, in their dealings with the military, and in corporate life. They constantly repeat their mistakes; they operate in a way that is self-centered in the extreme. And there may be no way out for them or for the nation.

Unless, of course, the peerless US military was given leave to run corporate America. This may seem radical. Yet the selfless teamwork of America's men and women in uniform very likely holds the key to resurrection. So many times we have delivered this nation from the abyss, because America represents the greatest nation in history. Is it salvageable? Of course it is. If only we listen to that hidden voice that comes from the universe—a voice of fairness and reason that has always governed the United States.

I thus begin my story with a short factual account of Saddam Hussein's operations room, illustrating precisely what we were up against. And why *no* civilian committee member could possibly understand the depth of the problem—solvable, as it was, essentially, by high explosives alone.

LIEUTENANT COMMANDER JEFFERY LAY
*United States Navy (Retired)*